Sisters

www.**booksattransworld**.co.uk

Also by Danielle Steel

*Published outside the UK under the title PASSION'S PROMISE

DANIELLE STEEL

Sisters

BANTAM PRESS

LONDON • TORONTO • SYDNEY • AUCKLAND • JOHANNESBURG

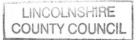
TRANSWORLD PUBLISHERS
61–63 Uxbridge Road, London W5 5SA
a division of The Random House Group Ltd
www.booksattransworld.co.uk

First published in Great Britain
in 2007 by Bantam Press
a division of Transworld Publishers

A CIP catalogue record for this book
is available from the British Library.

ISBN 9780593056691 (cased)
ISBN 9780593056707 (tpb)

Addresses for Random House Group Ltd companies outside the UK
can be found at: www.randomhouse.co.uk
The Random House Group Ltd Reg. No. 954009

The Random House Group Ltd makes every effort to ensure that the papers used in its
books are made from trees that have been legally sourced from well-managed and credibly
certified forests. Our paper procurement policy can be found at:
www.randomhouse.co.uk/paper.htm

Typeset in Charter ITC

Printed and bound in Great Britain by
Mackays of Chatham, Chatham, Kent

2 4 6 8 10 9 7 5 3 1

To my mother Norma,

and to my incredibly wonderful fantastic most fabulous in the entire world loving daughters: Beatrix, Sam, Victoria, Vanessa, and Zara.

May you always, always, always be there for each other, with tenderness, compassion, patience, loyalty, and love. You are each the best gift that I have given to the others.

And to Simon, Mia, Chiquita, Talulah, Gidget, and Gracie, the absolutely best, most adorable, and most beautiful dogs on the planet.

with all my love,
Mom/d.s.

Sisters

Chapter 1

The photo shoot in the Place de la Concorde, in Paris, had been going since eight o'clock that morning. They had an area around one of the fountains cordoned off, and a bored-looking Parisian gendarme stood watching the proceedings. The model stood in the fountain for hours on end, jumping, splashing, laughing, her head thrown back in practiced glee, and each time she did it, she was convincing. She was wearing an evening gown hiked up to her knees, and a mink wrap. A powerful battery-operated fan blew her long blond hair out in a mane behind her.

Passersby stopped and stared, fascinated by the scene as a makeup artist in a tank top and shorts climbed in and out of the fountain to keep the model's makeup perfect. By noon, the model still looked like she was having a fabulous time, as she laughed with the photographer and his two assistants between shots as well as on camera. Cars slowed as they drove by, and two American teenagers stopped and stared in amazement as they strolled by and recognized her.

"Oh my God, Mom! It's *Candy*!" the older of the two girls intoned with awe. They were on vacation in Paris from Chicago, but even

Parisians recognized Candy easily. She was the most successful super-model in America, and on the international scene, and had been since she was seventeen. Candy was twenty-one now, and had made a fortune modeling in New York, Paris, London, Milan, Tokyo, and a dozen other cities. The agency could barely handle the volume of her bookings. She was on the cover of *Vogue* at least twice a year, and was in constant demand. Candy was, without a doubt, the hottest model in the business, and a household name even to those who knew little about fashion.

Her full name was Candy Adams, but she never used her last name, just Candy. She didn't need more than that. Everybody knew her, her face, her name, her reputation as one of the world's lead-ing models. She managed to make everything look like fun, whether she was running through snow barefoot in a bikini in the freezing cold in Switzerland, walking through the surf in an evening gown in the winter on Long Island, or wearing a full-length sable coat un-der a blazing sun in the Tuscan hills. Whatever she did, she looked as though she was having a ball doing it. Standing in the fountain in the Place de la Concorde in July was easy, despite the heat and the morning sun, in one of Paris's standard summer heat waves. The shoot was for another *Vogue* cover, for the October issue, and the photographer, Matt Harding, was one of the biggest in the business. They had worked together hundreds of times over the last four years, and he loved shooting with her.

Unlike other models as important as she was, Candy was always easy—good-natured, funny, irreverent, sweet, and surprisingly naïve after the success she'd enjoyed since the beginning of her career. She was just a nice person, and an incredible beauty. She didn't have a single bad angle. Her face was virtually perfect for the camera, with no flaws, no defects. She had the delicacy of a cameo, with finely carved features, miles of naturally blond hair that she wore long most of the time, and blue eyes the color of sky and the size of saucers. Matt knew she liked to party hard and stay out late, and amazingly it never showed in her face the next day. She was one of the lucky few who could get away with playing and never have it show afterward. She wouldn't be able to get away with it forever, but for now she still could. If anything, she only got prettier with age, although at twenty-one, one could hardly expect her to be touched by the ravages of time, but some models started to show it even at her age. Candy didn't. And her natural sweetness still showed through just as it had the first day he'd met her, when she was seventeen and doing her first shoot for *Vogue* with him. He loved her. Everyone did. There wasn't a man or woman in the business who didn't love Candy.

She stood six foot one in bare feet, weighed a hundred and sixteen pounds on a heavy day, and he knew she never ate, but whatever the reason for her light weight, it looked great on her. Although she was thin in person, she always looked fabulous in the images he took of her. Just like *Vogue,* which adored her and had assigned him to work with her on this shoot, Candy was his favorite model.

They wrapped up the shoot at twelve-thirty, and she climbed out of the fountain as though she had only been in it for ten minutes, instead of four and a half hours. They were doing a second setup at the Arc de Triomphe that afternoon, and one that night at the Eiffel Tower, with the sparklers going off behind them. Candy never complained about difficult conditions or long hours, which was one of the reasons photographers loved working with her. That, and the fact that you couldn't get a bad photograph of her. Her face was the most forgiving on the planet, and the most desirable.

"Where do you want to go for lunch?" Matt asked her, as his

assistants put away his cameras and tripod and locked up the film, while Candy slipped out of the white mink wrap and dried her legs with a towel. She was smiling, and looked as though she had enjoyed it thoroughly.

"I don't know. L'Avenue?" she suggested with a smile. She was easy. They had plenty of time. It would take his assistants roughly two hours to set up the shoot at the Arc de Triomphe. He had gone over all the details and angles with them the day before, and he didn't need to be there until they had the shot fully ready. That gave him and Candy a couple of hours for lunch. Many models and fashion gurus frequented L'Avenue, also Costes, the Buddha Bar, Man Ray, and an assortment of Paris haunts. He liked L'Avenue too, and it was close to where they were going to shoot that afternoon. He knew it didn't matter where they went, she wasn't likely to eat much anyway, just consume gallons of water, which was what all the models did. They flushed their systems constantly so they didn't gain an ounce. And with the two lettuce leaves Candy usually ate, she was hardly likely to put on weight. If anything, she got thinner every year. But she looked healthy, in spite of her enormous height, and ridiculously light weight. You could see all the bones in her shoulders, chest, and ribs. Just as she was more famous than most of her counterparts, she was also thinner than most. It worried Matt for her sometimes, although she just laughed when he accused her of having an eating disorder. Candy never responded to comments about her weight. Most major models flirted with or suffered from anorexia, or worse. It went with the territory. Humans didn't come in these sizes, not after the age of nine. Adult women, who ate even halfway normally, just weren't that thin.

They had a car and driver who took them to the restaurant on the Avenue Montaigne, and as usual at that hour and time of year, it was mobbed. The couture collections were being shown the following week, and designers, photographers, and models had already started to fly in. In addition, it was high tourist season in Paris. Americans loved the restaurant, but so did trendy Parisians. It was always a scene. One of the owners spotted Candy immediately, and showed them to a table on the glassed-in terrace, which they referred to as the "Veranda." It was where she liked to sit. She loved the fact that she could smoke in any restaurant in Paris. She wasn't a heavy smoker, but indulged occasionally, and she liked having the freedom to do it, without getting dark looks or ugly comments. Matt commented that she was one of the few women who made smoking look appealing. She did everything with grace, and could make tying her shoelaces look sexy. She simply had that kind of style.

Matt ordered a glass of white wine before lunch, and Candy asked for a large bottle of water. She had left the giant water bottle she usually toted around in the car. She ordered a salad for lunch, without dressing, Matt ordered steak tartare, and they settled back to relax, as people at tables around them stared at her. Everyone in the place had recognized her. She was wearing jeans and a tank top and flat silver sandals she had bought the year before in Portofino. She often had sandals made there, or in St. Tropez; she usually got there every summer.

"Are you coming down to St. Tropez this weekend?" Matt asked, assuming she was. "There's a party on Valentino's yacht." He knew that Candy would have been one of the first to be asked, and she rarely turned down an invitation, and surely not this one. She usually stayed at the Byblos Hotel, with friends, or on someone's yacht. Candy always had a million options, and was in huge demand, as a celebrity, a woman, and a guest. Everyone wanted to be able to say she'd be there, so others would come. People used her as a lure, and proof of their social prowess. It was a hard burden to carry, and often crossed the line into exploitation, but she didn't seem to mind, and was used to it. She went where she wanted to, and where she thought she'd have the best time. But this time she surprised him. Despite her incredible looks, she was a woman of many facets, and not the mindless, superficial beauty some expected. Candy was not only gorgeous but decent, and very bright, even if still naïve and young, despite her success. Matt liked that about her. There was nothing jaded about Candy, and she enjoyed it all, whatever she did.

"I can't go to St. Tropez," she said, picking at her lettuce. So far, he had seen her actually swallow two bites.

"Other plans?"

"Yeah," she said simply, smiling. "I have to go home. My parents give a Fourth of July party every year, and my mother would kill me if I didn't show up. It's a command performance for me and my sisters." Matt knew she was close to them. None of her sisters were models, and if he remembered correctly, she was the youngest. She talked about her family a lot.

"Aren't you doing the couture shows next week?" More often than not, she was Chanel's bride, and had been Saint Laurent's before they closed. She made a spectacular bride.

"Not this year. I'm taking two weeks off. I promised. Usually I go home for the party, and come back just in time for the shows. This year I figured I'd stay home for a couple of weeks and hang out. I haven't seen all my sisters in one place since Christmas. It's pretty hard with everyone away from home, mostly me. I've hardly been in New York since March, and my mom's been complaining, so I'm staying home for two weeks and then I have to go to Tokyo after that for a shoot for Japanese *Vogue*." It was where a lot of the models made big money, and Candy made more than most. The Japanese fashion magazines ate her up. They loved her blond looks and her height.

"My mom gets really pissed when I don't come home," she added, and he laughed. "What's so funny?"

"You. You're the hottest model in the business, and you're worried about your mom getting mad if you don't go home for the Fourth of July barbecue, or picnic, or whatever it is. That's what I love about you. You're really still a kid." She shrugged with an impish smile.

"I love my mom," she said honestly, "and my sisters. My mom gets really upset when we don't come home. Fourth of July, Thanksgiving, Christmas. I missed Thanksgiving once, and she gave me shit about it for a year. As far as she's concerned, family comes first. I think she's right. When I have kids, I want that too. This stuff is fun, but it doesn't last forever. Family does."

Candy still had all the same values she'd been brought up with, and believed in them profoundly, no matter how much she loved being a supermodel. But her family was even more important to her. Much more so than the men in her life, who thus far had been brief and fleeting, and from what Matt had observed were usually jerks, either young ones just trying to show off by being out with her, or older ones who often had a more sinister agenda. Like many other beautiful young women, she was a magnet to men who wanted to use her, usually by being seen with her, and enjoying the perks of her success. The most recent one had been a famous Italian playboy who was notorious for the beautiful women he went out with—for about two minutes. Before that, there had been a young British lord, who looked normal but had suggested whips and bondage, and Candy found out later he was bisexual and deep into drugs. Candy had been startled, and ran like hell, although it was not the first time she'd had that kind of offer. In the last four years, she'd heard it all. Most of her relationships had been short-lived. She didn't have the time or the desire to settle down, and the kind of men she met were not the kind she wanted to stay with. She always said that she'd never been in love, although she had been out with a lot of men, but none of them worthwhile, since the boy she'd been involved with in high school. He was still in college now, and they had lost touch.

Candy had never gone to college. Her first big modeling break had happened in her senior year in high school, and she had promised her parents she'd go back to school later. She wanted to take advantage of the opportunities she had, while she had them. She put aside a ton of money, although she'd spent plenty on a penthouse apartment in New York, and a lot of great clothes and fancy pastimes. College was becoming an ever more unlikely plan. She just couldn't see the point. Besides, as she always pointed out to her parents, she wasn't nearly as smart as her sisters, or so she claimed. Her parents and sisters denied it, and still thought she should go to college when her life slowed down, if it ever did. But for now, she was still going at full speed, and loving every minute of it. She was on the fast track, fully enjoying the fruits of her enormous success.

"I can't believe you're going home for a Fourth of July picnic, or whatever the hell it is. Can I talk you out of it?" Matt asked hopefully. He had a girlfriend, but she wasn't in France, and he and Candy had always been good friends. He enjoyed her company, and it would be much more amusing having her in St. Tropez for the weekend.

"Nope," she answered, obviously unswayable. "My mom would be heartbroken. I can't do that to her. And my sisters would be really pissed. They're all coming home too."

"Yeah, but that's different. I'm sure they don't have choices like parties on Valentino's yacht."

"No, but they have stuff to do too. We all go home for the Fourth of July, no matter what."

"How patriotic," he said cynically, teasing her, as people continued to walk past their table and stare. You could see Candy's breasts through her paper-thin white tank top, which was a man's undershirt, a "wife beater" as they called it in the business. She wore them a lot, and didn't need a bra. She had had her breasts enlarged three years before, and they contrasted sharply with her rail-thin body. The new ones weren't huge, but they were spectacular looking and had been done well. They were still soft to the touch, unlike most breast implants, particularly those that cost less. She had had hers done at the best plastic surgeon in New York, much to her mother and sisters' horror. But she explained that she needed to do it for her work. None of her sisters or her mother would have considered doing such a thing, and two of them didn't need to. And her mother still had a great figure and was beautiful at fifty-seven.

All the women in the family were knockouts, although their looks were very different from each other. Candy looked nothing like the other women in her family. She was by far the tallest, and she had her father's looks and height. He was a very good-looking man, had played football at Yale, was six foot four, and he had blond hair like hers when he was young. Jim Adams was turning sixty in December. Neither one of her parents looked their age. They were still a striking couple. Like Candy's sister Tammy, her mother was a redhead. Her sister Annie's hair was chestnut brown with coppery auburn highlights, and her sister Sabrina's hair was almost jet black. They had one of every color, their father liked to tease them. And in their youth, they had looked like the old Breck ads, eastern, patrician, distinguished, and handsome. The four girls had been beautiful as children, and often caused comment, and still did when they went out together, even with their mother. Because of her height, weight, fame, and profession, Candy always got the most attention, but the others were lovely too.

They finished lunch at L'Avenue. Matt ate a pink *macaron* with raspberry sauce on it, while Candy grimaced and said it was too sweet, and drank a cup of black *café filtre,* allowing herself one tiny square of chocolate as a treat, which was rare. The driver took them to the Arc de Triomphe after lunch. They had a trailer for her there, parked on the Avenue Foch, behind the Arc de Triomphe, and after a short time she emerged in a startlingly beautiful red evening gown, trailing a sable wrap behind her. She looked absolutely breathtaking, as two policemen helped her cross through the traffic to where Matt and his crew were waiting for her under the huge French flag flying from the Arc de Triomphe. Matt beamed as he saw her coming. Candy was truly the most beautiful woman he'd ever seen, and possibly in the world.

"Holy shit, kid, you look unbelievable in that dress."

"Thanks, Matt," she said modestly, smiling at the pair of gendarmes, who also looked dazzled by her. She had nearly caused several accidents, as crazed Parisian drivers came to a screeching halt to stare as the two policemen led her through the traffic.

They finished shooting under the Arc just after five o'clock. She went back to the Ritz for a four-hour break then. She took a shower, called her agency in New York, and was at the Eiffel Tower for the last of the shoot at nine P.M., when the light was soft. They finished shooting at one A.M., after which she went to a party she had promised to attend. And she walked back into the Ritz at four o'clock in the morning, full of energy, and none the worse for wear. Matt had dropped out two hours before. As he had pointed out, there was nothing like being twenty-one years old. At thirty-seven, he couldn't keep up with her, nor could most of the men who pursued her.

Candy packed her bags, took a shower, and lay down for an hour after that. She had had a good time that night, but the party she had gone to had been standard fare, nothing new and different for her. She had to leave the hotel at seven A.M., and be at Charles de Gaulle airport by eight o'clock for a ten A.M. flight, which would get her into Kennedy by noon, local time. With an hour to get her bags and go through customs, and a two-hour drive to Connecticut, she would be home at her parents' house by three P.M., in plenty of time for their Fourth of July party the next day. She was looking forward to spending the night with her parents and sisters before the craziness of the party the following night.

Candy smiled at the familiar concierges and security as she walked out of the Ritz, in jeans, and a T-shirt, her hair in a ponytail she had barely bothered to comb. She was carrying a huge old alligator Hermès bag in a brandy color that she had found in a vintage store at the Palais Royal. A limousine was waiting outside for her, and she was on her way. She knew she'd be back in Paris again soon, since so much of her work was there. She had two shoots already scheduled in Paris in September, after her trip to Japan at the end of July. She hadn't figured out August yet, and was hoping to take a few days off, either in the Hamptons, or the south of France. She had endless opportunities for good times and work. It was a great life for her, and she was looking forward to spending a couple of weeks at home. It was always fun for her, even though her sisters teased her about the life she led. The little girl who had been Candace Adams, the tallest, most awkward girl in every grade, had turned into the swan who was known simply as "Candy" around the world. But even though she loved what she did, and had a great time wherever she was, there was no place like home, and no one on the planet she loved as she did her sisters and her mom. She loved her dad as well, but they shared a different bond.

As they drove through Paris in the early morning traffic, she settled back against the seat. And as glamorous as she looked, at heart she was in many ways still her mom's little girl.

Chapter 2

The sun beat down on the Piazza della Signoria in Florence, as a pretty young woman bought a gelato from a street vendor. She asked for lemon and chocolate in fluent Italian, and savored the combination as the two scoops of ice cream dripped from the cone onto her hand. She licked the excess gelato away, while the sun glinted off her dark copper hair, and she walked past the Uffizi gallery on her way home. She had lived in Florence for two years, after finishing college with a bachelor's degree in fine arts at the Rhode Island School of Design, a respected institution for people with artistic talent, mostly designers, but there had been a number of fine arts students there too. After Rhode Island, she got a master's degree at the École des Beaux Arts in Paris, which she had loved too. She had dreamed of studying art in Italy all her life, and had finally come here, after Paris, and this was where she knew she was meant to be.

She took drawing classes every day, and was learning the painting techniques of the old masters. In the past year, she felt she had done some very worthwhile work, although she still felt she had much to learn. She was wearing a cotton skirt and sandals she had bought from a street vendor for fifteen euros, and a peasant blouse she had bought on a driving trip to Siena. She had never been as happy in her life as she was here. Living in Florence was her dream come true.

She was planning to attend an informal life drawing class with a live model, at an artist's studio at six o'clock that night, and she was leaving for the States the next day. She hated to leave, but had promised her mother she'd come home, as she did every year. It was wrenching for her to leave Florence even for a few days. She was returning in a week, and then leaving for a trip to Umbria with friends. She had seen a lot of Italy since she'd been there, gone to Lake Como, spent some time in Portofino, and it seemed as if she had visited every church and museum in Italy. She had a particular passion for Venice and the churches and architecture there. She knew with absolute certainty that Italy was where she was meant to be, she had come alive since she'd been there. It was where she had found herself.

She had rented a tiny garret apartment in a crumbling building, which suited her to perfection. The work she was doing showed the fruits of her hard work for the past several years. She had given her parents one of her paintings for Christmas, and they had been astounded by the depth and beauty of her work. It was a painting of a madonna and child, very much in the style of the Old Masters, and using all of her new techniques. She had even mixed the paint herself, according to an ancient process. Her mother said it was truly a masterpiece, and had hung it in the living room. Annie had carried it home herself, wrapped in newspapers, and unveiled it for them on Christmas Eve.

Now she was going home for the Fourth of July party they gave every year, which she and her sisters moved heaven and earth to attend. It was a sacrifice for Annie this year. There was so much work she wanted to do, she hated to pull herself away, even for a week. But like her sisters, she didn't want to disappoint her mother, who lived to see them, and thrived having all four of her girls home at the same time. She talked about it all year. There was no phone in Annie's quaint apartment, but her mother called her often on her cell phone to see how she was, and she loved hearing the excitement in her daughter's voice. Nothing thrilled Annie more than her work and the deep satisfaction she derived from studying art, here at its most important source, in Florence. She got lost for hours at times in the Uffizi, studying the paintings, and drove often to see important work in neighboring towns. Florence was Mecca for her.

She had recently become romantically involved with a young artist from New York. He had arrived in Florence only six months before, and they had met only days after he arrived, when she got back from spending Christmas with her family in Connecticut. They met at the studio of a fellow artist, a young Italian, on New Year's Eve, and their romance had been hot and heavy ever since. They loved each other's work, and shared their deep commitment to art. His work was more contemporary, and hers more traditional, but many of their views and theories were the same. He had taken some time out to work as a designer, which he had hated, calling it prostitution. He had finally saved enough money to come to Italy to paint and study for a year.

Annie was more fortunate. At twenty-six, her family was still willing to help her. She could easily see herself living in Italy for the rest of her life, nothing would please her more. And although she loved her parents and sisters, she hated to go home. Every moment away from Florence and her work was painful for her. She had wanted to be an artist ever since she was a little girl, and as time went on, her determination and inspiration grew more intense. It set her apart from her sisters, whose pursuits were more worldly, and who were more involved in the moneymaking world, her oldest sister as an attorney, her next sister as the producer of a TV show in L.A., and her youngest sister as a supermodel whose face was known around the world. Annie was the only artist in the group, and could not have cared less about "making it" in the world as a commercial success. She was happiest when deeply engrossed in her work, and never even considered whether it would sell. She realized how lucky she was to have parents who supported her passion, although she was determined to become self-supporting one day. But for now, she was soaking up ancient techniques and the extraordinary atmosphere of Florence like a sponge.

Her sister Candy was in Paris often, but Annie could never tear herself away from her work to see her, and although she loved her youngest sister deeply, she and Candy had very little in common. When she was working, Annie didn't even care if she combed her hair, and everything she owned was splattered with paint. Candy's world of beautiful people and high fashion was light-years from her world of starving artists, and discovering the best way to mix her paints. Whenever she saw Candy, her supermodel sister tried to convince Annie to get a decent haircut and wear makeup, and Annie just laughed. It was the farthest thing from her mind. She hadn't been shopping or bought anything new to wear in two years. Fashion never made a blip on her radar screen. Annie ate, slept, drank, and lived art. It was what she knew and loved, and her current boyfriend Charlie was as passionate about it as she. They had been nearly inseparable for the past six months, and had traveled all over Italy together, studying both important and obscure works of art. The relationship was really going well. As she had told her mother on the phone, he was the first noncrazy artist she had ever met, and they had so much in common. Annie's only concern was that he planned to go back to New York at the end of the year, unless she could convince him to stay. She worked on him every day to extend his stay in Florence. But as an American, he couldn't work legally in Italy, and his money would run out eventually. With her parents' backing, Annie could live as long as she wanted in Florence. She was well aware of and deeply grateful for the blessing they provided her.

Annie had promised herself to be financially independent by the time she was thirty, hoping to sell her paintings in a gallery by then. She had had two shows in a small gallery in Rome, and had sold several paintings. But she couldn't have managed without her parents' help. It embarrassed her at times, but there was no way she could live on the sales of her paintings yet, and maybe not for many years. Charlie teased her about it at times, without malice, but he never failed to point out that she was one lucky girl, and if she was living in a threadbare-looking garret, it was something of a fraud. Her parents could have afforded to rent her a decent apartment, if she so chose. That was certainly not the case for most of the artists they knew. And however much he might have teased her about her parents supporting her, he had a deep respect for her talent and the quality of the work she produced. There was no question in his mind, or anyone else's, that she had the potential to be a truly extraordinary artist, and even at twenty-six she was well on her way. Her body of work showed depth, substance, and remarkable skill with technique. Her sense of color was delicate. Her paintings were a clear indication that she had a real gift. And when she mastered a particularly difficult subject, Charlie told her how proud of her he was.

He had wanted to travel to Pompeii with her that weekend, to study the frescoes there, and she had told him that she was going home for the week, for the Fourth of July party her parents gave every year.

"Why is that such a big deal?" He wasn't close to his family, and had no plans to visit them during his sabbatical year. He had mentioned more than once that he thought it was childish of her to be so attached to her sisters and parents. She was twenty-six after all.

"It's a big deal because my family is very close," she explained. "It's not about the Fourth of July as a holiday. It's about spending a week with my sisters, and my mom and dad. I go home for Thanksgiving and Christmas too," she warned, so there would be no disappointment or misunderstanding about it later on. The holidays were sacred times for all of them.

Charlie had been mildly annoyed, and rather than waiting for another week to go to Pompeii with her, he said he would make the trip with another artist friend. Annie was disappointed not to go with him, but decided not to make an issue of it. At least that way he'd have something to do while she was gone. He had recently hit a slump in his work, and was struggling with some new techniques and ideas. For now, it wasn't going well, although she was sure he'd pull out of it soon. He was a very talented artist, although an older artist who had advised him in Florence said that the purity of his work had been corrupted by the time he had spent doing design. The senior artist thought there was a commercial quality to his work which he needed to undo. His comments had insulted Charlie profoundly, and he hadn't spoken to his self-appointed critic for weeks. He was extremely sensitive about his art, as many artists were. Annie was more open to critiques, and welcomed them, in order to improve her work. Like her sister Candy, there was a surprising modesty about her, and who she was. She was without artifice or malice, and was astonishingly humble about her work.

She had been trying to get Candy to visit her for months, and between her trips to Paris and Milan, there had been ample opportunity, but Florence was off Candy's beaten path, and Annie's scene among starving artists wasn't for her. Candy loved going to places like London and St. Tropez between jobs. Annie's art scene in Florence was light-years from Candy's life, and the reverse was true as well. Annie had no desire to fly to Paris to meet her sister, or stay in fancy hotels like the Ritz. She was much happier wandering around Florence, eating gelato, or going to the Uffizi for the thousandth time in her sandals and peasant skirt. She preferred that to getting dressed up or wearing makeup or high heels, as everyone in Candy's crowd did. She disliked the superficial people Candy hung out with. Candy always said that Annie's friends all looked like they needed a bath. The two sisters lived in totally different worlds.

"When are you leaving again?" Charlie asked her, when he came to her apartment. She had promised to cook him dinner the night before she left, after her class. She bought fresh pasta, tomatoes, and vegetables, and she planned to make a sauce she had just heard about. Charlie brought a bottle of Chianti, and poured her a glass while she cooked, as he admired her from across the room. She was a beautiful girl, completely natural and unassuming. To anyone who met her, she seemed like a simple girl, when in fact she was extremely well educated in her field, highly trained, and came from a family that he had long since guessed was very well off, although Annie never mentioned the advantages she had had in her youth, and still did. She led a quiet, hardworking artist's life. The only sign of her somewhat upper-class roots was the small gold signet ring she wore on her left hand, with her mother's crest. Annie was quiet and modest about that too. The only yardstick she measured herself and others by was how hard they worked on their art, how dedicated they were.

"I'm leaving tomorrow," she reminded him, as she set down a big bowl of pasta on the kitchen table. It smelled delicious, and she grated the Parmesan herself. The bread was hot and fresh. "That's why I'm cooking for you tonight. When are you and Cesco going to Pompeii?"

"Day after tomorrow," he said quietly, smiling at her across the table, as they sat down on two of the unmatched, slightly shaky chairs she had found discarded in the street. She had acquired most of her furniture that way. She spent as little as possible of her parents' money, just for rent and food. There were no obvious luxuries in her life. And the little car she drove was a fifteen-year-old Fiat. Her mother was terrified it wasn't safe, but Annie refused to buy a new one.

"I'm going to miss you," he said sadly. It was going to be the first time they'd been separated since they met. He told her he was in love with her within a month of their first date. She liked him better than she had anyone in years, and was in love with him too. The only thing that worried her about their relationship was that he was going back to the States in six months. He was already nagging her to move back to New York, but she wasn't ready to leave Italy yet, even for him. It was going to be a hard decision for her when he left. Despite her love for him, she was loath to give up the opportunity for ongoing studies in Florence for any man. Until now, her art had always come first. This was the first time she had ever questioned that, which was scary for her. She knew that if she left Florence for him, it would be a huge sacrifice for her.

"Why don't we go somewhere after we get back from Umbria?" he suggested, looking hopeful, and she smiled. They were planning to go to Umbria with friends in July, but he loved and needed time alone with her.

"Wherever you want," she said, and meant it. He leaned across the table and kissed her then, and she served him the pasta, which they both agreed was delicious. The recipe had been good, and she was a very good cook. He often said that meeting her had been the best thing that had happened to him since he'd arrived in Europe. When he said it, it touched her heart.

She was taking photographs of him to show her sisters and her mom, but they had figured out that this was an important relationship for her. Her mother had already said to her sisters that she hoped Charlie would convince Annie to move back. She respected what Annie was doing in Italy, but it was so far away, and she never wanted to come home anymore, she was so happy there. It had been a great relief when she'd agreed to come home for the Fourth of July, as usual. Her mother was afraid with each passing year that one of them would break tradition and stop coming home as they always had. And once that happened, it would never be the same again. So far none of the girls were married or had children, but their mother was well aware that once that happened, things would change. In the meantime, until it did, she savored her time with them, and cherished their visits every year. She realized that it was nothing short of a miracle that all four of her daughters still came home three times a year, and even managed to visit whenever possible in between.

Annie came home less frequently than the others, but she was religious about the three major holidays they celebrated together. Charlie was far less involved with his family and said he hadn't been home to New Mexico to see them for nearly four years. She couldn't imagine not seeing her parents or sisters for that long. It was the one thing she missed in Florence, her family was too far away.

Charlie drove her to the airport the next day. It was going to be a long journey for her. She was flying to Paris, had a three-hour layover at the airport, and was catching a four P.M. flight to New York. She was getting to New York at six, local time, and expected to be home just after they finished dinner around nine. She had called her sister Tammy the week before, and they were getting home within half an hour of each other. Candy was arriving earlier, and Sabrina only had to drive in from New York, if she could drag herself out of the office, and of course she was bringing her awful dog. Annie was the only member of the family who hated dogs. The others were inseparable from theirs, except Candy when she traveled for work. She had her absurdly spoiled toy Yorkshire terrier with her the rest of the time, usually dressed in pink cashmere sweaters and bows. Annie had missed out on the dog-loving gene, although her mother was happy to have them home, with or without dogs.

"Take care of yourself," Charlie said solemnly, and then kissed her long and hard. "I'm going to miss you." He looked tragic and abandoned as she left.

"Me too," Annie said softly. They had made love for hours the night before. "I'll call you," she promised. They stayed in touch by cell phone when they were apart, even for a few hours. Charlie liked to stay in close touch with the woman he loved, and to have her near at hand. He had told her once that she was more important to him than his family. She couldn't say the same, and wouldn't have, but there was no question in her mind that she was very much in love with him. For the first time, she felt as though she had met a kindred spirit, and maybe even a possible mate, although she had no desire to marry for the next several years, and Charlie said the same. But they were thinking of living together for the last months of his stay, and had talked about it again the night before. She was thinking about suggesting it to him when she got back. She knew it was what he wanted, and she was ready to consider it now. They had gotten extremely close to each other in the last six months. Their lives were completely intertwined. He often said to her that he would love her no matter what, if she got fat, old, lost her teeth, her talent, or her mind. She had laughed at what he said, and assured him that she would do her best not to lose her teeth or mind. What mattered most to both of them was their art.

They called her flight then, and they kissed one last time before she left. She waved before disappearing through the gate, and her last sight of him was a tall, handsome young man waving at her with a look of longing in his eyes. She hadn't invited him to join her this time, but she was thinking of doing so for her Christmas trip, particularly if it was around the time he was going back. She wanted him to meet her family, although she knew that her sisters could be a little overwhelming at times. They all had strong opinions, particularly Sabrina and Tammy, and were all so different from Annie and the life she led. In many ways, she had more in common with Charlie than with them, although she loved them more than life itself. Their sisterly bond was sacred to each of them.

Annie settled into her seat for the brief flight to Paris. She sat next to an old woman who said she was going to visit her daughter there. After they landed, Annie wandered around the Paris airport. Charlie called her on her cell phone, the moment she turned it on after the flight.

"I miss you already," he said mournfully. "Come back. What am I going to do without you for a week?" It was unlike him to be that clingy, and it touched her that he was. They had been together so much that this trip was hard for both of them. It made her realize how attached to each other they had become.

"You'll have fun in Pompeii," she reassured him, "and I'll be back in a few days. I'll bring you back some peanut butter," she promised. He'd been complaining about missing it since he arrived. There was nothing about the States that Annie missed, except her family. Otherwise she loved living in Italy, and had adapted totally to the culture, language, habits, and food in the past two years. In fact, it was always a form of culture shock now when she went back. She missed Italy more than she did the States, which was part of why she wanted to stay. She felt so totally at home there, as though this were meant to be her place. She hated to give that up, if Charlie wanted her to go back to the States with him in six months. She felt torn between a man she loved, and a place where she felt so comfortable and at ease in her own skin, as though she had lived there all her life. Her Italian was fluent as well.

The Air France flight left Charles de Gaulle airport on time. Annie knew Candy had left the same airport six hours before, but Candy hadn't wanted to wait and go on Annie's flight, mostly because Candy flew first class, and Annie flew economy. But Candy was self-supporting and Annie wasn't. She wouldn't have considered flying first class at her parents' expense, and Candy said she'd rather die than fly in economy, squashed into a seat, with no leg room, and people squeezed into their seats on either side, unable to lie down. The first-class seats turned into proper beds, and she had no desire to miss out on that. She told Annie she'd see her at home. She had thought of paying the difference in her fare but knew that Annie would never take charity from her sister.

Annie was perfectly content in her economy seat as the plane took off. And although she missed Charlie, just thinking about seeing her family made her impatient to get home. She sat back in her seat with a smile, and closed her eyes, thinking of them.

Chapter 3

Tammy's day in Los Angeles was totally insane. She was at her desk by eight o'clock that morning, trying to get everything done before she left. The show she had produced for three years was on hiatus for the summer, but she was already busy organizing the following season. Their star had announced she was pregnant with twins the week before. Their male lead had been arrested for drugs, and it had been hushed up. They had fired two of their actors at the end of the last season, and they still had to be replaced. There was a threatened strike of the sound technicians that could delay the start of their next season, and one of their sponsors was threatening to move to another show. She had messages on her desk from lawyers about contracts and from agents who were returning her calls. She had about six hundred balls in the air, all of them part of the complicated logistics of producing a hit prime-time TV show.

Tammy had majored in television and communications at UCLA, and stayed on in Los Angeles afterward as the assistant executive producer of a longtime successful show. She'd worked on two shows after that; done a brief stint in reality TV, which she had hated; and worked on a dating show. For the last three years she had produced *Doctors,* a show about the practice of four women doctors. It had been the number-one show for the past two seasons. All Tammy ever did was work. Her last relationship had ended nearly two years ago. Since then she'd had two dates with men she had hated. She felt like she never had the time to meet anyone else or the energy to go anywhere when she finally left the office at night. Her best friend was Juanita, her three-pound toy chihuahua who sat under her desk and slept while Tammy worked.

Tammy was turning thirty in September, and her sisters teased her that she was going to be an old maid. They were probably right. At twenty-nine, she had no time to date, meet men, get her hair done, read magazines, or go anywhere for the weekend. It was the price she was willing to pay for creating and producing a hit television show. They had won two Emmys for the last two seasons. Their ratings had gone through the roof. The network and sponsors loved them, but she knew better than anyone that that would be the case only as long as their ratings stayed up. Any downward shift would drop-kick them into oblivion. Hit shows had gone from the top to the bottom faster than anyone could blink. Especially with their major star pregnant and on bedrest. It was going to be a major challenge to overcome, and Tammy didn't know how she would do it. Yet. She knew she'd solve the problems, as she always did. She was a genius at pulling rabbits out of a hat and saving the day.

By ten-thirty that morning, Tammy had returned all her phone calls, spoken to four agents, answered all her e-mails, and given her assistant a stack of letters to type. She needed to sign them before she left, and she had to leave for the airport at one for a three o'clock flight to New York. It was impossible to explain to her family what her life looked like on an everyday basis, and what kind of pressure she was under to keep the show on top of the ratings charts. After grabbing her third cup of coffee, she walked back into her office, glancing down at the tiny dog sleeping soundly under her desk. Juanita lifted her head, blinked, rolled over on her side, and went back to sleep. Tammy had had Juanita since college and took her everywhere with her. She was cinnamon-colored and shivered whenever she wasn't wearing a cashmere sweater. When Tammy left her office to do errands or go to lunch, she stuck Juanita in her purse. She carried an Hermès Birkin bag that was the perfect carrier for her tiny friend.

"Hi, Juanie. How're you doing, sweetheart?" The little dog moaned softly, and went back to sleep under the desk. People who came to see Tammy often in the office knew to watch where they walked. If anything happened to Juanita, it would kill Tammy. She was unnaturally attached to her dog, as her mother had commented more than once. She was a replacement for everything Tammy didn't have in her life, a man, children, women friends to hang out with, her sisters on a daily basis since they had all left home. Juanita seemed to be the sole recipient of all of Tammy's love. Juanita had gotten lost in the building once, and everyone had joined the search, while Tammy cried uncontrollably and even ran out to the street, looking for her. They had found her sound asleep next to a space heater on the set. She was famous all over the building now, as was Tammy, for her enormous success with the show, and her obsession with her dog.

Tammy was a stunning-looking woman, with a mane of long curly red hair that was so lush and luxurious that people accused her of wearing a wig sometimes, but it was all her own. It was the same color as her mother's, a bright fiery red, and she had green eyes, and a dusting of freckles across her nose and cheekbones, which made her look impish and young. She was the shortest of her sisters with a young girl's body, and irresistible charm when she wasn't running in fourteen directions and a nervous wreck about her show. Getting out of her office and onto a plane was almost like severing an umbilical cord, but she always went home for the Fourth of July to be with her sisters and parents. It was a good time of year to go, with the actors on hiatus.

Thanksgiving and Christmas were harder for her, as it was the middle of their season and the ratings battles were always tough. But she went home then too, no matter what. She took two cell phones with her and her computer. She got e-mails on her BlackBerry and was in constant communication with her staff wherever she went. Tammy was the consummate professional, the archetypal female television executive. Her parents were proud of her but were worried about her health. It was impossible to be as stressed as she was, have as much responsibility as rested on her shoulders, and not wind up with health problems one day. Her mother kept begging her to slow down, while her father admired her openly for her huge success. Her sisters cheerfully said she was nuts, which she was to some degree. Tammy herself said you had to be crazy to work in television, which was why it suited her so well. And she was convinced that the only reason she survived it was because she had had a normal home life while growing up. It had been what most people dreamed of and never had. Loving parents who were deeply devoted to each other, who had been rock solid for their four girls and still were. She missed their happy home life sometimes. Her life had never seemed entirely complete since she left. And they were all so spread out now. Annie in Florence, Candy all over the world shooting layouts for magazines or doing runway shows in Paris, and Sabrina in New York. She missed them so much at times, and usually when she finally had a chance to call them late at night, the time difference was all wrong, so she e-mailed them instead. When they called her on her cell phone, when she was running from one meeting to another, or on the set, they could only exchange a few words. She was really looking forward to spending the weekend with them.

"Your car is downstairs, Tammy," her assistant Hailey told her at twelve-forty, as she stuck her head in the door.

"Do you have the letters for me to sign?" Tammy asked, looking anxious.

"Sure do," Hailey said, clutching a file to her chest, and then set it on Tammy's desk and handed her a pen. Tammy glanced at the letters briefly, and scribbled her signature at the bottom of each of them. At least now she could leave with a clear conscience. All the most important things had been done. She couldn't stand leaving for the weekend without clearing her desk, which was why she usually came in on Saturdays and often Sundays, and hardly ever went anywhere for the weekend.

She had a house in Beverly Hills, which she loved. She'd had it for three years and still hadn't finished it. She didn't want to hire a decorator and was determined to do it herself, but never had time. There were still boxes of china and decorative doodads that she hadn't bothered to unpack since she sold her last house. One day, she told herself and promised her parents, she was going to slow down, but not yet. This was the high point of her career, her show was hot, and if she lost the momentum now, maybe everything would go down the drain. And the truth was she loved her life just as it was, hectic, crazy, and out of control. She loved her house, her work, and her friends when she had time to see them, which was almost never, she was always too busy with the show. She loved living in Los Angeles, as much as Annie loved Florence, and Sabrina loved New York. The only one who didn't care where she lived was Candy, who was happy anywhere as long as she was staying in a five-star hotel. She was just as happy in Paris, Milan, or Tokyo as she was in her penthouse in New York. Tammy always said that Candy was a nomad at heart. The others were far more attached to the cities where they lived, and the place they had carved out for themselves in their own worlds.

Although Candy was only eight years younger than Tammy, she seemed like a baby. And their lives were so incredibly different. Candy's professional life was all about how beautiful she was—no matter how modest she was about it. Tammy's work was about how beautiful others were, and how smart she was, although she was an extremely attractive woman, but she never thought about it. She was too busy putting out fires to even think about her looks, which was why there hadn't been a serious man in her life for more than two years. She didn't have time for men, and rarely liked the ones who crossed her path. The men she met in show business were not the kind of men she wanted to be involved with. Most of them were flaky, self-centered, and so full of themselves. She often felt she was almost too old for them now. They preferred dating actresses, and most of the men who asked her out were married and more interested in cheating on their wives than in having a serious relationship with a single woman. She had no patience with the bullshit, the lies, the narcissists, and she certainly had no interest in being anyone's mistress. And the actors she met seemed like freaks to her. When she first came to L.A. and started working in the business, she had had a million dates, most of which had turned out badly or been disappointing for one reason or another. She had been set up on dozens of blind dates. Now, when she finally left the office, she was just as happy relaxing in her house with Juanita and decompressing from the insanity of her day. She didn't have the time or energy to spend bored to death with some loser at a fancy restaurant, while he explained to her how bad his marriage had been, how crazy his soon-to-be-ex-wife was, and how his papers were coming through any day. Healthy single guys were hard to come by, and at twenty-nine she was in no rush to get married. She was far more interested in her career. Her mother reminded her every year that time went by quickly, and one day it would be too late. Tammy didn't know if she believed her, but she wasn't worried about it yet. For now, she was on the fast track of Hollywood, and thoroughly enjoying it, even if she didn't have a social life or even a date. It was working for her.

At five minutes after one she grabbed Juanita and put her in her Birkin, grabbed a stack of files and her computer, and shoved them in her briefcase. Her assistant had already sent her suitcase to the car waiting downstairs. Tammy didn't need much for the weekend, mostly blue jeans and T-shirts, a white cotton skirt for her parents' party, and two pairs of high-heeled Louboutin espadrilles. She had a row of bangle bracelets on her arm, and despite her lack of effort in that department, she always looked stylish and casual. She was still young enough to get away with whatever she wore. Juanita looked around with interest from inside the purse, and shivered as Tammy flew out of the office with a wave at her assistant and got into the elevator. Two minutes later she was in the car, heading for LAX. She had time to make calls on her cell phone from the car, and was annoyed to find that others had left the office early and were heading out for the holiday weekend too. By the time they were halfway to the airport, there was nothing for her to do but put her head back against the seat and relax. She had brought work to do on the flight. She just hoped she didn't have a talker sitting next to her.

Her mother always reminded her that she might meet the man of her dreams on a plane. Tammy smiled at the thought. She wasn't looking for Prince Charming. Mr. Normal would have been fine, but she wasn't looking for him either. She wasn't looking for anyone at the moment. She just wanted to get through another season of the show, and keep their ratings where they were. That was hard enough, especially with curveballs like their star getting pregnant. She still hadn't figured out how they were going to work around that. She'd figure out something. She had to. Tammy always came up with some idea that saved the day. She was famous for it.

A VIP service was waiting at the curb when they got to the airport, and the greeter recognized Tammy immediately. They had taken care of her before. Her assistant had arranged it. They checked her bags in for her, carried her briefcase, and commented about how cute her dog was.

"You hear that, Juanie?" Tammy said, bending to kiss the chihuahua. "She said you're a cutie. Yes, you are." Juanita shivered in response. Tammy had shoved her pink cashmere sweater into the bag with her, and would put it on her on the plane. She always complained that you could hang meat in the first-class cabin, they kept it so damn cold. She had brought a cashmere sweater for herself too. She always froze on planes. Probably because she skipped meals and never got enough sleep. She was looking forward to sleeping late at her parents' house that weekend. Something about being there made her feel as though she were back in the womb. It was the only place in her universe where she felt loved and nurtured and didn't have to take care of anyone else. Her mother adored fussing over them, no matter how old they were. She was looking forward to talking to her sisters about their parents' thirty-fifth anniversary, which was coming up in December. They wanted to throw a big party for them. Two of her sisters wanted to do it in Connecticut, and Tammy thought they should throw a big, fancy party at a hotel in New York. It was a landmark anniversary after all.

The VIP service left her at security, and Tammy made her way through on her own. She held Juanita as she went through the metal detector while the little dog shook miserably, and as soon as they got through it, she put her back in her bag. And she was relieved to discover that there was no one beside her on the plane. She put her briefcase on the seat next to her, and took her work out. Then she put the sweater on Juanita since the cabin was icy cold. She put her own sweater on, and was already working by the time they took off. She refused the champagne, which would just make her sleepy, took out the bottle of water she had brought with her, and gave some to the dog. They were halfway across the country by the time she finally stopped working, laid her head back against the seat, and closed her eyes. She hadn't even bothered to stop for lunch, and she had seen all the recent movies on DVD that she got from the Academy or at private screenings she went to when she had time. She put her seat back and slept for the rest of the trip. It had been a crazy week, but now finally out of the office, she started to unwind. She wanted to be wide awake and rested when she saw her sisters. They had so much to catch up on, and always so much to talk about. And even better than seeing her sisters, she couldn't wait to hug her mom. No matter how much clout she had in Hollywood or television, she was always thrilled to go home.

Chapter 4

Sabrina left her office at six o'clock. She had meant to leave earlier, but there were documents she had to proofread and sign. Nothing was going to get done over the holiday weekend, but she was taking an extra day off and her secretary had to file the papers with the court when she got back to the office on Tuesday. Sabrina never liked leaving loose ends. She was a family law attorney in one of the busiest practices in New York. Mostly, she handled prenuptial agreements and divorces and tough custody cases. What she had seen in her eight years as an attorney had convinced her that she never wanted to get married, although she was crazy about her boyfriend and he was a good man. Chris was an attorney in a rival firm. His specialty was antitrust law, and he got involved in class-action suits that went on for years. He was solid, kind, and loving, and they had been dating for three years.

Sabrina was thirty-four years old. She and Chris didn't live together, but they spent the night with each other, at his apartment or hers, three or four times a week. Her parents had finally stopped asking her if and when they were getting married. The arrangement they had worked for them. Chris was as solid as a rock. Sabrina knew she could count on him, and they loved the time they spent together. They enjoyed the theater, symphony, ballet, hiking, walking, playing tennis, and just being together on weekends. By now most of their friends were married and were even having second kids. Sabrina wasn't ready to think about it yet and didn't want to. They had both been made partners in their law firms. He was almost thirty-seven, and made noises occasionally about wanting children, and Sabrina didn't disagree with him. She wanted kids one day maybe, but not now. Although at thirty-four she was among the last of her friends still holding out. She felt that what she and Chris shared was almost as good as being married, without the headaches, the risk of divorce, and the pain she saw in her practice every day. She never wanted to be like one of her clients, hating the man she had married, and bitterly disappointed by how things had turned out. She loved Chris, and their life, just as it was.

He was coming to her parents' party the next day and would spend the night at the house in Connecticut. He knew how important these weekends with her family were to her. And he liked all of her sisters and her parents. There was nothing about Sabrina he didn't like, except maybe her aversion to marriage. He couldn't really understand it, since her parents were obviously happily married. He knew the nature of her law practice had put her off. At first, he had thought they'd be married in a couple of years. Now they had settled into a comfortable routine. Their apartments were only a few blocks apart, and they went back and forth with ease. He had a key to her apartment, and she had the key to his. When she worked late, she called him, and he went by her place and picked up her dog. Beulah, her basset hound, was their substitute child. He had given her the dog for Christmas three years before, and Sabrina adored her. She was a black and white harlequin basset, with the mournful look of her breed and a personality to match. When Beulah didn't get enough attention, she got severely depressed, and it took days to cajole her out of it. She slept at the foot of their bed, although she was a sixty-pound dog. But Chris couldn't complain since he had given her the dog. The gift had been a huge success at the time and ever since.

Sabrina left her office and went home to pick her up, and found Beulah sitting in her favorite chair next to the fireplace in Sabrina's living room with an insulted look. It was obvious that she knew her mistress was late to pick her up, walk her, and feed her.

"Come on," Sabrina said to her as she walked in, "don't be such a sourpuss. I had to finish my work. And I can't give you dinner before we go, or you'll get sick in the car." Beulah got carsick, and hated long rides. It was going to take at least two hours to get to Connecticut, Sabrina knew, or more in the holiday weekend traffic. It was going to be a long, slow ride. And Beulah hated missing meals. She was on the heavy side, from lack of exercise. Chris took her on runs in the park on weekends, but lately they'd both been busy. He was working on a huge case, and Sabrina was currently handling six major divorces, at least three of which were going to trial. She had a heavy workload, and was very much in demand as a divorce attorney among the elite of New York.

Sabrina handed Beulah a dog cookie, which the portly basset turned her nose up at and refused to eat. She was punishing Sabrina, which she did often. It only made Sabrina smile. Chris was better at getting the dog out of her dark moods, he had a lot more patience with her. And Sabrina was anxious to get on the road. She had packed the night before, and all she had to do was change out of her work clothes, a dark gray linen suit she had worn for a court appearance that morning, with a gray silk T-shirt, a string of pearls, and high-heeled shoes. She changed into jeans and a cotton T-shirt and sandals for the drive to Connecticut. She was anxious to get there, and knew it would be close to ten o'clock by the time she arrived. Her sisters Candy and Annie would already be there.

She knew that Tammy wouldn't get to the house until around two o'clock in the morning. Her plane was arriving at eleven-thirty that night, and after that she had to drive from JFK to Connecticut. Sabrina could hardly wait for all of them to be together. As far as Sabrina was concerned, they didn't see enough of each other. She and Chris had gone to California to visit Tammy two years before, but they hadn't been able to since, although they kept promising to make time to go out there again. They had had a great time with Tammy, although she was constantly working. The two oldest sisters in the group definitely had the strongest work ethic and Chris accused them both of being workaholics. He was much better about leaving the office at reasonable hours, and refusing to work on weekends. Sabrina always had her overstuffed briefcase near at hand, with things she had to read, or prepare for a case. Chris was a good lawyer too, but he had a more relaxed attitude about life, which made them a good combination. He made her loosen up a little, and she kept him on track, and didn't let him procrastinate, which he had a tendency to do. Sabrina sometimes nagged him, but he was a good sport about it.

She wished Tammy would find a man like him, but there were none in her world. Sabrina hadn't liked a single man that Tammy had gone out with in the past ten years. She was a magnet for self-centered, difficult men. Sabrina had chosen someone like their father, easygoing, kind, good-natured, and loving. It was hard not to love Chris, and they all did. He even looked a little like her father, which the others had teased her about when they first met him. Now they all loved him as she did. She just didn't want to be married to him, or anyone else. She was afraid it would screw things up, as she had seen so often. So many times couples told her that everything had been great while they were living together, sometimes for years and years, and then it all fell apart when they got married. One or both of them turned into monsters. She wasn't afraid that Chris would do that, or even that she would, but why take the chance? Things were so perfect as they were.

Beulah looked at Sabrina miserably as she set her suitcase down next to the front door. She thought she was being left behind.

"Don't look like that, silly. You're coming with me." As she said it, she picked up the dog's leash, and Beulah bounded out of the chair, wagging her tail, finally looking happy. "See, things aren't so bad after all, are they?" She clipped the leash on, turned off the lights, picked up her bag, and she and Beulah walked out the door.

Her car was in a nearby garage. She never used it in the city, only when she went out of town. It was a short walk to the garage. She put her bag in the trunk, and Beulah sat majestically in the front passenger seat and looked out the window with interest. Sabrina was relieved that her parents were good sports about their daughters' dogs. They had had cocker spaniels when they were children, but her parents hadn't had dogs now for years. They referred to the three visiting dogs as their "grand dogs" since her mother said she was beginning to think they would never have grandchildren. It looked that way so far.

Sabrina always assumed that one of the younger girls would get married first, probably Annie. Candy was still too young, and her head was all over the place about men. She was always meeting the wrong ones, drawn to her for her looks and celebrity alone. Tammy seemed to have given up dating in the last two years, and never seemed to meet decent men in the crazy business she was in. And she and Chris weren't going anywhere, they were happy as they were. Annie was the only one who seemed even remotely likely to get married. And as she drove out of the garage, Sabrina found herself wondering how serious this new boyfriend of Annie's was. She sounded pretty keen on him, and said he was terrific. Maybe not terrific enough to marry. She had said vaguely to Sabrina that he was moving back to New York at the end of the year. Sabrina figured it was probably the only thing that might get her to leave Florence. She loved it so much there, which worried Sabrina too. What if she never moved back from Europe? It was even harder to get to Florence than it was to get to L.A. to see Tammy. She hated the fact that they were all so spread out now. She really missed them. She saw Candy now and then when they both had time. Sabrina made a point of meeting her for lunch or dinner, or even coffee, but she hardly saw the other two and seriously missed them. Sometimes she thought she felt it more than the others. Her bond to her sisters and sense of family was strong, stronger than her bond to anyone else, even Chris, much as she loved him.

She called him from her car phone once she got on the highway. He had just come home from playing squash with a friend and said he was exhausted, but happy he had won.

"What time are you coming out tomorrow?" she asked. She already missed him. She always missed him on the nights they didn't spend together, but it made the nights they did spend with each other even sweeter.

"I'll get there in the afternoon, before the party. I thought I'd give you some time alone with your sisters. I know how you girls are. Shoes, hair, boyfriends, dresses, work, fashion. You have a lot to talk about." He was teasing her, but he wasn't far off the mark. They were still like a bunch of teenagers when they got together, they laughed

and talked and giggled, usually late into the night. The only difference now from when they were young was that they smoked and
drank while they did it, and they were a lot kinder about their parents than they had been as kids. Now they realized how lucky they
were to have them, and how great they were.

As teenagers, she and Tammy had given their mom a tough time.
Candy and Annie had been easier, and had enjoyed the freedoms
that Tammy and Sabrina had fought for earlier—and that in some
cases had been hard-won. Sabrina always said that they had worn
their mother down, but she had held a hard line at times. Sabrina
knew it couldn't have been easy to raise four girls. Their mom had
done a great job, and so had their dad. However, he often left a lot of
the difficult decisions to their mother and often deferred to her,
which always made Sabrina mad at him. She had wanted his support, and he refused to get in the middle of their battles. He wasn't
a fighter, he was a lover. And their mother had been more outspo-
ken and more willing to be unpopular with her daughters, if she
was convinced she was right. Sabrina thought she had been very
brave, and respected her a great deal. She hoped she'd be as good a
mother herself one day, if she was ever brave enough to have kids
of her own. She hadn't decided yet—it was another one of those decisions she had decided to put off for now, like marriage. At thirty-
four, she hadn't found her biological clock yet. She was in no hurry.

Tammy was the one who was nervous about missing out on having kids, if she didn't find the right guy. At Christmas, she had admitted that she would go to a sperm bank one day if she had to. She
didn't want to miss the chance to have children, just because she
never found a man she wanted to marry. But it was still early days
for that, and her sisters had urged Tammy not to panic, or she'd end
up with the wrong man again. She had done that often, and now

seemed to have given up entirely. She said the men she met were all too crazy, and Sabrina didn't disagree, from what she'd seen of them over the years. She thought all of Tammy's men were creeps.

Fortunately, there was nothing crazy or creepy about Chris. They all agreed on that. If anything, Sabrina was a lot crazier than he was, at least in her reluctance about marriage. She didn't want a husband or baby yet, just him the way things were, for now, and maybe even forever. She didn't want anything to change between them.

"What are you doing tonight?" she asked Chris on the phone as she sat in traffic. It was going to take forever to get there at this rate, but it was nice chatting with him. It always was. They rarely had arguments, and when they did, they blew over quickly. He was like her father that way too. Her father hated arguments of any kind, particularly with his wife or even his daughters. He was the easiest man on the planet to get along with, and so was Chris.

"I thought I'd cook myself some dinner, watch the game on TV, and go to bed. I'm beat." She knew how hard he'd been working on an oil company case. It was about environmental pollution, and the case would go on for years. He was lead counsel on the case, and had gotten a lot of publicity for it. She was very proud of him. "How's Beulah doing?"

Sabrina glanced at her in the passenger seat and smiled.

"She's falling asleep. She was pissed at me when I got home. I was late. You're a lot nicer about that than she is."

"She'll forgive you when she gets to play in the grass and chase rabbits." She was a hunter in her soul, although she was a city dog, and the only thing she ever got to chase were pigeons in the park when Chris took her for a run. "I'll give her some exercise tomorrow when I come out."

"She needs it. She's getting fat," Sabrina responded. As she said it,

Beulah jerked awake as the car lurched forward, and glared at her, as though she had heard what she'd said and was insulted again. "Sorry, Beulie, I didn't mean that the way it sounded." The dog curled up on the seat then, with a loud snort and went to sleep. Sabrina really loved her and enjoyed her company. "I hope Juanita doesn't attack her again," Sabrina said to Chris. "She scared the hell out of Beulah last time."

"That's embarrassing. How can Beulah be afraid of a three-pound dog?"

"Juanita thinks she's a Great Dane. She always attacks other dogs."

"I eat tacos bigger than she is. She's ridiculous, she looks like a bat." He smiled, thinking of the three dogs in their family, each one sillier than the other. Candy's Yorkie was a little princess, and always wore bows in her hair, which the chihuahua ripped out whenever she got the chance. She was a three-pound attack dog.

"Don't say that," Sabrina warned him. "Tammy thinks she's gorgeous."

"I guess love is blind, even about dogs. At least your sister Annie is sane."

"She's always hated dogs. She thinks they're a nuisance. She shaved my mother's cocker spaniel once. Mom put her on restriction for three weeks. Annie said the dog looked too hot with all that hair in the middle of summer. The poor dog looked totally pathetic." They both laughed at the image, and as traffic picked up again, Sabrina said she'd better hang up. He told her he loved her, and would see her the next day at her parents'.

Sabrina thought about him as she drove, and felt lucky to have met him. It wasn't easy to meet good men, and one as nice as Chris was rare. She was well aware of it, and deeply grateful that they were so happy with each other. It just got better from year to year, which was why her mother couldn't understand her lack of interest in getting married. It was just the way Sabrina was, and she always said it wasn't due to any failing on Chris's part. He was more than willing to get married, but patient with the fact that she wasn't. He never pushed, and accepted her as she was, phobias and all.

The drive to Connecticut was long and slow that night. She called home to apologize for the delay, and her mother told her that both Annie and Candy had arrived, and were sitting by the pool. She said they both looked terrific, although Candy hadn't gained any weight, but at least she was no thinner. And Annie was telling them about Charlie. Their mother said it sounded serious to her, which made Sabrina smile.

"I'll be there as soon as I can, Mom. I'm sorry to be so late."

"I figured you would be, sweetheart. Don't worry about it. I know it's hard for you to get out of the office. How's Chris?"

"He's fine. He'll be out tomorrow afternoon. He wanted to give us some girl time. He's always nice about that."

"Yes, he is," her mother agreed. "Drive safely, Sabrina. Don't rush. We'll be up late anyway. Tammy won't be in till after two. She had to work today too. Both of you work too hard, but with good results, I have to admit. I'm not sure where you two get your work ethic. I don't think your dad or I ever worked as hard as you two."

"Thanks, Mom." Their mother was always generous with praise. She was proud of all four of her girls, and in their own way, each of them was doing well. More important, all four of them were happy, and had found their niche. Their mother never compared them to each other, even as children, and saw each of them as individuals, with different talents and needs. It made their relationship that much better with her now. And each in her own way was crazy about their mom. She was like a best friend, only better. They had her unconditional love and approval, and she never lost sight of the fact that she was their mother, and not a friend. Sabrina liked it that way, and all of her friends had liked her mother too. As kids, all their friends had loved hanging out at their house, and knew they were always welcome there, as long as they were polite and behaved. Their mother had never tolerated alcohol or drugs when they were young, and with few exceptions, their friends had respected the rules. And when they didn't respect them, she had been tough.

It was just after ten o'clock when Sabrina pulled into their driveway. She let Beulah out of the car, and walked to the pool, where she knew she'd find everyone. The girls were in the water, and her parents were sitting on deck chairs, chatting with them. Sabrina's arrival was met with excitement and squeals of delight. Candy leaped out of the pool and hugged her, and Sabrina was instantly soaking wet, and then she hugged and kissed Annie, and all three girls laughed with delight. Annie said it had been worth the trip all the way from Florence just to see her, and she said Sabrina looked great. She had cut her almost-jet-black hair, which hung just past her shoulders and had been longer before. As a child, Annie always said that Sabrina looked like Snow White, with creamy white skin, dark blue-black hair, and big blue eyes, just like Candy's. Their father's eyes were blue. Both Tammy and Annie had their mother's green eyes. And her mother's hair was as red as Tammy's, although hers had always been straight. She wore it short now. Tammy was the only one in the family with wildly curly hair, and she had hated it growing up. She had ironed it for years. Now she just let it run wild, in a mane of soft curls. Sabrina had always been jealous of Tammy's hair. Sabrina's was thick and dark and straight. And like her sisters, but in a totally different way, she was a beautiful young woman. She had long legs and a trim figure. She wasn't as tall as Candy, but she was tall. Tammy was tiny, like their mother, and Annie was somewhere between the two and of average height, but she was an unusually pretty girl too.

"So what's with this guy Charlie?" Sabrina asked Annie, as she dangled her feet in the pool, and her mother handed her a glass of lemonade. She looked thrilled to have three of her girls at home and the fourth one only hours away. This was what she loved best, her entire family in one place. She looked lovingly at her husband, and he smiled at her. He knew how much it meant to her. He leaned over and kissed her. After nearly thirty-five years, they were still very much in love, and it showed.

They had had their arguments over the years, though never serious ones. Their marriage had been stable since the day they married. Sabrina wondered sometimes if that was why she was hesitant about marriage. She couldn't imagine being lucky enough to have a marriage like theirs, and she didn't want anything less. If anyone was likely to be a good husband, Chris was, but she couldn't imagine being as good a wife as her mother had been for all these years. Jane Adams seemed like the perfect wife and mother to her. Sabrina had said that to her once, and her mother was stunned. She said she had the same insecurities and flaws as everyone else. She gave Jim the credit for how good their marriage was, and said he had been the perfect mate. It was easy to see that in retrospect, but she said that when she got married, she had been scared too. Marriage was a big step, but she had told Sabrina she thought it was well worth taking the risk.

"So tell me about Charlie," Sabrina insisted. "How serious is it? Are you two getting engaged?"

"Hell, no," Annie said lightly. "Not yet anyway. He's a great guy, but it's only been six months. I'm twenty-six, I don't want to get married yet. You first. How's Chris?"

"He's terrific," Sabrina answered, and then they were all distracted as Candy's tiny Yorkshire terrier barked furiously at the basset, and Beulah, looking terrified, hid under a bush, while the Yorkie, wearing a small pink bow, kept her at bay. On her way out, Candy had stopped to pick her up at the place where she boarded her. She had missed her too much while she was in Paris, and was delighted to have her back. "My dog is a total wuss," Sabrina said, laughing at her. "I think she has self-esteem issues or something. She's very neurotic. She gets depressed."

"Wait till Juanita attacks her," Candy said, laughing. Even Zoe, the Yorkie, was afraid of her.

"How was Paris, by the way?" Sabrina asked her.

"It was great. Everyone was going to St. Tropez for the weekend. I'd much rather be here."

"Me too," Annie said, beaming.

"We all would," Sabrina said, smiling at her parents. Everything around them seemed so idyllic and peaceful. It reminded them of their childhood, and being safe, loved, and protected again. She always felt happy here.

They sat outside and chatted for another hour, and then their father went to bed. Their mother was staying up to wait for Tammy. She wanted to be awake to welcome her. Sabrina went to put her bathing suit on and joined her sisters in the pool. It was a hot balmy night, the fireflies were dancing, and it was warm in the pool. Eventually, they went back into the house and changed into their nightgowns at nearly one o'clock in the morning. Their mother put sandwiches and cookies with more lemonade out on the kitchen table.

"If I still lived here, I'd be too fat to work," Candy commented, took a bite out of one cookie, and then put it down.

"I don't think you're in any danger of that," Annie commented. Like the others, she worried about Candy's weight. She got too much positive reinforcement, and made too much money, for being too thin.

They were sitting in the kitchen, talking, when Tammy's limousine drove up. They heard the car door slam, and a moment later she ran into the kitchen, and they were all in each others' arms again, hugging and laughing and talking all at once while Juanita barked fiercely at everyone. She was on the floor for all of two seconds before she ripped Zoe's bow out, and had Beulah cowering under a chair. Her personality did not reflect Tammy's, but she was definitely the fiercest dog in the pack, although the smallest. Tammy picked her up and scolded her, but the minute she set her down again, she had both dogs on the run.

"She's hopeless," Tammy apologized, and then looked her sisters over carefully. "God, you all look great. I missed you so much." Tammy put her arms around her mother and hugged her, and a few minutes later Jane stood up. Her job was done. She had welcomed them all home and could leave them to their own devices now. She knew they'd sit up for hours, catching up, and exchanging secrets and stories about their respective lives. It was time for her to retire and leave them alone.

"I'll see you in the morning," she said with a yawn, as she left the kitchen. It was so good to have them home. These moments were the high point of her year.

"Sleep tight, Mom, see you tomorrow," they all said, and kissed her goodnight, just as they had as children.

They helped themselves to a bottle of wine after she left, and sat

and talked until after four in the morning, and then they walked upstairs. Their home had been unusual in that each of the girls had had
her own room as a kid. They all commented on how strange it felt at
times to be back here, and in their old beds, where they had grown
up. It made them feel like children again, and brought back so many
memories. They all said that they thought their mom looked well,
and they promised to discuss the anniversary party the next day, to
make a plan. They had so much to talk about, and share, and whatever tensions had existed between them over the years had vanished
when they met as adults. The only one who still seemed childlike to
them was Candy, but she was still very young. The others felt very
grown up, and however young she was, Candy led a very grown-up
life. Money and success had come to her early, and in some ways it
made her seem more mature than she really was. Sabrina and Tammy
worried about her, and talked about it sometimes. Candy was exposed to some pretty scary stuff, in the course of her career as a supermodel. They just hoped she could handle it. Her eating issues
were a serious concern to them. Annie was more relaxed about
it, and always said she thought she was fine. But in some ways, she
was less aware of the challenges that Candy faced on a daily basis,
and the dangers in her world. Annie's life was so simple and arty, she
couldn't really conceive of the life that Candy led. It was life on another planet to her. Her older sisters were far more aware of the dangers and risks, and the toll they could take on her.

They kissed each other goodnight and went to their own rooms,
and a few minutes later Sabrina walked back into Tammy's room and
told her how happy she was to see her. Tammy was sitting in bed,
wearing a pink nightgown, with her halo of red curls.

"I wish you didn't live so far away," Sabrina said to Tammy sadly.

"So do I," Tammy said. "I miss you guys so much. It comes back to me in a rush every time I see you. But there's no decent work for me here. All the big shows are done out of L.A."

"I know," Sabrina said, nodding. "I should come out to see you more often. I get so bogged down here," she said with regret.

"We all do," Tammy said, nodding. "It all goes by so fast. I hate waiting six months to see you. Sometimes I wish we all still lived here, with Mom and Dad, and we weren't all grown up."

"Yeah, me too," Sabrina said, and hugged her again. "I'm glad we still come home like this. At least that's something. Maybe we should organize a trip and all go over to see Annie in Florence. That would be fun. Maybe Mom and Dad would come too."

"I'm not sure he would, but Mom might. He always thinks they won't survive without him in the office." And then Tammy laughed. "I guess I think that too, about myself, and so do you. We really ought to try and spend more time together. Right now we're all free, we're not married, we don't have kids. Later it will be even harder to get together. We should try to do it while we still can."

"I agree," Sabrina said seriously, as Juanita popped her head out from under the covers and growled at her. She jumped, surprised by the threatened attack from a dog that was barely bigger than a hamster. The basset was sound asleep in her room. "Why don't we organize some kind of trip before we leave here this time? I can take a week off, if I plan it far enough ahead."

"Me too," Tammy said, wanting to do it, though not sure how easily she could get away. During the season, her life was insane.

"Let's talk about it tomorrow," Sabrina said, and left the room again. She was so happy to be with her sisters. They all were.

And in her room, their mother could hear them moving around, visiting each other's bedrooms. She smiled as she turned over next to Jim. It reminded her of the old days, when she knew that all was well because all four of them were home at night. She reveled in the comforting sounds of having her whole family under one roof. She counted her blessings, as she always did, as she fell asleep, thinking how lucky she was to have them, and that they would all be there for three more days. For her, they were life's greatest gift.

Chapter 5

When the girls got up one by one the next morning, their mother was waiting in the kitchen for them, ready to prepare a special breakfast for each of them. She loved cooking for them, as seldom as it was. Their father had eaten breakfast hours earlier and was outside by the pool, reading the paper. He liked to leave them time with their mother, and planned to get back in the thick of things again later. He knew how crazy things were going to get with all five of his women buzzing around him. He preferred his mornings peaceful and quiet.

Sabrina was always an early riser and was the first to get up. She came downstairs, found her mother in the kitchen, and offered to help her cook breakfast for the others. Jane insisted that she loved doing it herself. Sabrina noticed how happy her mother seemed that morning, and knew how much it meant to her that they were all at home, even for a brief time. She had put a pot of coffee on, and Sabrina helped herself to a cup of the steaming brew, and sat down at the kitchen table to chat with her mother while waiting for the others. She had only taken two sips when Tammy walked in with Annie right behind her. Candy was still the latest riser. Some things never changed even after all these years. She was still sound asleep upstairs in her bedroom, although her Yorkie had wandered downstairs and was playing in the kitchen with Juanita. Sabrina had let the basset out to check things out for herself, and hopefully she would find something to chase.

"Good morning, girls," Jane said brightly. She was wearing white shorts with a pink top and low-heeled sandals. Sabrina couldn't help noticing that she still had great legs. All three older sisters had been blessed and got their legs from her. Candy's were endless and were more like their dad's. "What can I make you?" They all started out by muttering that they didn't normally eat breakfast, no one was hungry, and coffee was fine. They were on a wide variety of time zones. It was already nearly dinnertime for Candy, who was still sleeping, and for Annie, who didn't want to admit it but was starving. She grabbed an orange from a bowl of fruit on the counter, and started unwinding the rind, as her mother poured coffee for Annie and Tammy. For Tammy it still felt like the middle of the night, but she was wide awake. They all were. In spite of the late night the night before, they all were energetic. Jane suggested scrambled eggs, and put a plate of muffins on the table, with butter and jam. All three girls helped themselves while chatting. Sabrina suggested that one of them should wake Candy, so she didn't get up in the middle of the afternoon. Annie silently disappeared from the room and went to rouse her, and ten minutes later they both came down. By then, their mother was making scrambled eggs and bacon. They all insisted they weren't hungry, but as soon as the eggs were ready, they helped themselves to generous portions, including several strips of bacon. Sabrina was pleased to see that Candy took some of the eggs too, half a muffin, and a single strip of bacon. It was probably the most she'd eaten for breakfast in several years.

Jane even sat down with them and had a plate of eggs herself. "What do you all want to do this morning?" she asked with interest. There wasn't much to do, since it was the holiday and everything was closed. But she thought they might want to call some of their friends who still lived in town. Many had moved away, gotten married, or had jobs in other cities, but the girls still stayed in touch with some.

"I just want to hang around with you guys and Mom," Annie said, echoing what they all felt. "And Dad, if he doesn't feel too outnumbered." They knew he enjoyed having them home too, but he had always been someone who needed his own space. When they were younger, he had spent a lot of time playing tennis and golf with friends, and they knew from their mother that he still did.

At fifty-nine, he still acted and moved like a young man, and hadn't changed much. There was more gray in his hair, but still the same spring in his step. And they all agreed that their mother looked better than ever. Her face was still beautiful and hardly lined. She could easily have lied and taken ten years off her age. It was hard for all of them to believe that she was old enough to have children their age, despite the fact that she had started young. She had almost no wrinkles at all, and took fairly good care of herself. She went to an exercise class three times a week, and had mentioned taking ballet to stay in shape. Whatever she was doing had paid off. Her figure was even better than it had been when she was young.

"Mom, what do we need to do to get ready for the party tonight?" Annie asked.

Her mother said that the caterers would be arriving at four o'clock. Guests were invited for seven. "But I need to go to the store at some point," Jane announced. "There's a supermarket open today on the other side of the highway. I forgot to get pickles for your father."

They were having hot dogs, hamburgers, fried chicken, and everything that went with them. The caterers were doing a full buffet, with salads, french fries, onion rings, several platters of sushi, and an assortment of ice creams and pies. "You know how your father is if he doesn't have pickles, and I think we're almost out of mayonnaise. I didn't think of it till last night. I can do it after lunch," she said, not wanting to tear herself away from them for even a minute. Annie looked over and smiled at her and understood.

"I can go with you, Mom. Why don't we go after breakfast and get it done? It won't take long." It was a ten-minute trip to the market their mother was referring to. "I can do it for you, if you want."

"I'll come with you," Jane said, rinsing off their dishes and putting them in the dishwasher, as Sabrina helped. It was times like this when Jane was glad she still had two machines. They still had two washing machines and two dryers as well. There had been a time when they couldn't have managed with anything less. But now, most of the time, when she and Jim were alone, it took days to fill the machines. Normally, she turned them on long before they were full. But with all the girls home, everything would be in use again.

With so many hands at work, it took them only a few minutes to clean up the kitchen, and their mother ran upstairs to get her car keys and purse. She was back a minute later, as the three other girls headed toward the pool to check on their father, while she and Annie went out the back door to the car.

Jane started the engine in her Mercedes station wagon, and they drove off, as she and Annie chatted. She told her mother about the classes she was taking in Florence and the new techniques she had learned. They were all based on ancient principles, and she was even learning how to mix her own paints, in some cases with egg.

"Do you think you'll ever move back?" her mother asked, trying to sound casual, and Annie smiled. Annie knew it pained her to have even one daughter far away.

"Eventually, but not yet," Annie said honestly. "I love what I'm learning there, and it's a good life. It's a wonderful place for an artist."

"So is New York," her mother said, trying not to be pushy about it. "I just hope you don't stay there forever. I hate having you so far away."

"It's not that far, Mom. I can fly home within a day, if you ever need me."

"It's not that. Your father and I are fine. It's just that I enjoy seeing more of you than just three times a year when you come home for holidays. That never seems like enough. I don't mean to sound ungrateful, and I'm glad you come home. I just wish you were around the corner, or in the city like Sabrina."

"I know, Mom. You and Dad should come to see me. Florence is such a beautiful city. It will be hard to leave when I finally decide to." She didn't tell her that Charlie was planning to leave, and she was thinking about it. She didn't want to give the relationship that much importance, particularly in her mother's eyes, who was ever hopeful that Annie would come home. And she didn't want to give her mother false hope.

They found a parking space at the supermarket easily, and went inside together. They put the few items they wanted in a cart, and qualified for the express lane. They were back in the parking lot in less than five minutes. The weather was extremely hot, and they were both anxious to get home and jump in the pool. It was hours before the guests would come. Jane was looking forward to spending the day with them, mostly in and around the pool. The temperature was supposed to go over a hundred that afternoon. She just hoped it would cool off a little by that night. If not, the guests were going to be sweltering outside at seven o'clock, and it would still be sunny and bright. It wouldn't get dark till after eight o'clock.

"This is even hotter than Florence," Annie commented as they got back in the air-conditioned car. She was grateful for the blast of cool air on her face when her mother turned on the ignition.

They had to cross the highway to get back to the house, and Annie was talking about Charlie as they got behind a truck that was carrying a load of steel pipes on a flatbed behind it. Jane was listening to her intently, and as Annie talked, they both heard a loud snap, and saw the steel pipes begin to fall off the truck. Some rolled off to the sides, causing cars on the other side of the road to swerve to avoid them, and the rest of the pipes shot backward off the truck toward Jane's Mercedes. She was trying to slow down as Annie gasped and saw three of the pipes shoot off the truck straight at them. Instinctively, she reached out toward her mother and shouted "Mom!" But it was already too late. Like a scene in a movie she couldn't stop, Annie saw the pipes come straight through the windshield into the car, as Jane lost control of the wheel, and the car plunged into the oncoming lane. Annie heard herself screaming and tried to grab the steering wheel, and as she did there was a sound of metal being crushed, breaking glass, and brakes screaming all around them. She looked toward her mother and couldn't see her anywhere. The door on the driver's side was open, the car was moving at full speed, and Annie saw the driver of the car they hit just as everything went black around her and she lost consciousness.

Two of the steel pipes had gone straight through their car, as it careened wildly and finally stopped after it had hit two oncoming cars. Cars behind them and ahead of them came to a screeching stop, and traffic backed up instantly, as someone called the police.

There was no sign of movement in any of the cars that had been hit, and the driver of the truck stood by the side of the road crying, as he looked at the scene of carnage his truck had caused. By the time the police came, he was in shock and unable to speak. Fire trucks came, ambulances, highway patrol, local police. The drivers of all three vehicles had been killed, along with a total of five passengers. There was only one survivor, the firemen were able to ascertain, and it took half an hour to get her out of the car. She had been pinned under the steel pipes, and she was unconscious as the ambulance drove her away. The rest of the victims were taken out of the cars, laid down on the highway, and covered with tarps, as they waited for more ambulances to arrive. The police on the scene looked solemn as the traffic backed up for miles. It was what always happened on the Fourth of July. People got in car accidents, tragedies happened, people died and became statistics. Jane had flown out of the car when the pipes hit them, and died instantly. And as they drove Annie to the trauma unit at Bridgeport Hospital, she was barely alive, clinging to life by a thread.

At the house, her sisters chatted with their father, innocently enjoying a hot sunny summer day. They were expecting their mother and sister back at any moment, and had no inkling that they would never see their mother again, and that their sister was fighting for her life.

Chapter 6

Two men from the highway patrol rang the Adamses' doorbell shortly after twelve-thirty. They had left the scene of the accident as Annie was taken away in the ambulance. They had found Jane's driver's license in her handbag in the car, and they could tell from Annie's that she was Jane's daughter. She still had her parents' Connecticut address on her U.S. driver's license. She had an Italian license in her handbag as well. If necessary, highway patrolmen were allowed to notify next of kin by phone, in case of an accident. But Chuck Petri, the officer in charge at the scene, thought it was inhuman to do that. If something had happened to his wife or daughter, he would want a real live human being to come and tell him, not a phone call. So he sent two patrolmen to the Adamses' address and handled traffic at the scene himself, as they directed a single file of cars to move past the crushed cars and tarped bodies, going five miles per hour. The highway would be tied up for hours.

The two patrolmen ringing the bell looked acutely uncomfortable. One was a rookie and had never done anything like it before.

The senior officer with him was his partner and had promised to do the talking when someone answered.

It took a few minutes for someone to come to the door, since they couldn't hear the doorbell clearly from the pool. Sabrina had just said she wondered where their mom and Annie were. They had been gone for nearly an hour, a lot longer than it took to get to the store they had in mind. Maybe the store was closed and they had had to go somewhere else for the pickles and mayonnaise. Tammy went to answer the door when they heard it; she was going to the kitchen to get something to drink anyway. She pulled open the front door and saw them through the screen door, and as soon as she did she could feel her heart pound, and forced herself to believe that this couldn't be as ominous as it appeared. They were probably there about some minor infraction, like the sprinkler leaving spots on the neighbor's window, or the dogs making too much noise. That had to be it. The young officer was smiling nervously at her, and the older officer looked at her with a somber frown.

"Can I help you, officer?" Tammy asked, looking him directly in the eye, reassuring herself silently again.

"Is there a Mr. James Adams here?" He was listed with the DMV as Jane's next of kin. His young partner had gotten it off the computer for him on the drive over.

"Of course," Tammy said respectfully, and stepped aside so they could come in out of the heat. The house was cool to the point of being chilly. Their mother liked to run the air conditioning full blast. "I'll get him for you. May I say what this is about?" She wanted to know herself, more than for her dad. But suddenly her father was right behind her, as though he had sensed that the doorbell signaled something important. He looked puzzled when he saw the two officers in highway patrol uniforms.

"Mr. Adams?"

"Yes. Is something wrong?" Tammy saw her father's face go pale, just as Sabrina and Candy walked in.

"May I speak to you alone, sir?" the senior officer asked, having taken his hat off in the house. Tammy noticed that although he was bald, he was a nice-looking man about her father's age. The officer with him looked about fourteen years old.

Without saying a word, their father led them into the library he and their mother used as a den in the winter. It was a pretty wood-paneled room with a fireplace, lined with antique books they had collected for years. There were two comfortable couches, and several large leather chairs. Jim sat down in one of them, and waved them both to the couch. He had no idea whatsoever why they were there. He had the insane idea suddenly that one of them was about to be arrested, and he couldn't imagine why. He hoped that one of the girls hadn't done something stupid. Candy was still young and was the only one he could think of who might. Maybe she had smuggled some drugs through customs when she came from Paris, or Annie in the spirit of her artistic life. He hoped not, but it was the only thing that came to mind. His daughters were hovering in the hallway just outside, looking worried, as the senior officer took a deep breath, clutching the hat in his hand. It was a while since he had done anything like this, and it was hard.

"I'm sorry to tell you, sir, there's been an accident. About twenty minutes ago, on Highway 1, about five miles from here."

"An accident?" Jim looked blank, and in the hallway Sabrina gasped and clutched Tammy and Candy's hands. It wasn't computing in their father's brain.

"Yes, sir. I'm sorry. We wanted to come and tell you in person. There was an incident with a truck, a bunch of steel pipes got loose and caused a three-way head-on collision. Some of the pipes went through one of the cars. The driver was Jane Wilkinson Adams, her date of birth was June 11, 1950. You're listed as next of kin with the DMV. I believe she was your wife." His voice dwindled to nothing as Jim stared at him in horror.

"What do you mean, she 'was' my wife? She still is!" he insisted.

"She was killed instantly in the accident. The pipes went through her windshield and ejected her from the car, which hit two other vehicles head-on. She was dead on impact." There was no way to dress it up. The terms were ugly. And Jim's face suddenly contorted in pain as it finally hit him, and all that it meant.

"Oh my God . . . oh my God . . ." The girls could hear a sob in the room, and not being able to stand it any longer, they rushed in. All they had heard was "dead on impact," but they still didn't know who, Annie or Mom or both? They were desperately frightened as their father cried.

"Who is it? What happened?" Sabrina was the first to enter the room and ask, with the other two close behind her. Candy was already crying, although she didn't know yet for whom, or why.

"It's Mom," their father said in a choked voice. ". . . There was an accident on . . . a head-on collision . . . steel pipes fell off a truck . . ." Tammy and Sabrina's eyes filled instantly with tears as well, as Sabrina turned to the officer with a look of panic, and he told them how sorry he was about their mom.

"What happened to my sister? She was in the car with Mom. Her name is Anne." She couldn't even let herself think that they had both been killed. She held her breath and braced herself the moment she asked.

"She's still alive. I was going to tell your father, but I wanted to give him a minute to catch his breath." The officer looked apologetically at them all, as tears filled the rookie's eyes. This was even worse than he had imagined. These were real people, and they were talking about their mother. He didn't look it, but he was Candy's age. He had three sisters, close in age to them, and a mother close to their mother's age. "She was badly injured in the accident, they just took her to Bridgeport Hospital. She was unconscious when they got her out of the car. It was a miracle—she was the only survivor in all three cars." In all, eight people had died, but the officer didn't tell the Adamses that. He had come here first, because Annie was still alive. And they had to be notified quickly so they could go to the hospital. The time factor was less crucial in the cars where everyone had died.

"What happened to her? Is she going to be okay?" Tammy interjected quickly, as Candy just stood there and sobbed, looking like a gigantically tall five-year-old.

"She was in critical condition when they took her. I'll drive you folks down there if you like. Or I can lead the way with the siren on, if you want to take your car." Jim was still staring at him in disbelief. Nearly thirty-five years with a woman he had loved deeply since the first hour he met her, and now suddenly in the flash of an instant, in an incredibly stupid freak accident, she was gone. He hadn't even fully understood what they'd said about Annie. All he could think of now was his wife.

"Yes," Sabrina answered before anyone else could, "we'll follow you." The officer nodded as she and Tammy sprang into action. They ran upstairs and grabbed their handbags, and with sudden forethought, Sabrina took the address book and party list from her mother's desk. They were going to have to call off the party that night. Tammy made sure all three dogs were inside and took bottles of water from the fridge and threw them into her bag. A moment later they were all running toward their father's car. It was a large recent-model Mercedes sedan. Sabrina got behind the steering wheel and told him to get in. He got into the passenger seat next to her, as Candy and Tammy slid into the backseat and slammed the doors. All Sabrina could think of was that maybe Annie would be dead before they even arrived. She was praying she'd still be alive.

The officers turned on the siren before they left the driveway, and took off at a terrifying speed with Sabrina right behind them. They hit ninety when they got on the highway, and she stayed within two feet of him for the entire drive. They were at Bridgeport Hospital within minutes. Their father hadn't stopped crying since they left the house.

"Why didn't I go to the store for her? I could have done it. I didn't even think to ask her." He was blaming himself, as Sabrina parked in the hospital lot and looked at him for a minute before they got out, and then took him in her arms.

"If you had done that, she'd have been here crying over you, Dad. It happened. We can think about that later. We have to see what happened to Annie, and get her through this somehow." Sabrina was hoping that she wasn't as badly injured as they all feared. With any luck at all, their sister would be spared. It was bad enough to lose their mother, unthinkable in fact, but right now all she could allow herself to think about was Annie. She waited for the others to get out, which seemed to take forever, set the alarm on her father's car, and waved her thanks at the highway patrolmen for getting them there so fast. They ran straight into the emergency room and were sent to the trauma unit, where the woman at the desk said Annie had been taken. Sabrina ran down the hall, with Candy and Tammy behind her, and her father bringing up the rear. Sabrina wanted to console him, but they had Annie to think about right now. There was nothing they could do for their mother. Somehow, as they walked into the trauma unit, Sabrina felt sure she would see her mother waiting for them, telling them Annie was going to be okay. The reality they encountered was far different.

The chief resident in the trauma unit came out to see them immediately, as soon as Sabrina gave their names. He said that Annie was barely clinging to life and needed brain and eye surgery as soon as possible, to relieve pressure on her brain and hopefully save her sight. But as he looked at all of them, he didn't pull any punches and said that Annie's injury was greatest in the part of her brain that affected her vision.

"I don't know if we can save her sight," he said bluntly. "Right now I'm more concerned with keeping her alive."

"So are we," Tammy said, as Candy stared at him in horror.

"She's an artist! You have to save her eyes!" He nodded and said nothing, showed them the CT scans and X-rays on a light box in the waiting room, and told them he was waiting for the best possible brain surgeon and ophthalmologist to come in. Both had been called. Since it was the Fourth of July, neither of them was on duty, but luckily their answering services had reached them. The brain surgeon had phoned to say he was on the way, and they had just reached the eye surgeon at a family barbecue. He had said he would be there in less than half an hour. Annie was on life support in the meantime. Her heart had stopped twice on the way in, and she was no longer breathing on her own. But her brain waves were normal. As far as they could tell, there was no major brain damage so far. The swelling of her brain was going to cause some real problems very shortly, but what the resident said he was most worried about were her eyes. If she survived the accident at all, there was a good chance her brain would return to normal. From what he had seen of the damage Annie had sustained in the accident, he couldn't imagine their being able to save her sight. His greatest concern was that her optic nerves were damaged beyond repair. But miracles did happen, and they needed one now.

The brain surgeon walked in as they were looking at the films of Annie's brain. After looking at them himself, he explained what the procedure would be, what the risks were, and how long it would probably take. He didn't pull any punches either, and said that there was a very real possibility that Annie could die in surgery. But they had no other choice. He said clearly that without surgery to relieve the swelling, Annie could be severely brain-damaged forever, or might die.

"Annie would hate that," Tammy whispered to her sisters, about her being brain-damaged. They agreed to let him operate, and both Sabrina and Tammy signed the release forms. Their father was in no condition to do anything except sit in a chair in the waiting room, crying for his wife. His daughters were afraid he'd have a heart attack, and Candy had to sit down, saying she thought she was going to faint. Candy and their father sat there together, crying and holding hands. Sabrina and Tammy were just as shocked as they were, but they were on their feet and talking, and in the front lines.

Moments after the brain surgeon left to examine Annie again, the ophthalmologist walked in, and explained his part of the procedure to them. It was infinitely delicate surgery, and he was honest when he looked at the films. He said it was a very, very long shot for him to be able to save Annie's sight, but he thought it was worth a try. Between the two procedures, they were told by both surgeons that the combined operation would take somewhere between six and eight hours, and they warned them that there was a very real chance that their sister might not survive. She was hovering near death now.

"Can we see her before the surgery?" Tammy asked the resident, and he nodded.

"She's in pretty bad shape. Are you sure you're all right?" Sabrina and Tammy both nodded and then turned to where their father and Candy were sitting. They walked over to them and asked if they wanted to see Annie before she went into surgery. They didn't say it, but it was possible that it was the last time any of them would see her alive. Their father just shook his head and turned his face away. He was already dealing with more than he could handle, and he had been told he would have to identify his wife's body, which was downstairs in the morgue. Candy looked at her two oldest sisters in horror and sobbed louder.

"Oh my God, I can't...oh my God...Annie...and Mom..." Their baby sister was completely falling apart, which didn't surprise either of them. They left Candy and their father in the waiting room and followed the resident into the trauma unit, where Annie was.

She was in a small curtained-off area with a forest of tubes and monitors hanging from her. She had been intubated for the respirator and her nose taped closed. Four nurses and two residents were working on her, watching her vital signs closely. Her blood pressure had dropped, and they were fighting to keep her alive. Tammy and Sabrina tried not to get in their way, and the resident showed them where to stand. They could only get to her one at a time. Her face had been badly lacerated, and one of her cheekbones was broken. There were cuts up and down both arms, and a nasty gash on one shoulder, which was bare. Sabrina gently touched her hand and kissed her fingers, as tears streamed down her cheeks.

"Come on, Annie girl . . . you can do it . . . you gotta hang in, baby, for all of us. We love you. You're going to be okay. Be a big girl now. We're all right here with you." She was suddenly reminded of when she had taken Annie to the playground when she was thirteen and Annie was five. She got on the seesaw when Sabrina wasn't looking, fell off, and broke her arm. Sabrina had been sick over it, and a mother she knew had driven them to the emergency room, where she had called their mom. Their mother wasn't angry and didn't scold her—instead she praised Sabrina for keeping a cool head and getting Annie to the hospital. She told her that it could have happened when she was with Annie too. Things happened to kids. She said it was a lesson to keep a closer eye on her next time, but it could have happened anyway. And she praised Annie for being brave. She hadn't scolded either of them for being stupid or careless, or Sabrina because her sister broke her arm. It had been one of her first major lessons about who her mother was, how she handled things, and how loving and kind she was. She had never forgotten it, and was reminded of it now. "You gotta be brave, Annie. Just like the time you broke your arm." But this was so much worse, and unthinkable if Annie lost her sight. But worst of all if she lost her life. Sabrina was willing to settle for anything they could get, even if Annie was brain-damaged and no longer herself for the rest of her life. They would love her just the same. She kissed her fingers again, and gave up her place to Tammy, who stood looking at her, with tears rolling down her cheeks in streams. She could hardly speak.

"You heard Brina, Annie . . . she's gonna kick our asses if you don't hang in." It had been her threat to her next-youngest sister when they were kids. She and Annie were the closest in age. Sabrina was eight years older than Annie, and five years older than Tammy. As children it had always seemed like a big difference, but it didn't matter now. "You be a big girl, Annie. We'll be right here when you wake up. I love you . . . don't forget that," Tammy said as she dissolved in sobs and had to walk away. Sabrina came to put an arm around her and they walked out to the waiting room again. Their father and Candy hadn't moved since they left them and looked even worse than before, if that was possible, which gave Tammy an idea.

She looked up their family doctor's phone number in the address book they'd brought with them. She put it into her cell phone and walked discreetly away. They were able to patch her through to the doctor at his home, and she explained to him what had happened. She asked if he could come to the hospital to identify her mother's body so her father wouldn't have to do it. She didn't want any of them remembering her that way, and the resident had warned her that the damage to her mother had been extensive and she looked pretty grim. Their family physician promised to meet them at the hospital immediately. She told him that her father and youngest sister were in pretty bad shape and might benefit from some form of sedation, if that seemed reasonable to him.

"Of course. And how are you?" He sounded concerned.

"I don't know," Tammy said honestly, glancing at Sabrina, who had walked over to be near her. "In shock, I think. We all are. This is pretty tough, and Annie's in bad shape." She explained what they were planning to do to her in surgery, and he promised to be there within the hour, to offer moral support, if nothing else. It was something at least, and would relieve her father of the horrifying task of identifying his beloved Jane's remains. Tammy couldn't bear to think of her that way, nor could he. She explained to her father that their doctor was coming, and that he would identify Mom for them. After that she could be released to a funeral parlor, but none of them had thought of that yet. They were too stunned by everything that had happened, and too worried about Annie. While Tammy was on the phone, the resident had come to say that Annie was already in surgery, and they'd be starting in a few minutes. He promised to send them reports as soon as they knew anything, but he warned them again that she would be in surgery for many hours.

"Shouldn't I say goodbye to her?" their father said about his wife, when Tammy explained to him that their doctor was coming to identify her, so he didn't have to. Tammy hesitated before she answered her father's question, looking for the right way to say it, and relieve him of guilt at the same time.

"I don't think so, Dad," she said honestly. "I don't think Mom would want you to remember her that way. You know what she looks like, and how beautiful she was. She wouldn't want you to be that sad," Tammy said gently, fighting back tears again. They were ever present now.

"You mean I can't hold her again?" His question nearly tore out his daughters' hearts, and the look of anguish in his eyes was even worse. He was a broken man. Only that morning he had been the lively, handsome, youthful father they had always known. And now, suddenly in a matter of hours, he was a frightened, agonized old man. It was horrifying to see.

"You can, Dad," Sabrina explained, "of course you can, but I think it would be so awful for you, and for Mom. Sometimes we don't get to say goodbye to the people we love most. If she'd gone down in a plane crash, you couldn't hold her either. All that's left now is a shell, not Mom, not Jane. She's gone, Dad. If you need to say goodbye to her, you can. No one's going to stop you. I just don't think it's what Mom would want." She had devoted a lifetime to making life happy and easier for him—the last thing she would have wanted was to cause him more anguish now.

"Maybe you're right," he said softly, looking relieved, and a little while later their doctor walked in. He was wonderful with Jim and the girls. He was deeply sympathetic, compassionate, and kind. He handed Sabrina a bottle of Valium and told her to distribute it as needed. He thought her father would benefit from one now and suggested someone take him home. He was in good health, but had always had a mild heart murmur, and he'd been through so much that day. He could see that Candy was a mess too. She had hyperventilated twice since they'd arrived, and said she felt as though she was going to vomit. She felt sick every time she stood up. Sabrina gave each of them a pill with a paper cup full of cold water, and conferred with Tammy quietly as soon as the doctor went downstairs to the morgue to identify Jane. He asked the girls if they had contacted a funeral parlor yet, and they said they hadn't had time. They had come straight to the hospital to see Annie. No calls had been made. Neither of their parents had siblings, and their grandparents were all dead and had been for years. The entire family was at the hospital. All decisions could be made right here, although Sabrina and Tammy were obviously in charge and had the clearest heads, in spite of the fact that both were deeply affected by what had happened. But their father and Candy were falling apart. Tammy and Sabrina weren't, no matter how heartbroken they were.

The doctor had told them what funeral parlor to call, and as soon as he left, Sabrina called them and said they would try to come in the next day to discuss arrangements, but circumstances were difficult, with their sister in critical condition. She just hoped they wouldn't be planning two funerals. One was bad enough, their mother's, which was beyond their worst nightmares and fears. The worst had happened to them. Sabrina refused to think of Annie dying too.

"I think one of us should take them home," Tammy said to Sabrina as they stood next to the water cooler down the hall from where Candy and their father were sitting. They were both beginning to look a little woozy from the Valium they'd taken, and their father looked like he was going to sleep. It had all been too much for him.

"I don't want to leave you here alone," Sabrina said, looking worried. "And I want to be here for Annie too. We both should."

"We can't," Tammy said practically. If anything, she was pragmatic and had common sense, even in circumstances as awful and emotional as these. And Sabrina was levelheaded too. They looked entirely different, but were sisters to the core, and had a lot of their mother in them. She would have handled this just as they had. Sabrina was aware of it herself. "Neither of them is in any condition to stay here. We've got to get them home to bed. I think you and I have to take turns being here for Annie. There's no point in our being here together, and leaving Dad and Candy alone at home. We can't. They're in terrible shape. And Annie's going to be in surgery for hours. I don't think she'll be out of surgery till nine or ten o'clock tonight."

"Why don't I get Chris here? He can stay with them tonight so you can come back when Annie's out of surgery. He's good with Dad. He was coming out anyway, for the party."

"Oh Jesus, we have to call everybody." The party was only hours away, and they didn't want a hundred people ringing their doorbell. It had to be called off.

"If you take Candy and Dad home," Sabrina suggested sensibly, "I'll stay here and make the calls. There's nothing else for me to do. I just want to be around if something goes wrong." Tammy wanted to be there too, but what Sabrina was suggesting made sense.

"Okay. When Chris gets here, he can stay at the house, and I'll come back and sit with you, or you can go home by then if she's okay and out of the woods."

"I don't think it'll happen that fast," Sabrina said sadly. "I think we're going to be in the woods for a while."

"Yeah, I guess," Tammy said, looking devastated. They both were. They just took comfort in action, like their mother. Annie and Candy were more like their father, dreamers, and more high-strung, although Tammy had never thought of her father that way. She had always assumed he was strong, but saw now that he wasn't, and without her mother he was collapsing like a house of cards. The shock was still fresh, but she had somehow expected him to be more solid than he was.

They both walked back to talk to Candy and their father then, and said the doctor thought they should go home and rest. Nothing was going to happen with Annie for many hours, they hoped. So Sabrina explained that Tammy was going to take them home.

"What about the party?" her father asked, looking worried. It had just occurred to him.

"I'll make the calls, Dad." It was a terrible way of breaking the news to their friends, but the only one they had. "I've got Mom's address book with me." She showed it to him in her bag, and his eyes filled with tears again as he nodded.

"I don't know where the guest list is," he said in a hoarse croak, as Candy stared at them, looking stoned. She weighed so little that the Valium had hit her hard. She had taken the same dose as her father, she was nearly as tall, but half his weight. Sabrina had forgotten to adjust the dosage, but she knew Candy had taken them before when she was upset, usually over guys, or some crisis at a shoot.

"I have the guest list too, Dad." It was suddenly like talking to an old man. "Don't worry about anything. Just go home and get some rest. Tammy will take you home." Sabrina told Candy to go too, and both of them followed Tammy out to the car, like docile children, after Sabrina and Tammy hugged for a long moment, and choked on sobs again. Sabrina said she'd call to check in.

The first thing she did when they left was call Chris. He was just leaving his apartment, and asked if she had forgotten anything she needed him to bring. He sounded in great spirits, and hadn't had time yet to notice that Sabrina wasn't. All she had said so far was hello, in a shaking voice.

"I need you to come out right away," she said, which confused him.

"I was just leaving. What's the rush? Something wrong?" He couldn't imagine what it was, unless the dogs had eaten all the food for the party. Beulah the basset was capable of it.

"I . . . uh . . . yeah," she said as tears choked her throat, and suddenly all the calm and false bravado were gone and she was a mess too. She couldn't stop crying long enough to tell him, as he listened at the other end, deeply worried. He had never heard Sabrina sound like that. She was always so calm and in control. She was sobbing openly on the phone.

"Baby . . . what's wrong . . . tell me . . . it's okay . . . I'll be there as fast as I can." He couldn't even imagine what it was.

"I . . . uh . . . Chris . . . it's my mom . . . and Annie . . ." His heart started to pound as he listened, and he had a premonition, which terrified him. He loved her family as much as his own, maybe more. Hers was nicer to him, and had been nothing but wonderful during the years he and Sabrina had been together.

"What happened?" He was scared to death to ask.

"They had an accident, a couple of hours ago." She took a deep breath, but her voice continued to shake and her tears to flow. She could let it all out with him, and now she couldn't stop. "A head-on collision, and a thing with a truck . . . Mom was killed instantly . . . and Annie . . ." She could hardly go on but forced herself to. "She's in surgery now for a brain injury, she's in critical condition, on a respirator. They think she may be blind, if she survives."

"Oh shit... oh my God... Sabrina... baby, I'm so sorry... I'll be there as fast as I can."

"No!" She almost shouted at him. "Don't drive too fast! Please!" And then she started to cry again.

"Where are you?" He wished he had a helicopter or could just beam himself down. He hated every moment he was away from her, and he knew it would take several hours to get there, at best. The holiday traffic was always awful on the Merritt Parkway.

"At Bridgeport Hospital. In the trauma unit, I'm in the waiting room."

"Who's with you?" He sounded on the verge of tears himself, for her. They weren't married, but he loved her as much as if they were, and all he wanted was to be with her now and take her in his arms.

"I just sent Tammy home. Candy and my father are a wreck. We gave them Valium. And Annie will be in surgery till late tonight. It's better if Tammy and I take turns."

"I can sit with you, or babysit your dad and Candy if you want."

"I was hoping you would," she said with a sigh. She could always count on him. "But Chris... will you come here first? I need you," she said, bursting into tears again, and this time she could hear that he was crying too when he spoke to her again.

"Sabrina, I love you. I'm so sorry this is happening to you. I'll be there as soon as I can. Call me on my cell phone when I'm on the way, whenever you want. I'll leave now. And I'll drive carefully, I promise." And then he thought of something. "What are you doing about the party?" They obviously had to call it off, but how? He was overwhelmed just thinking about it, and was sure she was too.

"I have my mom's address book here. I'm going to call everybody now."

"I'll help when I get there if it's not too late by then." But he suspected it would be. The party was in four hours, and it would take him three to drive out.

"I'll get there as soon as I can," he said again. "I love you, Sabrina." He was already thinking about taking some time off from work, if he could. It was the least he could do for her, and the funeral would be in the coming days, and awful for them. He just hoped Annie would be okay. That would just be too much for them. Losing their mother was bad enough and a terrible shock. Losing Annie too would drive them all over the edge. He couldn't even think about it. Or the possibility of her surviving blind. For an artist, on top of it. He just hoped that she'd survive, in whatever condition.

Sabrina called the caterers first, to cancel, and then everyone on the list. It took two hours, and was nearly unbearable. She had to tell each person what had happened. And all of their friends were in shock once she had. Many of them offered to go over and see her dad, but she told them she thought it was too soon. He had been in no state to see anyone when he left the hospital. She had called Tammy at the house several times, and she said they were both sound asleep, mercifully. The Valium had done its job. Tammy had taken nothing. She wanted to be alert, just as Sabrina was.

It was six o'clock when Chris arrived, looking flustered and worried about her. He found her in the waiting room, staring into space, thinking. Annie had been in surgery for four hours by then. The resident said they were halfway through the surgeries, and it was going well so far. Her vital signs were holding firm, which was something at least, but not enough. They hadn't started the eye surgery yet, and were still operating on her brain. Sabrina tried not to think about it, and collapsed in sobs in Chris's arms when he walked in. They sat together and talked for several hours, about her mother, Annie, her father, all of them. There was so much to think about and so little that any of them could do right now. All they could do was wait, and pray for Annie.

Tammy had called the funeral parlor again from the house, and started to make arrangements, and decisions. She told Sabrina that they had to go there in the morning and pick a casket. And they had to go to the church too, and set a day and time for the funeral, pick the music, find a photograph of their mother for the program. It was nightmarish thinking about it. How could this be happening to them? But it was. It was all too real.

At eight o'clock Sabrina sent Chris to the house to take over from Tammy. She said that their father had woken up and was crying again. She wasn't sure whether to give him another Valium or not. Candy was still out like a light. Chris told Sabrina he'd cook dinner for them, and Tammy could come back to the hospital to wait with Sabrina. Half an hour later Tammy was back, and the two sisters sat in silence in the waiting room, huddled together and holding hands. Eventually they had their arms around each other and just held each other that way. They couldn't seem to get close enough to each other, as though if they did, nothing bad could happen to them. Or at least nothing worse than what already had.

"How was Dad when you left?" Sabrina asked her, looking worried.

"He was happy to see Chris. He just sobbed in his arms. The poor guy is just a mess. I don't know what's going to happen to him when we all leave."

"Maybe I can commute for a while." Sabrina looked pensive. It would be a tough commute for her, with the hours she kept, but others did it. Her father did, although his office hours weren't as long as hers. He had been lightening his load for several years, to spend more time with his wife. And now what? He would come home every night to an empty house. Sabrina didn't want that for him.

"That's crazy. You can't do that," Tammy said.

"Maybe he could stay with me," Sabrina said cautiously.

"That's even worse. You won't have a life. And he's not ninety years old, for chrissake. He's fifty-nine. He'll want to be out here, in his own house."

"Without Mom? Don't be so sure. I'm beginning to wonder if he can manage without her. After all these years, he was totally dependent on her. I don't think I realized that till today."

"You can't judge by today," Tammy said, sounding hopeful. "We're all in a state of shock. He is too. He'll have to get used to managing on his own. Other men his age do, and even older ones, who lose their wives. Maybe he'll get married again," she said, looking upset, and her older sister looked horrified.

"Don't be ridiculous. Dad? Are you kidding? Mom was the love of his life. He's never going to get married again. But I'm not convinced he can take care of himself either."

"He's not an invalid. And he's an adult. He'll have to figure it out like everyone else does. He can visit you, if he wants. But don't ask him to move in. It would be impossible for you, and not good for him either. He was dependent on her. He can't transfer it to you now, unless you want to give up your life and become the spinster daughter," Tammy teased.

"I already am," Sabrina said, and laughed for the first time that day.

"Don't make it a lifetime habit," Tammy warned her, "or you'll be sorry. And it wouldn't be fair to Chris. This is your time, not Dad's. He had his life with Mom. Now he has to move into a different stage.

Maybe he should see a shrink." They were busily planning his life, without consulting him, but it distracted them from the agony of their mother's death only hours before, and their sister fighting for her life.

"Do you suppose we should call Charlie?" Sabrina asked after a momentary lull. The time ticked by too slowly, waiting for news of Annie.

"Annie's Charlie? In Florence?" Tammy looked surprised by the suggestion.

"Yeah. I just thought maybe he'd want to know. I think they've been pretty serious for the last few months. Annie says he's a great guy, rock solid. I think she might move back to New York with him. Mom was hoping she would."

"Have you met him, or talked to him?" Tammy asked, and Sabrina shook her head. "Then I think we should wait. We don't know anything yet. Things could get a lot better, or worse. Let's not shake him up more than we have to. This is pretty heavy stuff, for a guy who's just been dating her for six months, and they're young." Sabrina nodded. It sounded sensible to her too.

It was nearly ten when Annie finally came out of surgery. She had been there for almost eight hours, and as far as the doctors were concerned, it had gone well. She had survived it. She was still on the respirator, but they were going to try and take her off it in a few days. She was young and strong, and her vital signs were good, even during surgery. They had managed to take the pressure off her brain, and they were hopeful that there was no long-term damage. If she regained consciousness soon, it would bode well for her future. They gave them all the good news first. She was still in critical condition, but as they told her sisters, they were guardedly optimistic, depending on how she came through the next forty-eight to seventy-two hours. But they were hopeful that she would live, without long-term damage to her brain.

And then came the bad news. They had saved the worst for last. The most important was that she had survived the surgery, and the operation on her brain had gone well. But the eye surgery hadn't. Her optic nerves had been severed and could not be repaired. The damage to her eyes was so severe that even a transplant could not help her. There was no question and no hope. If Annie lived, she would be blind.

Tammy and Sabrina sat in shocked silence when they heard it, and made not a sound. They were too stunned to move, and then finally Sabrina spoke up.

"She's a very talented artist," she said, as though that would change their verdict, but it didn't. The ophthalmologist just shook his head and told them he was sorry. He felt she would be very lucky if she lived, and they agreed. But what kind of life would she have if she was blind? Knowing her as they did, they couldn't imagine it, and suspected she would rather be dead than blind. Everything in her life was about art and sight. What would Annie do without that? Her entire education and life were related to art. It was horrifying to think about, but losing her completely would be worse.

"Are you sure about her sight?" Tammy asked softly.

"Completely sure," the eye surgeon said, and he left a little while later, as the two sisters sat in the waiting room alone again, holding hands, and then silently they both began to cry, for their sister and each other and themselves, for the mother they loved so much and would never see again. They clung to each other like two lost children in a storm. The nurses saw them and kept their distance, sorry for them. They knew how much they'd been through, and could only imagine how hard it was.

Chapter 7

The doctors told them that Annie would not wake up that night, she was too heavily sedated, and they needed to keep her that way, to avoid movement of her brain. And there was no point for them to stay in the waiting room all night. Annie was in no imminent danger, and the nurses in the ICU promised to call if there was a problem. They suggested that Sabrina and Tammy go home and come back in the morning. They were exhausted when they walked through the front door of the house. Sabrina hadn't been there since they got the news, and Tammy had been at the hospital for hours. It was hard to believe it was the same day as the one in which they'd left the house, after learning of their mother's death, and going to find Annie. The day had been a thousand years long, and every one of them bad.

"How's Annie?" Candy asked as they walked into the kitchen. She was sitting groggily at the kitchen table with Chris, having just woken up. She had gotten a lot of mileage out of the single pill. Their father had gone back to bed after taking a second one, which Chris gave him, per Tammy's instructions before she left. He had liked talking to Chris, and they had both cried about Jane, and Chris told him how sorry he was.

"She's doing okay," Sabrina answered. "She came through the surgery very well, so they told us to come home." She and Tammy had agreed not to say anything about her sight that night. It was just too much to absorb, another huge blow, and this time late at night. They had agreed to wait until the next day to share the news that she was irreparably blind. It was going to be a lot to swallow, and for Annie most of all. She was going to need all of their support.

"How are her eyes?" Candy persisted.

"We don't know yet," Tammy said quickly. "We'll know more tomorrow." Chris watched her face and then looked at Sabrina. He didn't like the way Tammy had said it, or the look in Sabrina's eyes, but he didn't question them, nor did Candy, who just nodded, and drank from her water bottle, while the dogs scurried around the kitchen floor. Chris had fed them and let them out several times. There wasn't much else for him to do, since both Jim and Candy had been asleep most of the time. He just sat quietly, thinking, and played with the dogs. He was afraid to call Sabrina and disturb her, so he just waited to hear the news when they got back. Officially, it sounded pretty good. Privately, he was not so sure, but said nothing. He was there to help, not to probe.

He asked no further questions until he and Sabrina were alone in her room with the door closed. Candy was sleeping with Tammy that night. They both needed the comfort. "Is your sister really doing okay?" he asked Sabrina, looking worried, and she stared at him for a long, quiet moment.

"Brain-wise, yes, I think. As well as she can be, after brain surgery."

"And the rest?" he asked softly, and she met his eyes.

She sat down on her bed and sighed. She didn't even have any tears left. She was totally wrung out, and just grateful Annie was still alive, and hopefully would stay that way. She had a headache from crying all day. "She's blind. They can't fix it or do anything about it. If she lives, she will always be blind." There was nothing else she could say. She just looked at him with the depths of her sorrow for Annie. It seemed bottomless and without measure. She couldn't imagine any kind of life for Annie without sight, or what would happen to her now. A blind artist? How cruel was that?

"My God . . . what does one do with that? I guess it's a gift that she's alive, but she may not look at it that way." He looked as devastated as Sabrina felt.

"I know. It scares me. She's going to need a lot of support." He nodded. That was an understatement.

"When are you going to tell your dad and Candy?"

"Tomorrow. We just couldn't face it tonight. It was too much, for all of us," she said sadly. They hadn't even had time to properly mourn her mother, they were too worried about Annie. But maybe that was a blessing in its own way.

"But you know anyway, poor baby," Chris said about Annie's eyes, and then took Sabrina in his arms and held her. He put her to bed as though she were a child, which was just what she needed. It was as though overnight she and Tammy had become the parents. Her mother was gone, her father was falling apart, and her sister was blind. And she and Tammy were carrying it all on their shoulders. With one single moment and act of fate, their whole family had been struck down, and nothing would ever be the same again. For Annie most of all, if she survived, which wasn't sure yet either. Nothing was anymore.

Sabrina fell asleep in Chris's arms, and had never been so grateful for any human in her life, except her mother. But Chris was a close second, and he cradled her and comforted her all night. She knew she would never forget it, and would be grateful to him forever.

She, Chris, and Tammy got up early the next morning. He cooked breakfast while the girls showered and got ready to go to the funeral parlor. Candy and their father were still asleep. Chris took care of the dogs, and was waiting at the breakfast table with scrambled eggs and bacon and English muffins. He told them they had to eat to stay strong. Sabrina had called the hospital as soon as she got up, and they said that Annie had had a good night and was doing well, though still heavily sedated so she didn't move too much and jostle her brain so soon after the surgery. They were going to start reducing the sedation the next day. She and Tammy were planning to go back and see her, but they had so much to do first, and all the "arrangements" to make. Tammy said she had always hated that word, and all that it implied, and even more so now.

They went to the funeral home and were back in two hours. They had done all the awful things they had expected, chosen a casket, funeral programs, mass cards, a room to hold "visitation" in, where their friends could come to visit the night before the funeral. There was no "viewing" because it was a closed casket, nor a rosary, because their mother was Catholic but not religious. The girls had decided to keep things simple, and their father had been enormously relieved to let them make the decisions. He couldn't bear the thought of doing it himself. They both looked pale and tired when they came back, and by then their father and Candy were at the kitchen table, and Chris was making the same hearty meal he had cooked for them, and he even teased Candy into eating. Much to their amazement, their father cleaned his plate, and for the first time in twenty-four hours, he wasn't crying.

Sabrina and Tammy had agreed, they had to tell them about Annie then. It couldn't be put off. They had a right to know. Sabrina started to tell them after breakfast, and found she couldn't. She turned away, and Tammy stepped into the breach, and explained everything the ophthalmologist had said the night before. The bottom line was that Annie was blind. There was stunned silence in the kitchen after she said it, and her father looked at her as though he didn't believe her or hadn't heard her correctly.

"That's ridiculous," he said, looking angry. "The man doesn't know what he's talking about. Does he know she's an artist?" They had had the same reaction, so they couldn't fault him. But it didn't change anything. This was going to be a huge adjustment for all of them, but nothing compared to what it would be for Annie. It would be catastrophic for her, a tragedy beyond measure. Telling her would be the worst moment of their lives, other than their mother dying, living with it the worst moments in hers, forever. That was the hard part. Two impossible concepts for any of them to fathom, particularly related to Annie. Blind. Forever. It boggled the mind, and made the heart ache just thinking about it. The only thing worse was their mother gone forever.

"You mean like with a white stick?" Candy said, looking stunned about her sister, and sounding like a five-year-old again. She seemed to have regressed back into adolescence or childhood since the day before when her mother died. In contrast, her two older sisters felt four thousand years old.

"Yes. Maybe. Something like that," Sabrina said, feeling exhausted. They had shared enough bad news for a lifetime, and Chris reached over and patted her hand. "Maybe a seeing-eye dog, or an attendant. I don't know how all this works yet." But she was sure they were all going to learn, if they were lucky enough to have the chance. That wasn't sure yet either. But the shock of Annie's blindness kept them from thinking about what would happen if she died.

Their mother's funeral had been scheduled for Tuesday afternoon, after the long weekend. Tammy had contacted caterers to serve the throngs of people who would come to the house afterward. Interment would be private, and both older sisters had decided to have her cremated. Their father had said it was all right with him, and her mother had left no instructions as to her preference.

"Annie hates dogs," Candy reminded them all. Sabrina hadn't thought of that.

"That's true. Maybe now she'll have to change her mind. Or not. It's up to her."

Their father said very little, other than that he thought several specialists should look at her. He was convinced that the doctor who had operated on her was out of his mind, and the diagnosis completely wrong. Sabrina and Tammy doubted that was the case since Bridgeport Hospital was a Level I Trauma Center, but agreed to ask their doctor to bring in someone else. But the surgeon had been so specific with them, and so thorough, that it was hard to believe he might be mistaken. It would have been nice if he was, but Sabrina thought her father just wasn't ready to give up hope. She couldn't blame him. Everything about this experience had been excruciating for all of them. And Annie hadn't even started to face the challenge yet, or the rest of her life without her sight.

Candy went upstairs to shower then, and their father to lie down. He didn't look well, his coloring was sort of a greenish gray. And when they had gone upstairs, Sabrina mentioned Annie's boyfriend Charlie in Florence again. This time Tammy agreed that they should call. If he was calling her cell phone, he might be getting worried. It had disappeared somewhere under the truck. Luckily for them, there was an address book in the suitcase in her room, and Charlie's cell phone number was in it. It was all too simple to find him. Sabrina said she'd make the call, as Chris and Tammy sat at the kitchen table with her while she did. He answered on the second ring. By then it was dinnertime in Florence. Sabrina explained who she was, and he knew immediately, and laughed.

"Is the big sister checking up on me?" He didn't sound in the least daunted or surprised to be hearing from her, or even worried.

"No, I'm not actually," Sabrina said cautiously, not sure yet how to tell him. It would have been easier if he'd been worried by the call, and suspected something was wrong. He seemed to have no concerns at all about why she might be calling, which seemed odd to Sabrina.

"How was the Fourth of July? Annie never called," he said blithely.

"No . . . that's why I'm calling. There was an accident here yesterday. We never had the party," she explained. There was silence at the other end of the phone. He was getting it finally, as Sabrina went on. "My mother and Annie were in a head-on collision with two cars and a truck. Our mother was killed instantly, and Annie was very severely injured, but she's alive." She wanted to give him the good news about Annie first. He sounded stunned.

"How severely? And I'm sorry about your loss." It was a phrase she was beginning to hate. She had heard it at the funeral parlor, the hospital, the florist. It seemed to be the pat phrase everybody said now, although she was sure he meant well. It was hard to know what to say in the face of such enormous shock. She would have been hard-pressed for words herself, and after all she and Annie's boyfriend were strangers. All they had in common was her sister, which was a lot.

Particularly now. Although he didn't sound quite as distraught as Sabrina would have hoped. Mostly surprised.

"Very severely," Sabrina said honestly. "She's still in critical condition, and she had brain surgery last night. She seems to be doing well, but she's not out of the woods yet. I thought you should know, as I gathered from her that you two are very close, and very much in love. I didn't want you to feel that we didn't let you know, especially if you'd want to come over. She's still heavily sedated and will be for the next few days, if everything goes well. She's on a respirator, but they're hoping to take her off it tomorrow, if we're lucky."

"Jesus, is she going to be a vegetable or brain dead or something?" The way he said it upset Sabrina. It sounded cruel to her, particularly given what Annie would be facing. But he didn't know that yet.

"There's no reason to think so, and the surgery went well, to reduce the swelling to her brain. She had a good night last night."

"For a minute you had me worried. I can't imagine Annie suddenly being retarded or a vegetable. If that were the case, she'd be better off dead." He was remarkably insensitive, particularly for a man who'd just been told that the woman he loved had nearly died. Sabrina already didn't like him, but made no comment. He was after all the man her sister loved, and she owed him some respect for that, or at least some leeway, and the benefit of the doubt, which she gave him.

"I don't agree with you," Sabrina said quietly. "We don't want to lose her, whatever condition she's in. She's our sister and we love her." And supposedly he did too.

"Does that mean you won't unplug her if she's brain dead?" Sabrina not only didn't like him, she was beginning to hate him, for the ugly things he said. He had the sensitivity of a rubber duck.

"That's not the issue," Sabrina said. The rest was coming, and she was curious about his reaction now, particularly as an artist, who shared that world with her. "The impact of the accident caused some other damage. Some pretty important stuff. She had eye surgery last night, which didn't go as well as the brain surgery." She took a breath and finished it off, as Tammy and Chris watched her. They could read her displeasure on her face. She hated the guy and didn't even know him. "Charlie, if she survives, Annie is going to be blind. She already is. There's nothing they can do to restore her sight. It's going to be a huge adjustment for her, and I thought that you should know so you can support her."

"Support her? How?" He sounded panicked, although he knew her parents had money. But maybe, he told himself, they didn't want to support a blind kid and wanted to foist her off on him. If that was the case, they had called the wrong number. Sabrina thought she had anyway, in every possible way. She felt deeply sorry for her sister. But not everyone was lucky enough to find a man like Chris. He was a gem.

"She's going to need your love and support. This is going to be a huge life change for her, the biggest she'll ever face. It's not fair and it's awful, and all we can do is be there to help her. If you love her, you're going to be very important to her." There was a long silence at the other end of the phone.

"Now wait a minute. Let's not go crazy here. We've been dating for six months. I hardly know her. We have a good time, we share a passion for art, she's a fantastic girl, and I love her, but you're talking about a whole new deal here. Art is a piece of history to her now. Her career as a painter is over. Shit, her life could still be over. And she's going to be blind for the rest of her life? What am I supposed to do about that?" He was running scared, and she could hear it.

"You tell me," Sabrina said coldly. "How do you see yourself participating in her life?" Chris winced when he heard the question, and they could both tell it was not going well. Just listening to their end of the conversation, Tammy had decided he was a jerk. Chris was more inclined to give him the benefit of the doubt, as Sabrina had, but so far he wasn't impressed. Sabrina had had to say nothing to console him, which said it all to him.

"How do you expect me to participate in her life?" Charlie asked Sabrina. "I'm not a seeing-eye dog, for chrissake. I've never had a blind girlfriend. I don't know what that's about or what it feels like. It sounds pretty heavy to me. And why are you calling me like this? What do you want from me?" He was moving rapidly from scared to angry.

"Nothing, actually." Sabrina bit the words off at him, trying to hold her temper. She would have liked to give him a piece of her mind, but for Annie's sake, she didn't dare. She didn't want to make things worse, or scare Charlie off forever. It sounded like he was headed that way anyway, but Sabrina didn't want to be the cause of his disappearing into the sunset prematurely. Annie had a right to do that herself, or not if she preferred it. She needed him more than ever now. And it wasn't up to Sabrina to tell him what to feel or how to behave. "I'm calling because my sister is under the impression that you're in love with her. She's in love with you. She had a terrible accident and almost died yesterday. Our mother did. And as a result of the accident, we found out last night that she's going to be blind for the rest of her life. If you love her, I figured you'd want to know. I have no idea what you want to do about it. That's up to you. You can send her a get-well card, come to visit her, be there for her, or walk out on her because it's too much for you. It's your choice to make, and I'm sure it's not easy. I just figured you'd want to know what's going on. She has a lot of very, very hard stuff to face. And as far as I know, you're important to her."

Charlie sighed as he listened to her, wishing he'd never heard any of it. But he had, thanks to her. And he knew that ultimately, he'd have decisions to make. This wasn't easy for him. He had no money, had taken a year off from a job in New York, and was committed to being an artist. He'd had a good time with Annie, and thought he was in love with her. But a blind girl, whose talent and career as an artist had just gone down the tubes? It sounded like heavy furniture to him. Way too heavy for what he had in mind, or thought he could handle in his life. He decided to be honest with Sabrina, since she had been honest with him.

"I don't know what to say to you."

"You don't have to say anything. I just called to inform you. I figured you'd want to know, or might be worried if you hadn't heard from her."

"Actually, I was. But not that worried. I had no idea something this crazy could happen to her. To be honest, Sabrina, I don't know if I can do this, or even if I want to. She's a great woman, and she was a terrific artist. But she's going to need a lot of care and support. She'll probably be depressed out of her mind for the next several years, maybe forever. That's too much for me to carry. I can't. I don't want to be a psych nurse, or a guide dog for the blind. I can hardly keep my shit together myself, I can't take on hers too. Not major stuff like this. I don't want to kid her into thinking I'll be there for her now. She needs people she can count on, and I don't think I'm one of them. I'm sorry. But I just don't think I have it in me." He sounded sad as he said it, and he was surprisingly open with her. "I think she needs someone a lot stronger and less self-centered than I am."

Sabrina was inclined to think he was right. He knew himself well, and was brave enough to say it. She had to give him a few points for that, but not many. She had expected a whole lot better from him, and from all that Annie had said, Sabrina thought he loved her. As it turned out, he didn't, or not enough to overcome what had happened. "What are you going to say to her?" he asked, sounding worried.

"I can't say anything to her yet. She's not conscious. But if and when she is, what do you want me to say, if anything? I don't have to tell her I called you. You can call her yourself and tell her whatever you want to say, when she's further down the road to recovery, although that's going to be a very hard time for her." Sabrina dreaded the impact of his leaving her, on top of everything else.

"Yeah, it is." He thought about it for a long moment, mulling it over. "Maybe I should write her a letter, or tell her I found someone else. That makes me look like a shit, which I am, I guess, but it won't be about her because she's blind, which might spare her a little." He sounded hopeful, as though he had found a solution that would work for him, although surely not for Annie. Sabrina's heart ached for her, as she listened to him. She thought he was a selfish, cowardly little shit.

"It's going to be a blow either way. I think she was considering moving back to New York for you. So this was a big deal for her," Sabrina said sadly.

"It was for me too . . . until this. This is such shit luck for her." It was the understatement of the century. "I don't know. I guess I'll write to her. I'll send it to you, and you can give it to her whenever you think she's ready." How about never, Sabrina wanted to say.

"She'll figure it out anyway, when you never call and don't show up."

"Yeah. I guess. Maybe that's the best way then. Just disappear out of her life." Sabrina couldn't believe what she was hearing. He sounded relieved.

"That doesn't sound very noble to me," Sabrina said clearly. In fact, it sounded chickenshit to her, the cowardly way out, but it no longer surprised her. Annie's Prince Charming in Florence was a total lemon.

"I never said I was noble. I'm going to Greece next week anyway. Maybe I'll just write to her after that, and tell her I met someone else, or hooked up with an old flame."

"I'm sure you'll think of something. Thanks for your time," Sabrina said, wanting to get off. She'd had enough of him. All she wanted was to drive a stake through his heart, on her sister's behalf. Maybe two stakes, to be sure. He deserved worse than that, for what he was about to do to her sister, whatever his excuse.

"Thanks for calling. Sorry I can't do better than that."

"So am I," Sabrina said, "for Annie's sake. You're missing out on one of the great women of our time, blind or not."

"I'm sure she'll find someone else."

"Thanks," Sabrina said, and hung up on him, before he could say another word. She was steaming when she hung up, and Tammy and Chris had gotten the gist.

"What a sonofabitch," Chris muttered under his breath, and Tammy looked devastated for her sister, as did Sabrina. This wasn't how it was supposed to be.

They visited Annie in the hospital that afternoon. She was still unconscious, and would remain that way for another day or two, from the sedation. As it turned out, she was going to sleep through their mother's funeral on Tuesday, which the others thought was a blessing for her.

They had dinner together at the house that night, and Sabrina and Chris cooked. They were tired and depressed, and their father hardly said two words all night and went back to bed. Candy stuck around at least, and the four of them sat and talked long into the night, about their childhoods, their hopes and dreams, the crazy memories that surfaced at hard times like this.

On Monday the doctors took Annie off the respirator. Tammy and Sabrina were with her, and Candy and Chris were in the waiting room, in case anything went wrong. It was a tense moment, but they got through it. The two older sisters clutched each other's hands and cried when she took her first breath on her own. Sabrina looked at Tammy afterward and said that she felt as though she had just given birth to her herself. They reduced the sedation after that and expected her to wake up gently on her own in the next few days.

The visitation at the funeral parlor was that night, and was beyond awful. Hundreds of their parents' friends came, childhood friends of theirs, people Jane had been on committees with, others whom none of them even knew. They spent three hours shaking hands and accepting condolences. The girls had placed beautiful photographs of their mother around the room. They were all drained when they got home, and that night everyone went straight to bed. They were too tired to talk, think, or move. It was hard to believe that their mother had still been alive only two days before. Everyone at the visitation asked for Annie, and they had to explain what had happened to her as well, although they hadn't told anyone yet that she was blind. For the sake of her dignity, and out of respect for her, her sisters had decided that Annie ought to know first.

The funeral was the next day, at three in the afternoon. Tammy and Sabrina went to visit Annie in the morning, and she was still peacefully asleep. In some ways, they were both relieved. It would have been too much having Annie discover her blindness that day too. They had gotten a reprieve for another day.

The funeral itself was exquisite agony. It was simple, beautiful, elegant, and in perfect taste. There were lilies of the valley and white orchids everywhere. It looked more like a wedding in some ways, and the church was full, as was their house afterward. Three hundred people came to the house to remember her, drink, and eat from the buffet. Sabrina said to Chris afterward that she had never been so tired in her life. They were just about to sit down in the living room, when the hospital called. Tammy's heart stopped as she answered. All she could think of when the chief resident identified himself was that if Annie died now, it would kill them all. They had already been through so much more than they could take.

"I wanted to give you the good news myself," the resident said to Tammy as she held her breath. Was it possible? Was there still such a thing? Was there any good news left? It seemed hard to believe. She had made it off the respirator and was no longer listed in critical condition, which was a huge step, but she had made another leap that night. "I thought you might like to come over," he said quietly, as Tammy was about to tell him there was no way any of them could muster the energy after the emotions of the past few days and her mother's funeral that afternoon, but she never got to say the words. "She's awake," he said victoriously, as Tammy closed her eyes, and tears of grief and gratitude rolled down her cheeks.

"We'll be there in half an hour," she promised, thanking him for the call. And she knew as she hung up that for Annie, the hard part had only just begun.

Chapter 8

Annie's eyes were still bandaged when they got to her, and the chief resident assured them that they would be for at least another week. It gave them time to prepare for what they were going to say to her. She complained that she couldn't see anything with the bandages on, and asked weakly to have them taken off. Sabrina explained that her eyes had been hurt in the accident, she'd had surgery on them, and it would hurt if they took the bandages off. They kissed her and held her hands and told her how much they loved her. All three of her sisters and Chris had come to visit her. Their father was just too wiped out to face yet another emotional event. He promised to visit her the next day. They still had their mother's burial to get through the following afternoon. It was going to be a short ceremony at the graveside, and then they'd leave her there. The girls were anxious to get that over with. It was another day of torture for their father and them, and in the past four days they'd had more than enough. Their mother's burial was the last step in the series of traditions that seemed barbaric to all of them now, and this would be the final one.

Seeing Annie talking and moving again, and speaking to each of them was an affirmation of life. She asked where their parents were, and Tammy said simply that they hadn't come. They had all agreed not to tell her about her mother's death yet. She had only just woken up, and it seemed cruel to hit her with that before she regained at least a little of her strength, particularly with the shock she had in store about her sight.

"You scared the hell out of us," Tammy said, kissing her again and again. They were so grateful to have her back, and Candy lay down next to her on the bed, and dangled her feet off, which made them all laugh. She snuggled up to Annie, and smiled for the first time in four days.

"I missed you," Candy said softly, lying as close to her as she could, like a child cuddling up to her mother.

"Me too," Annie said in a tired voice, reaching out to touch each of them. Chris even came into the room for a few minutes, but said he didn't want to wear her out. "You're here too?" she said when she heard his voice, and smiled. He was like a big brother to all of them.

"I am. I came out for the Fourth of July, and never left." He didn't tell her he'd been cooking for all of them, or she would have wondered where their mother was.

"This wasn't how I was planning to spend my vacation," she said with a wan smile, and touched the bandages on her eyes again.

"You'll be up and running in a few days," Tammy promised.

"I don't feel like running yet," she admitted. "I have a terrible headache." Tammy and Sabrina promised to tell the nurse. She came in to check on Annie a few minutes later, and reminded them not wear Annie out. She offered her medication for the headache, and after kissing and hugging her, a few minutes later, they all left. Every one of them looked drained. It had been an unbelievably tough day. Their mother's funeral, all the guests at home afterward, and now Annie was awake. All in one day.

"When are they taking the bandages off?" Chris asked as he drove them home.

"I think in about a week," Sabrina said with a worried look. She had already called her office that morning, and was taking the next two weeks off. Chris had finagled four days, so he could spend the rest of the week in Connecticut with her. And Tammy had done the same, but she had to go back without fail by the coming Monday. She didn't see how she could stay even another day. Candy had called her agency and asked to get out of the booking in Japan. They were furious about it, but she insisted she was too upset to work, and told them why. So at least for the rest of the week, they could all be together, and at Annie's side. Sabrina knew she was going to need each one of them, maybe for a long time, or even forever. They hadn't worked out the future yet. First Annie had to wake up, and now that she had, they had to make plans. Sabrina was relieved that Annie hadn't said anything about Charlie that night. She was still too tired, but sooner or later, she would ask. It was yet another blow coming her way, along with her mother's death and the loss of her sight. It just wasn't fair for one human being to have to face so much. Sabrina would have done anything to lighten the load for her, but no one could.

They were sitting in the kitchen late that night, after their father went to bed, when Sabrina looked at her sisters with a frown.

"Uh-oh," Tammy teased her, and poured herself another glass of wine. She was beginning to enjoy the gatherings they shared every night, in spite of the reason they were still there. She was deriving enormous comfort from her sisters, more than ever before. Even their collective dogs were starting to get along. "I know that face," Tammy commented as she took a sip of the wine. They were raiding their father's wine cellar every night, just as they had when they were young. And when he found out then, he had had a fit. Tammy smiled at the memory, and savored his excellent wine. She reminded herself to send him a case of good Bordeaux after she left. They had been drinking some of his best wines. "You've had an idea," Tammy finished the thought, looking at her older sister. Sabrina looked as though she were hatching a plan. In the old days, when they were kids, it would have meant something forbidden, like giving a party when their parents went away for the weekend. She used to pay Tammy five dollars not to squeal. "I used to make money on these deals," she explained to Chris. "So what is it now?"

"Annie," she said succinctly, as though they could read her mind.

"I figured. What about her?" They were all dreading telling her about their mom. They would have to do it soon. It wasn't fair to her not to know for much longer, and inevitably, she would wonder where she was. Even that night, it had been hard to explain. Their mother would have been there in a flash, and camped out in the room. Her absence was sorely felt by them all, and would be by Annie too.

"She can't go back to Florence, and Charlie is a jerk."

"Yes, I think we all agree on that." He had been a huge disappointment to all of them, and would be to Annie most of all. But now she had bigger problems to solve. He was just one more source of grief. "You're right, she can't go back to Florence. I don't see how she could manage there in a fifth-floor apartment, no matter how independent she wants to be. She should probably move home, with Dad. It would be company for him."

"And way too depressing for her. She'll feel like a child again. And without Mom here, she'd be really sad." They were all feeling her absence in the house. Even in the three days since she had died, it felt as though everything had changed. And they knew their father was feeling it too. The housekeeper had come that day, and all she did was cry. And at twenty-six, Annie would not want to come home, not after living on her own in Italy for two years.

"She can stay with me, if she wants to. But I don't think she knows anyone in L.A., and without being able to drive or get around, she'd feel trapped. And I'm out all day." They all knew that Tammy worked impossible hours, and Sabrina did too, but at least she was in New York, which was familiar to Annie. She had lived there briefly before she left for Paris four years before, although she said it was too hectic for her. She had liked France, and then Italy much better, but now it was out of the question. She needed to be closer to home, for a while anyway, until she adjusted to her situation. They all agreed on that.

"She can stay with me if she wants," Candy chimed in, and then looked at them apologetically. "But I'm away a lot."

"That's my point. We'd all love her to live with us, but we each have some kind of problem that makes it difficult. Or at least you two do. I work crazy hours, but I think she could handle New York."

"So? What part of this plan are you not telling us?" Tammy asked as she sipped her father's wine. She knew how Sabrina's brain worked. There was a master plan here somewhere that she hadn't exposed to them yet.

"What if she lives with all of us?" Sabrina said, smiling. The master plan was emerging.

"You mean move around and stay with each of us for a while?

Don't you think that would be unsettling for her? I wouldn't mind, but I can't see Annie wanting to live out of a suitcase like a nomad, just because she's blind. I think she'd want her own place, though I have no idea where. I think we have to ask her," Tammy said, looking pensive.

"Better than that," Sabrina said, looking at her sisters. "I think eventually Annie will figure it out for herself, where she wants to be, and how she wants to live. But right now everything will be different for her, and she's going to need a lot of help at first. What if we all move in together for a year? Rent a big apartment, and all four of us live under one roof, until she gets on her feet? We can see how we all feel about it after a year. If it doesn't work, we move into our own apartments again, and if we like it, we sign on for another year. By then, Annie should be more adjusted. But for this year it could make a huge difference for her. What do you think?" Both Candy and Tammy looked stunned, and Chris looked surprised too. He wasn't sure where he fit in, although Sabrina kissed him reassuringly, whatever that meant.

"Am I part of this plan?" he inquired delicately.

"Of course. The way you are now. You could stay over whenever you want."

"My very own harem," he said with a wry grin. It sounded a little crazy to him, but was typical of them. He had never known four sisters quite like them, and without question, they took care of their own, more than most. And without their mother at the helm, he could sense Sabrina stepping into her shoes, to mother all of them. He knew that if she took it seriously, it was going to be a challenge for her, and maybe for him too. But he was willing to listen and see where they went with her idea. He could see advantages to it too, particularly for Annie, in her moment of need, initially anyway. In the long run, as hard as it was, Annie would have to find her way. Sabrina knew that too. But at least at first, they could help. And Sabrina had the feeling her mother would have approved of her plan.

"That's great for you," Tammy said practically, looking a little unnerved by the idea. "You both live in New York. I live in L.A. What am I supposed to do? Quit my job? And then what? I'd be out of work in New York. And the show is going to be bigger than ever this year." She loved her sister, but she couldn't give up everything for her. She had worked so hard for what she had.

"Can't you work in television here?" Sabrina asked. She knew embarrassingly little about her sister's business, despite how successful she was.

"There are no decent shows here," Tammy said quietly. Sometimes she hated it when Sabrina came up with these harebrained schemes. "The only shows here are soaps, and a couple of reality shows. That's a major step down for me. And a huge salary cut." She could afford it, since she had put plenty of money aside, but she didn't like playing with her career, and she really didn't want to leave the show. It was her baby now.

"What about you?" Sabrina asked Candy, who was thinking about it.

"I hate to give up my penthouse," she said wistfully, and then smiled. "But I guess I could sublet it for a year. It would be fun living with the two of you." She actually liked the idea. She was lonely at times in her own place, and she wouldn't be if she lived with them. Her sisters were great company, and she knew Annie needed them.

"Why don't I see what I can find that would be big enough for the three of us? And when Annie is ready for it, we can suggest the idea to her. I don't care about my apartment. I don't love it anyway. Chris, would you care?" she asked him, as part of the family, and he shook his head.

"As long as I can stay over and your sisters don't mind. It might get a little crazy at times. That's a lot of women under one roof, with three of you, but it might be fun for a year. And you can always stay with me," Chris pointed out to Sabrina, and she nodded. As long as someone was home to help Annie, which was the whole point of it. But Candy was in town at least some of the time. The whole idea was to help get Annie on her feet and used to her blindness. And knowing how resourceful and determined Annie was, Sabrina thought a year might do it, as long as she wasn't in the depths of depression, which she hoped she wouldn't be.

"I really like the idea," Sabrina said, and Candy giggled.

"Yeah, me too. Like going to boarding school," which she had always wanted to do, and their mother wouldn't let her. She wanted to enjoy her last child at home, and she had never believed in boarding school. She believed in family. And so did they, which was at the root of Sabrina's idea. Their main goal was to help Annie. She was going to need them now, and this was one way to help her. Chris was actually impressed by the idea. Tammy was the only holdout, understandably, since she had a major career in L.A.

"And we'll be close enough to Dad, if he needs us. This is going to be a tough adjustment for him too."

"What if you all hate it?" Tammy asked cautiously.

"Then I guess we give it up, and go back to our own places. A year isn't very long. I think we could stand each other for a year, don't you?"

"Maybe," Tammy answered. "We haven't really lived together since before college. You left sixteen years ago. I left eleven. Annie left eight years ago, and Candy was an only child after we left. This should be interesting," Tammy said with a grin. "Maybe the reason we get along is because we don't live together. Did you ever think of that?"

"I think it's worth a try for Annie," Sabrina said stubbornly. She had been trying to think of a way to help their sister without making her feel humiliated and dependent. This might do it. And she was willing to sacrifice a year of her life for her, and so was Candy. That was something, at least. And even Sabrina could see why Tammy didn't want to do it, and didn't hold it against her. She had an important job on the West Coast, and they couldn't expect her to jeopardize that. She had worked hard to get there, and Sabrina respected her for it, so she didn't push her. "I'll call a realtor tomorrow and see if she can come up with something that would make sense for the three of us. I don't make as much as Candy, and Annie is subsidized by Mom and Dad. Maybe Dad would pay her share of the rent here instead of Florence, although I'm sure that's a lot cheaper. But she'll really need his help now." And they all knew he could afford it. And then Sabrina frowned. "That reminds me. I guess someone is going to have to go over and close her apartment. She's in no shape to do it."

"What if she wants to stay in Italy?" Tammy asked.

"I guess she could try it in a year, if she can take care of herself, but not right away. She has a lot to learn first, about surviving as a blind person and living on her own. She's better off doing that with us, and then she can always go back later."

"I could pick up her stuff the next time I'm in Europe," Candy volunteered, which was a nice gesture although Tammy and Sabrina knew that she was the least organized of the sisters, and very young. The others were always helping her, but this might help her grow up. She made an incredible living as a supermodel, but she was still very immature. And she was only twenty-one. As far as they were concerned, she was a baby. But maybe she could handle closing the apartment in Florence. It was worth a shot. Neither Tammy nor Sabrina had time to do it, nor their father.

"Well, I have to admit, it's an intriguing idea," Tammy said, smiling, feeling faintly guilty for not participating, but she just couldn't, and the others knew that. "And it might really help her. It might cheer her up." They still had huge hurdles to overcome, telling Annie about their mother, her blindness, and all that that would mean to her, and even about Charlie, who was now history, just because she was blind. It all seemed so cruel, and if living with her sisters would help her for the first year, they all agreed that it was worth a try. They toasted each other with their father's vintage Bordeaux wine, and Chris joined them. Sabrina agreed to spearhead the project and keep them all informed as to what she found in the way of an apartment for them, or even a brownstone, if the rental price was right.

"You sure don't let the grass grow under your feet, do you?" Tammy said admiringly, looking at her older sister. "I've been trying to think of what I can do for her too, but I don't think she'd be happy in L.A."

"Neither do I," Sabrina agreed. "Now all we have to do is sell it to her." They had no idea how Annie would react. She had so much to adjust to in the coming days, it was staggering to think about.

"To sisters," Sabrina said, raising her glass again.

"To the most interesting women I've ever known," Chris added.

"To Mom," Candy said softly, and they were all silent for a long moment and took a long sip from their glasses.

Chapter 9

Their mother's burial on Wednesday was the last painful ritual the Adams family had to endure. And as Sabrina had asked him to do, the priest kept it short and sweet. Her mother's ashes were in a large handsome mahogany box. None of them liked to think about her having disappeared out of their lives and being reduced to something so seemingly insignificant and small. Her impact on them had been huge for all of their lives. Now they were leaving her here, to be buried at a cemetery with strangers, in the family plot.

They didn't wait to see the box lowered into the ground. Serena and Tammy had agreed at the funeral parlor that no one could have tolerated the agony of it, and when they checked with him, their father had agreed.

The priest made a point of saying during the brief ceremony that they had something to celebrate now, the survival and hopefully full recovery soon of their daughter and sister Anne, who had been spared the same fate as her mother during the accident on the Fourth of July. The priest had no idea that Annie was now blind, nor did anyone else. People would become aware of it gradually later when they saw her, but the family was keeping it quiet for now. It still felt like a very private, painful thing, for them, and above all for Annie herself, once she found out. They had no idea when they were going to tell her, and wanted to discuss it with her doctors first. Sabrina was afraid of telling her too soon, and having her get severely depressed, on the heels of their mother's death, but she knew they couldn't wait too long, and her bandages from the surgery were due to come off by the end of the week. There would be no way of keeping it from her then. And their father still insisted the diagnosis they'd made was wrong. It was inconceivable to him that one of his beautiful daughters was now blind. In the past five days everything had gone so wrong. Their family, which had never been touched by tragedy before, had been dealt a double blow, which had staggered them all.

As each of her daughters left her mother's graveside, she dropped a long-stemmed white rose next to the wooden box that contained her ashes, sitting on a stand. Their father felt each gesture like a blow. He stood alone next to the graveside for a long time, and his daughters respectfully left him there, and then finally Sabrina walked back to him, and tucked her hand into his arm.

"Come on, Daddy, let's go home."

"I can't just leave her here like this, Sabrina," he said as tears rolled down his cheeks. "How could this happen? We all loved her so much."

"Yes, we did," his daughter said, brushing away tears of her own. They were all dressed in somber black, and looked elegant and dignified. They had always been a beautiful family, and now, even without her, they still were. People who saw them were always struck by how handsome they were. And Jane had been Jim's bright, shining star. He couldn't bring himself to believe that she was gone. "Maybe it's better like this," Sabrina said softly, as he continued to stand there, staring at the box where her ashes were. "Now she'll never get sick or old. She didn't suffer. She lived to see all her children grow up. You'll always remember her still beautiful and young." She had hardly ever changed. Her beauty was timeless, and she exuded warmth, energy, and youth. She had been a dazzling woman right till the end. They would always think of her that way. Their mother had had enormous grace. He nodded at what his daughter had just said, without saying a word in response. He took one of the long-stemmed white roses and laid it on top of the box with the others, and then he took a second one, held it in his hand, and walked away with his head down. The past few days had been the hardest of his life, as his children knew only too well. He looked as though he had aged a decade in five days.

Her father got into the limousine without comment and sat next to Sabrina. He sat staring out the window on the way home. Tammy was in the car with them as well. Chris and Candy were riding in the second limousine. They had kept the interment private, and all three daughters were relieved that the painful rituals associated with their mother's passing had come to an end. It had been a rigorous three days, between visitation, funeral, hundreds of guests at the house afterward, and now this last poignant event, leaving her in the place of her final rest. They had talked about keeping her ashes at home, but Sabrina and Tammy had decided that it would be too hard for them, and especially for their father. It was better to leave the discreet wooden box at the cemetery. Sabrina had a sense that her mother would have preferred it that way. Since she had left no directions about funeral arrangements, they had had to guess all along the way, and they had consulted their father about each minute detail. He just wanted the nightmare to end, and for her to come back to them. Sabrina had a strong sense that the reality of it hadn't sunk in yet for any of them. She had been gone for only these few days, as

though she had gone away for the long weekend and might still return.

Sabrina knew they had to concentrate on Annie now, her full recovery from the brain surgery, and her adjustment to a whole new,
challenging life now that she was blind. They hadn't even begun to
travel that road with her yet, and she was fully expecting the transition from artist to woman who no longer had sight to take a long
time. This was no small cross for her to bear.

Her father said when they got back to the house that he needed to
go to the bank that afternoon. Sabrina offered to take him, but he
said he wanted to go on his own. Like the others, she was trying to be
there to support him, when he wanted, and to give him space when
he seemed to want to be alone. Like all of them, his spirits went up
and down. Sometimes the full weight of the tragedy nearly crushed
him, and at other times he felt all right for a few hours, and then fell
through a hole in the floor again, suddenly, brutally, with all the force
of her loss weighing on him. He felt as though his whole world were
upside down, and in many ways it was.

He had told his office not to expect him at all that week and
maybe not the following week as well. He wanted to wait to see how
he felt. He had been a personal investment adviser for all of his career, and his clients would be sympathetic about his absence after
the death of his wife. The most important ones had been notified,
and many of them had sent flowers.

The family was going to be together till the end of the week, and
then Tammy was going back to California, Chris was going back to
work, and eventually their father would too. Sabrina thought it would
be good for him, but some of the others didn't agree. He looked tired
and worn and frail, and had already lost several pounds. They were
all afraid that the loss of their mother would impact his health, and

that he would turn into an old man overnight. He already nearly had. It was frightening to see how shattered he was, how lost without her.

When Sabrina was alone in the library after the burial ceremony, she called the realtor in New York who had found her current apartment, and told her what she was looking for. Three bedrooms, since Tammy had decided not to join them but would stay in California so she could still produce her hit show. Sabrina told the realtor she wanted a bright, sunny apartment, preferably on one floor, with three good-sized bedrooms, three separate bathrooms, a good-sized living room, a dining room if possible, and maybe even a small den, although that was optional. They wanted a building with a doorman and some kind of security, since Candy came in at all hours, and Annie would need help when she came and went from the building, and she and Candy wouldn't always be there to help, if they went out, or were at work. They wanted the Upper East Side more than they wanted SoHo, Tribeca, or Chelsea. Sabrina was happier uptown, and Candy insisted she didn't care where she lived as long as she was with them. She had a gorgeous penthouse apartment she was planning to rent. Its beauty and views had done nothing for her. She had never bothered to decorate it, or put the finishing touches on it. She was out of town too much to really care. Like Sabrina, she was interested in their safety, and a sense of protection when she came home at night. The others didn't go out as much as Candy did, they led more sedentary lives.

"That's a tall order," the realtor told her honestly, "unless I find you some kind of fluke, like someone renting their co-op for a year." Sabrina had said they didn't care about terraces or views. And a cozy apartment in an old building would suit them too. The main thing was that they could live together, and provide an environment where Annie could flourish and feel comfortable, and above all safe, while she learned to handle the challenges of her new life. Sabrina was also hoping they'd find a place with a decent kitchen where they could cook. And hopefully, thanks to Sabrina, Chris would come often and whip something up for them to eat. He was very nearly a gourmet cook. Sabrina wanted to learn from him, but she never had time, and some of the time she skipped meals. From the look of her and what they'd seen her not eat in the past several days, Candy ate none at all. Tammy was somewhere in between, concerned about her weight but not obsessed by it. And Sabrina alternated real meals with salads, to compensate for it when she indulged, which wasn't too often.

The realtor promised to call her back as soon as she had something to show her. Sabrina knew they might not find it right away, and she was open to renting a brownstone too, but she didn't want to start with that because they were so often more expensive. She had explained their plan to her father on the way home from the cemetery, and he smiled as she talked about it.

"That's going to be so good for you. Just like the old days, when you girls all lived together at home. I can just imagine the mischief the three of you will get into. What about Chris in all this, Sabrina? Living with that many women could be challenging for any man. Even your dogs are females, and your friends of course." Sabrina said Chris was used to it by now. Wherever she lived, particularly with her sisters, was always chaotic to visit and even more so to stay there. They loved the lively atmosphere they created among them, and Chris seemed to adjust to it well.

In any case, the realtor had their requirements, and she didn't think it would be an impossible task to find something. Of course it made it more challenging that Sabrina told her they needed it soon. Annie would be out of the hospital in a few weeks, and Sabrina wanted to get them all moved in. She'd have to give notice on her own apartment, and Candy was planning to rent out her penthouse once they found something. If need be, she could pay rent at the apartment she planned to occupy with her sisters, and pay maintenance on her penthouse at the same time, since she owned it. She made such staggering amounts of money from her modeling that she could afford luxuries the others couldn't, even though she was the youngest of the group. Even Tammy, with her big Hollywood job as a producer, didn't make the kind of money Candy did. Candy readily admitted herself that the fees supermodels raked in were insane, and she was more in demand than ever.

Their father had said on the way home from the cemetery that he would pay Annie's share of the rent, and even a little more if it helped them. He was willing to pay as much as half, because he thought their project to help their injured sister was noble of them, although he still refused to believe that she would be permanently blind. He now said that maybe her vision would come back one day. The blow of her new reality was just too much for him to endure. Sabrina knew he would have to come to believe it over time. But losing his wife, nearly losing his daughter, and her becoming permanently blind were almost too great a shock for him to bear. His mind refused to take it all in, or believe what had happened in the past five days. It was barely easier for his daughters to understand. And Annie knew nothing about any of it yet.

Tammy and Chris made sandwiches when they got back. People had been dropping food baskets off to them, and there was a wide assortment of delicacies, snacks, and cooked meals crowded into the kitchen. It looked like Christmas, when friends and their father's clients sent baskets of gourmet treats and wine. But this was by no means Christmas. In fact, Sabrina was already dreading the holidays now that her mother was gone. They would be agonizing for all of them this year. She knew that their mother's absence would be felt even more acutely then, by all.

Their father went to the bank when the girls went to visit their sister that afternoon. Chris had offered to drive him. He was so distracted at the moment that his daughters didn't want him to drive. None of them wanted another accident to happen, like the one that had happened over the holiday weekend, although they all agreed it had been a freak thing. Chris was startled to notice, when Jim came out to the car, that he was carrying a tote bag and a small valise. Chris had no idea what he was doing, but he seemed very intent, and said little to Chris as they drove to the bank, which was unusual for him.

When Tammy, Candy, and Sabrina got to the hospital, Annie was sleeping. They sat quietly in her room for a while, and waited for her to wake up. The nurse said she was having a nap, but was in fairly decent spirits that day. Her sisters knew she wouldn't be for long. By the end of the week, reality would have hit. Like a tsunami.

She woke up finally as they sat whispering close by her. She could feel Tammy sitting near her bed. She was developing a sixth sense for people's movements with the heavy bandages over her eyes. Her hearing seemed much more acute, and she correctly guessed which of her sisters was standing closest to her almost every time.

"Hi, Tammy," she said, as her next-oldest sister smiled and kissed her cheek. The two sisters exchanged a smile, even though Annie couldn't see her.

"How did you know?" Tammy looked surprised.

"I could smell your perfume. And Sabrina's over there." She pointed to where Sabrina was standing.

"Now that's weird," her oldest sister commented. "I'm not wearing perfume. I forgot mine in the city."

"I don't know," Annie said, yawning. "I just feel you guys, I guess. And Candy's lying across the foot of my bed." They all laughed at what she said—she had been entirely accurate. "Where's Mom?" she asked, as she had yesterday. She sounded both casual and concerned about it.

"Dad had to go to the bank," Tammy said, hoping to distract her. She made it sound as though their mother had gone with him, without actually lying to her.

"What did he go to the bank for? Why isn't he at work? What day is this, by the way?" She had been unconscious for days, until the day before.

"It's Wednesday," Sabrina answered. "Dad took the week off."

"He did? He never does that." Annie frowned as she thought about what they'd said. All three girls exchanged a worried look. "You guys are lying to me, aren't you?" she said sadly. "Mom must have gotten hurt, or she'd be here by now. She'd never go with Dad, if she knew I was sick. What happened?" Annie asked them pointedly. "How bad is it?" There was silence in the room for long minutes. They hadn't wanted to tell her about their shocking loss this soon, but she wasn't giving them much slack. She never did. Annie was someone who wanted answers to her questions and to tie up loose ends. She hated it when things were messy in any way. And despite her artistic background, she was meticulous, precise, and direct. "What happened to Mom, you guys? Where is she?" None of them knew what to say, and were afraid to give her too big a shock. "Come on, you're freaking me out." She started to look extremely anxious, and so did they. It was agonizing, and they hated to tell her now, when she was just beginning to recover herself.

"It was pretty bad, Annie," Tammy finally said softly, as she approached the bed, so she could stand near her. Instinctively, they all did. And Candy reached across the bed and took her hand. "It was a very ugly accident. There were three cars and a truck."

"I remember when Mom lost control of the wheel. I looked over and tried to grab it before she went into the oncoming traffic, but when I looked, she was out of the car. I don't know where she went." Across the lanes into oncoming traffic, but the highway patrol had said that by then she was already dead. She had died on impact, when the steel pipes shot out of the truck and hit her. They had nearly taken off her head, and had missed Annie by only a hair. "I don't remember anything after that though," she said softly.

"You were trapped in the car, and you got a nasty bump on the head. It took them half an hour to get you out. Thank God they did in time," Sabrina added to what Tammy had said. They were a tightly knit group that often spoke with one mind, one voice. Their mother had loved calling them the four-headed monster when they were growing up. If you spoke to one, or crossed one, you dealt with all four. And God help you if they felt you had been unjust to one or more. Nothing much had changed. They were just older and calmer, and got worked up less often, but they still stuck together and had similar views about many things, and were quick to defend each other.

"You still haven't told me where Mom is." They knew that there was no way they were going to be able to avoid her question. She was too insistent, and too wide awake. It was hard to put her off.

"Is she in another room nearby?" Tammy looked at Sabrina and shook her head. They all approached the bed, and each one of them was touching her, her hand, her arm, her face. She could feel them all around her, and their presence was both comforting and ominous. She could sense that something terrible had happened. Her senses were as acute as ever, and her brain was working fine, much to everyone's relief, although in this case it made her harder to ignore.

"She didn't make it, Annie," Tammy said softly, since she was the closest. "It all happened too fast, and too much happened. She was hit by the steel pipes. She was killed instantly." Annie gasped. She opened her mouth in terror but no sound came out. And then she began flailing wildly, trying to touch them, and clutched hard at their hands. All three of them were crying again as they watched her, and so was she. They could see their own shock and pain mirrored in hers. But they had had four days to get used to it. To Annie it was raw and fresh.

"Mom died?" she said in a terrified whisper. She would have liked to look at them, and hated the bandages that kept her from it. The doctor said they had to stay on for a few more days. They were taking them off a week early as it was. But this was terrible not being able to see her sisters' faces or eyes if they had lost their mother. She wanted her bandages off, but tugging and clawing at them did nothing. She had already tried, to no avail.

"Yes, she did," Sabrina answered her awful question. "I'm so sorry, baby. I'm so sorry you had to go through all this."

"Oh God, that's so awful," she said as tears slid into the bandages from her eyes, and she could feel them burn, even though her eyes were covered. It just made it worse. She sat and cried for a long time while they held her, like three guardian angels taking care of her. But the sweetest angel of all was gone. Annie just couldn't understand it or absorb it any more than they could. It was the worst thing Annie had ever heard, and the same for her sisters, even after four days. None of them were feeling philosophical about it, although they tried to make their father think they were. "How's Dad doing?" Annie asked finally, worried about him too.

"Not good," Candy volunteered, "but we're not so great either. I keep falling apart. Sabrina and Tammy took care of everything. They've been so great." Candy filled her in. Annie had missed so much of what had happened. Everything in fact.

"Did I miss the funeral?" she asked, sounding shocked. She didn't really want to be there, but she felt mildly left out now, knowing that she hadn't. But there had been no other choice. They didn't know when she'd wake up, and they couldn't wait. It would have been too hard for their father, and even for them. They needed to get the agonizing formalities behind them, even without Annie.

"It was yesterday," Sabrina said. Annie couldn't believe it. Their mother was dead. She couldn't get her mind around the words or the concept. It hadn't been easy for them either. They were still having trouble adjusting, and so would she. Their mother was just too strong a loving presence for them to be able to understand her sudden death, or even able to cope with the aftermath, which so far had been very well handled, by her sisters above all.

"Poor Dad . . . poor us . . . poor Mom," Annie wailed in agony. "What a terrible thing to happen." It was, even more than she knew. Now it was poor her, even more than their mom. She had lived her life, had died too young, but had lived fully and joyously till the end. It was Annie who was going to have such enormous challenges to meet now, whose suddenly limited life was going to be so hard, who would never again be able to see a painting, or create one, when all her life she had lived for art. It was Annie who had been cheated out of her sight and was still so young. Their hearts ached for her, as much as for their mother.

They stayed with Annie for a long time that afternoon. They didn't want to leave her alone after they had told her the news about their mom. Sometimes they talked about it, sometimes they just sat in silence and held hands, sometimes they cried together, or laughed through their tears at a story one of them remembered and the others had forgotten. As close as they had been before, losing their mother had created an even stronger bond. They were four very different young women with a powerful love for each other and deep respect, which had been a gift to them above all from their mother, but from their father as well. They clung to him and each other, as the remaining powerful symbols of their damaged world.

It was seven o'clock when they finally left the hospital. Annie was exhausted, and so were they. They drove back to the house, talking about her, and found Chris chatting quietly with their dad. He said that at least a dozen people had come by, to check on them and pay their respects. It was such a strange time for all of them. Their mother had left such a huge hole in their lives, and their community, where for years she had been so loved and admired, as a wife, mother, friend, human being, and hard worker at many charities. She had been so much more to so many than just their mother or Jim's wife.

Tammy suggested they order Chinese takeout or sushi so Chris didn't have to cook again, but their father said he had something he wanted to do with them first. He looked sorrowful and shaken, as he had since Saturday, but determined. He asked them to follow him into the dining room. Chris knew what was happening, and hung back, not wanting to intrude. This was between them, a private moment in their family. It had startled him when Jim had told him what he was doing, after they went to the bank that afternoon. It seemed soon to him, but the older man had pointed out that it would be months before all his daughters would be home again at the same time. And he knew that this was what his wife would have wanted. It was early, but it was time. She had been generous with her husband, daughters, and friends all her life.

As the girls followed their father into the dining room, they were shocked at what they saw there. They hadn't been prepared for this, and he hadn't warned them. Tammy gave a little gasp of pain and took a step back. Sabrina covered her eyes for a moment with her hand. And Candy just stood there and started to cry.

"Oh Dad . . ." was all Tammy could say. She didn't want to face this yet. It hurt just looking at the familiar pieces, but it was now one of her many gifts to them, with their father's grace.

He had laid out all of her jewelry on the dining room table, in neat rows, the familiar rings and bracelets and earrings she had worn, the string of pearls from her own mother, the gifts he had given her over the years, for important birthdays, Christmas, major events, like their births. With his success in business, the gifts had grown over the years. They weren't important jewels, like some of what Tammy had seen in Hollywood, or Candy wore in fashion layouts for *Vogue,* or ads for Tiffany or Cartier. But they were lovely pieces that her mother had worn and loved. Each piece on the dining room table would remind them of their mother each time they wore them, although it felt a little like stealing them from her, raiding her jewel box while she was out, and having to explain it to her when she got back. They all still wanted to believe that she was coming back. Laying her jewelry out as he had was a way of acknowledging that she was gone forever, and they had to step into the world as adults now, with nothing to buffer them from what life had in store for them, good or bad. Suddenly, no matter what age they were, they were adults. They no longer had a mom. It felt much too grown-up.

"Dad, are you sure?" Sabrina asked with wide eyes full of tears. Tammy was crying softly too. This was hard.

"Yes, I am. I didn't want to wait till Thanksgiving when you'll all be home again. Annie isn't here, but she can't pick the pieces now anyway, and you know what she likes. You can pick for her, or make exchanges later if you want. I want you to take turns, one by one. Each of you pick something, then the next one takes a turn, by order of age, one turn each, until you divide it all up. Mom wanted you to have it. There's some very pretty stuff there. It belongs to you," he said quietly, and then walked out of the room, wiping the tears from his cheeks. He was leaving it up to them, knowing they'd be fair. In addition, he had taken out her four fur coats, two minks, a fox, and a beautiful lynx he had bought her the Christmas before. Each one was draped across a dining room chair. It was a lot to absorb.

"Wow," Sabrina said, sitting down on a dining room chair, and staring at what was on the table. "Where do we start?"

"You heard Dad," Tammy said somberly. "By order of age. That means you, then me, Annie, Candy. Who'll pick for Annie?"

"We all can. We know what she likes." She wore very little jewelry, and had very eclectic arty tastes, mostly silver bangles and a lot of turquoise. Her mother had more serious pieces than that, but there were some that would look well on Annie, if she wanted to appear more grown up. And even if she never wore it, it was a memory of their mother, and nice to have. They each knew the piece she had gotten when they were born. A narrow sapphire bracelet for Sabrina, a ruby band ring for Tammy, a pearl necklace for Annie, and a beautiful diamond bracelet for Candy, who had come along thirteen years after Sabrina, in more prosperous times. As they stood at the dining room table, they chose those items first. And then began to loosen up. They put the first items on. The ruby band was exactly the right size for Tammy, and she swore she'd never take it off. She was exactly her mother's size.

One by one, they began to choose items that they remembered so well. There were a few pieces of their grandmother's, which were outdated but pretty. They had the look of the forties, some big topaz pieces, some aquamarines, and a beautiful cameo they chose for Annie, because she could feel it and they agreed that the face on the brooch looked like her. It wouldn't have surprised their mother, or their father, that they were extremely respectful of each other. When one of them loved an item, the others immediately backed off and urged her to take it. There were a few pieces that looked like none of them, but they chose them out of sentiment. There was a handsome sapphire brooch their father had given her for her fiftieth birthday, which they all said Sabrina should have and she took. There were beautiful diamond earrings that looked great on Tammy, and some long diamond and pearl drop earrings she had worn when she was young, which were perfect for Candy, as well as a gorgeous diamond bangle that they all thought Annie should have, and set aside for her. They were lovely things, and halfway through they began to look less sad, and smiled and laughed with each other as they put them on, and commented on how they looked. It was bittersweet, both happy and sad.

They wound up with exactly the same number of pieces. Each of them had two or three fairly important items, and a number of others that were of less value but meant a lot to them, and they were satisfied with what they'd picked for Annie, and more than willing to make trades if she didn't like what they described. It was all a little more grown up than they were used to wearing, but they agreed that they'd grow into it over time, and even wear it now, to remind them of their mother. There was something very tender and moving about having her jewelry now. And when they had finished dividing it up, they tried on the furs. They worked out perfectly too.

They all agreed that the fox coat looked like Annie. It was almost the same color as her chestnut hair, it was full and long, it would undoubtedly fit her, and she could wear it with jeans. There was a black mink coat that looked gorgeous on Sabrina and fit her since the style was loose and her mother wore her fur coats a little on the long side. Sabrina looked very elegant in the coat. And the rich brown mink looked spectacular on Tammy, who said she would wear it to the Emmys next year. It was very chic. And the three-quarter lynx was pure Candy. She put it on and looked fabulous in it. She was so thin that it fit, and the length looked great with her long legs. The sleeves were a little short, but she said she liked it that way. Her mother had worn it only once, and all four of the coats were in great shape and seldom worn. She only wore them when they went to dinner in the city, or some major event. Their mother had had a penchant for fur, and had indulged it only in recent years. She had had a Persian lamb coat of her grandmother's from the thirties that she had worn when she was young, but it was long gone. These coats were almost brand-new, very stylish, and looked fabulous on them. They all set the coats down respectfully when they had chosen, and went back to the den to thank their dad.

He saw them walk into the room with smiling faces, and they each kissed him and told him how much it meant to them to have their mother's things. He had kept her wedding ring and engagement ring, which had a very small stone, and put them in a little box on his desk, where he could see them whenever he wanted. He couldn't have parted with them.

"Thank you, Daddy," Candy said, sitting down next to him, and holding his hand.

They were well aware of how hard it must have been for him to lay her things out and give them away so soon, and what a loving gesture it had been. "You can go through her other things later and see if there's anything you want." She had had some beautiful handbags, and some lovely clothes, which only Tammy could have worn since she was so small. But there was no rush for that. The jewelry had seemed important to him, as they needed to be together to do it, and he didn't want to wait five months, when they came back for Thanksgiving. It had shaken them to see her things at first, and to help themselves to them, but it had been done in an orderly, loving way. They had been as respectful to each other as they had been to their mother. It was typical of them, and what she had taught them as they grew up, to love each other, with kindness, generosity, and compassion. They had learned the lesson well.

Their father and Chris had ordered dinner while the sisters were looking at the jewelry. They had ordered curry from a nearby Indian restaurant, and it was very good. They chatted over dinner, and for a moment life almost seemed normal as they talked and laughed and teased each other. It was hard to believe they had just divided up their mother's jewelry, buried her that afternoon, and had a funeral for her yesterday. It was all so surreal.

As they cleaned up the kitchen, Tammy realized how much she was going to miss her sisters when she went back to L.A. Despite the sad occasion, she loved being with them. This was where she was happiest, in their midst. And whenever she was with her family, her life in California seemed so distant and without meaning. This was what mattered most to her. It was hard to compare the two worlds, and yet that was where she lived and worked, and what seemed so important when she was there, especially the show she had helped to create and which was so precious to her. But it was nothing compared to all this. She looked at her sisters as they left the kitchen, and Sabrina put an arm around her, and gave her a hug.

"We're going to miss you when you go back. I always do."

"Me too," Tammy said sadly. Her life there seemed so empty, without her sisters. Here they shared family meals, she could talk to them at any hour of the day, and their father looked over them benevolently. It reminded her of their childhood, which she thought had been perfect in every way, and so rare. And nothing had changed, except that they all lived all over the world. Or they had—now they'd all be living together, when Annie got out of the hospital, and she'd be living three thousand miles away. But there was no other way. She couldn't give up what she had there. It would have destroyed the career she had worked so hard to build. It was a tough choice for her to make.

The three dogs followed each other out of the kitchen, as the sisters went upstairs. It appeared to be a temporary truce of sorts, but Beulah and Juanita had become best friends in the past few days. Candy's Yorkie Zoe never left her side, or was always sitting on her lap. Juanita and Beulah had taken to sleeping together, and the chihuahua nipped playfully at Beulah's long silky ears. They had even chased a rabbit together in the backyard. They made everybody laugh. Zoe was the most elegant of the trio with a rhinestone collar and pink bows. Juanita was the fiercest, and Chris commented that Beulah hadn't looked depressed since they arrived. He said she needed siblings and clearly didn't like being an only child. Candy promised to send rhinestone collars for the others, which made Chris roll his eyes.

"She's a hunting dog, Candy, not a supermodel."

"You need to give her a little style," Candy said with a grin. "That's probably why she's been depressed." Her old leather collar was faded and worn, and as they said it, the basset looked up and wagged her tail. "See, she knows what I mean. I have a fabulous woman who makes Zoe clothes in Paris. I'll measure Beulah before we leave and get her some stuff."

"Now I'm getting depressed. You're corrupting our dog," Chris said firmly. Beulah was the only thing that he and Sabrina officially shared. They had their own apartments, never commingled money, and were careful to keep things separate. As attorneys, they knew the mess it could make otherwise, if they ever broke up. But Beulah was the child they shared. Sabrina always laughed and said they'd need a joint custody agreement for her if they ever split up. Chris had a better idea and would have preferred getting married, if nothing else to protect the dog, he liked to tease her. But marriage just hadn't been in the cards for her so far, and wouldn't be for a while.

"Why not?" Tammy asked her the next day, as they were sitting in the kitchen drinking coffee. Everyone else had gone out. Their father and Chris were doing errands, and Candy was checking out a new gym nearby. She said she was falling apart not doing her Pilates for the last week, and she said she was gaining weight, which seemed like good news to all of them. She said her body was turning to mush, or it felt that way to her. Hard to believe at twenty-one.

"I don't know," Sabrina said with a sigh. "I just can't see myself getting married. I hear such bad stories all day, about how people screw each other over, cheat, used to love each other and messed it all up when they got married. It doesn't make it very appealing, no matter how nice a guy Chris is. They all are in the beginning, and then everything gets fucked up."

"Look at Mom and Dad," Tammy pointed out. They were her role

models for the perfect marriage. She still wanted one of those, if she
ever found a man like their dad. The ones she met in L.A., particularly in show business, were all crazy, players, narcissists, or gener-
ally bad guys. She seemed to meet them all. She said she was a
magnet for nuts and shits, mostly nuts.

"Yeah, look at Mom and Dad," Sabrina said, looking glum. "They
were perfect together. How could we ever find something like that?
It only happens once. Mom used to say that too. She always said
how lucky they were. I'm not sure I'd have the same luck, and if I
didn't, I'd feel cheated, I don't want anything less. They set the bar
pretty high."

"I think Chris comes pretty close. You found a good one. That's
not easy to do. Besides, Mom and Dad worked at it. It didn't just
happen. They used to fight when we were kids."

"Not often. And usually about something we did, that they didn't
agree on. Like when I sneaked out at night during the week. Dad
thought she should say something and let it go at that. Mom put me
on restriction for three weeks. She was a lot tougher than he was."

"Maybe that's why they got along. But I can't remember them ever
having serious fights. Maybe once, when he got drunk on New Year's
Eve. I don't think she talked to him for a week." They both laughed
at the memory. Even with a little too much to drink, he had been
cute. Their mother had said he embarrassed her with their friends.
Neither of them had been a heavy drinker, and none of their daughters were, although they drank more than their parents had. Candy
partied harder than the others, but she was still young, and moved
in a faster crowd, because of her work. None of the others were out
of control, and Candy was still within the norm. They knew Annie
smoked dope with her artist friends, but she was so serious about
her work, she didn't like getting stoned often. She had done more of

it when she was in college, but none of them had substance abuse problems, and neither had their parents. They were a pretty wholesome group. Chris drank more than Sabrina did, and liked his vodka when he went out, but he didn't do it to excess. He seemed like the perfect man to Tammy, particularly compared to the freaks she met.

"I think it will be really sad if you and Chris don't get married one day," she commented as she put their cups in the dishwasher. "You're turning thirty-five in September. If you want kids, you shouldn't drag your ass forever. Besides, he may get tired of waiting. You don't even live together. I'm surprised he doesn't put the heat on you. He's not getting any younger either."

"He's only thirty-six. And he does put the heat on me at times. I just tell him I'm not ready. I'm not. I don't know if I'll ever be. I like things the way they are now, and we spend the night together three or four times a week. I like having time off, to myself. I work a lot at night."

"You're spoiled," Tammy commented.

"Yeah, I guess I am," Sabrina admitted.

"Let me tell you, if I found a guy like him, I'd nail him to the floor. What if you lose him because you won't get married?" Tammy had wondered about that before. She thought Chris was incredibly patient with her sister, and she knew he wanted kids. Sabrina wasn't sure about that either. She didn't want to lose her children half time to joint custody if she ever got divorced. She had been deeply affected by her work, and the ugly problems she handled for her clients every day.

"I don't know. I guess I'll worry about that when it happens, if it ever does. For now, it works."

Tammy shook her head in disgust. "Here I am, telling myself I'll go to a sperm bank when I'm your age, if I haven't found the right guy, which I probably won't, and you have the greatest guy on the planet, who *wants* to get married and have children, and you want to live alone and be single forever. Shit. Life just isn't fair."

"No, it's not. And don't you dare go to a sperm bank yet, you twit. The right guy will come along."

"Not in my business. And not in L.A. That's almost a sure thing. You don't know how crazy those guys are. I can't even be bothered dating anymore. If I hear one more bullshit story from some guy who just hasn't met the right woman in the twenty years he's been divorced, while he's cheating on me and dating twenty-year-old starlets, is a vegan, and has to have a high colonic twice a week to keep his head straight, whose politics are to the left of Lenin's, and by the way can I get him a major part in the show . . . I will throw up, and have. I'd rather TiVo my favorite shows and stay home with Juanita, checking scripts, after I leave the office at ten-thirty, which is what I do most of the time. It's just not worth putting on makeup and high heels for those guys. I really think I will wind up alone. It's better than what's out there." At twenty-nine, she had almost given up. "I tried computer dating a couple of times last year. They were even worse. One guy took me to dinner, and didn't have enough money to add a tip, and he asked me if he could borrow gas money to get home. The other one admitted he'd been gay all his life, and made a bet with his boyfriend that he could date a woman, just once. I was it. I've had it with the Freaks of the World Club. I'm their oldest member, and I'm way in the lead for number of dates with hopeless geeks." Sabrina had to laugh at what she said, but knew it was true, for Tammy anyway. She was in a tough spot to meet men. She was successful, powerful in her industry, in a world of narcissists and operators who all wanted something from her and gave nothing back. And yet she was beautiful, smart, successful, and young. It was hard to believe she couldn't meet a decent man, but she hadn't yet.

She worked too hard, had almost no spare time, and didn't even try anymore. She spent weekends working, or at home with her dog. "Besides," she added, "it would be too traumatic for Juanie if I got involved with a guy. She hates men."

"She loves Chris," Sabrina added with a smile.

"Everybody loves Chris. Except you," she scolded, and Sabrina denied it hotly.

"That's not true. I love him, enough to not want to screw up what we've got."

"Don't be such a chickenshit," Tammy told her. "He's worth the risk. You'll never find a better guy. Trust me, I've seen the worst. I've dated them all. Chris is a hottie, in every sense of the word. You've landed the big one. Don't ever throw him back. Or I'll beat you up." Sabrina laughed in response.

"Why don't you move to New York, if the guys out there are so awful?" Sabrina had thought of it before. She knew how lonely her sister's life was in L.A., and she worried about her. She knew their mother had too, for all the same reasons. She used to say that Tammy would never get married if she stayed in L.A., and it was a high priority to her. Their mother thought marriage and family were the best things since sliced bread. But look who she was married to. Their dad.

"I can't move to meet a guy," Tammy said, looking disgusted. "That's crazy. Besides, I'd starve to death. I can't give up my career, I've been at it for too long and put too much into it to just walk away. I love what I do. I can't give that up. Besides, maybe I wouldn't meet anyone here either. Maybe it's me."

"It's not you, it's them," Sabrina assured her. "Your business is full of weird guys."

"I seem to find them everywhere. I used to meet nuts when I went on vacation too. They're just drawn to me like moths or cockroaches or something. If there is a nutcase in the area, I'll find him, believe me. Or he'll find me."

"What are we talking about?" Chris asked as he stuck his head in the kitchen door. He and Jim had just gotten back after a long run to the hardware store. Chris had promised to fix some things around the house. They were looking for distractions to keep busy, and as long as he was going to be there for three more days, he thought he might as well help out. He enjoyed that kind of thing.

"We're talking about my nonexistent dating life. I'm the head of the Date-a-Freak Club. The main chapter is in L.A., but I've opened branches in other cities too. It's a very successful thing, huge membership, low dues, lifetime opportunities. You'd be amazed." All three of them laughed at what she was saying, but her sister knew it was all too true, and so did she. Chris said he always found it hard to believe that Tammy hadn't found a guy. She was gorgeous, smart, and made a hell of a good living. She'd be a plum for any guy. He said they were all fools.

"You'll meet the right one, one of these days," he assured her.

"I'm not sure I still care," Tammy said, and shrugged. "What time are we going to see Annie?" she asked, changing the subject.

"After lunch, when Candy gets back from the gym. If she ever does. She exercises too much."

"I know," Tammy said with a worried look. They all commented on her weight constantly. At least she ate somewhat more decently when she was at home, but not much. She kept track of her weight, and insisted that her livelihood depended on it. Her sisters reminded her that her health did too. Tammy had warned her that she'd wind up sterile from starving for so many years. It wasn't a high priority for Candy yet. She was much more interested in staying on top in her field, and she certainly had the right look. Being superthin was essential to her.

The three of them went out to the pool then and went for a swim. Afterward their father joined them, and sat chatting with Chris, while the two women talked about Annie, and the adjustment she'd have to make. Sabrina was still excited about her apartment idea, and hoped she'd hear from the realtor soon. It was going to make a big difference to Annie if she could live with them for a year.

"I wish I could do it too," Tammy said again. "I feel so guilty not moving home for her. But I just can't."

"I know," Sabrina said, lying in the sun, glancing over at Chris and her dad. They got along well, and it was nice for her father to have a man around. He had been outnumbered by women for years. Chris was like the son he'd never had. "You can fly in and spend weekends with us when you have time." Tammy tried to remember the last time she'd spent a weekend when she hadn't worked, and there hadn't been a crisis on the show. It had been at least six months, maybe more. And maybe a year before that.

"I'll try," she promised, as they both lay in the sun and dozed. They were both thinking the same thing, that if they closed their eyes, in a minute their mother would stand in the kitchen door and call them in for lunch. Maybe she had just disappeared for a few days, or had gone to the city, and would be back soon. It wasn't possible that she was gone. Those things just didn't happen. She was out. Or resting in her room, or visiting a friend. She wasn't gone. Not forever. And Annie wasn't blind. It just couldn't be.

Chapter 10

The girls spent Thursday afternoon and Friday morning at the hospital with Annie. She was getting restless and her head still hurt, which was hardly surprising. A physical therapist came to work with her, and she broke down and cried several times about their mother. She still couldn't believe what had happened, and neither could they. But they were focusing their worries on her now. Within days, she would know that she was blind. The bandages were due to be taken off on Saturday. And all three of her sisters felt sick, thinking about the impact it would have on her. Reality was coming toward her with lightning speed.

Their father went to see her on Thursday night, and dropped by again while the girls were there on Friday morning. She thanked him for her mom's jewelry, she hadn't seen it yet, but she remembered the pieces that the girls described, and she liked them all. She was happy with the choices they had made on her behalf, and she had always loved her mother's fox coat. She said it would be fun to wear in Florence, because the winters were so cold, and Italian women wore a lot of fur. No one seemed to get upset about it there. She said she would have been nervous wearing it in the States.

She was anxious to know too when she could go back to Italy, and worried that she hadn't heard from Charlie. She had asked her sisters several times to put a call through for her. She had called him on his cell phone, and it always went straight to voice mail. She assumed he was in Pompeii with his friends, and maybe the reception was bad there. She didn't want to leave a message that her mother had died and she'd been in an accident, and worry him, but it was upsetting not being able to get hold of him for so long. It had only been a week. So much had happened since then. More than she could even imagine, since she didn't know yet about her sight. Sabrina never mentioned having spoken to him, of course, and her sisters were silent when she talked of him in glowing terms. It was all Sabrina could do not to snarl. But they said nothing to her.

Annie spent the whole day surrounded by her sisters. Candy's agency had called about a shoot in Paris, but she turned it down. She was staying home for now. She was in no mood to work, and neither were the others. Sabrina still had another week off the following week, having changed her vacation, and Tammy was going back to L.A. on Monday. She hated to leave, but had no choice. Fires were burning at her office, and they still had to find a replacement for their star, and alter the scripts once they did. It was going to be a knotty problem to work out, and she was in no mood to think about it now. All she could think about were her mother and Annie. It was going to be very hard being so far away, and leaving it all on Candy and Sabrina's shoulders. And she wanted to be there for Annie, and her father. Annie already knew that she was going to have to spend a couple of weeks at her father's home, convalescing. The doctors had told her that she needed to stick around till the end of the month, if all went well. They thought she could leave the hospital in another week. But she had no idea that when she did, she would be blind. She kept saying that she couldn't wait until they took the bandages off her eyes, and every time she said it, her sisters silently cried. When the bandages came off, Annie's world would still be dark, forevermore. It was a tragedy beyond words.

When they left the hospital late Friday afternoon, all three of her sisters looked tired. They had all agreed to be there the next day when the ophthalmologist came. When the bandages came off, Annie was going to feel that her entire life had come to an end. The others were all dreading it for her. And they talked about it with their father that night. They had agreed amongst themselves that he shouldn't be there. It was going to be too emotional for him. He had enough on his plate, adjusting to the loss of his wife.

When Sabrina walked into the kitchen of her parents' house, she saw two messages from the realtor she had called, and thought it was a hopeful sign. She called her back, and caught her just before she left her office for a weekend in the Hamptons.

"I've been trying to get hold of you all day," she complained.

"I know. I'm sorry. It's a crazy time. My cell phone was turned off. I was visiting my sister in the hospital, and they don't let you keep it on. Did you find anything?" It seemed too soon, but at least they had gotten a start.

"I have two very interesting options for you. I think they're both excellent choices, depending on what you want. I wasn't sure. We didn't talk a lot about neighborhood, and sometimes people have very different ideas. I wasn't sure what you have in mind. All you said was East Side. How do you feel about downtown?"

"How far downtown?" Sabrina's office was in the fifties, on Park Avenue, and she and Chris lived within blocks of each other uptown, by design. Downtown would make it hard for him to just drop by, which he did often, even on the nights they weren't staying together. And when she worked late, he came over to walk the dog.

"I have a fabulous apartment in the old meatpacking district. It's a co-op, but the people aren't ready to move in yet. They want to sell their house first, so they're willing to rent it for six months or a year. It's in fabulous condition, since everything's brand-new. State-of-the-art equipment. It's a penthouse, and there's a pool and a health club in the building."

"It sounds expensive," Sabrina said practically, and the realtor didn't deny it.

"It is. But it's worth every penny." She told Sabrina the price, and she whistled.

"Wow, that's way out of our range." It worried her that the price was so high. Even with their father helping them, she couldn't come close to that, although maybe Candy could. But it was way beyond Sabrina's means. "I was hoping we could find something a lot more reasonable than that."

"It's a very unusual place," the realtor said, sounding miffed. But she wasn't easily daunted. "And they won't take dogs, by the way. They have white carpeting and brand-new floors." Sabrina smiled.

"Now, I feel better. We have dogs. Small ones, of course," she said, so as not to alarm her. They'd have to hide Beulah under a bush somewhere. She was short-legged, but certainly not small. "But I guess that rules us out of the meatpacking district apartment, whatever the price."

"Absolutely. They're not flexible on that. The place is just too new. I have something else though. It's kind of the opposite end of the spectrum, and a whole different mood. The one downtown is very white and airy, and everything is fabulous and new. The one uptown has a lot of charm." Uh-oh, Sabrina thought to herself, and not so fabulous and falling apart? But maybe a more reasonable price. They couldn't go totally out on a limb. She made a decent living, but she couldn't afford what her baby sister could, not by any means.

"What's it like?" Sabrina asked cautiously. If not light and airy, then dark and gloomy? But if so, maybe they could have dogs.

"It's a brownstone on East Eighty-fourth Street, and it's pretty far east. But that puts it near Gracie Mansion. It's a nice old neighborhood. It's not as trendy as downtown, of course. But it's a good house. It belongs to a doctor who just lost his wife. He's taking a sabbatical year off. I think he's a shrink. He says he's going to London and Vienna. He's writing a book about Sigmund Freud, and he has a dog, so he probably won't object to yours. It's a very pretty little house, not state of the art, but it has a lot of charm. His wife was a decorator, so she made the most of it. He wants to rent it for a year, and if the tenant is willing, he'd like to leave some of his furniture in it. If not, he said it can be stored."

"How many floors?" She was thinking about Annie. An apartment on one level would probably be easier for her than a house, and there was no security if they lived in a brownstone. If she needed help, there was no one she could call.

"Four. The top floor is kind of a family room. The house has a garden, nothing special, but it's nice. The bedrooms are small, you know how brownstones are. But there are four of them. You said you only need three, but you could use the fourth one as a home office. And the kitchen and dining room are in the basement, so it's a hike from the fridge to the bedrooms, but there's a fridge and a microwave in the family room upstairs. You have to be creative about brownstones in New York. There's a living room and den on the main floor, two bedrooms on each floor above it, which gives you four, and each bedroom has a bathroom, which is rare, they're small but very nicely done. His wife had a lot of style. And then the family room upstairs.

"It sounds like it has all the rooms you need, if you don't mind having the kitchen and dining room in the basement, which is fairly cozy. The garden leads off of that, so it's pretty light and faces south. It's all north-south exposure. Washing machine and dryer, the house is fully air-conditioned, and the price is right, but you can't extend it beyond a year. He wants his house back after a year. He sees patients in the house. He's a fairly well-known guy in his profession. He's written several books." None of which meant that they would love his house. Sabrina was thinking that they could put Annie on the second floor, with Candy maybe, and she could take one of the bedrooms on the next flight up, so she and Chris could have some privacy, and they could all hang out upstairs. With luck and a little planning, it might work, if Annie could get around.

"How much?" That was an important factor for her. The realtor told her, and Sabrina wanted to whistle again, but this time because it was so cheap. It was less expensive than her current apartment, and she could easily have paid half the rent or all of it, and she only had to pay a quarter, since her father had agreed to pay half of their rent for Annie, to help them out. "Why so cheap?"

"He doesn't care about the money. He just wants to know that there are nice people in his house. He doesn't want to leave it empty for a year. His kids don't want to live there. One lives in Santa Fe and the other one in San Francisco. He tried to get someone to house-sit for him, and he couldn't. He doesn't want people giving wild parties, or trashing it. It's a cute little house, and he wants to come back and find it in good shape. He set the price, and I told him he could get twice that, but he doesn't care. If you're interested, you'd better see it quick. I don't think it will be on the market for long. People are away this week because of the holiday, but as soon as other brokers get wind of it, I think it will get snapped up. He only put it on the market last week. I think she died two months ago." Poor guy. Sabrina felt sorry for him. Losing their mother had taught her a lot about the impact of losing someone you loved.

"I'm not sure my sister could manage all those stairs. But she might. It wouldn't be as easy as an apartment, especially with the kitchen in the basement. But I'd really like to see it. I like everything else about it." And it was still within walking distance of Chris. Not quite as close as her current apartment, but close enough.

"Is your sister handicapped?" the realtor asked, and Sabrina caught her breath. It was the first time she'd been asked, but yes, now she was.

"Yes," she said, measuring her words. "She's blind." It was hard saying the word.

"That shouldn't be a problem," the agent said matter-of-factly. "My cousin is blind. He lives in a fourth-floor walk-up in Brooklyn, and he manages fine. Does she have a seeing-eye dog?"

"Uh . . . not at the moment, but she might." She didn't want to tell her that it had just happened only days before. It was too hard to talk about.

"I'm sure he wouldn't mind. He has an English sheepdog, and I think his wife had a dachshund. He didn't say anything about not wanting dogs. He just wants good tenants who'll pay the rent and take care of his house." She knew Sabrina was an attorney, financially solvent, and had had good references before. That was all they needed to know. "When can you see it?"

"Not till Monday." They were taking Annie's bandages off the next day, and it was going to be a traumatic weekend. Sabrina needed to be around. "I could come into town for a few hours."

"I hope it holds till then." Sabrina hated the way real estate agents did that. They always made you feel as though you were about to miss the deal of your life if you didn't snatch it up within the hour.

"I might be able to get in on Sunday afternoon, but not before that." She didn't want to leave Annie the day her bandages came off. There was no way she was going to abandon her now. They had forbidden all the nurses on the floor to discuss Annie's blindness in her presence.

"I guess Monday will be all right. I think he said he was going away for the weekend, so no one else can get in to see it. Ten o'clock?"

"That sounds fine." She gave Sabrina the address, and she said she'd check to see if there was anything else before they met on Monday, but she said again that if Sabrina didn't mind a brownstone, she thought this might be the one. And the price was so good. It didn't have the security most young women wanted, with a doorman, but you couldn't have everything, she pointed out, and then added that houses and apartments were like romance. You either fell in love or you didn't. She hoped Sabrina would.

She told Tammy and Candy about it when she got off the phone. Their project was taking form, if the house was really any good. And it sounded perfect. It was almost too good to be true.

"Wait until you see it before you get excited," Tammy warned her. "I must have seen forty houses before I found mine. You can't believe how awful some people's houses are, or the conditions in which they're willing to live. The black hole of Calcutta was a palazzo compared to some of the hovels I saw. I was really lucky to find mine."

She loved her house, had decorated it beautifully, and kept it in immaculate condition, for herself and Juanita. She had a lot more room than she needed, a lovely view, and fireplaces in every room. She had bought some pretty antiques and wonderful art, and although the house wasn't finished, it was a pleasure to come home to at night, even if she was alone. Like Candy, her income allowed her to live in a wonderful place and buy pretty things. Sabrina lived on a tighter budget than her sisters. And Annie lived on a shoestring, out of respect for her parents, since she had almost no income except for the occasional painting she sold. She had simple needs. And none of them could imagine Annie making any kind of income now that she was blind. There was nothing she was trained for except art. Painting hadn't been her hobby, it was her life. She could have taught art history, because of her master's degree, but Sabrina couldn't imagine that blind teachers were in high demand. She just didn't know. This was a whole new world for her, and it would be for Annie too. Aside from the physical aspects, depression was her greatest fear for her sister now, and all too real. She couldn't imagine it being otherwise.

All three girls thought the brownstone sounded like a good possibility, and even Chris was enthused. He had never loved Sabrina's apartment—she had taken it because it was close to his, the building was clean, and it was cheap. But it had absolutely zero charm. The brownstone sounded much more interesting, even if somewhat impractical and a little quaint.

"Annie ought to be able to manage the stairs once she gets used to it. I think there are things you can do to make places easier to get around for people who don't have their sight. There are probably a lot of tricks we can all learn to help her out." It was new to all of them, and Sabrina thought he was sweet to say it.

Sabrina mentioned the house to her father that night, and he thought what they were planning to do for Annie was wonderful. He would worry about her a lot less knowing that she was living with two of her sisters, especially Sabrina, since she was considerably more responsible than Candy, and nearly fourteen years older. Candy was still a kid in many ways, and hadn't grown up yet. Sabrina was someone they could all count on, and so was Tammy. Unfortunately, she wouldn't be there, but promised to try and visit often. With a fourth bedroom in the house, if they took it, she'd have that option.

All three sisters left for the hospital at ten o'clock the next morning, with a fair amount of trepidation. The eye surgeon was due at ten-thirty. None of them had had the guts to prepare Annie for what was coming. The doctor in charge of her case had said to leave it to the surgeon. He was used to dealing with these things and would know what to tell her, and how. They already knew that she would have to have special training. She could go away to a rehab place for blind people for several months, or she could do it on an outpatient basis. What she needed now were life skills adapted to her blindness, and eventually maybe, if she was amenable, a seeing-eye dog. Knowing how Annie hated dogs, none of her sisters could imagine her doing that. She always claimed she thought dogs were noisy, neurotic, and dirty. A seeing-eye dog might be different, but that was still a long way off. She had a lot of very basic things to learn first.

At least Annie didn't have long months or years of surgeries ahead of her, Sabrina said on the way to the hospital, looking for the bright side. But other than that, there was none. A blind artist was about as depressing as it could get, and they were all sure that Annie would feel that way too. She had lost her career, and everything she had trained for, as well as her mother. She had been torturing herself all week about what she should have done in the accident, and how it might have been different if she could have grabbed the steering wheel from her mother, but there hadn't been time. She had classic survivor guilt, and her sisters told her over and over, to no avail, that it wouldn't have made a difference. It all happened too fast. They assured her again and again that no one blamed her, but she clearly blamed herself.

Annie was lying in bed quietly when they walked into the room. Candy was wearing short shorts, a thin white T-shirt, and silver sandals, and heads had turned when she walked down the hall. She looked incredible, although Sabrina had complained about the see-through T-shirt. She didn't think every worker, doctor, and visitor in the hospital needed a clear view of her sister's nipples.

"Oh, don't be so uptight. In Europe everyone goes topless," Candy grumbled.

"This isn't Europe." She went topless at their pool, which embarrassed Chris and her father, but Candy was oblivious to people seeing her body. She had made a career of showing it off.

"What's Candy wearing?" Annie asked with a grin. She could hear them crabbing at each other as they walked in, and Tammy had put her two cents in, saying that if she had paid as much for her breasts as Candy had, she'd be selling tickets and holding viewings to amortize the investment.

"She's not wearing much," Sabrina complained, "and what she is wearing, you can see through," she said as Annie laughed.

"She can get away with it," Annie commented.

"How're you doing?" Tammy asked her as they gathered around her bed, waiting for the doctor.

"Okay, I guess. I can't wait to get these bandages off. The tape itches, and I'm so sick of sitting here in the dark. I want to see you guys," she said, smiling, as her sisters said nothing. Sabrina handed her a glass of juice with a straw and helped her get it to her lips. "How's Dad?"

"He's doing okay. Thank God for Chris, he's keeping him occupied. I think they're fixing every door in the house, making sure every drawer rolls smoothly, changing lightbulbs. I have no idea what they're doing, but they seem very busy." Annie laughed at the image. And the doctor walked in five minutes later. He exuded an air of quiet confidence, and smiled as he looked at all four sisters. He had already seen them several times that week, and had commented that Annie was a lucky woman to have such strong family support. He said it wasn't always that way between sisters. And he realized now that he was facing all four, not just one, for this painful moment.

He told Annie that when he took the bandages off, she was not going to see anything different than she did now. As he said it, Sabrina held her breath, and Tammy reached out and squeezed her hand. This was awful. Candy was standing beside them.

"Why won't I see anything different?" Annie asked, frowning. "Does it take a while for my vision to come back?"

"Let's try it," he said calmly, and carefully began removing the bandages she had worn for the last week. Annie asked him then if there were stitches he had to take out, and he said there weren't. The stitches were all dissolving ones, and were inside. Many of the cuts on her face had begun to heal by then. Only the gash on her forehead was likely to leave a scar, but if she wanted to, she could cover it with bangs. Or have it taken care of later. Candy had been putting vitamin E oil on her sister's face all week.

Once the gauze bandages were removed, the only thing left were the two round patches that covered her eyes. The doctor glanced at Annie's sisters then, and finally back at her.

"I'm going to take the eye patches off now, Annie," he said carefully. "I want you to close your eyes. Will you do that for me?"

"Yes," she said in a whisper. She had the feeling that something was happening, and it didn't feel right. She didn't know what it was, but the tension in the room was palpable and she didn't like it.

He took the patches off, and Annie had done what she was told and closed her eyes. He shielded her eyes with his hand then, and asked Sabrina to close the venetian blinds. Even in her blindness, the sunlight could be a shock. Sabrina did it, and they waited, as he asked Annie to open her eyes. There was a moment of terrifying silence in the room, as Sabrina expected her to scream, but she didn't. Instead she looked puzzled and mildly frightened, but he had warned her.

"What do you see, Annie?" he asked her. "Do you see light?"

"A little, like a very pale gray," she said specifically, "kind of a pale gray, and black around the edges. I can't see anything else." He nodded, and tears rolled silently down first Tammy's cheeks, and then Sabrina's. Candy tiptoed from the room. She couldn't stand it. It was just too painful to watch. Annie heard the sound of the door whooshing closed but didn't ask who it was. She was concentrating on what she saw, and didn't. "I can't see anything, just that pale gray light in the middle of my field of vision."

He held a hand in front of her face then, with his fingers spread apart. "What do you see now?"

"Nothing. What are you doing?"

"I'm holding my hand in front of your eyes." He signaled to Sabrina to open the blinds again, which she did. "And now? Is the light any brighter?"

"A little. The gray is a little lighter, but I still don't see your hand." She sounded breathless, and was beginning to look very frightened. "How long will it be before I can see normally again? I mean everything, like shapes and faces and color?" It was a painfully direct question, and he was honest with her.

"Annie, things happen sometimes that can't be fixed. We do every single thing we can to fix them, but once they're broken, or connections are severed, we can't link them up again, no matter how hard we try. One of those pipes that hit you in the accident severed your optic nerves, and the veins that feed them. Once that happens, it's pretty close to impossible to repair the damage. I believe that you will see light and shadows in time. You may even see forms and outlines, and you may even have an impression of color, very much like the way you do now. The light is very bright in this room now, that's the pearl-gray color you see. Without that, the gray would be darker. That may improve slightly over time, but only very slightly. Annie, I know this is hard to conceive of now, but you're very lucky to be alive. The damage could have been far greater—your brain was not permanently damaged in the accident. Your eyes were. But, Annie, you could have lost your life." It was a tough speech to make, even for him, and he was well aware that she was an artist. Everyone in her family had told him, but it didn't change the damage that had been done to her eyes. And no matter how much he wanted to, there was nothing he could do about it. That didn't make it any easier for Annie now.

"What are you saying to me?" Annie said, looking panicked. She turned her face toward where she thought her sisters were, and could see nothing. And even the gray she had seen at first seemed dimmer now, as she turned her face away from the light. "What do you mean? Am I blind?" There was an infinitesimal pause before he answered, as her sisters stood there looking as though their hearts would break for her.

"Yes, Annie, you are," the doctor said quietly, and held her hand. She yanked it away from him and started to cry.

"Are you serious? I'm *blind*? I can't see *anything*? I'm an *artist*! I *have* to see! How can I paint if I can't see?" How could she cross a street, see a friend, cook a meal, or even find her toothpaste? Or get out of the way of traffic? Her sisters were far more concerned about the more basic issues than her art. "I *have* to see!!" she said again. "Can't you fix it?" She was sobbing like a child, as Sabrina and Tammy reached over to touch her so she would know they were still there.

"We tried to fix it," the surgeon said miserably. "We had you in surgery for five hours, just working on your eyes. The damage was too severe. The optic nerves had been destroyed. It really is a miracle you're alive. Sometimes miracles come at a high price. I think this is one of those. I'm really sorry. There are a lot of things you can do to have a good life. Jobs, travel, you can lead a fully independent life. People without sight do remarkable things in the world. Famous people, important people, ordinary people like you and me. You just have to take a different approach than the one you had before." He knew his words were falling on deaf ears. It was too soon, but he had to say something to give her hope, and she might remember it later. But for now, she had to absorb the shock of being blind.

"I don't want to be 'a person without sight'!" she shouted at him. "I want my eyes back. What about a transplant? Can I have someone else's eyes?" She was desperate and ready to sell her soul to get back her sight.

"There's too much damage," he said honestly. He didn't want to give her false hope. She might see light and shadows one day, but she would never have her sight. She was blind. At her father's request, another ophthalmologist had examined her records that week, and had come to all the same conclusions.

"Oh my God," she said, as her head dropped back onto the pillow, and she sobbed uncontrollably. Her sisters stepped up to her bedside then, one on either side of her, and the doctor patted her hand and left the room. There was nothing more he could do for her right now.

She needed them. He was the villain who had just destroyed all hope of life as she had known it until now. He would meet with her again, and help design a treatment plan for her, and make suggestions about the training she would need. But it was too soon for that. Although he was usually more dispassionate, these four women, and especially his patient, had moved him deeply. He felt like an ax murderer as he left the room, and wished he could have done more for her, but he couldn't. No one could have. At least he had managed to preserve her eyeballs so she wasn't disfigured. She was such a beautiful girl.

Candy saw him leave the room with a grief-stricken face, and slipped back in. She saw Sabrina and Tammy on either side of her, and saw Annie sobbing uncontrollably as they held her.

"Oh my God ... I'm blind ... I'm blind ..." Candy started to cry the moment she saw her. "I want to die ... I want to die ... I'll never see anything again ... my life is over...."

"No, it isn't, baby," Sabrina said softly as she held her. "It isn't. It feels that way, but it isn't. I'm sorry. I know this is hard. It's awful. But we love you, and you're alive. You're not brain-damaged, you're not crippled or paralyzed from the neck down. We have a lot to be grateful for."

"No, we *don't!*" Annie shouted at her. "You don't know what it's like. I can't *see* you! I can't see anything ... I don't know where I am ... everything is gray and black ... I want to die...." She sobbed in her sisters' arms for hours. They took turns consoling her, and finally a nurse came in and offered her some mild sedation. Sabrina nodded— it seemed like an excellent idea. This was just too much for her. Losing their mother and finding out she was blind, all within a week. After listening to Annie cry for three and a half hours, she felt as though she needed sedation herself.

Annie lay in Tammy's arms, crying, as they gave her the shot. Twenty minutes later she was nodding off, and the nurse said she would sleep for several hours. They could leave and come back, and on tiptoe they left her room, and said nothing until they reached the parking lot. They all looked as though they had been beaten up.

Tammy lit a cigarette with shaking fingers, and sat down on a large rock next to their father's car. "Jesus, I need a drink, a shot, heroin, a martini . . . the poor kid . . ." It had been awful.

"I think I'm going to throw up," Candy announced as she sat down next to her, took one of Tammy's cigarettes, and lit it, while Sabrina looked for the car keys. She felt as shaken as the others.

"Just don't throw up on me," Tammy warned her. "I couldn't take it."

The doctor had given Sabrina the name of a psychiatrist earlier that week, who specialized in working with blind people. After what they had just been through, Sabrina was going to call her.

She finally got the car keys out of her bag, and opened the doors. The others got in, and looked as though they'd been through the wars. It was two o'clock, and they had been with her for four hours, three and a half since she heard the news. Annie had sobbed non-stop. The three sisters didn't even have the strength to talk to each other on the way home. Tammy said she wanted to go back at four, in case she woke up then from the sedation. Sabrina said she'd go with her, and Candy said she wouldn't.

"I can't stand it. It's too awful. Why can't they give her someone else's eyes?"

"They just can't, there's too much damage. We have to help her make the best of it," Sabrina said, but when they got home, they all crawled out of the car, and walked into the kitchen, looking totally disheartened. Their father and Chris were just finishing lunch. It was easy to see how the morning had gone. Both men looked stricken when they saw the three sisters' faces.

"How was it?" Chris asked softly.

"How did she take it?" her father asked them. He felt like a coward now for not going with them. He knew Jane would have, but she was their mother and so much better at that kind of thing than he was. He would have felt like a bull in a china shop at her bedside. And Tammy and Sabrina reassured him that it wouldn't have made a difference. She wanted her eyes, not her father.

"Can she see anything?" Chris asked, as he put a plate of sandwiches on the kitchen table, but none of them could eat. No one was hungry. Candy disappeared and came back, said she had thrown up and felt better. It had been an awful morning for everyone, but especially excruciating for Annie.

"Just grayness and a little light apparently," Sabrina answered. "He said she may see shadows eventually, or even some color, but that's not even a sure thing. This is pretty much the way it's going to be forever, a gray and black world and nothing she can distinguish." Chris shook his head as he listened, and touched Sabrina's cheek with gentle fingers.

"I'm sorry, sweetheart."

"Me too," she said sadly, moving closer to him with tears in her eyes.

"How was she when you left her?"

"Sedated. She sobbed for hours and the nurse finally offered to give her something. I was ready to take some too. This is going to be a nightmare while she adjusts to this. I have to call that shrink he recommended. I'm worried she's going to wind up in a major depression, or worse." People had committed suicide for less, which was now her greatest fear. No one in the family had ever had suicidal tendencies, but none of them had ever lost their mother and their sight either. She wanted to do everything possible to help and protect her sister. That was what sisters were for.

Tammy went upstairs to lie down, and took Juanita with her. Candy went outside to stretch out at the pool, and Chris and Sabrina went with her, with Beulah and Zoe. The Yorkie jumped into the pool and looked like a drowned rat when she came out. Beulah liked walking across the steps at the shallow end to cool off, but preferred not to go swimming. It made Sabrina smile to watch them, and lightened the mood of the hour.

They sat and chatted quietly for a while, and eventually Jim came out to join them. He swam laps with powerful strokes up and down the length of the pool, and was tired when he finished. He was in excellent physical shape, but his whole body seemed to droop when he came to sit next to them. It was hard to believe that his beloved Jane had been gone for exactly a week.

"I'll go with you when you go back to see Annie," he said to Sabrina, and she nodded. Her sister needed all the love, support, and help she could get. And their father was an important person in their life. He was less hands-on than their mother had been with them, but he was always there in the background, protecting them and loving them, lending an ear or his support. Annie needed everything he had to give right now. "What can I do?"

"Nothing," Sabrina said honestly. "She just found out. It was a hell of a shock."

"What about her boyfriend in Florence? Do you think he'd come over to see her? That might cheer her up." Sabrina hesitated for a long moment, and then shook her head.

"I don't think so, Dad. I called him a few days ago, and he wasn't very supportive." She didn't have the heart to tell her father that he was a jerk, and he was gone. "This is a lot for any guy to deal with, and he's young."

"Not that young," her father said sternly. "I was married and had you when I was his age."

"Things are different now." He nodded and went to get dressed. He was ready to leave when she was, and Tammy came with them, Candy begged off. She said she had a headache and was still feeling sick. They had all been through so much that week that Sabrina didn't want to push. She could stay with Chris.

Their second visit of the day to Annie was even worse than the first. She was still sleepy from the sedation and had sunk into a depression. She just sat in her bed and cried and hardly talked. Their father cried when he saw her and tried to tell her, in a broken voice, that everything would be all right. He told her she could stay with him, and her sisters would take care of her, which only made her cry more.

"I'm not even going to have a life. I'll never have a boyfriend again. I won't get married. I can't live alone. I can't paint. I'll never see another sunset or a movie. I won't know what any of you look like. I can't comb my own hair." As she went down the list of all the things she could no longer do, it ripped out their hearts.

"There are a lot of things you still can do," Sabrina reminded her. "Maybe you can't paint, but you can teach."

"How am I going to teach? I couldn't see what I was talking about. You can't teach art history if you can't see the art."

"I'll bet you could, and lots of blind people get married. Your life isn't over, Annie. It's just different. It's not the end of everything. It's a change."

"That's easy for you to say. My life is over, and you know it. How can I go back to Italy like this? I have to live in my father's house, like a child." She started to sob again.

"That's not true," Tammy said quietly. "You can live with us for a while, till you get used to it. And eventually you can live on your own. I'm sure most blind people do. You're not retarded, you lost your sight. You can figure it out. There are schools that teach life skills to blind people. After that you can live on your own."

"No, I can't. And I don't want to go to school. I want to paint."

"Maybe you can do sculpture," Tammy suggested, as Sabrina gave her a thumbs-up from the other side of the bed. She hadn't thought of that herself.

"I'm not a sculptor. I'm a painter."

"Maybe you can learn. Give yourself time to figure this out."

"My life is over," Annie said miserably, and then cried like a child, as their father wiped his eyes. It occurred to Sabrina then that they might have to get tough with her, and force her to make efforts that she wouldn't make otherwise. Tammy was thinking the same thing. If Annie was going to feel sorry for herself, and refuse to cooperate, she would have to be pushed. But it was way too soon to tell. She had just found out, and everything was still horrifying and new.

They stayed with her until dinnertime, and then much as they hated to do it, they had to leave. They were all exhausted, and she needed to rest. They had been with her most of the day, and promised to come back in the morning, which they did.

Sunday was more of the same, if anything it was worse than the day before, as the reality sank in. It was what she had to go through, in order to accept what had happened to her. They left her at six o'clock. It was Tammy's last night. She still had to pack, and she wanted to spend some time with their father. Chris had promised to make lasagne, and he was going back to New York that night.

Tammy kissed Annie as she lay in bed, with tears rolling down her cheeks. Her eyes were open, but she couldn't see them. Her eyes were still a vibrant green, but they were useless to her now.

"I'm leaving in the morning," Tammy reminded her, "but I want you to kick some ass while I'm gone. I'll come back for a visit, maybe on Labor Day weekend, and by then I want to see you doing lots of stuff on your own. Is that a deal?"

"No." Her younger sister glowered at her, but for the first time she looked mad instead of sad. "And I'm never going to comb my hair again." She sounded five years old, and they all smiled. She looked so beautiful and vulnerable lying there in bed. Sabrina had brushed her coppery hair, and it shone. The nurses had washed it for her.

"Well, in that case," Tammy said practically, "I guess you're right. You won't find a husband or a boyfriend, if you stop combing your hair. I hope you plan to bathe."

"No, I won't," Annie said, sitting in bed with her arms crossed, and they all laughed. In spite of herself, Annie did too, for just an instant at least. "This isn't funny," she said, starting to cry again.

"I know it's not, baby," Tammy said as she kissed her. "It's not funny at all. But maybe all together we can make it a little bit more okay. We all love you so much."

"I know," Annie said, sinking into her pillow. "I don't know how to do this. It's so scary." Tears were streaming from her eyes.

"It won't be after a while," Tammy reassured her. "You can get used to anything, if you have to. You have the whole family behind you," she said, with tears in her own eyes.

"I don't have Mom," Annie said sadly, as two big tears rolled down her cheeks, and her father turned away.

"No, you don't," Tammy conceded, "but you have us, and we love you with all our hearts. I'll call you from L.A., and you better tell me some good stuff. If Sabrina tells me you're smelly, I'll come back and give you a bath myself, with my loofah that you hate." Annie laughed again. "So be a good girl. Don't be a big pain in the ass." It was what she used to tell her when they were kids. They were only three years apart, and Annie had been a pest when Tammy thought she was nearly grown up. Annie had squealed on her a million times, especially about boys. And Tammy had actually threatened more than once to beat her up, but never had.

"I love you, Tammy," Annie said sadly. "Call me."

"You know I will." She gave her one last kiss and walked out of the room. The others kissed her, and left too. Sabrina said that she and Candy would be back the next day, but not before the afternoon. She didn't tell Annie, but she was going to see the house in New York the next morning. She was leaving for the city at the same time Tammy left for the airport, at eight o'clock. Sabrina was taking Candy with her too, so if they liked it, they could make a decision on the spot.

They all tried to come up with ideas for Annie that night over dinner. There was no question, she had to go to a special school for the blind. She was right, there were so many things she couldn't do now. She had to learn them all, and how to deal with them without sight— filling a bathtub, making toast, combing her hair.

"She has to see a shrink," Sabrina insisted. She had called the psychiatrist and left a message on her voice mail. "And I thought your sculpture idea was great," she said to Tammy.

"If she's willing. That's going to be the key. Right now she feels like her life is over. And it is, as she knew it. She has to make the transition to a new life. That's not so easy to do, even at her age."

"It's not so easy at mine either," their father said sadly, helping himself to the excellent lasagne that Chris had made. "By the way, I think you should give up law and become a handyman and cook."

Chris had been worth his weight in gold for the past week, being helpful in a thousand ways. "You can have a job here anytime you like."

"I'll keep it in mind, if I get tired of class-action suits."

But their father's comment made them all realize that his adjustment was going to be hard too. He had been married for nearly thirty-five years, and now he was alone. He wasn't used to taking care of himself. He had relied on his wife for more than half his life, and he was going to be lost without her. He couldn't even cook. Sabrina made a mental note to ask the housekeeper to start leaving him meals he could reheat in the microwave, once they were gone.

"Every widow and divorcee in the neighborhood is going to start knocking on your door," Tammy warned him. "You're going to be a hot commodity around town, and in great demand."

"I'm not interested," he said glumly. "I love your mother. I don't want anyone else." He hated the idea.

"No, but they'll be interested in you."

"I have better things to do," he growled. But the trouble was, he didn't. He had absolutely nothing to do without his wife. She had taken care of everything for him, organized their social life, planned everything. She had kept life interesting for him, with trips into the city for symphony, theater, and ballet. None of his children could imagine him doing any of that for himself. He had been totally pampered by her. And as a result had become dependent on her.

"You'll have to come into the city and have dinner with us, Dad." Sabrina reminded him about the house they were seeing the next day.

"It sounds cute."

"It might be, or could be a horror. You know how real estate agents are. They lie like dogs and have terrible taste." He nodded, suddenly thinking how lonely he was going to be in the house when the girls left again.

"Maybe I should retire," he said, looking depressed, and all three of his daughters responded at once.

"No, Dad!" And then they laughed. The last thing he needed was to strip his life down even more. He needed to keep busy, and do more now, instead of less. That much was clear. "You need to work, and see friends, and go out just the way you did with Mom."

"Alone?" He looked horrified, as Sabrina sighed and Tammy glanced across the table at her. Now they had Annie to take care of and their dad.

"No, with friends," Tammy said. "That's what Mom would want. She wouldn't want you sitting here alone, feeling sorry for yourself." He didn't answer, and a little while later, he went upstairs to bed.

Chris went back to the city after dinner, so he could get to work on time the next day. Sabrina hated to see him leave, but she was grateful for all his love and help. He kissed her tenderly before he left, when Sabrina walked him out to his car.

"It's been a hell of a week," she summed it up.

"Yes, it has. But I think everyone's going to be okay. You're lucky you have each other." He kissed her again. "And you have me."

"Thank God," she sighed, and put her arms around his neck as he sat in the car. It was hard to believe that the accident had happened only eight days before. "Drive safely. I'm coming into the city tomorrow to see the house. But I won't stay long. I have to get back out here. Maybe I can leave Candy with Dad, and come in for a night this week."

"That would be nice. See how it goes. I'll come on Friday, if you want me." It suddenly felt like being married, with a husband who came out on weekends, while his wife stayed in the country with the kids. Only in this case the "kids" were her father and two sisters. Sabrina felt as though she had suddenly become everybody's mom, including her own. "Try and take it easy, Sabrina. Remember you can't do it all." He had read her mind. "I'll call you when I get home." She knew he would. Chris was solid, reliable, a person you could count on. He had proved that yet again in the past week. But it wasn't news to her. It was part of what she loved about him. Other than her father, Chris was the best man she had ever known.

"If you don't marry him, I will," Tammy teased her when she walked back into the house. Beulah walked into a corner of the kitchen, glared at them miserably, and looked depressed. She was always sad when Chris left. "I want a guy like him. Normal, healthy, nice, helpful, good to my family, and he can cook. *And* a hunk. How did you get so lucky and I wind up with such jerks?"

"I don't live in L.A. Maybe that helps. Or I answered the right ad," she teased.

"If I thought I'd find the right one in an ad, believe me, I'd try."

"No, you wouldn't, and I wouldn't let you. Knowing your luck, you'd only get a serial killer in a personal ad. One of these days, Tam, the right guy will turn up."

"Believe me, I'm not holding my breath. I'm not even sure I care anymore. I say I do, but I think I'm just used to bitching about it. Everybody does. I'm actually happy at home alone at night, with my doggie and total control of the remote. And I don't have to share my closets."

"Now I'm worried about you. There is more to life than sole custody of the remote."

"I can't remember what. God, I hate to leave," she said with a sigh as they walked upstairs. It suddenly felt like the old days when they were kids. Candy had put music on, and it was too loud. Tammy was almost waiting for their mother to stick her head out of their bedroom and tell her to turn it down. "It's so weird here without Mom." She said it in a whisper so her father didn't hear her as they walked past his room.

"Yes, it is," Sabrina said. "It's going to be even weirder for Dad." They both agreed.

"Do you think he'd ever get remarried?" Tammy asked her. She couldn't imagine it herself, but you never knew.

"Not in a million years," Sabrina reassured her. "He was too in love with Mom to ever look at anyone else."

"He's still young. I've gone out with men his age."

"She'd be a tough act to follow, at any age. She was it for him." And she had been for all of them too, as a mother.

"I don't think I could deal with the wicked stepmother thing," Tammy confessed, and Sabrina laughed.

"I don't think we'll ever have to. Maybe he should come out to visit you sometime in L.A. Weekends are going to be lonely for him."

"That's a nice idea," Tammy said as she took out her suitcase to pack and Candy wandered in. The three sisters chatted as she packed her things, and it was after midnight when they all went to their rooms. Chris had called Sabrina by then. Their dogs were all asleep on their beds. Their father had gone to bed at ten. All was peaceful in the house, and as Sabrina got into bed, she told herself that if she closed her eyes, she could pretend that her mother was still there. In each of their beds, all three girls were thinking exactly the same thing. And even for an instant, as they drifted off to sleep, it was nice to pretend that nothing had changed, when in fact everything had, and would never be the same again.

Chapter 11

Tammy's airport shuttle came at exactly eight o'clock the next morning. She was up, dressed, and ready to leave when it arrived. Candy and their father came downstairs to say goodbye. Candy was wearing a cotton T-shirt and cut-off jeans. The T-shirt showed her breasts, as always, and as she stood outside waving goodbye, with her long blond hair tousled and sexy, every man in the shuttle stared at her with wide eyes.

She hugged Tammy, and Sabrina and their father did the same, and then Tammy got into the shuttle, with Juanita in her Birkin bag. They hated to see her leave. Two minutes later Candy and Sabrina got into the car to drive into town to see the house. They were in town by nine-thirty, and stopped by Sabrina's apartment, to pick up some more clothes, and mail.

Candy said she didn't need to go to hers. She seemed to have a limitless supply of see-through T-shirts with her. Sabrina felt as though she'd been gone for years. It felt strange to realize that the last time she had seen her apartment, her mother was alive and Annie wasn't blind. So much had changed in a short time. And she knew a lot more things would change now. Particularly if she moved. She wasn't attached to her apartment, so she didn't care so much about that. But living with Annie and Candy would be a big change for her. She had been on her own since college, nearly thirteen years. Moving in with her sisters would be a step backward in time for her. She would miss her independence. But it was for a good cause. And in a year Sabrina hoped Annie would be adjusted to her situation, and ready to live alone. Candy could then go back to her elegant penthouse, and Sabrina could get another apartment by herself. But for the next year, they all had to be good sports and pitch in to help Annie make the transition to the enormous challenges facing her. Challenges that were huge.

They left Sabrina's apartment at five minutes before ten, and as she parked her car on East Eighty-fourth Street, Tammy called on her cell phone. She said she was getting on the plane.

"I just called to say goodbye again." They were clinging to each other more than ever these days, as though they were trying to make up for the missing link. Their mother's disappearance had badly shaken them all.

"Have a good flight. We're just about to see the house," Sabrina said as she turned off the ignition.

"Tell me how it is." Tammy suddenly felt left out and wished she were there too.

"I will. Pick up a cute guy on the plane," Sabrina encouraged her.

"I only sit next to priests, elderly women, or children with earaches. I make it a firm rule."

"You're sick." Sabrina laughed.

"No. Just determined to be an old maid. I think it's my vocation."

"One of these days you're going to walk off into the sunset with some major movie star, or Hollywood hunk, and knock us all dead."

"From your mouth to God's ears, as they say in L.A."

Sabrina and Candy were standing in front of the house by then, the realtor was waiting for them, and Tammy was in her seat on the plane.

"Gotta go. Call you later. Fly safe. Love you. Bye," she rattled off, and handed the phone to Candy so she could say goodbye too, as the realtor walked toward them with a smile. She was one of those tall, portly, overly blond women who wore too much perfume and teased her hair. And from the deep rumble of her voice, Sabrina could tell she smoked. She had the keys to the house in her hand. Sabrina introduced her to Candy, once she was off the phone, and the realtor unlocked the door, turned off the alarm, and let them in.

"We'll see if you like it. I have some other ideas too, downtown, but I think this one would work best." Sabrina hoped that they'd agree. It would certainly be easy if the first house they saw was it. Finding a place to live was an agony she had never enjoyed. Candy looked a lot more excited than she did and thought it was fun. She wandered through the house, checking out every room, and opening every door.

The entrance hall was dark, and painted a forest green, which seemed gloomy to Sabrina, but the floor was done in white and green marble squares, and she noticed that there was a pretty antique mirror on the wall, and English hunting prints that gave the entrance a certain British air. The living room was open and sunny and faced south, the library was small and dark and cozy, and had a small, handsome fireplace that looked like it worked. The walls were lined with books, many of which Sabrina had read. Candy looked around and smiled and nodded her approval to Sabrina. Already on the first floor, they liked the feeling of the house. They communicated it to each other with a nod and a smile. It was inviting and warm. The ceilings were high, and there were attractive antique sconces on the walls. There was plenty of light. And even for a tall person like Candy, the scale felt right.

They walked into the basement to check out the kitchen and dining room after that. The kitchen was modern enough, serviceable, and there was a nice round table in it, big enough for eight or ten to eat at, and it opened out into the garden, which was friendly and unkempt. There were two deck chairs, a patio, and a built-in barbecue that looked well used. Sabrina knew that Chris would like that.

The dining room was more formal and had dark red lacquer walls. There were good-looking professional touches everywhere, although the house didn't look recently done. But Sabrina liked that about it. It wasn't like walking into a magazine. It was a home, and it wasn't overcrowded. Some of her furniture would fit, and she liked a lot of what they had. She might even put her own things into storage if they took it. The house had a great feeling, and she could see why the owner loved it and wanted it back. It was a great place to live. Candy expressed her excitement in a whisper when the realtor left the room. "I love it!" she said, looking excited.

"Me too." Sabrina smiled. So far it was a winner.

The bedrooms were small, as they'd been warned, but adequate with pretty windows, and good curtains in pastel silks with elegant tassels and tie-backs. There was a king-size bed in every room, which Candy loved, and the others would too, particularly if they had men in their lives. And a king-size bed was a must for Chris, he was so tall. The master bedroom was slightly bigger. The one next to it was a little small, but they didn't need it anyway, and as a guest room it was perfect. The rooms for Candy and Annie were nicely decorated and cozy. The bathrooms had baths and showers. The colors in the bedrooms were light and airy, and the bathrooms all had marble tile.

Sabrina looked at the realtor in amazement. There was absolutely nothing about the house she didn't like. And she could see that Candy loved it too. It had a great feeling, and "good energy," as Candy said. And as the realtor had promised, it had charm. Lots of it. It would be perfect for them, and there was nothing complicated that would be hard for Annie. The stairs were straightforward and easy, and it seemed like an easy place to get around, even for someone blind.

"Bingo!" Sabrina said, grinning. Candy was beaming, and nodding in agreement. She told Sabrina she liked it better than her penthouse. It was friendlier and warmer. Her penthouse was sophisticated and showy, and cold in many ways. It looked like a magazine shoot, not a home. Candy already felt more at ease here. It was the kind of place that made you want to curl up in a big, comfy chair and stick around. It had a wonderful vibe to it. And hopefully it would be a good place for Annie too, once she figured out where things were, which wouldn't take long. It was a small house, with two relatively good-size rooms on every floor.

"What do you say?" Sabrina asked her sister politely. She already knew how she felt about it, and Candy was in full agreement.

"I say yes! Let's grab it. I can have Zoe here, right?" She never went anywhere without her dog, although she had left her with their father that morning. She was afraid she would be too hot in the car, and she was company for Beulah, who had stayed in the country too. Sabrina hadn't wanted to scare the realtor with a bigger dog. And Beulah got carsick, so she wasn't fun to drive around.

Sabrina confirmed with the realtor that the owner had no problem with dogs.

"I checked with him this morning, and he said dogs are fine. He didn't even say small dogs. He just said dogs." He obviously hadn't specified how many either, which was great news for them too, since he had two of his own. The house had been made to order for them, in every way. Warm, cozy, pretty, comfortable, inviting, and the price was right. His furniture was better than their own, and they could have their dogs. Candy had already decided that she wanted to rent her penthouse furnished, which would make it more appealing to a tenant. She was going to put it on the market that week. Co-ops in her building rented all the time, at astronomical prices, so she would make money on the deal. The rent for the house on East Eighty-fourth Street was relatively cheap.

"We'll take it," Sabrina confirmed. "How soon is it available?"

"August first." The two girls looked at each other. That was soon, but it was probably just about right. Sabrina still had to get out of her lease, but thought she could, for a small fee. And Annie was getting out of the hospital in a week. She was going to spend a week or two at their dad's. And once Sabrina and Candy got the house ready, they could move in.

"That works for us," Sabrina confirmed. They were going to be busy, helping Annie, keeping an eye on their father, and moving in. Sabrina suddenly realized that it was lucky Candy had told her agency that she was taking the month of August off. And the rest of July. Sabrina had to go back to work the following week, and would be swamped, as usual, once she did.

"I can try and get it for you sooner, if you like," the realtor offered. "I think he's staying at his beach house, and he leaves for Europe in a couple of weeks."

"That might be a good idea," Sabrina agreed. "We need to move in pretty soon. My sister gets out of the hospital in a week."

"Is she sick?" The realtor looked surprised.

"She was in an accident over the Fourth of July weekend," Sabrina said solemnly, not wanting to give her the details. "That's how she lost her sight."

"Oh, I'm so sorry. When you said she was blind, I didn't realize it was so recent, I thought...The three of you are moving in together?"

"Until she gets used to things. It's going to be a big adjustment for her."

"I can certainly see that," the woman said sympathetically, and was even more inclined to help. "I'll talk to the owner and see what he says. It's nice of you girls to move in with her," she said, looking touched. Her early slightly hard edge had softened instantly and disappeared in the face of what they were doing.

"Of course. We're sisters," Candy said.

"Not all sisters are that close," the agent said. "I haven't seen mine in twenty years."

"How sad," Candy said.

"What do we have to sign?" Sabrina asked.

"It's a standard lease, first and last months' rent, and security deposit. I don't think he wants a big security. I'll write it all up and have it sent to your office."

"I'm not in this week. I'm in Connecticut at my dad's. I could drive in and pick it up."

"I can have it ready for you by tomorrow."

"That's fine," Sabrina confirmed. She wanted to spend a night with Chris anyway, and Candy could hold the fort for one night. "Do you need all our signatures?"

"Just yours will be fine for now. We can add the others when you're all back in town, if that's easier for you."

"It is. I'll get the others to you next week." They shook hands on the deal, took another walk around the house, and liked it even better the second time. Five minutes later they were back in the car, chortling with glee. They could hardly wait to tell Annie. Sabrina called Chris from the car, and he was happy for them. He said he couldn't wait to see it. And they were going to tell Tammy as soon as she got off the plane.

Their father was out when they got home, although he had taken several weeks off from work. Sabrina made lunch, which Candy didn't eat, and she scolded her for it.

"You're not working right now. You don't need to starve."

"I'm not starving. I'm just not hungry. It's the heat."

"You didn't have breakfast either." Candy looked annoyed, and got up to make some calls on her cell phone. She didn't like anyone keeping track of what she ate, or didn't. It was a sensitive subject with her, and had been for years. She even got mad at their mom whenever she used to mention it. She had started starving at seventeen, when her modeling career took off.

They went to see Annie at the hospital at two, and when they got there, she was asleep. She stirred when she heard them walk into the room.

"It's us," Sabrina said, smiling at her, which Annie couldn't see, but she could hear the excitement in her voice.

"I know it's you. I can smell your perfume, and I can hear the bracelets on Candy's arm." Sabrina didn't comment, but in subtle ways Annie was already instinctively adjusting to her disability, which seemed like a good thing, if you could call it that. Her hearing and other senses seemed to be getting more acute.

"We have a surprise for you," Candy chortled with a grin.

"That's nice," Annie said, looking glum. "Lately the surprises haven't been so good." They would all agree with her on that. But they were hoping that hearing about the house would cheer her up. "What have you been up to?"

"We just got back from the city," Sabrina explained. "We went right after Tammy left. She said to give you a kiss. So, kiss." Annie smiled, and waited for the rest. "We went to see a house."

"A house?" She looked suddenly panicked. "Is Dad moving to the city?" She didn't want everything to change so soon. She loved her parents' house, and staying there when she came to visit. She didn't want him to sell it, and hoped he wouldn't.

"Of course not," Sabrina went on. "We went to look at a house for us."

"Are you and Chris getting married, or moving in together?" She looked confused, and Sabrina laughed. Finding the perfect house for them on the first shot had been a major victory.

"Nope. Not now anyway. This is a house for you, me, and Candy. For a year, while you get organized, and . . . well . . . used to things." She tried to be delicate about it. "And a year from now, you can figure out what you want to do. You can get rid of us if you want. Or we can rent another place. This one's only available for a year anyway. It's really cute. On East Eighty-fourth Street."

"What am I going to do there?" She looked mournful and hopeless as she said it.

"Go to school, maybe. Whatever you need to do this year to get independent." Sabrina was trying to be upbeat about the changes she'd have to make. They weren't even fully aware of what they were yet. They were waiting for her treatment plan for when she'd be released.

"I was independent, up to a week ago. Now I'm going to be like a two-year-old, if that."

"No, you're not. We want to be your roommates, Annie, not your jailers. You can come and go as you please."

"And how do you think I'm going to do that? With a white stick?" she said, as tears filled her eyes. "I don't know how to use one." As she said it, all three of them thought of the people they had seen trying to cross the street in heavy traffic, and needing assistance. "I'd rather be dead. Maybe I'll just stay at Dad's." It sounded like the kiss of death to them. Even their dad would be going back to work in a few weeks, and she'd be alone at the house all day, unable to escape.

"You'll die of boredom out here. You'll be much better off in the city, with us." She could at least take cabs to get around.

"No, I won't. I'll be a burden to you. Forever probably. Why don't you just put me in an institution somewhere and forget me?"

"I might have liked that when I was fifteen and you were seven. But I think it's a little late for that. Come on, Annie. Let's try and make the best of this. It would be fun living together. Candy is going to rent the penthouse for a year, and I'll get out of my lease. And Tammy can come and visit for long weekends. Look at the opportunity. We keep talking about how much we miss being together. This is probably the only chance we'll ever have to do it. For a year. One year. And then we all grow up forever."

Annie shook her head as she lay in the hospital bed, looking morbid. "I want to go back to Italy. I've been trying to get hold of Charlie. He can stay with me at my place. I don't want to live here."

"You don't want to be in Florence on your own," Sabrina tried to reason with her. This truly was an idea that would work, if Annie would only agree to do it. And Charlie was history. She just didn't know it, and Sabrina didn't want to be the one to tell her. Annie had been trying all morning to reach him on his cell phone. She mentioned it to Sabrina, and her oldest sister couldn't help wondering if he had turned off his cell phone in case she called. She wouldn't put it past him, after the conversation she'd had with him the week before.

"I don't want to live with you like some kind of cripple," Annie said angrily. "I don't mean to sound ungrateful. But I don't want to be the blind sister that everyone feels sorry for and you two have to take care of."

"I can't anyway," Candy said practically. "I travel a lot. And Sabrina works. You have to learn how to take care of yourself. But we can help you."

"I don't *want* to be *helped*. I just want to go somewhere on my own. And I have an apartment in Florence. I don't need a house in New York."

"Annie," Sabrina said, trying to be patient with her, "you can live anywhere in the world once you get the hang of this. But it may take a little time. Don't you think you'd be better off living with us at first?"

"No. I'll go back to Florence and live with Charlie. He loves me," she said petulantly as Sabrina's heart sank. He didn't love her. And she could not go back to Italy on her own. Not yet anyway, and probably not for many months, if ever.

"What if Charlie doesn't want to? What if he can't handle it, or it's too much for him? Wouldn't you rather try your wings out with us?"

"No. I'd rather be with him."

"I can understand that. But you'd be making things hard on him. We're your family. He isn't. And there are some great rehab programs for the blind in New York."

"I don't want to go to a blind school!" Annie shouted at her. "I can figure it out for myself." She was crying again, and Sabrina was near tears herself, in frustration.

"Don't make it so hard for yourself. Come on, Annie. This is going to be hard enough. Let us help."

"No!" Annie said, and rolled over in bed with her back to them. Sabrina and Candy exchanged a long look and said nothing. "And don't look at each other like that!" she shouted. Sabrina jumped when she said it.

"So now you've got eyes in the back of your head? You have your back to us. And pardon me for mentioning it, but you're blind, so how do you know what we're doing?"

"I know you!" she said angrily, and Sabrina chuckled.

"You know, you're as big a brat as you were when you were seven. You used to spy on me, you little shit, and tell Mom."

"So did Tammy."

"I know, but you were worse. And she always believed you, even when you lied."

She still had her back to them, but Sabrina could hear her laughing in her bed.

"So are you still going to be a brat, or are you going to be reasonable? Candy and I found a great house, and I think you'd love it. We all would. And it would be fun to live together."

"Nothing I do is ever going to be fun again."

"I doubt that," Sabrina said sternly. She couldn't wait to hear from the shrink. Annie needed one badly. They all did. And maybe she could tell them how to deal with Annie. "I'm signing the lease tomorrow night. And if we lose this house because you're having a tantrum, I'll be really pissed." She had a right to more than a tantrum, but Sabrina figured that maybe being firm with her would work best. All she wanted to do was put her arms around her and hold her, but maybe Annie needed something stronger than that. Hard as it was to do, they couldn't let her wallow in feeling sorry for herself.

"I'll think about it," was all Annie would say, and she wouldn't turn around to face them. "Go away. Leave me alone."

"Do you mean that?" Sabrina looked shocked, and Candy hadn't said a word. She had always hated Annie's temper. For her, Annie was the big sister who had given her a hard time when she was growing up. They were five years apart.

"Yes," Annie said sadly. She hated the world.

Sabrina and Candy stayed for another half-hour and tried to jolly her out of her black mood, without success. And finally they took her at her word and left, promising to be back later, if she called them and wanted them to come back, or tomorrow.

Both sisters talked about it on the way home. Sabrina thought that maybe it was a good sign that she was angry. And she had no one else to take it out on but them. In truth, she was railing at the fates that had taken her mother from her in one fell swoop, and left her blind. They had been cruel fates indeed.

"What'll we do about the house?" Candy asked, sounding worried. "What if she won't move in with us?"

"She will," Sabrina said calmly. "She doesn't really have a lot of choice."

"That's sad." Candy was feeling sorry for her again.

"Yes, it is. The whole thing is sad. For her, for Dad, for us. But we have to make the best of it." She was still excited about the house they had found. It was perfect for them. "She'll come around," Sabrina said, hoping it was true.

When they got home, she found a message from the shrink. Sabrina called her back, told her what had happened, and she agreed to come out from the city to see Annie. She said her practice was in New York, but in special circumstances, she made exceptions and visited patients where they were. Annie's circumstances sounded special enough to her. She promised to come out on Wednesday, and was encouraged to hear that they were moving to the city in the next few weeks. She had time to take Annie on as a patient and sounded interested in her case. Sabrina was relieved, and thought she sounded nice on the phone. She had been highly recommended by Annie's surgeon.

Sabrina left a message on Tammy's cell phone then to tell her they got the house. And she spent the rest of the afternoon returning calls and making notes. She called her office and checked in, then called her landlord about how to go about releasing her apartment. It sounded like a fairly simple procedure to her. She explained the circumstances to them, and they were sympathetic and helpful.

They didn't visit Annie again till the next day. When they got there, a nurse was walking her down the hall, and Annie didn't look happy. She sensed them before they greeted her. She took Sabrina's arm then, and they walked back to her room. She looked skittish, and was anxious about bumping into things. More than ever, seeing her out of her room made her sisters realize how vulnerable she was. She was like a turtle without a shell. She was very quiet once back in her room, and then finally she told them. She had spoken to Charlie. She looked sad the moment she said it, and they both knew why.

"He was in Greece, and he said his phone wasn't getting reception till now." She hesitated and then went on. "He said he met someone else. That's cute, isn't it? I left Florence less than two weeks ago, and he was madly in love with me. And within days, he meets someone else. He was a shit on the phone. He didn't want to talk. I guess he went to Greece with her." Two tears crept down her cheeks as she said it, and Sabrina gently brushed them away.

"Guys are shits sometimes. I guess women are too. People can be. That was a lousy thing to do to you." Even lousier than she knew.

"Yeah, it was. I didn't tell him that I'm blind, so it wasn't that. I told him about the accident though, and that Mom had died. But I said I was okay. I didn't want him to feel sorry for me. If everything had been okay with us, I would have told him. So he could decide if he was okay with it. But I never got that far. He told me almost as soon as he answered." Listening to her, Sabrina decided it was better that way. And she was glad she'd called and warned him. If Annie had told him, and he'd rejected her, it would have been much worse. This way she thought she'd gotten dumped like anyone else. Rotten luck. And bad behavior on his part. But not the mortal blow of a man who no longer wanted her because she was blind. Losing him was for the best. He clearly wasn't a good guy.

"I'm sorry, Annie," Sabrina said, and Candy told her there would be other guys, and he was obviously a jerk.

"There won't be other guys for me now. No one wants a woman who's blind," she said, feeling sorry for herself. Sabrina decided not to tell her yet about the shrink, but she was glad that she was coming to see Annie.

"Yes, there will," Sabrina said gently. "You're just as beautiful and smart and nice as you were before. None of that has changed."

"You know, I get dumped all the time," Candy added, and both of her sisters laughed. It was hard to believe that with looks like hers. "A lot of the guys I go out with are assholes. Some guys our age just are. They don't know what they want. They love you today, and want someone else tomorrow. Or they just want to get laid, or get into a party. There are a lot of users out there." Sabrina realized it was probably one of the standard features of Candy's life. A lot of people wanted to use her. And she was young to handle all that. And Tammy wasn't having an easy time either with men her age and older. Men could be tough at any age.

"You two make me glad I'm not that young. I'd forgotten what jerks guys in their twenties are. I went out with some lulus before I met Chris."

After that Candy and Annie talked for a while about the horrors of dating, but underneath the joking around, Sabrina could see that Annie was profoundly sad. Charlie dumping her summarily, supposedly for someone else, had been a blow, especially now. She had been so sure that he was the right one. She had almost been ready to move back to New York for him. Sabrina didn't remind her of that.

"It won't kill you to live with us for a while. Besides, it might be fun."

"It won't be fun," Annie said stubbornly. "Nothing is ever going to be fun again."

"Tell me that in six months when you're dating some other guy."

"There won't ever be another guy," Annie said sadly, and they could both see that she believed it.

"Okay," Sabrina said, "I accept that challenge. Today is July fourteenth, Bastille Day. I hereby bet you a hundred dollars that six months from now, which will be January fourteenth, you will either have been dating someone for a while, or will be starting to date someone. A hundred bucks says you'll be dating again. And Candy is our witness. You're gonna owe me a hundred bucks, Annie, so you'd better start saving your money."

"You're on," her sister said. "I will bet you that in six months, or six years, I won't have had a date yet."

"The bet is for six months," Sabrina said firmly. "If you want a six-year bet, I'm going to charge you a hell of a lot more money. You can't afford it. Take the bet for six months. And remember, you're going to owe me a hundred bucks. Dead-ass certain."

Annie was lying in bed, smiling. She was depressed about Charlie, but she enjoyed being with her sisters. Even now they made her feel better. Tammy had called her when she got back to L.A. the night before, and had even made her laugh with stories about Juanita, and some crazy guy she sat next to on the plane.

They left her a little while later and went back to the house. Before they left the hospital, Sabrina told her that she was going into the city to sign their lease.

"I haven't said I'd do it," she said petulantly, still looking depressed, although better than when they'd arrived. She was understandably upset about Charlie. But at least now she wasn't trying to rush back to Florence. Being there alone and blind would have been impossible for her, and she knew it. But she insisted that she didn't want to give up her apartment in Florence. Sabrina told her to discuss that with their father. It was up to him, and she knew Annie's apartment there was dirt cheap so maybe he'd let her.

"Well, if you don't move in with us," Sabrina told her, "then Candy and I will live together and you'll miss out." Annie smiled slowly as she said it.

"Okay, okay . . . we'll see. I'll think about it."

"I can promise you one thing, Annie Adams," Sabrina said as they stood up to leave. "If you don't come to live with us, you'll miss out on the time of your life. We're great to live with."

"No, you're not." Annie laughed at her and looked straight at her as though she could see her. "I lived with you until I was ten years old, and I can tell you, you are a giant pain in the ass. And Candy is not a lot better. She is the messiest human on the planet." They all knew that she had been for years, but she seemed to have improved lately.

"I am not anymore!" Candy said, sounding insulted. "Besides, we need a maid if we're going to live together. I am *not* going to clean house."

"Gee, maid service too . . . now that is something to think about," Annie said, grinning. "I'll let you know," she said grandly, sounding more like herself for the first time.

"You do that," Sabrina said, kissed her, and walked out of the room with Candy right behind her. Sabrina turned to wink at Candy, who gave her a thumbs-up. Annie was going to do it. She had no other choice.

Chapter 12

The psychiatrist saw Annie at the hospital as promised on Wednesday afternoon, and she called Sabrina after she'd seen her. She couldn't disclose any of what Annie had said to her, due to the confidentiality laws, but she told Sabrina that she was satisfied with their meeting, and was planning to see her again, once more in the hospital before her discharge, and hopefully on a regular basis once she moved to New York. Annie still hadn't told Sabrina that she was moving into the house, but it sounded as though she would. And Sabrina had signed the lease the night before.

The psychiatrist reassured Sabrina that her sister was not suicidal, or even unusually depressed. She was going through all the emotions that were to be expected after that kind of trauma, and losing both her mother and her sight as a result. It was a major double blow. She suggested, as the surgeon had, that Annie needed to join a rehab program that worked with people who had lost their sight, but she said the doctor would make those referrals before Annie came home. In the meantime, she was satisfied with what she saw. For Sabrina, that was good enough.

The meeting had been particularly interesting for Annie, who had been furious when the psychiatrist walked into the room and told her who she was. She told her that Sabrina had called her, and at first Annie had refused to talk. She said she didn't want any help, and she was doing fine on her own.

"I'm sure you are," the psychiatrist, Ellen Steinberg, assured her. "But it never hurts to talk." Annie eventually exploded and said that the doctor had no idea what she was going through, and she didn't know what it was like to be blind. "Actually, I do," Dr. Steinberg said calmly. "I happen to be blind myself. I have been since I was in a car accident much like yours, right after I finished medical school. That was twenty-four years ago. I had some very tough years afterward. I decided to give up medicine. I had trained as a surgeon, and so as far as I was concerned, my career was pretty well shot. There aren't a lot of calls for blind surgeons." Annie was fascinated as she listened. "And I was absolutely sure that there was no other specialty I was interested in. I thought psychiatry was for the birds. What did I want to do with a bunch of lunatics and neurotics? I wanted to be a heart surgeon, which was pretty prestigious stuff. So, I sat home and pouted for a couple of years, and drove my family insane. I started to drink a lot, which complicated everything. My brother finally told me what a horse's ass I was, how everyone was sick of my feeling sorry for myself, and why didn't I get a job and stop punishing everyone for how miserable I was.

"I couldn't do anything. I had no training for any job except medicine. I got a job in an ambulance company, answering the phones. And as some kind of crazy fluke, I got another job on a suicide hotline, and I actually liked it, which led me to psychiatry. I went back to school, and studied psychiatry. And the rest is history, as they say. I met my husband when I went back to school, he was a young professor at the medical school. We got married and have four kids. I don't usually talk about myself this way. I'm here to talk about you, Annie, not about myself. But I thought it might help you to hear about what happened to me. I was hit by a drunk driver in the accident. He went to jail for two years. And I was blind for the rest of my life. But actually, if you want to look at it that way, maybe it was a blessing. I wound up in a specialty I love, married to a wonderful man, and have four pretty terrific kids."

"How can you do all that, being blind?" Annie was fascinated by her. But she couldn't imagine any of that happening to her. Not the good stuff anyway. She felt cursed.

"You learn. You develop other skills. You fall on your face just like everyone else does, blind or not. You make mistakes. You try harder than everyone else at times. You have disappointments and heartbreaks just like people who have their sight. It's not so different in the end. You do what you have to do. Why don't we talk about you for a while? How are you feeling right now?"

"Scared," Annie said in a little girl's voice, as tears started to flow. "I miss my mom. I keep thinking I should have tried to save her. It's my fault that she died. I couldn't grab the steering wheel. I didn't have time." She looked anguished as she spoke.

"It doesn't sound like you could have. I read the accident report before I came here."

"How did you read it?" Annie asked her.

"I had it translated into braille. That's pretty easy to do. I type all my reports in braille, and my secretary retypes them for sighted people."

They talked for over an hour, and then Dr. Steinberg left her. She said that if Annie wanted her to, she would come back again.

"I'd like that," Annie said softly. She felt like a child again, at everyone's mercy. She had told her too about Sabrina and Candy wanting her to move into a house with them.

"What do *you* want to do?" Dr. Steinberg had asked her, and Annie had said she didn't want to be a burden to them.

"Then don't be. Go to school. Learn what you need to know so that you can be independent."

"I guess that's what you did."

"Yes, but I wasted a lot of time feeling sorry for myself before that. You don't need to do that, Annie. It sounds like you have a good family. I did too. But I punished everyone for a long time. I hope you don't do that. It's a waste of time. You'll enjoy your life again, if you do what you need to. You can do almost everything that sighted people can do, except maybe watch movies. But there are so many things you can do."

"I can't paint anymore," Annie said sadly. "That's all I ever wanted to do."

"I couldn't be a surgeon either. But I like psychiatry a lot better. There are probably a lot of artistic things you can do. Talents you don't even know you have. The secret is to find them. To accept the challenge. You've been given a chance here, to be more than you were before. And something tells me that you're going to do it. You have a whole life ahead of you, and new doors to open, if you're willing to try." Annie didn't answer for a long time, as she thought about it. And a few minutes later Dr. Steinberg got up to leave. Annie could hear her cane sweeping the floor.

"You don't have a dog?"

"I'm allergic to them."

"I hate dogs."

"Then don't have one. Annie, you've got most of the choices you had before, and more. See you next week." Annie nodded, and heard the door close. She lay back in her bed, thinking of everything Dr. Steinberg had said.

Chapter 13

The next few weeks were insanely hectic for Sabrina. She took care of her father, and tried to buoy his spirits. Candy wasn't as much help as she'd hoped. She was easily distracted, disorganized, and still too upset about their mother's death to assist in the ways Sabrina needed. In so many aspects, Candy was still a child, and now she expected Sabrina to mother her. Sabrina did her best, but sometimes it was very hard.

After signing the lease, they went back through the house to decide which of the furniture they wanted to keep. There were a lot of pretty pieces that Sabrina and Candy both agreed they liked. She helped Candy put her apartment up for rent. It was off the market in three days, at a profit to Candy. She was going to make enough from it to cover her rent. And Sabrina got out of her lease, for a minimum penalty. She sold some of her furniture, put other pieces in storage, and earmarked what they'd need on East Eighty-fourth Street. Candy had rented her penthouse fully furnished, so they had nothing to move from there. Sabrina had told Candy to book the movers for August first. It was something she could do to help. And between the four hundred phone calls she had to make, Sabrina visited Annie every day. She had finally agreed to move in with them and see how it went. After her second meeting with Dr. Steinberg, Annie had told both of her sisters that if they babied her or made her feel helpless, she would move out. And both Candy and Sabrina had agreed, and said they would be respectful of her and wait until she asked for their help, unless she was about to fall down the stairs.

By the third week of July, when Annie was released from the hospital, all three girls were excited about the house and living together again, in spite of why they were moving there.

Annie's first days at her father's house were difficult. Being there without their mother was newer to her than to the others. They had already been there for three weeks without her. For Annie, it was all fresh. She knew the house perfectly, so could move around fairly easily, but in every room she expected to hear her mother's voice. She walked into her closets, and felt her clothes with her fingers and put them to her face. She could smell her perfume, and almost sense her in the room. It was agony at times being there, and reminded her again and again of her last vision of the steering wheel slipping out of her mother's hands as she flew out of the car. The memory haunted Annie, and she spoke of it during every session with Dr. Steinberg. She couldn't get it out of her mind, nor the feeling that she should have done something to stop it, but there hadn't been time. She even dreamed of it at night, and losing Charlie after the accident just made things worse. In some ways, she was glad she was moving to New York, and not back to Florence. She needed a fresh start. But her father had agreed not to give up her apartment there for a while.

Her treatment plan when she left the hospital was fairly straightforward, and the ophthalmologist explained it to Sabrina as well. Sabrina was beginning to feel more like Annie's mother than her sister. She was responsible for everyone now. Annie, Candy because she was still so young and irresponsible at times, and their father, who seemed to be getting more helpless by the hour. He lost things, broke things, cut himself twice, and couldn't remember where anything was, or worse, had never known. Sabrina commented to Tammy on the phone late one night that their mother must have done everything except chew his food for him. He had been totally pampered, protected, and spoiled. She had been the consummate wife, and it wasn't Sabrina's style. She tried to get him to do some things for himself, with very little success. He complained a lot, whined constantly, and cried often. It was understandable, but Sabrina was at her wit's end dealing with him and everything else.

Annie's doctor wanted her to have follow-up CT scans after her brain surgery, and he had strongly recommended that she attend a training school for the blind in New York for six months. He had told her and Sabrina that it would allow Annie to become independent, and able to live successfully on her own, which was ultimately their goal. Annie had been sullen about it for days after they talked, and wandered around her father's house looking depressed. She had a white cane, but wouldn't use it. In her parents' house she managed well, as long as no one moved anything. Candy left a chair out of place in the dining room, and as Annie cruised through the room unsuspectingly, she fell flat on her face. Candy apologized profusely as she helped her up.

"That was not cute!" Annie said, furious with her, but more at the fates that had humbled her this way. "Why did you do that?"

"I forgot . . . I'm sorry . . . I didn't do it on purpose!" It was the kind of thing Candy would have said as a child, and still did. Intent was all that mattered to her, not result.

Annie was determined to bathe herself alone, and forbade her sisters to come into the bathroom with her, although she'd never been modest before, and no one in the family really was. Their father was circumspect and never appeared at breakfast without a robe, and their mother had been as well, but the girls had always drifted in and out of each other's bathrooms, looking for hair dryers, curling irons, nail polish remover, clean panty hose, and a missing bra, in various states of undress. Now Annie went in fully dressed and closed and locked the door. Her second day home, her bathtub had overflowed, and as water poured through the dining room chandelier directly below it, Sabrina realized what had happened, and ran upstairs. She pounded on the door, and Annie finally let her in. Sabrina turned the tub off for her, standing in two inches of water on the marble floor.

"This isn't working," Sabrina said calmly. "I know you don't want it, but you need help. You need to learn some tricks of the trade here, or you're going to drive yourself and everyone else nuts. What can I do to help?" Sabrina asked, cleaning up the bathroom.

"Just leave me alone!" she shouted at her and locked herself in her room.

"Fine," Sabrina steamed, but said nothing more. In the end, she had to call an electrician, a carpeting firm to dry the carpets, and a painter to repair the damage. Annie was furious with both her sister and herself. It took two more incidents for Annie to agree to at least think about going to school in September, to learn how to deal constructively with being blind. Until then she pretended to herself that it was a temporary condition and she could deal with it on her own. She couldn't. That much was clear to all of them, and her anger at all of them was very wearing. She was no longer anyone they recognized. She wouldn't even let Sabrina or Candy help her comb or brush her hair, and the second week she was home she chopped it off herself. The results were disastrous, and Sabrina found her sitting in her room, on the floor, sobbing, with her long auburn hair all around her. She looked like she'd been attacked by a buzz saw, and when Sabrina saw her, she put her arms around her and they both cried.

"Okay," Annie said finally, resting her head on her sister's shoulder, "okay . . . I can't do this. . . . I hate being blind. . . . I'll go to school . . . but I don't want a dog."

"You don't have to have a dog." But she clearly needed help. Just seeing her in the mental state she was in was depressing their father too. He felt helpless when he watched her stumble and fall, pour hot coffee on her hand as she tried to fill the cup, or spill her food like a two-year-old.

"Can't you do something for her?" he asked Sabrina miserably.

"I'm trying," she said, doing her best not to snap at him. She was calling Tammy five and six times a day, who was feeling guilty for having left, and still hadn't found anyone to fill the pregnant star's place. Her life was in turmoil too, and she felt as though she was letting her family down by being in L.A. All of them were desperately unhappy in one way or another, and Annie most of all.

She finally let Candy fix her hair. She was too embarrassed to go to their mother's hairdresser to let them clean it up. She didn't want them to see her that way, blind, with hair that looked like it had been lopped off with a machete. She had used her desk scissors, and it looked pretty bad. Her hair had been beautiful, silky, and long, much like Candy's, only longer and a reddish-brown color instead of blond.

"Okay, new hairdo coming right up," Candy said, sitting on the floor with her the day after she'd cut off her hair. Until then, she looked like she'd just been let out of prison. Her hair was sticking up all over the place, some bits were short, others were slightly longer, and all of it was a mess. "I'm actually pretty good at this," Candy reassured her. "I'm always cleaning up people's hair after shoots, when some nutjob psycho hairdresser does something that fucks the model's hair up even if it looked great at the shoot. But the good news here," Candy said cheerfully, "is that you can't see what I'm doing. So if I fuck it up, you won't get mad." What she said was so awful that it made Annie laugh, and she sat, looking docile, for the entire procedure as Candy snipped, tugged, brushed, combed, and snipped some more. It looked stylish and adorable when she was through, and Annie looked like an elegant Italian elf with a slightly spiked top and a little longer on the sides, and all of it framed her face with its shining copper color and set off her green eyes. Candy was just admiring her work when Sabrina walked into her bedroom, and saw hair all over the floor. The room was a disaster, but Annie looked prettier than ever, as though she'd gone to a top hairdresser in London or Paris for her new style.

"Wow!" she said, as she stood in the doorway, impressed by how competent Candy was. It was her business, after all, to look stylish, sexy, and fashionable. It was the best haircut Sabrina had seen in years. "Annie, you look fantastic! It's a whole new you. And now we know what Candy can do if her modeling career ever tanks. You can definitely open a hair salon. You can do mine any day."

"Do I really look okay?" Annie asked, looking worried. It had been a major gesture of confidence to let Candy cut her hair. She had had no idea how bad it looked after her irate hack job—totally awful and scary-looking. And Candy had transformed it into something magical and cute. It was sexy and young, like Annie herself, and actually looked better on her than her long straight hair, which Candy had always told her made her look like a hippie, and half the time she wore it in a braid. She had gone from Mother Earth to movie star in half an hour, at Candy's hands.

"You look a lot better than okay," Sabrina reassured her. "You look like the cover of *Vogue*. Our baby sister definitely has a knack with hair. All these hidden talents we seem to have. I seem to have missed my calling as a maid. Which reminds me, ladies, if we're going to play Hair Salon in future"—it was a game they'd loved as children, doing each other's hair and nails, and creating a gigantic mess—"do you think we could do it in the bathroom? I'd like to remind you that Hannah is off this week, and the cleaning staff is me. So please . . ."

"Oops . . . ," Candy said, looking embarrassed. She hadn't even noticed. She never did. She was so used to other people waiting on her and cleaning up after her, on shoots and even in her apartment, that she was totally unaware of the mess she'd made. There was hair everywhere. "Sorry, Sabrina. I'll clean it up."

"Sorry," Annie added, wishing she could help, but there was no way she could see the hair, or even sense it, to help clean it up.

"Don't worry about it," Sabrina said to Annie. "You can do other stuff to help me out. Maybe you could help Dad load the dishwasher. He must have a vision problem too—he keeps putting dishes in it with food on them. I don't think he gets how it works. The dishwasher just cements the food onto the plates and cutlery. I guess Mom never let him help."

"I'll go downstairs," Annie said, getting to her feet and feeling her way out of the room. She looked absolutely beautiful with her new haircut, and Sabrina told her so again.

She found Annie and her father in the kitchen twenty minutes later. Annie could feel the food on the plates and rinsed them off. She did a much better job of it than their father, who wasn't blind, just helpless and spoiled. It was depressing to see how lost he was since their mother had died. The strong, wise father they had all looked up to had vanished before their eyes. He was weak, scared, confused, depressed, and cried all the time. Sabrina had suggested seeing a shrink to him too, and he refused, although he needed one as much as Annie, who seemed to be liking hers.

She let Annie babysit for him, while she and Candy went into the city to get ready for their move. Annie had already been to the house and felt her way around it. She said she liked her room, although she couldn't see it. She liked having her own space, and said it was a decent size, and she was pleased with having Candy across the hall, in case she needed help. But she didn't want anyone's assistance unless she asked. She had made that clear. She got into jams constantly, but tried valiantly to work them out for herself, sometimes with good results. At other times she didn't, which usually led to temper tantrums and tears. She wasn't easy to live with these days, but she had a more-than-valid excuse. Sabrina hoped that going to a training school for the blind would improve her attitude. If not, Annie was going to be tough to be around for a long time. Between their father's crushing depression over losing his wife and Annie's anger over her blindness, the atmosphere around them was extremely stressful for them all. And Sabrina noticed that Candy was eating less and less. Her eating disorder seemed to be in full bloom since their mother's death. The only normal person Sabrina could talk to was Chris, who had the patience of a saint, but he was busy too, with his latest mammoth suit. Sabrina felt as though she was being pulled in fourteen directions, caring for all of them and organizing the move, especially now that she was back at work.

"Are you okay?" he asked her worriedly one night. They were at her old apartment, and she had said she was too tired to even eat.

She had had a beer for dinner and nothing else, and she seldom drank.

"I'm exhausted," she said honestly, laying her head on his lap. He had been watching the baseball game on TV while she packed her books. They were moving in three days, and there was a heat wave in the city, which her air conditioner couldn't make a dent in. She was hot and tired and felt filthy after packing for several hours. "I feel like I'm caretaker to half the world. I don't even know where to stop. My father can hardly tie his shoelaces, and he does less and less every day. He refuses to go back to work. Candy looks like she just got out of Auschwitz, and Annie is going to kill herself slashing her wrists while she tries to slice the bread and won't let anybody help. And nobody is doing anything to make this move happen except me." He could see that she was near tears and completely overwhelmed.

"It'll get better once Annie goes to school." He tried to sound encouraging, but he had noticed everything she had said. It was incredibly upsetting being around her family these days, and it worried him too, mostly for her. She was carrying all the weight, and it was way too much for her, or any one person. He felt helpless as he watched, and did all he could to help her.

"Maybe. If she sticks with it, and is willing to learn," Sabrina said with a sigh. "Annie wants to do everything herself, and some things she just can't. And the minute she can't, she gets crazy and starts throwing things, usually at me. I feel like we all need a good shrink."

"Maybe that's not a bad idea. What are you doing about Candy?" It was always about what she was doing, as though they were all her children and it all rested on her. She had renewed respect for her mother now, for raising four children, and taking care of her husband as though he were her fifth child. She wondered how she did it. But she had done nothing else while they grew up. Sabrina was working at her law firm, trying to move into the new house, run back and forth from Connecticut to the city, and keep everybody's spirits up, except her own.

"I'm not doing anything about Candy. She used to see someone for her eating disorder when she was younger. And she's been better for a while, not great but better. Now it's completely out of hand again. I'll bet you anything she's lost five pounds, maybe ten, since Mom died. But she's an adult. She's twenty-one. I can't force her to go to a doctor if she doesn't want to. And when I mention it, she goes nuts. The danger is that she'll wind up sterile, lose her teeth or hair, or worse, develop a heart problem, or die. Anorexia is nothing to screw around with. But she won't listen to me. She says she doesn't want kids, she gets hair extensions so her hair looks great anyway, and so far her health doesn't seem to be affected. But one of these days it's all going to take its toll, and she'll wind up in the hospital with an IV in her arm or worse. Mom used to handle it better than I did, but she had more clout. No one listens to me, they just want me to solve the problems and get off their backs. I don't know how I got stuck with this, but it's a really shit job." They both knew how she had gotten stuck with it. Her mother had died. And Sabrina was next in line, as oldest child. And she had a personality that let her take on everyone else's problems and try to solve them, no matter what it did to her life. She did it at work too. And no matter what Chris said, or how often he urged her to take it easy, she always did just one more thing, for someone else. And the person who always got short shrift and didn't get her needs met was her, and now him as well. They had hardly had five minutes of peace alone in the last three and a half weeks since the accident. He kept her father entertained and cooked for the entire family every weekend, and she did everything else. They were suddenly like the parents of a large family, taking care of their many children, except that all of them, for one reason or another, were dysfunctional adults. She felt as though her family and her life were falling apart. But at least Chris was still around. Tammy had warned her that he wouldn't be, if Sabrina didn't take it easy and slow down. It was easy for her to say, living in California, three thousand miles away, while Sabrina was running the show, and picking up pieces everywhere. She felt as though their once-orderly life was in tiny shards all around her. She lay on the couch and cried.

"Come on," Chris said to her then. "I'm putting you to bed. You're wiped out. You can finish packing tomorrow."

"I can't. The movers are coming to take the stuff to storage, and I have to be back at my dad's tomorrow night."

"Then I'll do it. That's it. Bedtime. No discussion," he said, taking her by the hand, pulling her off the couch, and leading her into the bedroom. He undressed her as she smiled at him. He was truly the best man in the world. She was feeling a little giddy from the beer on an empty stomach.

"I love you," she said, climbing into bed in her thong and nothing else. Candy had given it to her as a gift. She never bought herself things like that. And Chris loved it.

"I love you too. And I love that too," he said, touching the black lace thong. "As soon as you move, I'm taking you away for the weekend. We're turning into a couple of old farts. Your sisters are just going to have to manage without us for two days." She knew that she needed to spend time with him too. It was only fair. They hadn't had a minute alone since her mother died, and by the time she fell into bed at night, she was too tired to even think about making love, and too sad. She was still in deep mourning for her mother, and so was everyone else. Chris understood that, but he missed the life they had led before it happened. He knew things would get better eventually, but it was hard to say when, particularly given the magnitude of Annie's problem.

And he wasn't at all sure what it would be like staying with Sabrina once she and two of her sisters were living together. It had the possibility of turning into some real high drama and chaos, or like sleeping in the dorm of a sorority. He wanted time alone with her and was afraid that he might not get any for the next year. It was a scary thought, but he didn't want to upset her by voicing his own fears or complaining. She had enough on her plate as it was, and he didn't want to add to it. But like Sabrina, he was getting short shrift too.

He lay down next to her on the bed, stroked her hair, and rubbed her back, and within five minutes she was sound asleep, as he lay next to her, wondering if they'd ever get married. Having the full responsibility of her entire family now wasn't likely to help his cause. He was going to give her a few months to calm down, and then talk to her about it. He wanted to get married and have a family. And one of these days he wanted her to bite the bullet and take the leap. He didn't want her to miss out on having kids because she was scared and had seen too many bad divorces and bitter custody battles through her work. That was no excuse to shortchange them. Not anymore, after three years together. In normal times, they had a wonderful relationship, and Chris wanted more. His worst fear was that normal would never come their way again, and her sisters would become her life.

When Sabrina woke up in the morning, he was gone. He'd had an early breakfast meeting with the associate counsel on his case, to bring him up to speed. He had left her a note, telling her to take it easy. She smiled when she read it. He said he'd see her in Connecticut on

Friday night. And then he was coming back into the city with her on Saturday to help her move. It was going to be a wild weekend. Candy was coming into the city to help. And their father would be babysitting Annie, or the reverse. Sabrina just hoped that everyone kept it together and no major disasters happened. She no longer had the same faith in life—that things would turn out okay—that she'd had a month before. Her mother's death had shown her that everything could change in the fraction of an instant. Life could end. And look what had happened to Annie.

Chapter 14

Candy, Chris, and Sabrina left Connecticut at six in the morning on Saturday. Chris drove, Sabrina checked her endless list, and Candy filed her nails. She said she had booked a massage at her health club that afternoon.

"How can you book a massage?" Sabrina asked with a look of panic. "We're moving!"

"This is very stressful for me," she said calmly. "I don't transition well to new places. My old therapist said it had something to do with Mom being older when she had me. Moving is a very traumatic thing for me. I never sleep well in hotels either."

"So you need a massage?" Sabrina looked at her blankly. She hated that kind of voodoo bullshit—karma, aromatherapy, incense, experiences recreated from the womb. She was a far too practical person to listen to all that stuff and not want to say something rude about it. Chris smiled to himself as he saw her face. He knew her well, and so did Candy.

"I know you think it's bullshit, but it helps me. I need to stay centered. I have a manicure and pedicure scheduled after."

"Do pedicures help you stay centered?" Sabrina was starting to steam, and it was only six-thirty in the morning, which was part of it. She had been up till two in the morning, helping Annie pack, and finishing some work she'd brought home from the office. Sabrina's work was never done. And now she was extremely tired, and they hadn't even started. The movers were coming at eight, to deliver everything they had picked up the day before. Everything Candy was bringing was in a stack of Louis Vuitton bags and two trunks that they had picked up at her penthouse apartment. She was only bringing clothes. The decor was being provided by Sabrina and their landlord.

"They massage my feet when I get a pedicure," Candy said primly. "Do you know that all your nerve centers are in your feet? You can heal almost anything with foot massage. I read a great article about it in *Vogue*."

"Candy, I love you, but if you don't shut up, I may have to kill you. I handled four new cases this week, my secretary quit, Annie had fourteen tantrums, and Dad hasn't stopped crying in a month. I packed up my apartment, Beulah *and* Zoe had diarrhea all over the house and I cleaned it up—you didn't, I might add—I have a hell of a goddamn headache, and today we're moving. Please don't talk to me about pedicures and get on my nerves."

"You're being very hostile and really mean," Candy said with tears in her eyes, "and that just makes me miss Mom more." She was sitting in the backseat of Chris's Range Rover, and Sabrina turned to look at her with a sigh.

"I'm sorry. I'm just tired. I miss Mom too. I'm worried about all of you. You're losing weight, Dad's depressed, Mom's gone, and Annie's blind. And we're moving. That's about all I can handle."

"Do you want me to book you a massage too?" Candy offered,

making an effort to bridge the gap. But the thirteen years and personality difference between them made it challenging, particularly at that hour of the morning, with very little sleep. Sabrina felt like she was on a merry-go-round at breakneck speed and was about to fly off into oblivion in a million shattered pieces. There was just more going on than she could handle, but in spite of that, she had to. There was just no other choice. She was it. And Candy wasn't—she was a baby. And so was their father. And now Annie was too, in spite of herself, by force majeure. All of them were the babies, and she was suddenly The Mom. And she had never wanted the job.

"I'd rather stay and get the house organized," Sabrina answered honestly. She wasn't used to being pampered, or even pampering herself. For Candy, it was part of her job, and had been for the last four years. "I'd rather get the place ready for all of you, so we can move in and stay there tomorrow."

"Do you think Dad's going to be okay without us?" Candy asked, looking worried.

"He has to be. There's no other choice. Other people survive it. He can't move in with us." That would have been just too much. "You and Annie can stay out there with him on and off this month. You're not going back to work till September, and she starts school then too. You can go back and forth. I have to work. He's going to be on his own in September though. He has to get used to it pretty soon." Candy nodded. They both knew it was true.

They were at the house on East Eighty-fourth Street at five minutes to eight o'clock, after stopping at Starbucks. Sabrina felt better with a cappuccino under her belt, and so did Chris. Candy had a grande iced black coffee, which should have kept her nerves raw for a week, but she claimed she loved it. She drank four of them every day when she was working in the city. No wonder she didn't eat. She was high on caffeine all the time, and smoked, which cut down her appetite too.

The movers were already there when they arrived, and got started quickly. By one o'clock they had unloaded the truck, and spent the rest of the afternoon unpacking the boxes and crates. By six o'clock, there were things everywhere, dishes, books, paintings, clothes. The place was a total mess, and Sabrina was trying to put her belongings away where she wanted them, with Chris's help. Candy had left two hours before for her massage, manicure, and pedicure, and said she'd be back by seven. Sabrina called her father and told him they were going to spend the night in the city, at the new house, to deal with the mess. He said he and Annie were fine. He said he was cooking dinner for her, which meant frozen egg rolls and instant soup. Sabrina smiled. He sounded better than he had all week. And he said Annie was helping. She had set the table. They were all children again. For now, it was the best any of them could do.

Chris was carrying a huge box of games upstairs to the top floor playroom, when she crossed him on the stairs, as she was coming down. He blew her a kiss and said the place was looking great. It would, she knew, but it wasn't yet. They still had a long way to go, and days of work. And they were supposed to move in officially the following night. She was thinking of asking Candy and Annie to wait a week to move in, so she and Chris could finish the job. Annie couldn't manage, with boxes all over the place and everything a mess. She couldn't have threaded her way through the obstacles. When she arrived, everything would have to be neat and in its place, so she could learn their locations. That much was obvious to Sabrina.

Candy called at seven-thirty and said she had run into a friend at her health club. She wanted to know if Sabrina would mind if she went out to dinner with him. She said she hadn't seen him in six months, since he moved back from Paris. Or did Sabrina and Chris want her to bring back something to eat for dinner?

Sabrina said they'd be fine, and she could order a pizza. She told Candy that she wasn't going back to Connecticut that night, and if Candy wanted, she could sleep at the house in the city, if she could find the sheets she'd brought in her suitcase, which Sabrina knew were Pratesi. Hers were from a white sale at Macy's, but they were fine with her. Candy said she'd be back later. They were going to Cipriani downtown, and probably clubbing, Sabrina guessed. Candy hadn't been out with friends in a while, and it had been a tough few weeks. She didn't begrudge her the relief, and she wasn't much help anyway. It was easier not having her underfoot.

"Why didn't you make her come back here to help us?" Chris asked, looking startled. He thought Sabrina was way too easy on her sisters, and too often they took advantage of her because she was forgiving and willing to do it all herself.

"Do you really think she'd be a lot of help? She'd mess up her manicure, and spend two hours on the phone. I'd rather get it done myself."

"That's why she doesn't learn," he scolded. "You give her too much slack."

"That's why I'm not a mom," Sabrina said simply, "and don't want to be. I'd be lousy at it."

"No, you wouldn't. You'd be great. And you're great with her. I just think you need to be a little tougher and more demanding. They are with you. Why should you do all the grunt work? Who made her the fairy princess and you Cinderella, scrubbing the castle floor? You have just as much right to be a fairy princess as she does. Let her do a little scrubbing for a change."

"I love you," Sabrina said, smiling at him, and then kissed him.

"I'd rather be alone with you anyway." The movers were finally gone, and they were working on their own. And they had peace. They took a break half an hour later, went upstairs and put the sheets on her bed, and wound up making love, and lying there in each other's arms for an hour afterward. It was perfect, just as it always was. She dozed in his arms, until they finally got up and went back to unpacking and putting things away. It was the first time in a month that Chris felt he had her full attention, and that for an hour at least she belonged to him again. It was sheer heaven and gave him hope that their life might return to normal again one day. He couldn't help but wonder when.

In Connecticut, her father had made Annie dinner. She didn't want to complain, but the frozen spring rolls had been awful, although the soup was halfway decent. He apologized for his shaky cooking skills, and Annie laughed with him.

"It must be genetic, Dad. I'm not such a great cook either." He handed her a Dove bar afterward, after asking her if she wanted chocolate or vanilla, and dark chocolate or milk. She chose vanilla ice cream with a dark chocolate shell and was savoring it when she heard the doorbell. Her father went to answer it, while Annie waited in the kitchen. She could hear a woman's voice talking to her father and the words "What a surprise," from her father, but she didn't pay any attention to it, until she finished her Dove bar, and followed the voices to see what he was doing and who it was. By then, he was standing outside on the front lawn, talking to a woman whose voice she didn't recognize. All she could tell was that she sounded young.

"You remember Annie, don't you?" he said to the unknown woman as Annie approached. "She's all grown up now."

"And blind," Annie added for shock value. She had been saying things like that for weeks. It was her way of expressing her anger. Sabrina had pointed out several times, as gently as she could, that being rude to people wouldn't bring her sight back. It was unlike Annie to act that way. Or had been, until then.

"Yes." Her father's voice grew instantly somber. "She was in the accident with her mother." Annie still had no idea who he was talking to.

"Who is it, Dad?" she asked as she reached where they stood. She could smell an unfamiliar perfume that was made of lilies of the valley.

"Do you remember Leslie Thompson? Her brother went to school with Tammy."

"No, I don't," Annie said honestly, as the young woman addressed her.

"Hi. My brother Jack went to school with Tammy. I'm his big sister. Sabrina and I were friends." Yeah, for about five minutes, Annie thought to herself. She remembered her now. She was older than Tammy and younger than Sabrina. They had been horrible social climbers, and her mother didn't like them. She remembered the girl being a pretty blonde whom Sabrina said was a slut, when she made a pass at Sabrina's boyfriend. Sabrina was seventeen then and a senior in high school. Leslie had been fifteen and what their mother had referred to as "fast." Sabrina never let her come over again. "I just moved back from California, and I heard about your mom. I came over to tell you both how sorry I am." Annie could hear something else in her voice, but she wasn't sure what. Her voice had changed when she spoke to Annie. Before that, speaking to her father, it had had a warmer lilting sound, and now she sounded annoyed, as though it bothered her that Annie was there. It was a curse to be so aware now. Annie was suddenly hearing nuances she never had before. It was like listening to people's minds and felt odd.

"She brought us an apple pie," her father said warmly. "Home-made. We were just about to have dessert. Would you like to come in and join us?" Annie frowned as she listened to them. Why was her father lying? They had had Dove bars. She figured he was just trying to be polite.

"No. That's fine. I've got to get back. I just wanted to say hi, and tell you how sorry I am. Jack said to say he was sorry too."

"When are you going back to California?" Annie asked, for no particular reason. But she made it sound as though she hoped it would be soon.

"I'm not, actually. I'm staying with my parents, while I look for an apartment in the city. I was living in Palm Springs and I just got divorced. I was out there for ten years and got pretty sick of it. So now I'm back," she said, with a lilt in her voice again, as Annie nodded, processing the information.

"I'm moving to the city too," Annie supplied, although Leslie hadn't asked her. "We're moving in tomorrow. Candy, Sabrina, and I."

"That's too bad," Leslie said, as Annie got another whiff of her perfume and decided it was too sweet. "I'll bet your dad will be lonely when you're gone."

"Yes, I will," he answered quickly, and then Leslie said she had to leave after saying goodbye to both of them. "Don't be a stranger, Leslie. Come by anytime," her father called after her, and then Annie heard a car door slam, and she drove away.

"Why did you say that?" Annie asked, frowning at him, even though she couldn't see him. She had to take his arm to get back into the house. She had gotten slightly turned around. "The thing about 'don't be a stranger'?"

"What am I supposed to say? She brought us an apple pie," which he was balancing in the other hand. "I didn't want to be rude, Annie."

"So how come she came by? We haven't seen her since Sabrina was a senior in high school." She thought about it for a minute as they walked into the house, and she let go of his arm. She could get around the house without assistance. "I smell a rat here." Actually, what she had smelled was lily of the valley, and a hell of a lot of it.

"That's silly, Annie. She's a nice girl who used to know you when you were kids, and she heard about your mother."

"That's my point, Dad. Don't be so naïve."

"Don't you be so paranoid. A girl that age is not going to go after me. And I already told you, I'm not going to be dating anyone. I'm in love with your mother and always will be." Annie was worried about it anyway. She wished that she could have seen her and evaluated the situation herself. She made a mental note to mention it to Sabrina when she came home. She didn't like the idea of women going after their father. Particularly not girls like Leslie Thompson, if she was anything like what she'd been when they were kids. All she really remembered was a lot of blond hair, and Sabrina saying she was a slut. Annie had only been nine years old. But she remembered her oldest sister being mad as hell. It was funny how things like that left a lasting impression. For the rest of time, she was a "slut" in Annie's mind, based on her behavior at fifteen.

Annie put the dishes in the dishwasher after that. Her father had a piece of the apple pie and said it was excellent, and Annie snorted in response. And afterward they both went upstairs. Annie was excited about the new house and moving in the next day. It was too quiet here, and she felt isolated. It was going to be nice to be in the city, even if her movements were still limited and she couldn't go out on her own. It was going to be a refreshing change.

She sat in her room quietly for a while, listening to music, and thinking about her life in Florence. Painting, visiting Siena, her endless hours in the Uffizi gallery, and her months with Charlie. She still missed him, and wished she could have called him, just to say hello. She was still in shock that he had found someone else so fast and dumped her. But at least she hadn't had to tell him she was blind, and he didn't feel sorry for her. She called Sabrina, who said everything was going well at the house, and Tammy in L.A., who was home alone on a Saturday night. She said she was giving Juanita a bath and doing laundry. It was sad realizing that she would never see their faces again, or look into their eyes. She could feel them and hear them, touch them, but for the rest of their lives she would remember them as they were now. They would never grow old in her mind's eye, and they would never change. She went to sleep thinking about it, and dreamed that she and Charlie were watching the sunset in Florence, and when she turned to say something to him, and tell him that she loved him, he had disappeared.

Chapter 15

Sabrina came out alone to pick Annie up on Sunday. Candy stayed in the city at the new house, after coming home at four in the morning. As Sabrina had predicted to Chris, she had gone clubbing with her old friend. And Chris had gone to a baseball game with friends that day, after spending the first night in the new house with Sabrina. They were comfortable in her room, and loved the bed, which was enormous, much better than her old one, which was queen size, lumpy, and too hard. The one in their new house was a dream. Sabrina loved everything about the place, and so did Chris. They had their own floor, so they didn't even hear Candy come in at four. And she was still asleep when Sabrina left in the morning.

She found Annie and her father sitting at the pool with the dogs. Zoe and Beulah were best friends now, and Candy had left Zoe there the day before. She didn't want her to get lost or hurt with the moving men going in and out. Sabrina asked her father if he'd mind keeping them there for a while. They had fun in the country, it was company for him, and she and Annie were going to be busy moving in, and so was Candy. She had enough on her plate at the moment without worrying about the dogs. Her father said he'd be delighted to babysit his grand dogs, and she and Annie drove back to the city after lunch. Annie seemed to be in a very somber, quiet mood, and Sabrina left her to her own thoughts. It happened often now. She had so much to adjust to, and she was an introspective person anyway, and something of a dreamer. She had always spent long, quiet hours, thinking about her art.

They were halfway to the city when she finally spoke up.

"Do you remember Leslie Thompson?" Annie said out of the blue, as though the name had just crossed her mind.

"No. Why? Who is she?"

"You hated her. Her brother went to school with Tammy, and she tried to put the make on one of your boyfriends."

"She did? When?" Sabrina looked completely baffled, and Annie laughed.

"I think you were a senior. I was nine, but I still remember you called her a slut."

"I did?" Sabrina laughed out loud. "Oh my God!" She turned to glance at her sister and then looked back at the road. She was much more nervous about driving, especially on the highway, since the Fourth of July. And Tammy said she was too, once she got back to L.A. "I do remember her! She was a total bitch, but pretty, in a cheesy way. She was a real operator. And Mom called her a hot number. Hot number, my ass. What made you think of her?"

"She dropped by yesterday."

"Why? I never saw her again after that day."

"She said she just got divorced and moved back from California, and she came to say how sorry she was about Mom. She brought Dad a pie."

"Are you kidding?" Sabrina made a face of pure disgust, and then she glanced over at her sister again, and wished she had her sight. They would have exchanged a look like no other. "Shit. Here it comes. The onslaught. But isn't she a little young? She must be about thirty-two. Thirty-three at most. She was fifteen then. I remember her perfectly now and how much I hated her. 'The slut.' I wish you could tell me what she looks like now, and how she looked at Dad."

"She sounds fake, and she was wearing cheap perfume, and too much of it."

"Ugh."

"Exactly. And she's smart. She brought the pie in a dish he has to give back. She must figure he has money."

"She can't be after a man that old. Shit, he's almost twice her age."

"Yes, but he does have money, and he's single now."

"She sure didn't waste any time." Sabrina looked annoyed. Their mother had only been dead for a month. "Maybe she was being sincere, and she just feels sorry for us."

"My ass," Annie said bluntly, and Sabrina laughed.

"Yeah, mine too. But hopefully not Dad's. The poor guy has no idea what's about to hit him. Every single woman within a hundred miles is going to be pounding down his door. He's a reasonable age, he's good-looking, he's successful, and he's alone. Waaaatttchhhh out!" They were all worried about it, and protective of him. He was so naïve, and totally unprepared for what was coming.

"I tried to tell him that, but he said I was paranoid."

"I trust your instincts. What did she sound like?"

"Slimy," Annie said. "What do you expect from a slut?" They both laughed.

They thought about it for a while in silence and then talked about other topics. Sabrina told her about the things she had discovered about the house that she hadn't known before, and how comfortable it was. They both agreed that they were sorry Tammy wasn't going to be there too, but there was no way she could leave her job. It was too much to give up.

When they arrived at the house, Candy was still sleeping. She eventually appeared at the top of the stairs in a pink satin thong and a see-through T-shirt, yawning, and happy to see them.

"Welcome home," she said to Annie, as her sister began feeling her way around. It was important to her to try to figure out where the furniture was so she could be comfortable getting from one spot to another with ease. After she got through the living room and den, concentrating intently, she made her way upstairs, and wound up in Candy's room instead of her own and instantly stumbled over a suitcase and nearly fell.

"Shit!" she said loudly, trying to get her bearings, as she rubbed her shin. "You're such a slob."

"Sorry." Candy jumped up to move the suitcase and clear a path for Annie. "Do you want me to show you where your room is?" she asked, trying to be helpful, and Annie snapped at her immediately. It was stressful for her trying to get acclimated to the house, but she knew it would be easier once she did it.

"No, I can find it myself," Annie said, barking at her again. She found her own room a minute later, and Sabrina had set her suitcase down on the bed. She knew Annie would want to unpack it herself. She came by a few minutes later to see if everything was okay. "Thanks for not unpacking my bag," she said softly. It meant a lot to her not to be treated like a child.

"I thought you'd rather put your own stuff away, so you know where it is. Yell if you want help."

"I won't," Annie said firmly, and then felt her way around the room, checking out the closet and opening the drawers. She found where the bathroom was and put her cosmetics away. With her new short hairdo, she had an easier time doing her hair than when it was long.

It was dinnertime by the time Sabrina checked on her again and Candy wandered in too. It seemed the perfect time to tell Candy that a girl she had known in high school had dropped by to hit on Dad.

"Are you kidding?" Candy looked stunned, as Annie chuckled and sat down on her bed. She was exhausted, but she had gotten everything unpacked. She hadn't brought much from Florence, and it was all she had. "How old is she?"

"Thirty-two, thirty-three at most," Sabrina answered.

"That's disgusting. Who is she?"

"The slut," Annie answered, rolling the words off her tongue with glee as all three girls laughed.

"What did Dad say?" Candy asked with interest. It was fun talking about it among the three sisters as long as nothing came of it, which they knew it wouldn't. They knew their dad.

"He insisted it was innocent," Annie answered. "He's such a baby. She reeked of cheap perfume."

"How disgusting. I'd give anything to know what she looked like."

"So would I," Annie said sadly, and Sabrina shot Candy a warning look. "I'll bet she's blond and has fake tits," she said, forgetting that that also described her youngest sister. "Oh . . . sorry . . . I didn't mean like you . . . I meant cheesy."

Candy laughed and was good-natured. "I forgive you. I bet you're right."

They told Tammy about it that night when she called, and Chris when he came by after the ballgame with a friend. He was another attorney from his law firm, a good-looking young guy, and he almost fainted when he saw Candy in short shorts and a skimpy halter top. She looked breathtaking as she pranced around. But Chris thought Leslie's visit was probably innocent.

"Oh, it was *not!*" Sabrina disagreed. "How can you say that? Why would a girl her age bring a pie over for Dad?"

"She's probably a nice person. Just because she tried to steal your boyfriend in third grade does not make her some kind of predator now."

"I was a senior, she was fifteen, and she *was* a *slut!* And it sounds like she still is."

"You guys are tough!" he said, laughing at them. They all seemed to be in high spirits, and happy in their new house. He liked it too.

"You're as innocent as my father," Sabrina said, rolling her eyes.

They all decided to go out to dinner, and went downtown to a little neighborhood Italian place in the Twenties. Annie didn't want to go initially, but they insisted she come with them. It was the first time she'd been to a restaurant since the accident. She wore dark glasses and kept a tight grip on Candy's arm. It was confusing for her, but afterward she admitted she'd had a good time, and said Chris's friend seemed nice.

"What does he look like?"

"Tall, nice-looking," Candy said. "African-American. He has kind of bluey-green eyes."

"He went to Harvard," Sabrina added. "But I think he has a girlfriend and she's out of town. I'll ask Chris, if you want." He had decided to sleep at his place that night and let them get settled on their own. He would have liked to stay, but he didn't want to intrude on Candy and Annie. That was the one thing he didn't like about Sabrina's new living arrangement. He didn't want to bother her sisters, although they all insisted that he didn't and that they loved him. But he went home anyway. He told Sabrina he'd spend the night on Tuesday, when Candy and Annie went back to Connecticut to stay with their father. Sabrina was staying in town all week. "I'll find out if Phillip has a girlfriend," Sabrina said matter-of-factly.

"Don't bother," Annie said quickly. She wasn't interested in men at the moment, or maybe ever again. "I just thought he sounded nice. I wondered what he looked like. I hate not being able to put a face with a voice." Saying it out loud brought the point home to her sisters again. This was so miserable for her, and all things considered, she was being a good sport about it. "I'm not going to be dating," she said firmly.

"Don't be stupid," Candy said bluntly. "Of course you are. You're gorgeous."

"No, I'm not. And that's beside the point. No one's going to want to date me like this. That would be pathetic."

"No," Sabrina said quietly, "it would be more pathetic if you gave up on life at your age. You're twenty-six years old. You're smart, beautiful, talented, well educated, well traveled, and fun to be with. Any guy would be lucky to go out with you, whether you have your sight or not. You have enough other attributes to make up for that. Any man worth a damn won't care if you can see or not. And fuck the others."

"Yeah. Maybe," Annie said, unconvinced. She and Dr. Steinberg had been talking about it. Annie couldn't imagine ever dating again, or any man wanting her in this condition.

"Give yourself some time, Annie," Sabrina said gently. "You just broke up with someone, we lost Mom, you got hurt in the accident. That's a lot to deal with." And the career she had studied all her life for had gone out the window. They were all aware of that. All of it was a major adjustment. More than most people would ever deal with in their life. And it had all hit her overnight.

They settled into their new rooms that night, and as Annie lay in bed, with her cell phone on her night table, it rang, and for the flash of an instant she hoped it would be Charlie, having changed his mind and dumped the other girl, wanting her back again. But if that was the case, what would she tell him? She almost didn't answer, and finally she did. She had caller ID, but couldn't see it. "Hello?" she said tentatively, and then was startled to realize it was Sabrina, calling her from her bedroom upstairs.

"I just called to say goodnight and tell you I love you," she said, yawning. She'd been thinking about her, and decided to call her before she went to sleep.

"You're crazy, and I love you too. For a minute, I thought it was Charlie. I'm glad it wasn't." That probably wasn't true, but Sabrina was touched that she would say it, and sorry she had to face such major challenges. It just wasn't fair. "I like our new house," Annie said happily, happy to have someone to talk to. She'd been feeling lonely.

"So do I," Sabrina said. She missed having Chris sleep there that night, but it was fun being with her sisters.

"Who are you talking to?" Candy asked, as she poked her head into Annie's room and saw her talking on her cell phone.

"Sabrina," Annie giggled.

"Goodnight!" Candy shouted up the stairs. "How come you didn't call me?" She was teasing, and leaned over to kiss Annie goodnight. "I love you, Annie," she said softly, and tucked her in.

"I love you too. I love both of you," Annie said into the cell phone and into the room so they could both hear her. "Thank you for doing this for me."

"We love it," Candy said, and hearing her say it, Sabrina agreed.

"Goodnight, sweet dreams," Sabrina said, and hung up, as their voices echoed in the house, and Candy went back to her room. Annie lay in bed afterward thinking that, in spite of everything that had happened, she was very lucky. In the end, no matter what happened, or what tragedy struck, they were all so lucky to have each other. They were sisters and best friends. It was all that mattered, and for now it was enough.

Chapter 16

Time seemed to be moving with lightning speed. Tammy had finally found a new star for the show, and was able to fly out on Friday night for the Labor Day weekend. Sabrina picked her up at the airport. Candy and Annie had been in Connecticut all week, and said their father was doing better. It was hard to believe that their mother had been gone for two months. So much had happened since.

And as always, Tammy had Juanita with her, sound asleep in her Birkin. She asked how they all liked the new house, and Sabrina said that they loved it. It was perfect. Her only concern was that she might not see as much of Chris. He seemed a little shy about intruding on her sisters.

"He'll get used to it," Tammy said easily. "He's part of the family. I assume he's coming out this weekend."

"Tomorrow. He wanted to give us a night alone. See what I mean? He kind of hangs back when we're all together."

"I think he's just being respectful."

They chatted easily on the way out to Connecticut, and got there at nine-thirty at night. The others were sitting at the pool, and the dogs were ecstatic when they saw Juanita. Her sisters and father were happy to see Tammy. They stayed up late that night, as they always did when they got together and hadn't seen each other for a while. Tammy had been gone for nearly six weeks. The time had flown for all of them.

In the morning Chris came out, and it was an easy, fun weekend. They played Scrabble, liar's dice, and read the Sunday paper. But Annie could do none of it, and at one point Sabrina saw the look on her face, and motioned to the others to put the games away. Annie knew instantly what they'd done and why, and insisted it didn't bother her, but it was obvious that it did. They lightened the moment by teasing their father about Leslie Thompson's visit and her gift of an apple pie.

"You girls are heartless," he said with a smile. "The poor thing just went through a terrible divorce. She started her own business, and the bastard cleaned her out."

"How do you know that?" Annie looked at him suspiciously. "She didn't say anything about that when she was here." Unless she had mentioned it before Annie came outside. But that wasn't the case, as their father made clear.

"She came back for her pie plate when you and Candy were in the city, moving into the house."

"That was fast," Tammy commented, glancing at Sabrina. Their father missed the look they exchanged. "What else did she say?"

"She's had a tough life. She was married to this guy for seven years. She lost her business to him. And she had a baby that died, of SIDS, her only child. After that she left, and came back here. I think it only happened last year. She said the divorce was just final. But that may be why she felt badly about your mom. She knows what it's like to lose someone now. The baby was only five months old, long enough to fall in love with him, and then he's gone." They could tell from what he was saying to them that their conversation had been deeply personal.

"How long did she stay picking up the plate?" Sabrina asked.

"Actually, I felt so sorry when she told me all that, I invited her to lunch. She's a sweet kid. She's staying with her parents till she finds her own place. You girls should give her a chance."

"Yeah, well...maybe..." Sabrina said, feeling sorry for her about the baby she lost, but her memories of her still weren't pleasant. Admittedly it had been eighteen years before, and people changed when they grew up. "That's too bad about her baby."

"She cries every time she mentions it. I think it's still pretty fresh." He looked embarrassed then. "I have to admit, I cried too when I talked about your mom."

"It must have been a real cheerful lunch," Tammy said under her breath to Sabrina, with a worried look in her eyes. Their father went inside shortly after that, and she commented that he was so innocent that he was going to be easy prey for some woman who wanted to take advantage of him, and she hoped Leslie wasn't it.

"I doubt it. She's too young. That's not his style," Sabrina reassured them all, and believed what she was saying.

"You never know," Tammy commented cynically. "You see a lot of that in L.A. Girls her age with men his. It's a pretty standard thing, especially if the man has money."

"He probably thinks of her like one of us, just a kid. I'm no kid, but Dad thinks of me that way. And she's a couple of years younger than I am," Sabrina said.

"That's my point," Tammy warned.

"We can't lock him up," Annie said. "Maybe we should, until he gets a little wiser in the ways of the world. Maybe there's a school for him too, to warn him about conniving women." They all laughed at the idea.

The rest of the weekend sped by too quickly, and they all left on Monday morning, so they could show Tammy the house in town. Their father looked sad when he waved goodbye, and Candy and Annie promised to come back soon, and this time they took their dogs with them, since they were settled into the house. He said he'd miss them all.

"Maybe we should buy him a dog," Tammy said thoughtfully. "He's going to be so alone in that house."

"I know," Sabrina said. "I felt guilty taking Beulah back, but Chris misses her too."

"I feel so sorry for him," Tammy said. "I really think a dog might be a good idea. If he's willing to take care of it. That's a whole other thing. But it would be good company for him."

Juanita and Beulah were peacefully asleep in the backseat. Annie had ridden with Candy, and they had Zoe with them. And Chris was meeting them at the house.

Tammy loved the house when she saw it, and said they had already done great things to it. It had a happy, cozy feeling to it. Sabrina's things looked pretty spread around the house, and she and Annie had gone to buy a carful of plants. The basic bones of the house were good, and the decor was charming, as the realtor had said. And when Tammy saw the small bedroom across from Sabrina's, she fell in love with it. Everything in it was pink. It looked like a candy box, and even though it was small, it had a nice feeling to it.

"That's your room for whenever you're here." Tammy looked delighted, and Juanita did too. She jumped on the bed and went right to sleep. Beulah had been running up and down the stairs, and Zoe was barking at everyone, delighted to have them all under one roof.

Annie was less delighted at the constant barking right outside her room. She came out to shout at Zoe, and fell over her, as she got tangled in Annie's feet. Annie fell flat on her face.

"Fucking dog!" she shouted at her, as Zoe came up and licked her face, and Annie smiled in spite of herself as Zoe licked her nose. "Hasn't anyone told you I hate dogs? And if you trip me up again, I'm going to drop-kick you into the garden."

"Don't you dare!" Candy shouted at her from her room. "She was just trying to say hi to you."

"Well, tell her to stay out from under my feet." As she said it, Beulah thundered past them, on her way upstairs to find Sabrina. "Oh, Jesus, this place is a lunatic asylum," Annie said, getting back on her feet. "Thank God I don't have a dog."

"I love this place," Tammy said enthusiastically. "I wish I could stay."

"Come anytime you want," Sabrina invited her. "You have your room." Admittedly, Chris liked being alone on the floor with her, so he could walk around in his boxer shorts. But she knew he wouldn't mind Tammy staying for the occasional weekend. He loved her sisters, and claimed them as his own.

They had dinner in the kitchen that night. Everyone pitched in. And afterward Sabrina drove Tammy back to the airport to catch the last flight to L.A.

"I hate to leave," Tammy said, looking at her sister sadly. They clung to each other for a long moment before she left her to board the flight. It reminded them both of what their mother had so often said, that the greatest gift she had given any of them was each other. They were indeed a precious gift in each other's lives.

"I love you, Tammy," Sabrina said in a choked voice.

"I love you too," Tammy whispered, and then picked Juanita up in her handbag, and with a last wave at her sister, she walked through security to walk to her gate and board the plane to L.A.

The flight arrived in Los Angeles at one A.M. Pacific time. It was too late to call her sisters again. When she turned her cell phone on, Tammy had a message from each of them, and as she walked into her house that night, she had never felt so lonely in her life, or so far away. Living in Los Angeles had always been perfect for her. She had been there since college. But now with their mother gone, and Annie blind, it was so much lonelier to be here. She felt guilty as she lay in her bed that night, as though she should be back there pitching in. But there was just no way she could. She loved her house, her job, and the career she had established here, but suddenly she felt cut off from all of them and as though she was letting them down. Even Juanita looked unhappy to be home. She lay down on Tammy's bed and whined. She missed the other dogs.

"Stop that. You're not helping anything," Tammy scolded her, and stroked her silky head. It was five in the morning for them, as Tammy turned out the lights and tried to get to sleep. She dreamed of them all night, in the house in New York.

She was exhausted the next morning when she went to work. And as usual, all hell broke loose the day after the holiday weekend. Sound technicians were having problems, directors were complaining, actors were throwing tantrums and threatening to quit. One of their biggest sponsors dropped out. The head of the network was blaming her for it. And their pregnant star was filing a suit for replacing her instead of giving her the option to work, even though her doctor said she couldn't.

"Now, tell me the logic in that," Tammy said, storming around her office with the star's attorney's threatening letter in her hand. "She told us she was on bedrest for six months. So now what, our character in the show is supposed to become a shut-in too? She *can't* work. She told us that. And now she wants to *sue* us? I hate fucking actors and goddamn TV!" She had to meet with the legal department about the validity and potential repercussions of the threatened suit. And absolutely everything that could go wrong that day did. Welcome to Hollywood, she muttered to herself as she walked off the set at nine o'clock that night and drove home, with Juanita in her purse.

Sabrina called her in the car when she was driving home. It was midnight for her. "How was your day?"

"Tell me you're kidding. How was Hiroshima the first day? Probably on a par with my day today. We're being sued, among other things. Some days I hate what I do."

"Other days you love it," Sabrina reminded her.

"Yeah, I guess," Tammy conceded. "I miss you guys. How's by you?"

"Okay. A little tense. Annie starts school tomorrow. She's in a rotten mood. I think she must be scared stiff."

"That's understandable." Worrying about her sister got Tammy's mind off her work. "It's probably like the first day of school for any kid, only worse. I was always afraid I couldn't find the bathroom at school. But I knew you were there, so it was okay." They both smiled at the memory. Tammy had been so shy as a little girl, and still was at times, except in her work. In social situations, she could still be very reserved, unless she knew people well. "Are you going with her?"

"She won't let me. She says she wants to take the bus." Sabrina sounded worried. She had become a mother hen in two brief action-packed months.

"Can she do that?"

"I don't know. She's never done it before."

"Maybe she should wait until they teach her that at school. Tell her to take a cab if she wants to go alone." It was a practical suggestion Sabrina hadn't thought of, and made perfect sense.

"That's a great idea. I'll tell her in the morning."

"Tell her to stop being so cheap. She can afford the cab." They both laughed. Annie was notoriously frugal—as an artist, she had been careful about money for years. With the salaries they earned, the others were less cautious.

"I'll tell her you said so." Sabrina smiled.

Tammy was at her house by then, and she sat in her car for a few minutes, chatting with Sabrina, and then said she had to go in. It was nearly ten o'clock and she hadn't eaten much since breakfast. She hadn't had time. She was used to it. She had eaten candy all day to keep going, and power bars.

"Call me tomorrow and tell me how it went," Tammy said, as Juanita stood up on the seat next to her, stretched, and yawned. She had eaten sliced turkey at noon. Tammy took better care of her than she did of herself.

"I will," Sabrina promised. "Get some rest. All the same problems will be there tomorrow. You can't fix everything in a day."

"No, but I try, and tomorrow there will be a whole new load of shit to deal with. Into each day, some shit must fall," Tammy said, and then they hung up.

And as it turned out, she was right. Hard as it was to believe, the next day was worse. They were hit with a wildcat strike. The light technicians were walking out. Everything on the set ground to a total halt. It was every producer's nightmare. And Tammy got word that their pregnant star had filed her suit. The press was calling her for comment.

"Oh Jesus, I don't believe this," Tammy said, sitting at her desk, fighting back tears. "This can't be happening," she said to her assistant. But it was. The rest of the day was worse. "Remind me again of why I wanted to work in television, and took my major in it. I know there must have been a reason, but it seems to have slipped my mind." She was at the office until after midnight, and never got to talk to Sabrina. She had had four messages from her, in the office, and two on her voice mail, saying everything was okay, but Tammy never got to return the calls, and it was too late now. It was three A.M. in New York. She wondered how Annie's first day of school had gone.

Chapter 17

Annie's first day at the Parker School for the Blind had been a disaster. Or at least the first part of the day was. She had liked Tammy's suggestion, passed on by Sabrina, and had taken a cab to the school, which was in the West Village, a lively neighborhood these days, but a long way from where they lived. Traffic was terrible getting there, and she was late when she arrived. She had taken her white stick with her, and insisted that she knew how to use it. She had refused to allow Sabrina to take her there, like a five-year-old.

"I lived in Italy and didn't speak the language when I arrived. I can manage in New York without my sight," she said grandly, but had allowed her older sister to hail her a cab. Annie gave the driver the address, and Sabrina's heart was in her mouth as she watched them drive away. She resisted the urge to call Annie on her cell phone to warn her to be careful. She was suddenly panicked that the driver might kidnap and rape her, because she was young, beautiful, and blind. She had a sinking feeling in her stomach, worrying about Annie, as she walked back into the house.

She shared her fears with Candy, who told her she was crazy. She had gone back to work that week, finally, and was leaving for Milan the next day, for a shoot for *Harper's Bazaar.* There were clothes and suitcases all over the place. Annie had tripped on two of them on the way out. Sabrina warned Candy again not to create an obstacle course for her sister. And as she said it to her, Sabrina fell over Candy's dog.

"This place is a madhouse," she said, as she went upstairs to finish getting dressed. She was late for her office, and had to be in court that afternoon, on a motion to suppress in a nasty divorce she hadn't wanted to take in the first place. But all she could think about was Annie as she stepped into her skirt, at the same time as she put on high heels.

As Sabrina learned later from Annie, she had arrived at the school, after paying the cab. She got out, unfolded her white stick as she'd been taught to do, extended it, and immediately fell over an unusually high curb, and skinned both her knees right through her jeans. She had torn them, and could feel blood trickling down her legs. It was an inauspicious beginning, to say the least.

A monitor standing outside the school came forward to help her, as Annie walked into the school. He took her to the office, and put Band-Aids on her knees himself, then escorted her upstairs for orientation. He pointed her in the right direction and she got lost immediately, and wound up in a sex ed class for advanced students, where they were showing them how to put condoms on bananas, and as she listened, Annie realized that she had come to the wrong room. They asked her if she had brought her condoms with her, and she said she didn't realize she needed them for the first day of school, but she promised to bring some the next day. After a ripple of laughter swept across the classroom, another person took her back to the right place, but everybody in her section had already left the room for a tour of the school. So she was lost again, and had to ask for help to meet up with her group. She confessed later to her sisters that by then she was in tears. Someone saw her crying, and escorted her to her group. She could feel that she had blood on her torn blue jeans, realized that she had skinned her hands too, was crying pathetically, had to go to the bathroom and had no idea where it was, and couldn't find a tissue to blow her nose.

"What did you do?" Sabrina asked, when she heard the story later. Just listening to it, she was ready to cry herself. She wanted to put her arms around Annie and never let her out of the house again.

"I used my sleeve," Annie answered practically, with a grin. "For my nose, I mean. I waited till later to find the bathroom. I held it in. And my group finally found me."

"Oh God, I hate this," Sabrina said, writhing in her seat.

"Me too," Annie said, but she was smiling by then, which she hadn't been in school.

At orientation they had explained to them what the next six months would be like. They would learn how to manage public transportation, live in their own apartment, take out the garbage, cook, tell time, type in braille, apply for a job—the employment office would find her one if necessary—shop for clothes, dress themselves, do their hair if it was something they wanted to learn, take care of pets, read braille, and work with a seeing-eye dog if that was what they wanted to do. There was an additional training program for working with the dog, which would extend her school year by eight weeks, and guide dog work was done off-site. They mentioned that there was a sex ed class for advanced students, and listed several other options including an art class. By the time Annie had listened to the whole list, her head was spinning. According to them, about the only things she wouldn't be able to do after six months at the Parker School were drive a car and fly a plane. There was even an exercise class and a swimming team, and an Olympic-size pool with lanes. Just hearing about all of it, she was overwhelmed. And after orientation, they went to lunch in the cafeteria, and were shown how to manage that too, how to handle money, how to choose what she wanted to eat. The signs were in braille, which was going to be their first class every morning. For today, there were teaching assistants who told them what the choices were and helped them get it on the trays, and to the tables. Today's lunch was free. Welcome to the Parker School. Annie had picked a yogurt and a bag of potato chips. She was too nervous to eat. The yogurt was pineapple, which she hated anyway.

"Boy, this is intense, isn't it?" a voice next to her said. "I graduated from Yale. It was a lot easier than this. How are you? Are you okay?" He sounded young and as nervous as she felt.

"I think so," she said cautiously. The voice was male.

"So what brings you here?"

"Research for a book," she said, sounding flip.

"Oh." He sounded disappointed. "I'm blind." She was suddenly sorry for what she'd said.

"Me too," she said more gently. "My name's Annie. What's yours?" She felt like one of two kids meeting in the sandbox, checking each other out on the first day of school.

"I'm Baxter. My mother thought I should come here. She must hate me. So what brought you here?"

"A car accident in July." There was something intimate about the darkness they lived in, like being in a confessional. It was easier saying things when she couldn't see his face, nor he hers.

"I had a motorcycle accident in June, riding with a friend. I was a graphic designer before this. So now I figure I'll be selling pencils in a cup on the street. There's not a lot of work out there for blind designers," he said, sounding half tragic and half funny. But she liked him, he had a friendly voice.

"I'm...I was a painter. Same problem. I was living in Florence."

"They drive like lunatics there. No wonder you got in an accident."

"It happened here, on the Fourth of July." She didn't tell him about her mother. That would have been too much, even in their shared darkness. It was impossible to say. Maybe later, if they really became friends. But it was nice to have someone to talk to the first day.

"I'm gay, by the way," he said suddenly, out of nowhere.

She smiled. "I'm straight. My boyfriend just dumped me, right after the accident. But he didn't know I was blind."

"That's rotten of him."

"Yeah, I guess."

"How old are you?"

"Twenty-six."

"I'm twenty-three. I graduated last year. Where'd you go to school?"

"Risdy," she said, which was the code among the knowledgeable for the Rhode Island School of Design. "I went to the Beaux Arts in Paris after I graduated, and picked up a master's degree. And I've been studying in Florence ever since. A lot of good all that hot-shot education does us now. Risdy, Yale, now this, so we can learn to use the microwave and brush our teeth. I fell flat on my face outside the school this morning, getting out of a cab," she said, and suddenly it didn't seem so tragic, it was almost funny. "I walked into the sex ed class by mistake and they asked me if I brought condoms. I told them I'd bring some tomorrow." He was laughing at what she said.

"Do you live with your parents now?" he asked with interest. "I've been staying with my mom since June. I was living with my boyfriend before that," he said, sounding solemn. "He died in the accident. It was his bike."

"I'm sorry," she said softly, and meant it, but she still couldn't tell him about her mother. "I'm living with my sisters for a year, till I get on my feet. They've been really nice to me."

"My mom's been pretty cool too, except that she treats me like a two-year-old."

"I guess it's scary for them too," Annie said, thinking about it.

And then they were told that it was time to go to the classroom. They were being divided into four groups.

"I hope I'm in yours," Baxter whispered. She did too. She had a new friend at school. They listened carefully for their groups and were ecstatic to discover they were in the same one. They followed the rest of the group to their classroom, and found their seats. It was Braille 101.

"I don't remember this class in college, do you?" he whispered, and she giggled like a kid. He was funny and irreverent, and smart, and she liked him. She had no idea what he looked like, tall or short, fat or thin, black or white or Asian. All she knew was that she liked him, they were both artists, and he was going to be her friend.

They were both exhausted by the end of the day. She asked him if he needed a ride home, if he lived uptown and was on her way. He said he had to take two buses and a subway to Brooklyn, where he had to take another bus to get home.

"How did you do that?" she asked with admiration.

"I just ask for help all along the way. It takes me about two hours to get here. But if I don't come here, my mother will kill me."

Annie laughed at what he said. "My sisters would too."

"Are you going to get a dog?" he asked her. "My mom thinks I should."

"I hope not. I hate dogs. They're yappy and they smell."

"In this case, I think they help," he said practically. "And it might be good company, when I live alone in my own place. I'm not sure there's a lot of interest in blind gay guys. I figure I may be alone a lot." He sounded sad as he said it, and echoed her fears about blind women.

"I've been thinking pretty much the same thing," she admitted.

"It's too bad I'm not straight," he whispered.

"Yeah, it is. Maybe you'll get cured."

"Of what?" He sounded shocked.

"Being gay."

"Are you serious?" Their friendship was about to end.

"No," she said, and he burst out laughing.

"I like you, Annie."

"I like you too, Baxter." They both meant it, which was sweet. It seemed like a miracle that they had found each other in the cafeteria and sat down at the same table. Two blind artists in a sea of people. There were eight hundred adults in the school. There was a youth section, but there were far more adults. And it was thought to be one of the best training schools for the blind in the world. They both suddenly felt lucky to be there, when it had seemed like a punishment before.

"Best friends?" he asked her before they left each other for their respective journeys home. Hers was a lot shorter and easier than his. His sounded like an odyssey to her.

"Forever and ever," she promised as they shook hands. "Have a safe trip home."

"You too. Try not to fall flat on your face again on your way out. It gives the school a bad name. It's okay on the way in, but leaving you should at least try to look like you know what you're doing." She laughed again, and he disappeared.

There were guides in the hallway to help the new students find the main door, and to assist them with transportation outside. Annie explained to one of them that she needed a cab, and he told her to wait, and he'd come to get her when he had the cab. She was standing in the main lobby, feeling lost again, when someone spoke to her. He had a calm, pleasant voice.

"Miss Adams?"

"Yes." She looked hesitant, and suddenly shy.

"I'm Brad Parker. I just wanted to say hello and welcome you to the school. How did your first day go?" She wasn't sure if she should tell him the truth. He sounded very grown up, unlike Baxter, who sounded like a kid, even younger than he was.

"It went fine," she said meekly.

"I hear you had a little mishap on the way in. We have to get the city to do something about that curb. It happens all the time." She felt less stupid about having fallen when he said it, which seemed kind, whether it was true or not. "Are you all right?"

"I'm fine. Thank you very much."

"Did you find your classes all right?"

"Yes." She smiled. She didn't tell him that she had stumbled into the lesson about condoms. She didn't know him well enough.

"I understand you're fluent in Italian and lived in Florence." He seemed to know all about her, and she looked surprised.

"How did you know that?"

"It's on your form, and I read them all. I was interested in that, because I spent a lot of time in Rome. My grandfather was the American ambassador there when I was a child. We used to visit him in the summer."

She suddenly wondered and decided to ask, since he knew so much about her, even that she had fallen down. "Are you blind?"

"No, I'm not. But both my parents were. I built the school in their memory, with a bequest they left for this purpose. They died in a plane crash when I was in college."

"That's pretty amazing." Annie was impressed, and he sounded like a nice man. She was touched that he had bothered to talk to her, had read her application prior to that, and even knew about her fall. He was well informed, particularly in a school that size.

"We've grown considerably since we started. We've only been here for sixteen years. I hope you enjoy it, and if there's anything I can do for you while you're with us, let me know."

"Thank you," she said demurely. She wouldn't have dared to call him Brad. She had no idea how old he was. But as the founder of the school, she had to assume he wasn't very young, and he sounded like he was a man, not a boy like Baxter, so she couldn't kid around, and didn't want to seem rude.

As they spoke, the guide came back inside to get her. He had a cab waiting outside. He greeted Brad informally, she said goodbye, and the guide took her outside and helped her into the cab. She thanked him and gave the driver her address. And as she promised she would, she called Sabrina at her office to tell her she was on the way home.

"How was it?" Sabrina asked, sounding anxious. She had worried about her all day.

"It was okay," Annie said noncommittally, and then smiled in the back of the cab. "Okay . . . it was pretty good."

"Well, that's nice to hear." Sabrina smiled in relief. "I felt like I'd sent my only kid to camp. I was a nervous wreck all day. I was afraid you'd hate it, or that someone would be mean to you. What did you learn?"

"Condoms 101." She laughed as she said it.

"Excuse me?"

"Actually, I wandered into the wrong class, after I fell on the curb outside. We studied braille."

"You'd better tell me about all this when I get home. I'll be home in about an hour." Annie had left the school just after five. They went to school from eight to five every day, five days a week, for six months. It was an intensive course.

When Annie got home, Candy was still packing for Milan, and there were suitcases all over her room. She was leaving for three weeks, but after Sabrina's lecture that morning, she had kept all of it in her room, so Annie didn't trip and fall when she walked in. And then she saw the knees of her jeans. They were torn and soaked with blood.

"What happened to you?" Candy looked instantly sympathetic.

"What do you mean?"

"Your knees."

"Oh, I fell."

"Are you okay?"

"Yeah, I'm fine."

"How was school?"

"Not too bad," Annie conceded, and then smiled at her, looking more than ever like a little kid. "Actually, it was almost cool."

"Almost cool?" Candy laughed. "Did you meet any guys?"

"Yeah. A guy in my class who's a graphic designer. He went to Yale, and he's gay. And the head of the school, who's about a hundred years old. I'm not going there to meet guys."

"That doesn't mean you can't meet them if you're there."

"That's true."

Candy could tell that she had been favorably impressed, and other than the skinned knees, no harm had come to her. It seemed like an acceptable first day, to all of them. Tammy called to check in the following morning, and she was relieved to hear about it too. Sabrina asked her if things were running more smoothly than before she left for the holiday.

"Not exactly. I'm dealing with a wildcat strike. And about four hundred other headaches, but I'm okay." She sounded stressed, and she had been worried about Annie. All of the sisters were pleased with Annie's first day at the Parker School, and so was she.

Sabrina hoped it was a good omen for the future, and they celebrated with a bottle of champagne that night.

Chapter 18

Tammy's week went from bad to worse. Problems with actors, problems with the network, problems with the unions and the scripts. By the end of the week, she was a total mess. And she felt guiltier every day for not being with her sisters to help deal with the aftermath of her mother's death. Her father sounded terrible. And Candy was in Europe for three weeks, so Sabrina was handling everything alone. She was singlehandedly supervising Annie, trying to bolster their father's spirits as best she could from the distance, and carrying an enormous workload at her office. None of it seemed fair. And now with Annie to take care of, and their father to visit whenever she could, she felt as though she hardly had time to see Chris. He slept at the house a few times a week, but she said she barely had time to talk to him. All of the responsibilities were on her shoulders, and no one else's. And even when she had been at home, Candy was too young and immature to really help. She was twenty-one going on twelve, or six.

Tammy spent a long, quiet, reflective weekend. The show was shut down because of the strike, and they already knew they weren't going to be able to shoot the following week because of it. The union said they could hold out for months. And the network was going to lose a fortune if they did. But there was nothing Tammy could do. What she was contemplating now was her own life. She spent a lot of quiet time with Juanita, stroking her quietly as the little dog slept on her lap. Holding the dog always gave Tammy a sense of peace, and by Sunday night she knew what she wanted to do. The decision had been hard. It was the scariest thing she'd ever done.

On Monday morning, she made an appointment with the senior executive producer of the show for later that afternoon. And another appointment with the head of the network the following day. She wanted to speak to them both. She owed it to them, and to herself.

She looked somber when she walked into the senior executive producer's office, and he smiled as he looked up.

"Don't look so depressed. The strike can't last forever. We'll settle it in a couple of weeks, and get back on track." His view was more optimistic than what she'd been hearing around the show.

"I hope that's true," she said, as she sat down. She didn't know where to start.

"By the way, I'm sorry about your loss." It was the expression she hated most. It always seemed to be said by rote, and was such an easy way out. Like Season's Greetings. Or All The Best. All the best what? It wasn't just a loss, it was her mother's life. And her sister's eyes. Which was why she was sitting in his office. But it wasn't his fault. He was a nice man, and had been a decent boss. And she loved the show. It had been her baby for all this time. And now she had come to give it back. It was like giving up her child. Tears filled her eyes even before she spoke.

"Tammy, what's wrong? You look upset."

"I am," she said honestly, pulling a tissue out of her pocket and dabbing at her eyes. "I don't want to do what I'm about to do, but I have to."

"You don't have to do anything you don't want to do," he said calmly. He could see what was coming, and he was trying to take some of the air out of the balloon, before it popped. But it already had.

"I came here to resign," she said simply, with tears running down her cheeks.

"Don't you think that's a little extreme, Tammy?" he said gently. He dealt with crises every day, and he was good at handling them. As a rule, so was she. But more than anything, she knew that right now this wasn't where she belonged. She needed to go home. L.A. had been home to her since college, she loved her job and her house. But she loved her sisters more. "It's only a strike."

"It's not about the strike."

"Then what is it?" He spoke to her like a child. She was just another hysterical woman sitting in a chair on the other side of his desk, although he had enormous respect for her. A scene like this was totally atypical of her.

"My mother died in July, as you know. And my sister was blinded in the accident. My father is a mess. I just need to go home for a while and lend a hand."

"Do you want a leave of absence, Tammy?" Normally, he couldn't have spared her, but he didn't want to lose her either. She was vital to the show.

"I would, but that wouldn't be fair to you. I want to go home for a year, so I came here to quit my job. I love it, I love everyone here. It drives me insane, but there's nothing I'd rather do . . . except be with them. They need me at home. My oldest sister is just carrying too much. My youngest sister is too young. And the one who's blind now needs all the help she can get. So, I'm checking out." She looked grief-stricken as she said it. It was the biggest sacrifice she'd ever made, but she knew it was right. Leaving the show was like leaving home too.

"Are you sure?" He looked shocked, but it was impossible to argue with what she had said. It was obviously a tough time for her. An extremely tough time, and he knew how close she was to her family. Unusually so, which was rare.

"Yes, I am."

"This is a lot for you to give up."

"I know. And I'll never have another job I love this much. But I can't let my family down," she said almost tragically. And yet in her heart, it felt clean and right and pure. It had been tormenting her ever since she got back to L.A.

"There are no decent shows for you to work on in New York."

"I know that too. But even if I work on some shit show, this is something I have to do for them. I'll never forgive myself if I don't. In the end, this is just a show. What they're dealing with is real life. My sisters need my help, and so does my dad."

"It's noble of you, Tammy, but a hell of a sacrifice for you. It could impact your whole career."

"And if I stay? What does that say about who I am as a human being?" she asked him, as her eyes bored into his. She never wavered in her resolve. He was stunned by the force of it as she sat on the other side of his desk.

"When do you want to leave?" he asked, looking worried.

"As soon as I can. That's up to you. I won't just walk out. But I'd like to get back there soon."

He didn't try to talk her out of it, he could see he couldn't. "If you give us till next week, maybe I can get one of the associate producers to step in. The strike will probably still be on, so that gives us time." In their business, no one stuck around once they gave notice. In fact, they were usually ushered out by security within minutes. He would never do that to her. It was entirely up to him. She was prepared to do whatever he wanted, even if he told her to leave within the hour. Her decision had been made.

"Next week will be fine. I'm sorry, I'm really sorry," she said, as she started to cry again.

"I'm sorry for you," he said kindly, as he stood up, walked around the desk, and hugged her. "I hope everything turns out for the best, and that your sister will be all right."

"So do I." Tammy smiled through her tears. "Thank you. Thank you for being so nice about it, and not throwing me out."

"I couldn't do that to you."

"I would understand if you did."

He thanked her again and wished her well as he walked her out of his office. They had agreed that she would leave by the following Friday. She had nine workdays left, and then her career in television was virtually over. For now anyway. And she might never get a decent job again. She knew that as she left his office, but she truly felt she had no choice.

Her meeting with the head of the network the next day was less emotional. He was angry at first, and then resigned. He thought that what Tammy was doing was a crazy thing to do. He told her she was throwing her career away. And as he pointed out, giving up her job, which was so much more than just a job, would not give her sister back her sight. Tammy pointed out that that was true, but it might help support her through a terrible time, and the others who were with her. He could see her point, but it was not the decision he would have made. Which was why he was the head of the network, and she wasn't. But Tammy also knew that his home life was a mess. His wife had left him two years before for another man, and both of his children were on drugs. So maybe from a career standpoint, he was right. But personally, she wouldn't have traded her life for his. She'd rather screw up her career than let her sisters down. And maybe one day there would be another opportunity for her, even at a different network. For now, she just had to trust the fates. She was doing her part right, maybe they'd do theirs.

She thanked the head of the network for his time, and left his office. The deed was done. All she had to do was finish out these two weeks. And she had decided not to tell Sabrina and Annie anything about it. She knew they would object for her sake. This was a gift she was giving them, and it was her choice.

She packed quietly over the next two weeks. She had decided not to rent her house. For now, she could afford to keep it as it was, and just close it. She had been careful with her money, and had plenty set aside, even if she didn't work for the next year, although she was planning to look for something in New York. You never knew what might turn up. And with luck, she'd be back here in a year. So she wasn't going to sell anything, or make any more brutal changes than she already had. At least she still had her house if not her job.

Her last day at work was heartbreaking for her. Everyone cried when she left, and so did Tammy. She went home absolutely drained that night, and lay in the dark, with Juanita sleeping on her chest. She had packed everything she wanted to take in four big suitcases. She was leaving the rest. She took a nine A.M. flight the next day, on Saturday, and landed at JFK in New York at five-twenty local time. She rang the doorbell on East Eighty-fourth Street just before seven. She didn't even know if they'd be home. If not, she could go to a hotel until Sunday night if they were in Connecticut for the weekend.

There was no sound inside for a few minutes, and then Sabrina opened the door and stared at Tammy, who was looking very solemn as she stood there, with four enormous bags, and Juanita in her tote.

"What are you doing here?" Sabrina looked stunned. She had had no warning that Tammy was coming, which was what Tammy had wanted. The decision wasn't theirs, it was her own.

"I thought I'd surprise you." Tammy smiled as she started to drag in her bags. It was still warm and balmy in New York.

"You brought all that shit for the weekend?" Sabrina asked as she helped her, suddenly wondering why she was there. There was a strange look in her sister's eyes.

"No," Tammy said quietly. "I'm not here for the weekend."

"What do you mean?" Sabrina stopped and stared at her with a worried look.

"I came home. I quit my job."

"You did *what?* Are you crazy? You love your job and you make more money than God."

"I don't know how much He makes." Tammy grinned at her. "But currently I'm unemployed, so He makes more money than I do right now."

"What the hell have you done?"

"I couldn't let you do this by yourself," Tammy said simply. "They're my sisters too."

"Oh you lunatic, I love you," Sabrina said, as she threw her arms around Tammy's neck. "What are you going to do here? You can't just sit around the house."

"I'll find something. At McDonald's maybe." She grinned. "So do I still have my pink room?"

"It's all yours." Sabrina stepped aside, as Annie appeared on the landing with headphones on. She'd been listening to a lecture from the Parker School, but as she took them off, she heard her sister's voice.

"Tammy? What are you doing here?"

"I'm moving in." She beamed.

"You are?"

"Yes. Why should you guys have all the fun without me?" As she said it and looked at her sisters, she knew she had done the right thing. There was absolutely no question about it. And as Sabrina helped her drag her bags up two flights of stairs, Tammy knew without a doubt that her mother would have been pleased. Better than that, she would have been proud of her.

And as they walked into the room that was going to be her home for the next year, Sabrina turned to look at Tammy and smiled with a look of relief and whispered, "Thank you, Tammy." It had been worth everything for the look on her sister's face.

Chapter 19

Tammy's arrival at the house changed the dynamics considerably. She was another responsible adult to share the burdens with Sabrina, which was precisely why she'd come. It made things more crowded than before, even though Candy was still away. And they all knew that when she got back, it would be even crazier. They were four women and three female dogs in a relatively small house. Chris said that he was feeling overwhelmed by estrogen overload these days, which was a mild understatement. There seemed to be women's shoes, hats, furs, coats, bras, and thongs everywhere. Tammy said after being there for a week that she felt as though she had given up her job to become a maid.

"This isn't working for me," she finally said one Sunday morning, after doing her third load of towels. Candy had gotten home the night before, and brought all her laundry home with her, although she could have had it done at the hotel where she was staying. But she said the hotel shrank everything the last time she was there, so she brought it all home, not to Mom anymore, but to her sisters. And Tammy had become the chief laundress, since she wasn't working.

"I love you guys," she announced at breakfast, as Chris tried to stay out of the way. Annie had named him an "honorary sister" the week before, which he said he didn't think was funny, although she meant it as a compliment. But he said he was beginning to feel like Dustin Hoffman in *Tootsie*, or worse, Robin Williams in *Mrs. Doubtfire*. "I need two things for total happiness," Tammy went on. "A job, and a maid." She had come to realize that as long as she wasn't working, she was going to become the chief cook, schlepper, maid, and bottle-washer. She needed to get out of the house and go to work. And they needed someone else to do the scut work. She hadn't done it in her own house in Los Angeles. Why should she do it here?

"That's a great idea," Sabrina said absentmindedly, as she handed the sports section of the Sunday *Times* to Chris. They were all crowded around the breakfast table, and were sharing scones, pains au chocolat, and blueberry muffins. The three older sisters were sharing them, and Chris had already eaten several. Candy hadn't touched a single one. They all had noticed, and also that she had lost more weight on her trip. But no one had mentioned it so far. Sabrina wanted to talk to Tammy about it later that day.

"I can see you're all really impressed by my suggestion," Tammy said, looking miffed, as she helped herself to another scone. Unlike Candy, she was eating too well. She had nothing to do now, except sit around the house and eat, between doing loads of laundry. They were wearing out the owner's machines. "Okay, ignore me. I'll find a maid myself." And a job, although God knew what that would look like here.

The five of them went to a movie that afternoon, and when they did, Tammy noticed that Annie had already gotten far more proficient with her white stick. The three weeks she had spent at the Parker School had already made a difference. She was more comfortable moving around the house, used the microwave easily, and had learned several handy tricks. She had fun with Baxter when she was at school, and he called her often on weekends. She hadn't encountered Brad Parker again. He had bigger fish to talk to than her.

The movie they went to wasn't much fun for Annie, but she went so she could spend time with them. And she was able to follow it just listening to the dialogue, although afterward she said it was stupid. They went out for pizza together after the movie, and Candy teased Chris about his harem.

"People are going to start thinking I'm a high-class pimp," he complained. But the four sisters stuck together like glue. Now that they were living together, he hardly ever got time alone with Sabrina. He didn't complain about it, but he let her know that he noticed. And before Tammy came, with Annie to take care of, she rarely spent a night at his place with him.

It was Sunday night so he went back to his place that night, after spending time with Sabrina alone for a while in her room. Wherever one went in the house, there was someone there, kitchen, den, living room, playroom, dining room. They were a lot of people living under one roof. He was a good sport about it, but Tammy had suggested to her that she shouldn't push it.

"He's a guy, after all, Sabrina. He must get sick of seeing all of us when he wants to be with you. Why don't you stay with him more often?"

"I miss you when I'm at his place." She had the constant awareness that this was only for a year. But Tammy wasn't as sure that that was clear to Chris. Tammy thought he looked annoyed about it at times, but Sabrina didn't think he did.

"You know him better than I do," Tammy told her, "but I wouldn't push it if I were you. One of these days he may go up in smoke."

The next morning Tammy did as she had promised, and called an agency for a maid. She explained the nature of what they wanted, and the head of the agency said she had two candidates that might work for her. One was a woman who had worked in a hotel for ten years, and didn't mind working for several people. She was only available twice a week however, which wasn't enough. Tammy thought they needed someone every day. With four of them living there, and Chris some of the time, there was just too much to do. The other candidate was a little more "unusual," she said. She was Japanese, spoke no English, but was immaculate, and worked like a Trojan. She had worked for a Japanese family that had moved away. The agency said they had an excellent reference on file for her, and they highly reccommended her.

"How can I talk to her, if she only speaks Japanese?"

"She knows what to do. The family she worked for had five kids, all boys. That's a lot harder than cleaning house for four adult women, and three dogs."

"I'm not so sure," Tammy commented, having done it herself. But a maid who spoke no English was better than nothing, and a lot better than doing it herself.

"Her name is Hiroko Shibata. Would you like me to send her over to meet you this afternoon?"

"Sure," Tammy said. She had nothing else to do.

Mrs. Shibata arrived promptly for the interview and was wearing a kimono. As it turned out, she didn't totally "not speak English," she said about ten words that she repeated frequently, whether appropriate or not. She did in fact look immaculately clean, and she left her shoes politely at the door when she got there. The only detail the agency had failed to mention, and probably wasn't allowed to, was that she looked about seventy-five years old and had no teeth. She bowed to Tammy every time she spoke to her, which made Tammy bow too. And she didn't seem to mind the dogs, which was something at least. And several times she said "Dog verry cute." Better yet. Somehow through using sign language, speaking loudly, which served no purpose, and pointing at her watch, Tammy managed to convey to her to come back the following morning to try out. She had no idea if she'd show up or not, but was delighted when she did.

Mrs. Shibata walked in the front door, took off her shoes, bowed politely to everyone, including Candy in a thong and see-through T-shirt, Annie as she flew out the door to school, Sabrina as she left for work, the dogs several times whenever she saw them, and turned into a whirling dervish. Much to Tammy's delight, she stayed till six and everything was impeccable when she left. The beds were changed and made with military precision, the refrigerator had been scrubbed out, their personal laundry was done, the towels were clean and folded. She had even fed the dogs. The only problem was that she had fed them seaweed, left over from the lunch she'd brought, of pungent pickles, seaweed, and raw fish, all of which smelled awful, and the seaweed made the dogs violently sick. Tammy spent more time cleaning up the mess they made than she would have cleaning the house. So when Mrs. Shibata came to work the next day, as Tammy had pantomimed her to, she pointed to the dog bowls, the dogs, the seaweed, and made faces worthy of kabuki, asking her not to do it again. Mrs. Shibata bowed at least sixteen more times in all directions and let Tammy know she understood.

Candy had managed to trash most of the house the night before when friends dropped by, so she had plenty of work to do. The arrangement was working well. Tammy told the agency she was hired, and Mrs. Shibata set to work keeping them clean and in good order, and Tammy felt like a free woman. She was never going to have to wash towels or take out the trash again. Which was comforting, since no one else did.

Problem number one was solved, but now Tammy had to solve a more important problem before she could look for a job. She and Sabrina had agreed that something had to be done about Candy's eating disorder before it destroyed her, so they confronted her that night. It was the perfect night to do it, since Chris was at a basketball game with friends, which was a good thing, because you could have heard Candy's screams of outrage and denial from there to Brooklyn. Her older sisters said they no longer cared what excuse she had for the weight she was losing. She had two choices, a hospital or a shrink. Candy looked stunned.

"Are you serious? How can you be so mean? It's so *rude* of you to make an issue of my weight like this. Mom would *never* have done that. She was a lot nicer than either of you."

"That's true," Tammy said, without denying it. "But we're here and she's not, and you're not going to be here much longer either if you don't do something about this. Candy, we love you and you're going to get really sick. We lost Mom. We don't want to lose you." They were loving but firm. She slammed the door of her room, threw herself on her bed, and cried for hours, but her sisters would not be moved. They were both aware that she made enough money to move out and get her own apartment, but she didn't. She didn't speak to them for two days, while she mulled it over, and finally, much to everyone's amazement, she gave in and opted for the shrink. She said there was nothing wrong with her eating, and they just didn't see her eat, and what she ate was healthy. For a canary maybe, or a hamster, but not a woman who stood six feet one in bare feet. They assured her that she didn't need to get fat to please them, and no, they weren't jealous of her. She even pointed out that Tammy was gaining weight, which was true, although she wasn't heavy either, but she was a lot shorter so whatever she gained showed, and she had gained about five pounds since arriving in New York. But the only issue of any consequence, as far as they were concerned, was that Candy's eating problem was out of control.

Tammy made the shrink appointment, and took her to the first meeting. She didn't go in with her, but called and spoke to the doctor first. Candy was furious when she came out, but she gave them a shopping list, which Tammy bought immediately, and at least they saw her eat now, and they weren't just ignoring the problem. This was what they were there for. Allegedly for Annie, but Candy obviously needed their support too. It was so much easier dealing with it while they were all living under one roof.

"Do you ever get the feeling that we gave birth to two grown kids this summer?" Sabrina asked Tammy, as she lay on the couch after a long, hard day at work. She had had three appearances in court.

"Yes, I do." Tammy grinned. "I have more respect than ever for Mom now. I don't know how she stood us when we were kids."

They were still worried about their father and hadn't had time to see him for several weekends. They were all too busy at home. Except for Tammy, who now spent her time directing Mrs. Shibata with kabuki faces, and dropping Candy and Annie off at their respective shrinks. She felt more than ever like the suburban mother of two teenage girls, which led her to project number three, finding work. She knew she wasn't going to find a job anything like the one she had in California, she had no delusions about that. But she needed more to do than what she was doing, otherwise Candy would be right, and all she'd do would be sit around and eat. She needed more than that in her life. Candy and Sabrina were working, and Annie was going to school. She was the only one of the sisters who had nothing important to do, except be there at night when they all came home. She felt like a housewife, and as though she was losing her identity.

Project number three took a lot more time than projects one and two. It was well into the middle of October before she had lined up some interviews. She talked to several soaps, and hated the way they were structured. They were so second rate compared to what she had done before. And she finally talked to a show that she had heard of but never seen. It was pure, outrageous, utterly cheesy reality TV. The show focused on couples who were having trouble in their relationships, and basically allowed them to fight with each other on TV. Fisticuffs were not allowed, but other than that, anything went. A psychologist followed them on the show, who turned out to be an outrageous woman who looked like a drag queen. The show was called *Can This Relationship Be Saved? It's Up to You!* It sounded so awful that in spite of herself, Tammy was intrigued. Professionally, it would be embarrassing to be associated with the show, but the ratings were good, and they were desperate for a producer. The one they'd started with had just quit for a prime-time show on network TV. They couldn't believe that someone with Tammy's credentials was actually willing to talk to them. And she couldn't believe it either.

She didn't tell any of her sisters that she was going to talk to them about a job. She was sure they would be horrified, and she was herself. But she was bored out of her mind, sitting around the house with nothing to do until the others came home at night. And Annie was doing remarkably well at the Parker School after five weeks. Tammy was the only one now with no purpose in her life, although she was still glad that she had moved, to spend the year with them.

She felt as though they all needed it, and were benefiting from it, she as much as the others, after losing their mother three and a half months before.

Tammy went to the appointment on a Thursday afternoon. She had already sent them her résumé, and they knew all about her creating the show in L.A. She was a major pro. And if she came to work with them, they wanted some fresh ideas to keep the show alive. It had started to slide a little, although much to Tammy's amazement, their ratings were still strong, and the concept mesmerized their viewers. The show seemed to represent or even mirror the problems people had in their relationships, from cheating to impotence, emotional abuse, or intrusive mothers-in-law. Substance abuse and delinquent children also seemed to be high on the list of what caused people problems and brought them to the show. It was a slice of life, and everything you didn't want to know about other people's relationships and lives. Except the audience apparently did. The Nielsen ratings said so.

Tammy went to the meeting with some trepidation, and met the executive producer in his office. Much to her surprise, he seemed like a normal human being. He had a psychology degree himself, from Columbia, and had preferred to keep the show based in New York when he set it up. He had been married for thirty years and had six kids of his own. He had been a marriage counselor for several years before getting into TV. He had entered TV in sports, and then finally got to put his concept on TV with the advent of reality shows. This was his dream come true, just as her show had been for her. It was just a very different breed of show. And like most reality TV, it catered to the lowest common denominator. But some of the couples they had filmed sounded reasonable, even to her. Although most of them were badly behaved, which the audience preferred.

They had an excellent conversation, and she had to admit she liked him, although the associate producer was a jerk and had an attitude about her. He was defending his turf, wanted the senior job himself, and was not being considered for it.

"So what do you think?" Irving Solomon, the executive producer, asked her, as their meeting drew to a close.

"I think it's an interesting show," she said, somewhat honestly. She didn't say she loved it, which wouldn't have been true. And in a lot of ways, it wasn't highbrow enough for her. She had never been inclined to exploit people's problems, nor to sink to that kind of sleaze. But on the other hand, she wanted to work. And this seemed to be all that was around. The pickings in New York were slim. "Have you ever thought of making it a little more serious?" she asked thoughtfully. She wasn't quite sure how to do it, but she was willing to ponder the idea.

"Our audience doesn't want serious. They have enough pain in their own lives. They want to see people slugging it out, verbally of course, not physically, the way they wish they could do with their mate, if they dared. We are their alter ego, and we have the guts they don't." It was one way to see it, although Tammy didn't quite see it that way. But they weren't hiring her to revamp the show, or improve it, just to keep it on the air, and drive their ratings up if she could. That was always the issue for any show on TV. How do we get the ratings higher? What they wanted was more of the same. "What brought you to New York, by the way? That's some terrific show you walked out on." She thought she heard a reproach in the way he said it, and shook her head.

"I didn't walk out," she corrected him. "I gave notice and left. There was a tragedy in my family this summer, and I wanted to be here," she said with quiet dignity, and he nodded.

"I'm sorry to hear it. Is it resolved now?" he asked with some concern.

"It's getting better. But I want to stay here now, to keep an eye on things."

"Do you have time to work on the show?"

"Yes, I do," she said confidently, and he looked relieved. She was a professional to the core, and he knew she wouldn't be talking to him if she wasn't interested in the job. He was hoping she was. He already knew he wanted her. He wasn't interviewing anyone else, and he said as much to her. He gave her several tapes of the show, and asked her to think about it and get back to him. They didn't want to mess with something that worked. And he wanted her to respect that too.

"I'll get back to you in a couple of days," she promised. She wanted to see the tapes of the show. She met the psychologist on the way out. She couldn't believe what she looked like. Flamboyant was far too tame a word. She was wearing rhinestone glasses and a skin-tight dress over an enormous bosom that poured out of her dress. She looked like a madam in a bad bordello, but he claimed the audiences and the couples loved her. Her name was Désirée Lafayette, which couldn't possibly have been her real name. She looked like a transsexual to Tammy, and she wondered if she was. Nothing would have surprised her on this show. Least of all a female psychologist who had once been a guy.

She went back to the house, and put the first tape on TV. She was watching it intently when Annie came back from school. She stood in the den for a minute and listened to what Tammy had on, and broke into a broad smile.

"What the hell is *that*?"

"A show I'm checking out," she said, still concentrating on the couple on screen. They were beyond belief, and had just called each other every name in the book.

"You're not serious, I hope."

"I think I am. For comic relief, if nothing else. How was school?"

"Good." She never said "Great," but at least she didn't say it was awful, and her sisters suspected that she liked it. Tammy glanced at her watch. She had to get her to her shrink, and reminded her of it, in case she wanted something to eat before she went.

"I'm twenty-six, not two. I can go by cab if you want to keep watching that crap."

"I can watch it later," Tammy said, as she turned it off. But she had already made her decision. It was awful, but what the hell, why not? Désirée Lafayette was too ridiculous for words. But the show had something, a kind of down-and-dirty misery to it, and yet behind all the window dressing was a thread of hope. Tammy liked that. They rarely seemed to tell people to give up on their relationships, and Désirée tried to give them ideas of how to improve them, even if they were slightly absurd, and the people on the show incredibly vulgar. There was nothing dignified about it.

"You must be desperate for work," Annie commented when they went out.

"I think I am," Tammy admitted. She thought about it while she waited for Annie in Dr. Steinberg's office. Annie's meetings with the psychiatrist seemed to be doing her some good. She appeared more accepting of her situation than she had been at first, and was noticeably less angry. And Tammy liked to think that being surrounded by her sisters, who loved her so passionately, was doing her good too.

She watched the rest of the tapes alone in her room that night. Some were better, others worse. She had a good sense of the show now. It would look odd on her résumé, particularly after the other shows she'd worked on, which were of high quality. But it was the only available job in town. She had called everyone she knew, and no one else needed a producer at the moment. And she had nothing else to do.

She called Irving Solomon the next morning, and told him she was interested. He named some figures, and she said her agent would call him. She had to call her in L.A., and her attorney. She was going to have a hell of a time explaining to them why she was doing this show. She had a "no compete" clause in her last contract, for another year, but nothing about this crazy show competed with her old one. She was clear on that. The salary he had offered her was healthy. And it was honest work, even if it was a sleazy show. And work was work. She wasn't someone who wanted to stay idle, and spend her life going shopping, or having lunch with friends. She had no friends in New York, and her sisters were all working. She wanted to be too. Irving said that if they could come to an agreement quickly, he wanted her to come in the following week. She said she would do what she could to get her agent moving.

She announced it at dinner that night, and her sisters looked at her and stared. Annie already knew, and Sabrina said she thought she was crazy. Candy said she had seen the show, and it was pretty raunchy.

"Are you sure?" Sabrina asked her, looking worried. "Will it hurt you later?"

"I hope not," Tammy said honestly. "I don't think so. It may seem a little strange, but it doesn't hurt to try reality TV again. I did it years ago, and it didn't hurt my career then. As long as I don't make a lifetime career of it."

It made Sabrina feel mildly guilty to think of what Tammy had given up to come there, and she had done it to help her. But to be with Annie too, which was the whole point. But Tammy didn't seem to regret leaving L.A. She had closed the door on her old show and never looked back. And now she was opening a new door. With angry couples and a psychologist named Désirée Lafayette waiting to greet her. The thought of it horrified Sabrina, and it made Tammy laugh.

Chapter 20

Once Tammy was working, life at the house on East Eighty-fourth Street seemed to speed up considerably. Sabrina was having a busy fall season, half the couples in New York seemed to want a divorce, and were calling her. After the summer, and once the kids went back to school, people called their lawyers and said "Get me out of here!" They usually did it after Christmas too.

Candy was on shoots every day once she got back from Europe. The intervention over her eating disorder had helped a little. She had never been bulimic, she just didn't eat, and was anorexic. But she was doing better, and was on weekly weigh-ins that Sabrina monitored diligently, and called the doctor to check on. They weren't allowed to tell Sabrina what Candy's weight was, but they could say if she had come in to be weighed. And when she skipped it, Tammy and Sabrina raised hell with her. They were keeping a close eye on the problem, and she looked as though she had gained a few pounds, although she was still grossly underweight, which was the nature of her business. She got paid a fortune to look that way. It was a tough battle to win, but at least they weren't losing ground. Her shrink had referred to it as "fashion anorexia" to Sabrina, when they talked about it. She didn't have deep-seated psychological problems about her childhood or womanhood. She just loved the way she looked when she was rail thin, and so did millions of women who read fashion magazines, and the people who put them together. It was cultural, visual, and financial, not psychiatric, which the shrink said was an important factor. But her sisters worried about her health. They had no desire to lose another member of the family, even if she died looking gorgeous, was rich, and was on the cover of *Vogue*. As Tammy said bluntly, "Fuck that."

After two months Annie seemed to be doing well at the Parker School, and she and Baxter were fast friends. They got together on weekends sometimes, and talked about art, their opinions, the things they thought were important about it, the work they had seen and loved. She talked to him for hours about the Uffizi in Florence, and instead of being angry now, she said she was grateful to have seen it before she went blind. She never talked about Charlie, he had been a huge disappointment, and she felt betrayed by him still. But not nearly as much as she would have if she had known the truth. Her sisters never said a word about it. And Baxter met a man he liked at a Halloween party he went to in the city. He had gone as a blind person, which Annie told him was disgusting. But the man he was dating seemed nice. He had lunch with Annie and Baxter at the school once, and Annie said he sounded like a good person. It cut into their time together somewhat, but she didn't mind. He was twenty-nine years old, a young fashion designer at a major house, and had gone to Parsons School of Design. He didn't seem to care that Baxter was blind, which was encouraging for him and Annie, and bolstered their spirits. There was life after blindness. Annie still doubted it for herself, but said she didn't care, which no one believed. But she was learning useful things at school.

Sabrina had assigned her to feed the dogs. Mrs. Shibata was incapable of it. She always fed them things that made them sick. She had fed Beulah cat food once, and she'd been at the vet for a week, which cost them a fortune. And she still sneaked seaweed into their diet from time to time. Annie was home more than the others, and came home earlier from school than they did from work, so Sabrina assigned her the task. And Annie was outraged.

"I can't. Anyway, you know I hate dogs!"

"I don't care. Ours need to eat, and no one else has the time. You have nothing else to do after school, except your shrink twice a week. And Mrs. Shibata is going to make them really sick, which costs a fortune at the vet. And you don't hate our dogs. Besides, they love you, so feed them." Annie had fumed and refused to do it for the first week. It had turned into a major battle with her oldest sister. But finally Annie learned how to use the electric can opener, measure the kibble and put it in the right bowls, which were of different sizes. She grudgingly put their food out when she got home, even with strips of cold cuts for Juanita, who was a picky eater and turned up her nose at the commercial dog food they bought. She made rice for them once when they were sick, after Mrs. Shibata gave them seaweed again, with one of her Japanese pickles as a special treat, which stank up the house. Tammy called them the thousand-year-old pickles. They smelled like they'd been rotten for years, and nearly killed the dogs.

"It is *not* my job to feed *your* dogs," Annie had said huffily. "I don't have one, so why do I have to do it?"

"Because I said so," Sabrina said finally, and Tammy told her she thought she was being a little tough.

"That's the whole point," Sabrina confessed. "We can't treat her like an invalid. I think she should do other chores too." Sabrina sent her to the mailbox with letters to mail as often as possible, and asked her to pick things up at the dry cleaner's down the street, because she was home before it closed, and the others weren't.

"What do I look like? An errand boy? What did your last slave die of?" Annie growled at her. It was a running battle between them, with Sabrina constantly asking her to do errands, pick things up at the hardware store, get a new hair dryer for her when hers broke. Her mission was to get Annie independent, and this was the best way to do it, even though it felt cruel to her sometimes too. She even bitched at her for spilling the dog food in the pantry and leaving a mess, and told her to clean it up before they got rats or mice in the house. Annie had been in tears over it, and didn't speak to Sabrina for two days, but she was becoming more and more independent and capable of taking care of herself.

Tammy had to admit the program was working, but it was definitely tough love. And more often than not, Candy sided with Annie, not understanding the motivation behind it, and called Sabrina a bitch. It was good cop, bad cop, with Tammy as the mediator a lot of the time. But Annie was becoming an independent woman again, sighted or not. And she was no longer frightened to go out into the world. The supermarket, drugstore, and hardware store no longer daunted her, blind or not.

Her biggest problem was that she had no social life. She had no friends in New York, and was shy about going out. She had always been the least social of her sisters and the most introverted, spending hours alone, sketching, drawing, and painting. Losing her sight had isolated her more. The only time she went anywhere was with her sisters, and they made every effort to get her out. But it was hard. Candy led a crazy life with photographers, models, editors, and people in the fashion world, most of whom Sabrina and Tammy thought were unsuitable for her, but they were who worked in her business and it was inevitable that she hung out with them. Sabrina worked long hours and wanted to spend time with Chris, and both of them were too tired to go out much during the week. And Tammy was living crazy hours in her new job, which had as many crises as her old job in Los Angeles. So most of the time, Annie had no one to go out with, and stayed home. It was a big deal for her to go out to dinner once a week with them, which they all agreed wasn't enough for her, but they didn't know how to solve the problem. And Annie insisted she liked staying home. She was starting to read in braille, and spent hours with her headphones on, listening to music and dreaming. It wasn't a full life for a twenty-six-year-old woman. She needed people and parties, and places to go to, girlfriends and a man in her life, but it wasn't happening, and her sisters feared it never would. She didn't say it to them, but so did she. Her life was as over as her father's, who sat in his house in Connecticut, crying for his late wife most of the time. Sabrina and Tammy worried about both of them, and wanted to do something about it, but neither of them had time.

Tammy's life was insane. As it turned out, Irving Solomon had basically wanted to turn the show over to her, and let her deal with it. He was in Florida half the week, and played golf whenever he could. He was tired, and wanted to retire early, but the show was a cash cow for him. When Tammy tried to discuss its problems with him, he waved her out of his office, and told her she had dealt with bigger problems in her last show, just deal with it. He trusted her completely.

"Shit, what am I supposed to do here?" she said to the associate producer one day. "I'm running a show where people beat each other up on TV, and they changed the time slot against a number-one show. All they know is what the ratings look like, and as long as they're good, no one wants to hear it."

She came up with the idea that their "couples" should at least look decent, and had her assistant call Barney's to see if they could get clothes for them, for credit on the show. They leaped at the idea.

"At least we won't have to look at their tattoos," Tammy said with relief. She was trying to upgrade the show, and give it a little class, which was risky business, she knew.

"Don't fix what ain't broke," the associate producer warned her, but Tammy was following her instincts, and thought people might relate to it better and care more, if the people looked less trailer park and more middle class. Jerry Springer was already the best of the business in that world. She wanted to carve out a niche of their own.

She hired two excellent hairdressers from a well-known soap to do the women's hair, and to try and get Désirée's look a little more under control. Désirée was furious that Tammy didn't like her look, but the audience loved the results. Tammy actually got their staff psychologist into some attractive beige suits by major designers, some more modest silk dresses where her gigantic tits weren't spilling onto her knees, and she suddenly looked like an authority in her field, and not a guy in drag. Her look had been very *Cage aux Folles* before that. And within three weeks of the changes Tammy had instigated, they got two new sponsors, one for dishwashing soap and the other for diapers. It was all squeaky-clean stuff. And the ratings soared.

That didn't rule out the problems they had with the couples, which were legion. One husband had pulled a gun on the host when he had goaded him Geraldo style, and called him a "rotten cheater." The guy was steaming for the rest of the show, and slammed the host up against a wall with a gun in his belly the minute they came off the air. No one had any idea how he had gotten the gun past security, but there it was, as Tammy happened to be walking by and saw it.

"I agree with you, Jeff," she said calmly. "The guy's an asshole. I don't like him either, but he's not worth going to prison for. And I thought it was pretty clear on the show that your wife's still in love with you. Why throw all that away? Désirée thought you two had a good shot at patching things up." Tammy tried to sound convincing and unflustered, and even sympathetic, as she tried to calm the potential shooter, while waiting for someone from security to show up before he shot her too.

"Really?" the man said, and then he got wound up again. "You're just saying that. You guys made assholes of us."

"I don't think so. The audience loved you, and our ratings were the best they've been all week." His wife was crying offstage somewhere, because it had come out that he had slept not only with her best friend but also with her sister, which she hadn't known. Could this relationship be saved? Hopefully not. The wife had also slept with his brother, and the entire neighborhood except their dog, to get even with him. As far as Tammy was concerned, they all belonged in jail, where "Jeff" had already been twice, for assault. What were they doing on the show anyway? And why was she producing it? That was the real question. It took them twenty minutes to talk him down. The cops had been called by then, and he was led away in handcuffs, which made the *New York Post* the next day. And that of course only helped their ratings. There was no question in Tammy's mind. It was a very sick show, catering to the absolute worst instincts of the public. They were Peeping Toms into other people's relationships and bedrooms, and what they saw there fascinated them. Most of the time, it made her sick.

"Well, that was fun," she said to her assistant, as she got back to her office and sat down at her desk, still looking pale. "Who the hell is screening these people, and where are we getting them? The parole board at Attica prison? Do you think we could do a slightly better job screening these lunatics before we put them on the show and piss them off?" She raised hell at their next production meeting about it, and the associate producer apologized profusely. Their host had actually been shot once before. He had gotten a huge salary increase because of it, and the position was now considered high risk.

"What am I doing here?" she asked herself as she left the meeting and Désirée waylaid her. She said she loved her new wardrobe, but did Tammy think she could talk to Oscar de la Renta about doing an exclusive wardrobe for her? She loved his clothes. A month before they'd been dressing her off the sale rack at Payless, and now she wanted Oscar de la Renta to design her clothes. They were all nuts.

"I'll try, Desi. But this may not be his kind of show." Particularly if their participants were going to be led away in handcuffs after every show. They had had a less traumatic incident the day before, when a wife had slugged her husband on the air and broken his nose. There had been blood everywhere. The audience had roared in sheer delight. "I loved your dress today."

"So did I," she said, looking pleased. "I loved the one yesterday too. But that idiot got blood all over it. All I had said backstage was that I thought his wife was gay. I didn't expect him to say it to her on air. Besides, she told me she was, she just didn't want him to know. So he tells her, and she breaks his nose on air. Go figure," Désirée said, looking nonplussed. "I hope they can get the blood out of the dress." She had just added a clause to her contract that allowed her to keep her on-air wardrobe. It was no wonder she wanted Oscar to do her clothes now. Tammy would have enjoyed a wardrobe too. Instead, she worked in sweatshirts, jeans, and Nikes most of the time. She needed to feel free to move around, and there was a lot of fancy footwork involved with the show.

"Yeah, go figure," Tammy agreed, thinking to herself that the psychologist was insane. But in spite of that she added two more new sponsors in the next two weeks. The show was skyrocketing to stardom, which was embarrassing, and *Variety* was attributing it to her, which was worse. She had been hoping to keep a low profile on this one, but that wasn't happening. Her old friends from L.A. were starting to call her and tease the hell out of her for what she was doing in New York.

"I thought you went back there to take care of your sister," one of them said.

"I did."

"So what happened?"

"She's in school, and I got bored."

"Well, you won't be bored on this show."

"No, I'll probably wind up in jail."

"I doubt it. You'll probably wind up running the network one day. I can hardly wait."

Worse yet, *Entertainment Tonight* asked her for an interview shortly after the husband had pulled the gun on their host, and Irving wanted her to do it. She tried to keep it brief and dignified, which was no mean feat. And to top it off, the day after, their host asked her out. He was fifty-five years old, had been divorced four times, had caps on his teeth the size of Chiclets, and a terrible hair weave he had done in Mexico. He had been a minor actor on soaps in his youth, and was a bodybuilder. From a distance, he was decent looking, but from up close he was terrifying. And he was a born-again Christian, which was a little too intense for her. She preferred her spirituality in smaller doses, and he regularly handed her religious pamphlets about being saved. Maybe he needed that in order to face the daily risk of getting shot.

"I . . . uh . . . that's very sweet of you, Ed. . . . I make it a policy never to go out with men on the shows I work on. It's such a mess if things don't work out."

"Why wouldn't they work out? I'm a great guy." He beamed at her. He had seven children by all four wives, all of whom he supported, which was honorable of him, and as a result, he drove a twenty-year-old car, and lived in a fourth-floor walk-up on the West Side. Getting shot in the gut had improved his financial situation immeasurably. He had said he was moving to a better neighborhood next month. "I thought maybe we could have dinner after work. You know, something simple. I'm on a vegan diet right now."

"Oh, really." She tried to look interested, if only to be kind. "Do you do high colonics?" Every freak she'd met in L.A. did them. It was her first clue he wasn't the man for her. She didn't want to date a man whose prize possession was an enema bag. She'd rather have entered a convent, and at this rate, might one day. It was becoming more appealing by the hour.

"No, I don't. I think they're bigger out west than here. I have a friend on *Match Point* who does them all the time. Do you do them, Tammy?"

"Actually, no, I don't. I'm a junk-food addict. My idea of gourmet food is KFC, and I have an incredible Ho-Ho and Twinkie habit. I've been that way since I was a kid. High colonics would be wasted on me."

"That's too bad." He looked sorry for her and then lowered his voice. "Have you found Jesus yet, Tammy?" Where? Under her desk? In the attic? Was he kidding? Did she have to "find" Him? Wasn't He everywhere?

"I think you could say I have," she said politely. "Religion has been important to me since I was a child." She didn't know what else to say to him, and it was somewhat true. They had gone to Catholic schools as kids, but she was no longer devout, although she believed.

"But are you a *Christian*?" He was intense as he looked at her, and she tried not to stare at his hair, which was badly dyed too. She made a mental note to get a decent hairdresser for him too. She didn't know why she'd never noticed that his hair color was this bad. She had been too distracted by the bad weave.

"I'm Catholic," she said easily.

"That's not the same thing. Being Christian is a lot more than that. It's a whole way of thinking, of being, of living. It's not just a religion."

"Yes, I'd agree with you on that." She tried to glance at her watch discreetly. She had a network meeting in four minutes, to avoid a strike. It was a big deal. She couldn't miss it. "I think we should talk about it some other time. I have a meeting in four minutes."

"Exactly. So how about dinner? There's a great vegan restaurant on West Fourteenth Street. How about tonight?"

"I...uh...no...remember my policy? No men from the show. I've never broken that rule, and I have to go home to take care of my sister."

"Is she sick?" He looked instantly concerned.

Tammy hated herself for what she was about to do. But it might get him off her back. With silent apologies to Annie, she looked up at him mournfully. "She's blind. I really don't like to go out and leave her on her own."

"Oh, I'm so sorry...I had no idea...of course...what a saintly person you are to take care of her. Do you live with her?"

"Yes, I do. It happened this year, and she's only twenty-six." It was pathetic to use her sister's handicap so shamelessly, but anything in a pinch. She would have invented a dying grandmother too.

"I'll pray for her," he assured her, "and for you."

"Thank you, Ed," Tammy said solemnly. And went to her network meeting. He was probably a perfectly nice human being, just unattractive and creepy. Her specialty. Men like him were the only ones who ever asked her out, on either coast.

She told her sisters about it that night as they were doing the dishes after dinner. Annie was rinsing and putting them in the dishwasher. Sabrina had checked the dogs' bowls, and Annie had fed the dogs. Annie said Sabrina treated her like Cinderella, which her older sister didn't comment on. Tammy had them all in hysterics describing Ed.

"See what I mean? Those are the only guys who ever ask me out. Weird teeth, hair weaves, vegan diets, and high colonics in L.A. I swear, I haven't had a date with a normal one in years. I'm not even sure what that looks like anymore."

"I'm not sure I do either," Candy admitted. "All the men I meet are bisexual or gay. They like women, but they like boys more. I never even see straight guys anymore."

Annie said nothing. She felt completely out of the running, and had since her accident this summer. Normally, after breaking up with

Charlie, she would have started dating again within a few months. Now, she felt that it was over for her. The only man she had talked to in months was her friend Baxter at school. His love life was a lot happier than hers. He had a boyfriend. She was sure she never would again.

"The only one in the family who can't complain is Sabrina," Candy commented. "Chris is the only normal man I know."

"Yeah, me too," Tammy agreed. "Normal *and* nice. It's an unbeatable combination. When I meet normal ones, or at least men who look that way, they turn out to be assholes, or married. I guess I could always start dating one of the participants on the show." She told them about the incident with the one that morning, and Sabrina shook her head. She still couldn't believe that Tammy had taken a job producing that show. Giving up the job she'd had had really been the ultimate sacrifice for her. She said very little about it, but they were aware of it. The show she was working on instead was at the opposite end of the spectrum, from the sublime to the ridiculous. Tammy never complained, she was a good sport about it, and she was happy to have found work. And Irving Solomon, the executive producer, was a fairly decent man to work for.

Another man asked Tammy out the following week. This one was extremely attractive, married, and cheating on his wife, although he explained they had an open marriage and she understood.

"She might," Tammy had said brusquely. "I don't. That's not my style, but thanks." She brushed him off, and more than flattered, she was insulted. She always felt that way when married men asked her out, as though she were a cheap slut, that they could have a good time with and then go home to their wives. If she ever wound up with anyone, which was beginning to seem unlikely, she wanted it to be her own man, not one she had stolen or borrowed from someone else. She had just turned thirty, and wasn't panicked about it.

On Sabrina's thirty-fifth birthday, she and Chris had gone away for the weekend, and he had given her a beautiful gold Cartier bracelet that she never took off her arm. Things were, as always, comfortable between them, although he was sleeping over less often than he had when she lived alone. She reminded him regularly that it was only for a year, until Annie got adjusted, and he rarely commented or complained. The only thing that got to him occasionally was Candy wandering around the house half naked, oblivious to the fact that there was a man in their midst. So many people saw her naked or at least topless during couture shows or on shoots that she didn't really care. But he did. And although he loved them, their flock of dogs occasionally got on his nerves. That and the lack of privacy, with Tammy now living on the same floor. That was challenging for him at times.

The only thing that unsettled all of them was the man Candy came home with in early November, when she got back from a three-day shoot in Hawaii. Sabrina said she had read about him. Tammy had never heard of him, and Annie said he gave her a creepy feeling, but since she couldn't see him, she couldn't pinpoint why. She said he sounded phony, like Leslie Thompson when she had visited their father with the pie. Kind of drippy and oozing sweetness, as Annie put it, when he had something else on his mind.

He said he was an Italian prince and he had an accent, Principe Marcello di Stromboli. It didn't sound real to Sabrina, and they were all shocked to realize that he was forty-four years old. Candy said she had met him the first time in Paris, at a party Valentino gave, and she knew another model who had dated him, and said he was very nice. He took Candy to all the trendy hot spots in New York, and some fabulous parties. They were in the tabloids almost immediately, and when Sabrina questioned her about it with a worried look, Candy said she was having a great time.

"Be careful," Sabrina warned her. "He's a very grown-up guy. Sometimes men his age prey on young girls. Don't just go off somewhere with him or put yourself in an awkward situation." Sabrina felt like the anxious mother hen of all time, and her baby sister laughed.

"I'm not stupid. I'm twenty-one years old. I've lived alone since I was nineteen. I meet men like him all the time. Some of them are a lot older. So what?"

"What do you suppose he's after?" Sabrina asked Tammy with a worried look a few days later. They had been in *W*, several tabloids, and on page six of the *Post* in the past two weeks. But there was no denying that Candy was a famous model, and he was a familiar socialite in New York. He had a famous mother who had been a well-known Italian actress. And he had a title. Princes were in high demand in lofty social circles, and made people overlook a multitude of sins. He had come to the house several times to pick Candy up, and treated her sisters like the maids who opened the door. He didn't even bother to speak to Annie, since she couldn't see how devastatingly handsome he was. And he was indeed remarkably attractive and aristocratic looking and exquisitely dressed in a European style. He wore beautiful Italian suits, perfectly starched shirts, sapphire cuff links, a gold ring with his family's crest on it, and his shoes were custom made by John Lobb. And with Candy on his arm, he looked like a movie star, and so did she. They made a dazzling couple.

"You don't suppose it's serious," Sabrina asked Tammy in a panic one night after he'd picked her up in a black Bentley limousine he had rented for the evening. Candy had been wearing a silvery-gray satin evening gown and silver high heels. She looked like a young queen.

"Not for a minute," Tammy said, without concern. "I see men like him in the movie business all the time. They go after famous actresses, supermodels like Candy. They just want an accessory for their narcissism. He's no more interested in Candy than he is in his shoes."

"She said he wants to meet her in Paris next week when she's there on a shoot."

"He might, but it won't last long. Someone bigger and more important will come along. Those types come and go."

"I hope he goes soon. There's something about him that makes me nervous. Candy's such a babe in the woods. She may be one of the hottest models in the world, but underneath all that gorgeousness and glamour, she's just a child."

"Yes, she is," Tammy agreed. "But she has us. At least he knows we're around, like parents, keeping an eye on her."

"I don't think he gives a damn about us," Sabrina said, still worried. "He's a lot slicker than we are. And we're no one in his world."

"I think Candy can handle it," Tammy said confidently. "She meets a lot of men like him."

"I sure don't," Sabrina said, smiling ruefully. Chris was light-years away from the Italian prince, and a much finer man. Chris was a man of substance and integrity. All of Sabrina's instincts told her that Marcello wasn't. It was easy to spot. But Candy thought he was exciting, even if her sisters found him much too old.

And when she got back from Paris, she said they had had a fabulous time. He had taken her to a string of parties, including a ball at Versailles, and introduced her to all of Paris. Everyone he knew had a title. He had turned her head much more than Sabrina liked, and she was looking thinner again. When Sabrina commented on it, Candy said she had worked hard in Paris. But Sabrina called her shrink anyway. The shrink made no comment but thanked Sabrina for her call.

Thanksgiving was the following week, and they all went out to their father's house in Connecticut. He looked thinner too. Tammy asked him if he felt all right, with a look of concern. He said he did, but he seemed quiet and lonely and grateful to see the girls.

They went through their mother's things that weekend, at his suggestion, took the clothes they wanted, and he was going to donate the rest. It was hard to do, but he seemed to want to clear it all out. And they helped Annie make selections from what they described to her. She had always particularly loved her mother's soft pastel cashmere sweaters, and they looked beautiful on her. She had the same color hair.

"How do I look?" she asked them, after she put one on. "Do I look like Mom?"

Tammy's eyes had filled with tears. "Yeah, actually, you do." But Tammy did too, although her red hair was brighter and much longer. But there was a definite similarity between their mother and those two daughters.

It was a quiet, easy weekend, and they had no social plans. The girls made the turkey dinner themselves, and had fun making the stuffing and all the vegetables. Annie helped too.

Chris had come out for Thanksgiving Day, and then went skiing in Vermont for the weekend with friends. Sabrina had opted to stay with her sisters and dad. It was a family weekend, which was important to them, especially this year.

It was Saturday when Tammy came across a pair of women's sneakers in the room off the kitchen where her mother used to arrange flowers. They were a size nine, and her mother had worn a size six.

And they didn't belong to any of the girls. And his housekeeper had small feet too.

"Who do these belong to, Dad?" Tammy asked after they had gone through her mother's clothes all day and sorted them in piles for each of them and to donate. "They're not Mom's."

"Are you sure?" he said vaguely, and Tammy laughed.

"Not unless her feet grew three sizes this year. Should I throw them out?"

"Why don't you just leave them wherever you found them? Maybe someone will claim them." He was preoccupied with fixing something when she asked, and had his back to her so she couldn't see his face.

"Like who?" she asked, curious now, and then decided to be brazen. She'd had a sudden thought. "You're not dating, are you, Dad?" He spun around as though she had shot him and looked at her.

"What makes you ask that?"

"I was just wondering. The shoes seem a little odd." He certainly had the right to date anyone he wanted. He was a free man, but it seemed a little soon to her. Their mother had been gone for five months, shy of a week.

"I had some friends over a few weeks ago, for lunch. One of them may have left her shoes here. I'll call." He hadn't answered her question, and she didn't want to pry. She just hoped it wasn't Leslie Thompson. She hadn't brought over any pies that weekend, and there was no evidence of a woman in the house. She mentioned it to her sisters in the car on the way back. They had left early Sunday morning to beat the weekend traffic.

"Stop spying on him," Candy scolded her. "He has a right to do what he wants. He's a grown man."

"I'd hate to see him fall into the clutches of some conniving woman just because he's lonely without Mom. Men do that sometimes," Sabrina said with genuine concern. He seemed so vulnerable right now, and had been since July. And at least during the summer he'd had his daughters with him. Now they hardly ever had time to go out and visit him. Although they were planning to spend Christmas with him too. It had been a nice Thanksgiving for all of them, although they all missed their mother. The holidays were really tough.

"I think Dad's too smart for some gold digger," Tammy reassured them. She had more faith in him than that.

"I hope you're right," Sabrina said.

And as soon as they got back to the house, Candy dressed to go out.

"Where are you going?" Tammy looked at her in surprise.

"Marcello invited me to a party." She mentioned some socialites whom Tammy had read about frequently in the papers, and she smiled.

"You lead a mighty fancy life, princess," Tammy teased her.

"I'm not a princess yet," she teased back. But she felt like one with Marcello, and she didn't say it to her sisters, but he was incredible in bed. They had taken Ecstasy a couple of times, which made sex even more exciting. She knew he did coke once in a while, and he didn't need it, but he used Viagra to stay hard, so he could make love to her all night. He was a very intoxicating man, and she was beginning to think she was in love with him. He was hinting about marriage. She was too young of course, but in a few years...maybe...he said he wanted to have babies with her. But right now it was more fun just having sex. She was planning to stay at his place that night, and mentioned it vaguely to her sisters as she walked out the door. She was meeting him at his apartment so she could drop off a small bag. She wondered if they would even make it to the party. Sometimes they never made it out the front door, and wound up in bed instead, or on the floor. She didn't mind that at all.

"I may not be home tonight," she muttered vaguely over her shoulder, halfway out the front door.

"Hey wait a minute...," Sabrina said. "What was that? Where are you staying?"

"Marcello's," Candy said blithely. She was twenty-one, had been on her own for two years, and her sisters didn't have the right to tell her what she could and couldn't do, and she knew it. So did they, although they worried about her.

"Be careful," Sabrina said, and came over to kiss her. "Where does he live, by the way?"

"He has an apartment on East Seventy-ninth. He has fantastic art." Sabrina wanted to say that that didn't make him a nice guy, but didn't. Candy was wearing a crotch-length black leather miniskirt and thigh-high black suede high-heeled boots. She looked incredible with a skin-tight black cashmere sweater, and a gray mink jacket.

"You look knockout gorgeous," Sabrina said with a smile. She was such a beautiful girl. "Where on East Seventy-ninth Street? Just in case something happens, it's nice to know where you are. And cell phones don't always work."

"Nothing's going to happen." It annoyed her when Sabrina acted like a mother instead of a sister, but she indulged her just this once. "One forty-one East Seventy-ninth. *Don't* drop by!"

"I won't," Sabrina promised, and Candy left.

Chris came back from his ski weekend, and they retired to her room to talk and cuddle and watch a movie on TV. He slept there that night, and Tammy slept in Candy's room, so they'd have the floor to themselves. She stuck her head in to see Annie before she went to bed. She was doing homework in braille.

"How's it going?"

"Okay, I guess." She looked frustrated, but at least she made the effort. All in all, things were going well for her, and they all agreed it had been a nice Thanksgiving weekend, even without their mom.

Chapter 21

The Monday after Thanksgiving, life went on as usual. Sabrina and Chris left for work together, Tammy had another network meeting to rush off to. And Annie left for school in a cab. She was planning to start taking the bus soon, but didn't feel ready yet. She had been at the Parker School for three months. Things were slightly more complicated that day because it had snowed the night before, which made the ground slippery and treacherous, and this time she slid on an ice patch in front of the school and wound up on her bottom instead of her knees. But unlike the first time, when she was near tears, this time she laughed.

She had just said hello to Baxter, who heard the sound she had made as she fell.

"What happened?" he asked, mystified by what was going on. Her voice was coming from lower to the ground, and she was laughing.

"I'm sitting on my ass. I fell."

"Again? You klutz." They were both laughing as someone helped her up. It was a firm, strong hand.

"No sledding in front of school, Miss Adams," the voice teased her, and she didn't recognize it at first. "You'll have to do that in Central Park." She realized as he helped her up that the seat of her jeans was wet. And she had nothing to change into. And then she remembered the voice. It was Brad Parker, the director of the school. She hadn't spoken to him since the first day.

Baxter could hear him talking to her, and they were late, so he told Annie he'd meet her in class and told her to hurry up.

"I take it you two are friends," Brad said pleasantly, as he tucked her hand into his arm and walked her in. There was ice on the ground. It had snowed early that year. And there were always mishaps outside school when it did, even if they were careful to shovel it.

"He's a great guy," she said about Baxter. "We're both artists, and we both had accidents this year. I guess we have a lot in common."

"My mother was an artist," Brad Parker said pleasantly. "She painted as a hobby actually. She was a ballerina, with the Paris ballet. She had a car accident at twenty, and it ended both careers. But she did some wonderful things in spite of that."

"What did she do?" Annie asked politely. It was amazing how many lives were destroyed or lost with car accidents. She had met several in the school, some of them artists like her. With eight hundred people in the school, there were countless stories and people from all walks of life.

"She taught dance. And she was very good. She met my father when she was thirty, but she taught even after they got married. She was a hard taskmaster," he laughed. "My father had been blind since birth, and she even taught him how to dance. She always wanted to start a school like this. I did it for her after she died. We have dance classes here too. Both ballroom and ballet. You should try it sometime, you might like it."

"Not if you can't see," Annie said bluntly.

"The people who take the class seem to like it," he said, undaunted, as he noticed that she touched the wet seat of her jeans. She was soaked from her fall, and wondering if she should go home. "You know, we have a closet with spare clothes in it for times like this. Do you know where it is?" She shook her head. "I'll show you. You're going to be miserable in those wet jeans all day," he said kindly. He had a gentle, easygoing voice, and sounded as though he had a sense of humor. There was always laughter just beneath his words. He sounded happy, she decided, and nice. In a fatherly sort of way. She wondered how old he was. She had the feeling he wasn't young, but she couldn't ask.

He took her upstairs to a storeroom with racks of clothes in it. They donated them to some of their scholarship students, or used them for incidents like this. He looked her over and handed her a pair of jeans. "I think these might fit. There's a fitting room in the corner, with a curtain. I'll wait here. There are others if you want." She tried them on, feeling slightly self-conscious, and they were big but dry. She came out looking slightly like an orphan, and he laughed. "May I roll them up for you? You're going to fall again if you don't."

"Sure," she said, still feeling self-conscious. He did, and they felt fine. "Thank you. You're right. My jeans are really wet. I was thinking about going home to change at lunchtime."

"You'd have caught cold by then," he said, and she laughed.

"You sound like my sister. She's always worried that I'm going to hurt myself, fall down, get sick. She acts like a mom."

"That's not an entirely bad thing. We all need one at times. I still miss mine, and she's been gone for almost twenty years."

Annie spoke softly when she answered, "I lost mine in July."

"I'm sorry," he said, and sounded genuine. "That's very hard."

"Yes, it was," she said honestly. And Christmas was going to be rough this year. She was grateful they had gotten through Thanksgiving. But they were all dreading Christmas without their mother. They had talked about it when they divided up her clothes.

"I lost both my parents at once," he said, as he walked her out of the storeroom and toward her classroom. "In a plane crash. It makes you grow up very quickly when there is no one between you and the great beyond."

"I never thought about it that way," she said pensively. "But maybe you're right. And I still have my dad." They had reached her classroom then. She had braille that morning, and kitchen skills that afternoon. They were supposed to make meat loaf, which she hated, but Baxter was in the same class and they always had fun clowning around. She could make perfect cupcakes now, and chicken. She had cooked both at home, to critical acclaim. "Thank you for the jeans. I'll bring them back tomorrow."

"Anytime," he said pleasantly. "Have a good day, Annie." And then he added, "Play nice in the sandbox," and she laughed. He had a major advantage over her. He could see what she looked like, and she couldn't see him. But he had a nice voice.

She slipped into her seat in braille class, and Baxter teased her mercilessly. "So now the head of the school is carrying your books for you, eh?"

"Oh, shut up," she chuckled. "He took me to get dry jeans."

"Did he help you put them on?"

"Will you stop? No. He rolled them up." Baxter hooted softly under his breath and continued to razz her about it all morning.

"I hear he's cute, by the way."

"I think he's old," Annie said matter-of-factly. Brad Parker hadn't been hitting on her. He was just being helpful, and acting like a head of school. "Besides, I didn't see you helping me get off my ass outside when I fell on the ice."

"I can't," Baxter said simply. "I'm blind, you ninny."

"And don't call me a ninny!" They were like twelve-year-olds. The teacher called them to order, and a little while later, Baxter added, "I think he's thirty-eight or thirty-nine."

"Who?" She was concentrating on her braille homework, and was furious to discover she had gotten almost half of it wrong. It was harder than she thought.

"Mr. Parker. I think he's thirty-nine."

"How do you know?" She sounded surprised.

"I know everything. Divorced, no kids."

"So? What's that supposed to mean?"

"Maybe he has the hots for you. You can't see him. But he can see you. And three people have told me you're gorgeous."

"They're lying to you. I have three heads and a double chin on each. And no, he was not hitting on me. He was just being *nice*."

"There's no such thing as *nice* between men and women. There's interested and not interested. Maybe he is."

"It doesn't matter if he is," Annie said practically. "Thirty-nine is too old. I'm only twenty-six."

"Yeah, that's true," Baxter said matter-of-factly. "You're right, he is too old." And with that, they both went back to work, trying to master braille.

When Annie got home from school that evening, both her older sisters were still out, and so was Candy. And Mrs. Shibata was about to leave. Annie fed the dogs, and started her homework. She was still working on it when Tammy came home at seven. She heaved a sigh as she came through the door, took off her boots, and said she was exhausted when she saw Annie, and asked her how her day was.

"It was fine." She didn't tell her that she had fallen. She didn't want her to worry, and they got nervous about things like that, and worried that she might hit her head. After brain surgery five months before, that would not be a good thing. But she had only hit her bottom. Sabrina came home half an hour later and asked if anyone had seen Candy. She had called her on her cell phone several times that afternoon, and it went to voice mail every time.

"She must be working," Tammy said practically, as she started dinner. She wasn't a baby after all, even if they treated her that way, and she had a major career. "Did she tell you what she was doing today?" she asked Annie, who shook her head, and then she remembered. "She was doing some kind of shoot for an ad this afternoon. She said she'd come home this morning and pick up her portfolio and her stuff." She usually carried a bag full of makeup and other things with her when she worked.

"Did she?" Sabrina asked, and Annie reminded her she'd been at school so she didn't know.

"I'll look," Sabrina said, and ran up the flight to Candy's room. The portfolio and work bag, a giant Hermès tote in dark red alligator, were still there. She carried Zoe around in it sometimes too. But Zoe had been home all day with the other dogs. It gave Sabrina a strange feeling to see the portfolio and bag in her room. She wondered if she should call Candy's agency to see if she had checked in, but she didn't want to act like a cop. Candy would have been furious if she did, even if her intentions were good, which they were. She just worried about her baby sister.

"Well?" Tammy asked when Sabrina came back down to the kitchen.

They were all downstairs by then except Candy, who still hadn't appeared.

"Her stuff is all in her room," Sabrina said, with a worried look.

They called her several times after dinner, but her phone still went to voice mail. It was obviously turned off. Sabrina wished she had asked her for Marcello's phone number, but she hadn't, only his address, and she couldn't drop by to ask him where her sister was. Candy would have gone insane. He lived in a good neighborhood at least, if that meant anything. And at midnight they still hadn't heard a word from her. Tammy and Sabrina were still up, and Annie had gone to bed.

"I would hate being a parent," Sabrina said miserably to Tammy. "I'm worried sick about her." Tammy didn't want to admit it, but she was getting concerned too. It was unlike Candy to just disappear like that and not check in. They didn't know what to do. And then Tammy remembered that there was a hotline at her agency to call anytime day or night, for models who had problems. Some of them were still very young, came from other cities or countries, and needed help or advice. Tammy looked it up in Candy's address book and found it. She dialed the number, got an answering service, and asked to be put through to the head of the agency if that was possible. A sleepy voice answered two minutes later. It was Marlene Weissman herself.

Tammy apologized for calling at such a late hour, but said they were concerned about their sister, Candy Adams. She hadn't come home since the night before, and they hadn't heard from her after she went out with a friend.

Marlene Weissman sounded instantly concerned. "She didn't show up for a shoot today. She's never done that before. Who was she with last night?"

"The man she's currently going out with, he's some sort of Italian prince. Marcello di Stromboli, he's quite a bit older than she is. They were going to a party on Fifth Avenue."

Marlene was now wide awake. She spoke quickly and distinctly. "The man's a phony and a bullshitter. He has some money, and preys on models. He's had some problems with the law, and he's roughed up two of my girls. I had no idea he was still going out with Candy or I would have said something to her. He usually goes after younger girls than she is."

"They've been in the papers a number of times," Tammy said, feeling weak at the knees.

"I know. I just assumed he had moved on by now. He usually does. Do you know where he lives?"

"She gave us the address." She read it off to Marlene.

"I'll meet you there in twenty minutes. I think we'd better go up there. He may have her there, drugged up or worse. Do you have a boyfriend or a husband?" she asked bluntly.

"My sister does," Tammy said.

"Bring him. If he won't let us in, we'll call the police. I don't like this guy, he's trouble." It was everything Candy's sisters didn't want to hear. Thank God they had called her.

Sabrina called Chris and woke him up, explained what was happening, and he said he'd pick them up in a cab in ten minutes. Tammy wasn't sure if they should wake Annie to tell her they were leaving. She was sound asleep, and there was no reason to think that she should wake up while they were gone. The two women bundled up and put heavy coats and boots on. It was snowing hard when Chris picked them up, and he said he was lucky to find a cab at twelve-thirty on a snowy night. They were at Marcello's address ten minutes later, slipping and sliding across the icy streets. Marlene was already there, in a mink coat over jeans. She was an attractive gray-haired woman in her late fifties with a silky voice.

She spoke in an authoritarian manner to the doorman, and said the prince was expecting them, and not to bother to call. She was so daunting that the doorman followed her instructions, aided by a hundred-dollar bill, and let all four of them up. He told them it was apartment 5E. They were silent in the elevator, and Tammy could feel her heart beating as she looked at the older woman, with her hair pulled back in a slick chignon, and the elegant mink coat.

"I don't like this at all," she said softly, and the others nodded.

"Neither do we," Sabrina answered, holding tightly to Chris's hand. He still looked half asleep, and wasn't entirely sure what was going on or what they hoped to find. It seemed obvious to him that if Candy was there, she wanted to be, and might be furious at the four intruders who had come to rescue her. Particularly if she didn't want to be. Whatever happened, it was going to be an interesting scene.

They reached the door to apartment 5E a moment later, and Marlene startled Chris by whispering to him to say he was the police. He looked less than enthused. He was beginning to think they would all get arrested for this caper.

"I'm an attorney. I'm not sure I should do something like that," he whispered. "I could be charged with impersonating the police."

"He could be charged with worse. Just say it," she said to him in a stern whisper, and feeling stupid, he rang the doorbell, waited for a male voice on the other side, and played the game dictated by Marlene. Tammy and Sabrina were deeply grateful to her, and to Chris, for being there.

"Open up. Police," Chris intoned convincingly. There was a pause on the other side, a long hesitation, and then the sound of unlocking bolts. He kept the chain on when he opened the door to them, and Chris looked immediately stern, and got into it. "I said open the door. I have a warrant for your arrest." Sabrina's eyes grew wide as she stared at Chris. Maybe that was going a little far.

"For what?" It was Marcello, and he sounded half asleep.

"Kidnapping and false imprisonment. And we believe you are dealing drugs from this address." The women were standing behind Chris where Marcello couldn't see them.

"That's ridiculous," he said, as he slid the chain off. "And who do you think I kidnapped, officer?" He hadn't asked to see a badge or any kind of ID, but Chris looked awe-inspiring, standing in a dark coat and jeans. He was a powerfully built man in excellent shape, with an air of authority when he chose. And right now he chose, although he thought they were all nuts. But he was doing it for Sabrina. The door was open wide by then. Chris stepped into the apartment so he couldn't close the door on them, and towered over Marcello, with at least fifty pounds and a lot of toned muscle to his advantage. Marlene stepped in beside him and didn't pull any punches with him.

"I didn't bring charges against you last time because the girl was seventeen and it would have been too hard on her. This one isn't. She's fully capable of bringing charges against you, and so am I. Where is she?"

"Where is who?" he said, looking pale, and it was obvious that he knew and hated Marlene.

"Hold on to him," Marlene said to Chris, and strode into the apartment as though she owned it.

"I will bring charges against *you*!" he screamed at her. "You are breaking into my apartment!"

"You let us in," she said as she hurried down a hall. He acted as though Tammy and Sabrina didn't exist, as Chris watched him closely, and he started to run after Marlene. It was too late. She had opened the door to the bedroom, guessing accurately where it was, and found Candy unconscious, with tape over her mouth, and her arms and legs tied to a four-poster bed with rope. She looked dead. And Marcello looked totally panicked as the others followed Marlene into the room. Candy was naked and unconscious, and parts of her body were severely bruised, her legs spread wide. Both of her sisters screamed, and Chris grabbed Marcello and slammed him up against the wall.

"You sonofabitch," he said through clenched teeth, shoving him hard. "I swear if you killed her, I'll kill you." Sabrina was sobbing as she helped Marlene untie her. Candy showed no sign of regaining consciousness, as Tammy dialed 911 with shaking hands and tried to describe what they'd found. She could hardly breathe. Marlene had checked the pulse in Candy's neck, and she was alive. Her head dropped down on her chest as they untied her and covered her with a sheet. The ambulance said they'd be there in five minutes.

"Call the cops," Chris said to Tammy, as he held Marcello in a death-grip against the wall.

"They're coming with the ambulance," Tammy said in a choked voice. Candy still looked dead, and Marlene said softly that Candy had been drugged. He might have killed her eventually, but he hadn't yet.

As though to reassure them, but it didn't, Marlene said, "The last one looked worse than this. He beat her up." They could hear sirens by then, and a moment later police and paramedics were in the room. They checked Candy, started an IV, put an oxygen mask on her, put her on a gurney, and left the room with her sisters hard on their heels, while the police put handcuffs on Marcello, and Marlene and Chris described the scene they'd found. They left the apartment, with Marlene and Chris bringing up the rear. He said in a subdued voice that he had had no idea they would find this. She hoped they wouldn't but was afraid they might.

The girls had already left in the ambulance, as Marcello was put in a squad car and driven away. They had taken her to Columbia-Presbyterian Hospital, and Marlene and Chris hailed a cab to join the others there.

The scene at the hospital was grim—gunshot wounds, two stabbings, a man who had just died from a heart attack. They rushed Candy into the trauma unit, while the others waited. After what they'd been through that summer with their mother and Annie, this was a painful déjà vu for Tammy and Sabrina.

But this time when the doctor came out to talk to them, the news was better than they'd feared, although it wasn't good. As they could well imagine, she had been raped. Her bruises were superficial, nothing was broken, and she had been heavily drugged. They said it would take another twenty-four hours for her to come around, and then they could take her home. They had taken photographs of all her bruises for the police files. But they said there would be no lasting physical damage, only the emotional trauma she had sustained, which was undoubtedly considerable. The only good news was that the doctor assumed she had been unconscious for most of what had been done to her, so she would have no memory of it, which was a mercy.

Both of her sisters were in tears as they listened, as was Marlene, and Chris looked murderous. He wanted to kill Marcello for doing something like this to a nice kid like Candy.

"You have no idea how many models this happens to," Marlene said grimly. "Usually it's the really young ones who don't know how to protect themselves."

"Candy thought he was a great guy," Tammy said, wiping her eyes.

The police had told her they would talk to all of them in the morning. Tammy volunteered to stay with her, so Chris and Sabrina could go home to Annie, and Marlene wanted to be there too. Tammy said it wasn't necessary, but the older woman insisted, and they sat on either side of Candy's bedside all night, talking softly of the evils of the world as Candy slept.

It was ten the next morning before Candy stirred. She had no idea where she was or what had happened. All she knew was that every inch of her hurt, especially "down there," as she said. "Where's Marcello?" she asked as she looked around. The last thing she remembered was having dinner with him in his apartment, before they were supposed to go to the party. He had put whatever he'd given her in her food.

"In jail, where he belongs," Marlene answered, and then gently stroked her hair. She left the hospital a few minutes later, looking tired and depressed, but relieved that Candy was okay.

They let her go home at five o'clock that afternoon. Tammy had called her office to say she wouldn't be in. And Sabrina left her office to help bring her home. They had told Annie what had happened, and all of them were fiercely upset. And Sabrina had called Candy's shrink to tell her what had happened. They were going to need her help, maybe for a long time. She recommended someone who specialized in trauma cases, and Sabrina called her too. It was just one more disaster they didn't need. Candy was crying when they brought her home, but had no idea why. She remembered nothing of the past two days, only Marcello's face as she went to sleep.

The police had come to talk to Sabrina and Chris before they left for work. And they had gone to the hospital to take reports from Tammy and Marlene. Candy was still throwing up from the drugs while they were there. Marcello was being prosecuted for rape, assault, battery, false imprisonment, and kidnap, and for drugging her. They were throwing the book at him, and the judge had set a five-hundred-thousand-dollar bail. A friend paid it for him that night, and he was free. To do it again.

Sabrina and Tammy pampered her in every way they knew how. Her lip was swollen, her eyes were battered, both her breasts were bruised, and she could hardly sit down. It had been an experience none of them would ever forget.

"I think I'll definitely give up dating after this," Tammy said somberly, and for the first time in days, they all laughed.

"I wouldn't go that far, but it certainly is a lesson to be extremely careful." As Marlene said when she came to visit them again, there were some very dangerous people out there who preyed on beautiful girls. It made Sabrina think how vulnerable Annie was. She was not only young and beautiful, but blind. But Candy had been blind in her own way too. Marcello had been charming, but a profoundly bad guy.

By the end of the week, Candy was on her feet again. Marlene told her to take a few weeks off, until the bruises healed. And she went to her shrink every day. But there was nothing to remember, no painful or frightening memories. All she had were the bruises, which slowly faded away. But her sisters would never forget what they had seen when they found her, nor would Chris. They were all deeply grateful to Marlene for responding so quickly, and being so brave. Despite what had happened, Candy was a very lucky girl. And much to everyone's relief, relative to other equally appalling charges, Marcello was deported and extradited to Italy by the end of the week. Marlene had used her connections to speed the process. There would be no scandal, no court appearances, no press. He would be punished in his own country, and Candy would never have to see him again. He was gone.

Chapter 22

On the last day of school before the Christmas holiday, Brad Parker stopped Annie in the lobby to say goodbye.

"Have a great Christmas, Annie!" he wished her, although he knew the holiday would be difficult this year. And then he did something he never did. He had a hard and fast rule but broke it for her. He had been thinking of her since the day he had helped her find dry jeans. She was such a pleasant, intelligent, nice girl, and seemed very mature for her age. And she'd been through so much this year. More than he knew. Candy's recent disaster had shaken her up too.

"I was wondering if you'd like to have coffee sometime, while we're on break." They were going to be on vacation for three weeks.

Annie was startled at first, and didn't know what else to say, so she said yes. She didn't want to be rude to him, and he was the head of her school, after all. She felt like a kid when he asked. But Annie was no kid anymore. She had grown up immeasurably this year, and had been on her own before that.

"I have your number in our files. I'll give you a call. Maybe sometime later this week. I don't know if you like sweets, but I have a terrible sweet tooth. There's a cute place called Serendipity. The desserts are outrageous."

"I'd like that," she said. It sounded harmless. He wasn't going to attack her over hot chocolate and apple pie. At least she hoped not. Candy's experience had upset them all. But she knew Brad Parker was fine. Even her sisters couldn't object.

On the contrary, when he called her that night, they hooted and jeered and went crazy, which embarrassed Annie as she hung up. They had all been listening while she and Brad made the date.

"That'll be a hundred dollars, thank you," Sabrina said, and touched her hand. Annie looked outraged.

"For what?"

"We made a bet in July. I said you'd have a date within six months. You said you wouldn't. We bet a hundred bucks. That was exactly five months and one week ago. Pay up."

"Wait a minute. This is *not* a date. This is coffee with the head of my school. That is not a date."

"Bullshit, it's not," Sabrina insisted. "The details were never specified. Nobody ever said it had to be black tie, or for dinner. Coffee is a date."

"It is *not!*" Annie said firmly. But Candy and Tammy sided with Sabrina and told Annie she had to pay up. Much to everyone's relief, Candy was in relatively good shape. Her bruises were healing, and she was in fairly decent spirits, considering what had happened. And they were all looking forward to Christmas. Mostly it was a relief to know that Marcello was gone and she wouldn't run into him anywhere. Marlene was also delighted. He was a danger to any woman he encountered. But Brad Parker was an entirely different story. And they were all thrilled for Annie.

He offered to pick Annie up, but she said she'd meet him at the restaurant. And he was right, the desserts were fantastic. She had something called a frozen mochaccino, which was chocolate ice cream, ice, and coffee all blended together, with whipped cream and chocolate shavings on top. He had an apricot smush, which was a fabulous confection, and they shared a piece of pecan pie.

"You may have to roll me out the door," she said, as she sat back in her chair, feeling like she might explode. He described the restaurant to her, and it sounded cute and Victorian, with Tiffany lamps, old ice cream tables, and amusing things to sell. He said he had come here since he was a child with his mother. Annie had heard of it before but never been there.

They talked about Italy and art, her time in Florence, his in Rome. He still spoke some Italian, and she said hers was getting rusty. They talked briefly about the school, and his hopes for it as it grew. He was hoping to open other schools like it in other cities. She reluctantly admitted that so far it had been very helpful.

"I've learned how to make chicken," she said, laughing, "and cupcakes."

"I hope we teach you more than that. Why don't you take the sculpture class? Everybody seems to love it. I've thought of taking it myself, but I'm not very artistic."

"I don't think I am anymore either," she said sadly.

"I doubt that. The brain has a way of rerouting itself when it has to. You might enjoy the class. And if you don't like it, you can drop it. I give you permission." They both laughed at that.

They had a very nice time together, and he walked her home up Third Avenue, as they talked about a multitude of subjects. It was a reasonable walk to the house she shared with her sisters, and she felt rude suddenly saying goodbye to him outside. She asked him if he'd like to come in for a minute. She knew Candy and Mrs. Shibata would be there. He said just for a minute, he still had Christmas shopping to do that afternoon. Annie had been stumped about how to do that this year, and was planning to ask her sisters to help.

He walked into the house, as Mrs. Shibata was vacuuming loudly, and Candy had her music on so loud, you could hardly hear. It was Prince. All three dogs were barking, the phone was ringing, and Juanita attacked him and tried to bite his ankle the moment he walked in the front door. With that, Mrs. Shibata turned off the vacuum cleaner and bowed low, just as Candy appeared at the top of the stairs, wearing a Christmas hat with bells on it and a bikini she had bought while Christmas shopping.

"Hi!" she shouted from the top of the stairs, and ran to put a robe on, so he didn't see the bruises, which were faint now.

"That's my sister Candy," Annie explained. "Does she have clothes on?" You never knew with Candy, even now.

"Actually, she was wearing a bikini and a Christmas hat."

"That's pretty dressed for her. She usually wears a lot less. Sorry about the dogs."

"It's fine. I like dogs."

"I don't. But you get used to them after a while. Things are pretty crazy around here most of the time. Especially when all four of us are home."

"Do you always live together?" He was fascinated. The atmosphere he felt the moment he walked into the house was inviting and warm. You could tell that people lived here who loved each other, and he was entirely right. It made you want to stay forever. He said as much to Annie, and she was touched.

"Actually, they did this for me this year. They rented this house so they could help me get organized, because of the accident. We only have the house for a year. Tammy quit a fantastic job in L.A. to do it.

She works on a terrible reality show here now. People try to shoot each other on it at least once a week. It's called *Can This Relationship Be Saved? It's Up to You!*"

"Oh my God, I've seen it." He laughed out loud. "It's awful."

"Yes, it is," Annie said proudly. "My sister Tammy is the producer of the show." She mentioned Tammy's previous show, and he was enormously impressed, particularly that she had given it up to come to New York for Annie. "My sister Sabrina was in New York anyway. She's an attorney. She has a boyfriend, Chris, who stays here some of the time. He's an attorney too. I was living in Florence before the accident, and I may go back, I haven't figured it out. I still have an apartment there. I keep meaning to give it up, but no one has had time to pack it up, and it's so cheap it doesn't really matter. And my sister Candy is all over the place. She's a model."

"Candy? *The* Candy? On the cover of *Vogue* practically every month?" He looked stunned. She had quite a family of overachievers, with a flock of unruly dogs.

"That's who you just saw in the Christmas hat and the bikini. She's taking a few weeks off." Annie didn't mention why. It was none of his business, and not something any of them ever planned to talk about. They didn't need to. Chris and Marlene were the only people outside the family who knew about it. They hadn't even told their father. It would have been too much for him to deal with right now.

"What a group!" Brad said admiringly. "This must be terrific." For a moment he forgot the tragic circumstances that had brought them together. There was nothing tragic about them.

"It is terrific actually," Annie said, smiling happily. "I was a little nervous about it at first, but it's been working out great."

"What's terrific?" Candy asked as she joined them.

"Living together," Annie explained. "Do you have your clothes on?"

"Yes," Candy laughed, "I'm wearing a robe and my Christmas hat. I thought we should go and get our tree tonight." Despite what had happened to her, she was in the Christmas spirit. She felt enormously blessed to have survived.

Brad couldn't stop himself from staring at Candy. He had never seen a woman so beautiful in all his life. And she was completely relaxed and in no way stuck-up. She was just like any other girl her age, only a hundred times more beautiful. Except that in her own way, he thought Annie was just as beautiful. She was smaller and had softer looks, but he loved her auburn hair and the pixie cut she wore.

"I got my tree last night," he said, as Candy invited him downstairs for a cup of tea. He hesitated, but it was hard to resist spending a few more minutes with them. He followed Candy downstairs to the kitchen, with Annie right behind him, and all three of them were bowled over by the smell.

"Oh my God," Candy said, as Annie translated for Brad.

"Mrs. Shibata eats these awful Japanese pickles. They smell like something died." He laughed openly at the craziness that went on in their house. Mrs. Shibata bowed low as they entered the kitchen and put the pickle jar away. She had just put some seaweed in the dogs' bowls, and Candy grabbed it immediately and explained to Brad that the seaweed the housekeeper gave them made the dogs sick.

"I thought you said you didn't like dogs," he said, turning to Annie.

"I don't. They're not mine. They belong to everyone else."

"Zoe's mine," Candy said as she picked up the Yorkie, as Beulah looked highly insulted, turned away, and sat down. He bent down to play with her, and Juanita tried to attack him again, but in the end, she gave up and licked his hand.

"You should get one too," he said to Annie. He had suggested a seeing-eye dog to her earlier, and she was unenthused. She had finally admitted to him that having a seeing-eye dog with her identified her immediately as a blind person wherever she went. She could put the white stick away in a public place or a restaurant once she sat down. It was a vanity she wasn't ready to give up.

Brad left a little while later, enchanted with his visit. He had enjoyed meeting Candy, loved talking to Annie, and couldn't wait to meet the others. He called her the next day and invited her to dinner three days later, before she left for Connecticut for Christmas with her father. Annie hesitated for a second, and then accepted. It was a little scary dating someone you couldn't see. But she liked him, and they shared a wealth of common opinions and ideas.

Sabrina got home just after Brad called Annie and invited her to dinner, and Annie marched up to where she was sitting, unwinding from her day. Annie dropped five twenty-dollar bills in her lap without comment, and Sabrina looked up at her in surprise.

"What, did you win the lottery today? What's this for?"

"Never mind," Annie growled at her, pretending to be annoyed, when in fact she was very pleased and excited about the dinner date with Brad. She was only twenty-six after all, and it was fun to have a date with someone who sounded as nice as he did. She had just paid off Sabrina's bet. And as she realized what it was, Sabrina scooped it up victoriously and laughed.

"I told you so!" she shouted as Annie slammed her bedroom door.

Chapter 23

All three of Annie's sisters helped her dress for her dinner date
with Brad. She tried on four different outfits, and each of them had
a different opinion about what she should wear for a first date. High
heels, low heels, something simple, a little more dressed up, a sexy
sweater, a light color, a flower in her hair, earrings, no earrings. In
the end, Candy picked out a soft pale blue cashmere sweater for her,
a good-looking gray skirt, suede low-heeled boots so she didn't fall
on high heels walking into the restaurant, and pearl earrings that
had been her mother's. She looked beautiful and young and unclut-
tered, and not as though she was trying too hard to impress him or
seduce him. They all decided it was a good look, just as the doorbell
rang. He found himself instantly surrounded by the entire group of
sisters, and all three dogs.

"This is quite a welcoming committee," he said, as Annie introduced him to Tammy and Sabrina for the first time. And two minutes later, Chris arrived.

"Now you know everyone," Annie said happily. They left five minutes later, for a small Italian restaurant nearby. It was so close, they

walked and didn't need a cab. Candy had loaned her her short gray mink jacket, so Annie was warm, and felt very fancy for her first real date in months. It was a far cry from her arty days in Florence with Charlie. This felt very grown up. And at dinner, he told her he was thirty-nine.

"You don't look it," she said, and they both laughed. "Or maybe I should say you don't sound it."

"You don't look your age either." She could hear the smile in his voice. "At first, I thought you were younger." He sounded embarrassed then. "I checked your records."

"Aha!" she chortled. "Insider information. That's not fair. You know a lot more about me than I know about you."

"What do you want to know?"

"Everything. Where you went to school, what you studied, where you grew up, who you hated in third grade, who you married, why you divorced." He looked surprised then.

"You have insider information too. How did you know that?"

"Someone told me at school," she admitted. But she was curious about him. Since she couldn't see him, she wanted to hear all the details. And she would have wanted to know them anyway. It was just that now she couldn't see the expressions on his face, of sadness, guilt, or regret. Those things were important. So she had to rely on what she heard, and how he said it.

"I was married for three years, to my college sweetheart. She's a wonderful girl. She's married to someone else now and has three kids. We're good friends. We wanted very different things out of life. She wanted a career in television, like your sister. I wanted a family and kids. I had lost my parents young, and wanted a family of my own. She didn't. It seems funny now that she has kids. But she's had all three of them in the last four years. We were divorced a long time ago. We were divorced by the time I was twenty-five, fourteen years ago. At the time, we were pretty angry at each other. She felt pressured. I felt cheated. We grew up in Chicago, but she wanted to live in L.A., I wanted to live in New York. I wanted to start the school. She hated the idea. It was a very stressful three years and terrible for both of us."

"So how come you never got married again?"

"Scared, burned, busy. Starting the school was a huge amount of work. I lived with someone for four years. She was a great woman, but she was French and wanted to go back to France. She missed her family too much. I had already started the school and didn't want to move away. I guess I've been married to the school for sixteen years. It's been my baby and my wife. Time flies when you're having fun, and I am." She could understand that to some extent. Both her older sisters felt that way about their work, and she had about her art. It hadn't precluded romance in her life, but it had in Tammy's case and even in Sabrina's, to some extent. They were both workaholics, and maybe he was too. You paid a high price for that, and sometimes wound up alone.

"What about you, Annie? No man in your life now?" She laughed dryly. She hadn't had a date since Charlie in Florence and thought she never would again.

"I had a boyfriend in Florence before the accident. He dumped me for someone else, before he found out I was blind." She always took comfort in that. "I thought it was serious, but I guess it wasn't. Or not as serious as I thought. And before that, I only had one real boyfriend, after college. I was always too passionate about my work as an artist to put a lot of energy into other stuff. It's been a huge change not having my art. Now I have no idea what I'm going to do when I grow up." She looked desolate for a minute and then shrugged and looked in his direction although she couldn't see him. But he could see how beautiful she was, and she touched his heart with her openness and sincerity. There was no artifice about her.

"You'll find something," he said gently. She was industrious, hard-working, passionate, and smart. There was no way she wasn't going to find the right path sooner or later. He wasn't worried about her at all.

They ordered dinner and kept on chatting. They sat at the table until the restaurant closed and then he walked her home. She didn't invite him in this time, because it was late, and she didn't feel ready to do that. And her sisters were probably in their pajamas and relaxing. She thanked him for dinner, and let herself into the house. She turned as she was about to step inside, smiled at him, and wished him a Merry Christmas, wishing she could see his face. Her sisters had all told her he was handsome. He was tall and blond with broad shoulders, and they thought that they made a cute couple.

"Merry Christmas to you too, Annie," Brad said softly. "I had a great time."

"So did I," she said, and closed the door behind her. Everyone was asleep by then, and she tiptoed to her room, looking happy. It had been a very nice first date, and worth every penny she'd paid Sabrina for their bet.

The last day on the show before the Christmas hiatus was predictably insane. Guests were hysterical, frantic about the holidays, and meaner than usual to their mates. One couple started slugging it out, and they had to cut to commercial. And for the first time ever, their psychologist, Désirée, got hit in the face and had hysterics. She took a Xanax and called her lawyer, she threatened to sue them, and said it

was going to cost them. The entire staff had hangovers and headaches from their Christmas party the night before.

"Life in the fast lane," Tammy said to someone as she ran to get an
ice pack for Désirée to try and calm her down. The fighting couple
had actually made up on the show, which Tammy told Désirée was a
major victory for her.

It was all the usual craziness and then some, and on top of everything else, two of the network executives were on the set to see the
show. They wanted to see what all the fuss was about. Since Tammy
had been there, sponsors were lining up around the block, and the
ratings were sky high. She was carrying the ice pack for Désirée when
she was introduced to the executives, and one of them asked her if
she took self-defense classes to work on the show.

"No, just Red Cross first-aid training," she said, as she held the ice
pack. "We administer electroshock therapy if they get too out of
hand." He laughed, and he was still hanging around after Tammy
came back from Désirée's dressing room. She had finally calmed
down.

"Is there some reason why you want to work in a psych ward?" he
asked. He had thought the show was hilarious though in incredibly
bad taste. There was a certain humanity and poignancy to it, but on
the whole, even Tammy knew it was bad.

"It's a long story. I had to come to New York for a year. So I gave
up my job in L.A." It was more than a job. He knew the show she'd
been on, and couldn't believe she'd given it up. Neither could anyone else.

"For a guy, I assume," he said knowingly, but she shook her head,
with a smile.

"No, for my sister. She had a bad accident and my other sisters and I decided to take care of her for a year. We moved in together, and it's been great. And I took this job. So here I am, Nurse Ratched in a psych ward, handing out ice packs and Valium." He was intrigued by her. She was an amazing woman. He was a few years older than she was and had just moved from Philadelphia. She liked him too, and thought he looked relatively normal, which only meant he was a freak in disguise, if she thought he was cute.

"Look, uh . . . I'm going to St. Bart's with my family for Christmas. I'd love to see you when I get back, after New Year's. It would be fun to see you then."

"Not to worry," she said, smiling at him. "I haven't had a date on New Year's Eve since kindergarten. And I cry when I hear 'Auld Lang Syne.' Have a great time in St. Bart's."

"I'll call you when I get back," he promised, which she knew was polite for "I hope to never lay eyes on you again and I'm going to flush your cell phone number down the toilet, or feed it to my cat." She had absolutely no expectation of ever hearing from him again. He was too cute and looked too normal. He didn't look like a vegan or like he'd ever had a high colonic.

"Thanks for visiting the show," she said politely, ran off to attend to the usual crises, and promptly forgot him. He said his name was John Sperry and she was absolutely certain she would never hear from him again.

The sisters all left for Connecticut together the next day. Chris came with them, and they all went to midnight mass together with their father. It was a solemn moment thinking about their mother, after going to mass with her in that same church every year. Tammy looked over and saw that her father was crying. She slipped her hand into the crook of his arm and hugged him. And at the sign of peace, they all hugged each other. It was a tender moment full of memories and love, and in its own way filled with hope. They were still together and had each other, whatever happened.

The weather was cold in Connecticut, and it snowed several times over the weekend. The girls and Chris got into snowball fights, and they built a snowman. Their father seemed more like himself at last. It was the perfect Christmas weekend for all of them. They gathered around the kitchen table on the last day, and ate an enormous lunch that they had all helped prepare.

Sabrina noticed that their dad was quiet and assumed it was because they were all leaving, and he would be alone again. She knew he hated being alone, and at the end of lunch, he cleared his throat uncomfortably, and said he had something to tell them. Tammy was afraid he was going to say that he was selling the house and moving into the city. She loved this house and didn't want him to sell it. She hoped that wasn't it.

"I don't know how to say this to you," he said unhappily. "You're all so good to me, and I love you so much. I don't mean to sound ungrateful." He was almost crying, and their hearts ached for him. "The last six months have been the most awful of my entire life, without your mother. There were times when I really thought I couldn't survive it. And then I realized that I could, that my life wasn't over because she died. And I owe it to all of you to go on." All of his daughters were touched and smiling as he said it.

"And I don't think your mother would want me to be alone and unhappy. I wouldn't have wanted that for her either. People our age aren't meant to be alone. You need companionship and someone to be there for you," he explained as they began to wonder what he was saying. He seemed to be veering off into some odd direction that was making less and less sense, and suddenly both Tammy and Sabrina began to wonder if he was getting senile. He was only fifty-nine, but maybe the shock of losing their mother had been too much for him. They were both frowning as he went on toward his conclusion. "I'm miserable alone, or I was. And I know this will be a shock for you, but I hope you understand that this is in no way a disrespect to your mother. I loved her deeply. But there have been changes in my life now, and Leslie Thompson and I are getting married." All four of his daughters nodded complacently as they listened to what he'd said, and then suddenly it hit them. Tammy heard it first.

"You're *what*??? Mom's been gone for six months, and you're getting married??? Are you *kidding*?" He was senile. He had to be, and then she realized who he said he was marrying, and it was even worse. "Leslie? The *slut*?" The word slipped out of her mouth, and he looked as outraged as she did.

"Don't ever speak of her that way again. She's going to be my wife now!" They were both standing at the table glaring at each other, as the others watched in horror, and Tammy sank back into her seat with her head in her hands.

"Oh, please God, please tell me this isn't happening. I'm dreaming this. I'm having a nightmare." She looked straight at her father with anguished eyes. "You're not really marrying Leslie Thompson, are you, Dad? You're just kidding?" She was pleading with him, and he looked devastated.

"Yes, I am marrying her. And I was hoping that all of you could at least try to be supportive. You don't know what it's like to lose the woman you've loved for thirty-five years."

"So you run out and find a replacement in six months? Dad, how could you? How can you do that to yourself, and to us?"

"You're not here. You have your own lives. And I need mine. Leslie and I love each other."

"I'm going to throw up," Candy announced to the table in general. She got up and disappeared, as Sabrina stared at their father.

"Don't you think this is a little hasty, Dad? You know how they tell people who've had a major loss not to make any big decisions for a year. Maybe you're rushing this a little." He was clearly out of his mind with grief, or experiencing some form of insanity. And Leslie Thompson? Oh no . . . anyone but her . . . Sabrina wanted to cry. They all did. And so did their father. He looked bitterly disappointed in them. He had been dreaming if he thought they were going to celebrate his marriage to another woman and be happy for him. "When did you have in mind?" Sabrina tried to sound calm, and didn't feel it, as Chris quietly left the table and went outside. He had a strong sense that he didn't belong there, and he was right. This was strictly family business.

"We're getting married on Valentine's Day. In seven weeks."

"How perfect," Tammy said, with her head still in her hands. "And how old is she, Dad?"

"She just turned thirty-three last week. I know it's a considerable age difference, but it doesn't matter to either of us. We're kindred spirits, and I know your mother would approve."

Tammy sat up in her seat then and took off the gloves. She was furious with their father.

"My mother would drop dead from a heart attack if she weren't dead already. Are you crazy? She would *never* have done this to you! Never! How can you do this to her, to us, and to her memory? It's absolutely disgusting."

"I'm sorry you feel that way," he said with an icy stare. He was twenty-six years older than the woman he was planning to marry seven months after his wife's death, and he expected his children to be happy for him. That was not going to happen, not in a hundred million years. Tammy stood up with a look of outrage, and so did Sabrina as Candy walked back into the room. They could all see that she'd been crying, after she threw up.

"Daddy, how could you?" she said miserably, throwing her arms around his neck. "She's younger than Sabrina."

"Age isn't important when you love someone," he said as his children wondered how he could make such a fool of himself. They had no idea if Leslie loved him or not, but they really didn't care. They wanted her to disappear. Candy took a step back and looked at her father with utter despair.

"Dad, why don't you put this off for a while?" Sabrina tried to reason with him, and talk him down off the ledge. "How about waiting a year?"

Tammy looked panicked then and thought of something else. "Oh my God, is she pregnant?"

"Of course not." Their father looked highly insulted, as Annie finally came to life. She'd been listening to all of them. She could hear the fury in Tammy's voice, the fear in Sabrina's, the heartbreak in Candy's, and the disappointment in their dad's.

"I don't know if you care what I think," Annie said, looking in her father's direction. "I doubt you do. But I think this is probably the single dumbest thing you've ever done, not for us, but for you. It's a lousy thing to do to Mom, Dad. And we'll get used to it if we have to. But to rush off and marry someone seven months after Mom died, just makes you look like a fool. Why is Leslie in such a hurry? Doesn't she realize that it's the surest way to make us hate her? Why can't the two of you at least wait a year, out of respect for Mom? Your getting married that fast is like a giant 'fuck you' to all of us, and to our mother." She stood up too then and said what she really thought. "I'm really disappointed in you. I always thought that you were better than that. You were when you were married to Mom. I guess Leslie doesn't give a damn how we feel, or how you look. It says a lot about her, and about you." Annie picked up her white stick then and left the room. She found Chris in the living room, sitting quietly. It had been a hell of a way to end Christmas.

Sabrina cleared the table and put the dishes in the dishwasher, and as soon as she finished, they said goodbye to their father. Without commenting further on his announcement, they left his house and drove home to New York.

The explosions in the car were extreme all the way home. Tammy swore she'd never see him again. Sabrina was afraid he had Alzheimer's and Leslie was taking full advantage of him. Candy said she was losing her father to a slut and cried all the way to the city. And Annie quietly said he was the biggest fool that ever lived, and there was no way on earth that anyone would ever convince her to go to the wedding. He hadn't asked them, as Sabrina pointed out. They didn't even know where the wedding was going to be. All they knew was that they hated her, and were furious with their father. And as they drove home from Connecticut, Chris very wisely said not a single word.

Chapter 24

None of them spoke to their father for the rest of the week. All of them were off work, so they had plenty of time to talk about it. No matter how they turned it around in their minds, they were outraged on their mother's behalf, hated Leslie's guts, and were furious with their father. And they got more so every day.

None of them had exciting New Year's plans, and they had decided to spend it quietly at the house. Sabrina and Chris hated going out on New Year's Eve, and Tammy didn't have a date. Candy said she had a friend coming in from L.A., and they were going to hang out at the house, and two days after Christmas Brad called Annie and asked her out for New Year's Eve, and she invited him over to the house instead. It seemed like a nice way to spend the evening, instead of going out.

On New Year's Eve, Chris and the girls cooked dinner. Brad brought several bottles of champagne. He and Chris had a good time talking before, during, and after dinner, and the biggest surprise of the evening was Candy's friend from L.A. He was probably the most famous young actor on the planet at the time, and it turned out that they had met three years before on a shoot and become good friends. He always hung out with her when he came in from L.A. There was nothing romantic between them, and he was great company. He had them laughing hysterically through most of the evening, and Brad couldn't believe the sort of people who dropped in at their house. Annie insisted she hadn't even known her sister knew him.

"Yeah, right. Who else is coming by? Brad Pitt and Angelina Jolie?"

"Don't be silly," she laughed at him. "I swear, most of the time, it's just us and the dogs, and Chris."

"Okay, let's see, your sister is the biggest supermodel in the country, or maybe the world. Your other sister was one of the hottest producers in L.A., and is now the producer of the worst show in New York, we just had dinner with an actor who makes women swoon from fourteen to ninety, and I'm supposed to believe you guys are just regular people? How do you expect me to believe that?"

"Well, maybe they're not. But I am. Until six months ago, I was just a starving artist in Florence. Now I'm not even that."

"Yes, you are," he said gently. "You'll find other outlets for your art. That just doesn't go away. Give it a little time to surface again in a different way." He sounded confident it would.

"Maybe," she said, but didn't believe him. And at midnight they all toasted each other and hugged. Brad stayed and talked with them until three o'clock in the morning. Candy's actor friend spent the night on their couch, after drinking too much champagne. And Chris and Sabrina slipped away early. He asked her to come upstairs with him shortly after midnight, and the others never saw them again.

When Chris closed the door to Sabrina's bedroom, he kissed her. Privacy was hard-won in their house. He had brought with him two glasses and a bottle of champagne he'd bought himself. Sabrina smiled at him. It had been a hell of a year. So many things had happened, and whatever tragedies befell them, Chris was always there. This latest outrage with their father was just one more bump in the road. She knew she could count on Chris to be there for her, no matter what.

And as he kissed her, he took a small box out of his pocket, held her close to him, opened it with one hand, and slipped a ring on her finger. She didn't know what he was doing at first, and then she realized and looked down to see it. It was an absolutely beautiful engagement ring he had picked out on his own, and slipped out of a Tiffany box. He had been planning this for months.

"Oh my God, Chris, what are you doing?" She looked stunned.

He got down on one knee before he answered, and gazed at her solemnly from the floor. "I'm asking you to marry me, Sabrina. I love you more than anything in life. Will you marry me?" As he asked her, her eyes filled with tears. This was not what she had in mind. It was just one more shock. And she had had far too many in far too short a time. From their mother's death to Annie's blindness, the assault on Candy, and now her father marrying a girl half his age whom they had always thought of as a slut—it was just too much. She wasn't prepared to marry him. She wasn't ready. She just wanted to get through this year of taking care of Annie and living with her sisters. And maybe after that she and Chris could go back to their old life, but not get married. She didn't feel ready for that yet, and maybe never would. She loved him but felt no need to marry him. What they had now was enough for her.

She took off the ring and handed it to him with tears running down her cheeks and sorrow in her heart. "Chris, I can't. I can't even think straight right now. So much has happened in the last year. Why do we have to get married?"

"Because I'm thirty-seven, you're thirty-five, I want to have babies with you, we've been together for almost four years, and we can't wait for the rest of our lives to grow up."

"Maybe I can," she said sadly. "I love you, but I don't know what I want. I loved what we had before, each of us living in our own space, being together whenever we wanted. I know it's been a little crazy living with my sisters, and I love you. But I just don't feel ready to make that kind of commitment for the rest of my life. What if we screw it up? I see people in my office every day, just like us, who thought they were doing the right thing, got married, had kids, and then everything went wrong."

"That's the kind of chance we all take," he said, looking anguished. "There are never any guarantees in life. You know that. You just have to take a deep breath, jump into the pool, and do your best."

"What if we drown?" she said miserably.

"What if we don't? But one thing I do know. I don't want to go on like this. Life is starting to pass us by. If we wait long enough, we'll be too old to have kids, or you will. And we'll never have a real life. I want that with you now." His eyes were pleading with her, and his heart sank as she shook her head.

"I don't. I can't." She looked panicked. "I won't. I'd be lying to you if I said I was sure."

"You don't have to be sure," he tried to reason with her. "We just have to love each other, Sabrina. That's enough."

"Not for me."

"What the hell do you want?" he said, starting to get angry.

"I want a guarantee that it's right."

"There are none."

"That's my point. I'm too scared to take the chance." He was still holding the ring, and then he slipped it back into the box and snapped it shut again.

"I love you. But I'm not sure I'm ever going to want to get married," Sabrina admitted to him. She couldn't lie to him. She just didn't know, and she didn't feel ready to be engaged, no matter how much she loved him.

"I guess that's my answer," he said, but he wasn't sorry that he'd asked her. Sooner or later he had to know. He turned as he stood in the doorway. "You know, I think your father is a fool to do what he's doing, especially so soon after your mother died, and with a woman younger than you. But however stupid it may seem to us, at least you've got to respect the guy for having the balls to take a chance."

Sabrina nodded. She hadn't thought of it that way, and she was furious at him. But Chris had a point. Her father still had enough life in him to take a chance. "I guess the bottom line is, I don't have the balls."

"No, you don't," he said, then walked out of her bedroom, closed the door, walked down the stairs, and out the front door. Instead of getting engaged, as he had hoped they would, they had broken up. It was not the New Year's Eve he had wanted or planned. He had dreamed of this moment for so long, and her reaction to it had pushed him right over the edge. And in her room, Sabrina sat on her bed and sobbed.

The others didn't hear about it until the next morning, and when Sabrina told them, they were shocked.

"I thought you two were upstairs all night, like lovebirds," Tammy said with a look of amazement.

"No, he was gone before one o'clock. I gave him the ring back and he left." She looked heartbroken as she sat at the kitchen table with her sisters, but she knew she had done the right thing. She didn't want to get married, even to Chris. For her, what they had now was enough. More would be too much.

They were all depressed about it when they heard what had happened, but no one as much as Sabrina. She really did love him, but she just didn't want to get married, and those things couldn't be forced, even with a lovely ring, and a great guy.

Between her breaking up with Chris, and their fury over their father getting married, January was a gloomy month on East Eighty-fourth Street. Chris never called her again, and Sabrina didn't call him. There was no point. She had nothing new to say. And he was still too upset to call her. He was devastated by her refusing his proposal. And he didn't want to resume the same relationship they'd had for years. He wanted more. She didn't. And suddenly there was nothing left to say, nowhere to go, but gone.

All of them were in the doldrums for the first few weeks of January, and then slowly things began to pick up. Annie had dinner with Brad several times. They always had a nice time. He had talked her into taking the sculpture class, and she was actually enjoying it. And even without being able to see what she was doing, her work was surprisingly good. He told her about a lecture series he was trying to organize, centered on cultural things, theater, music, and art. He asked her if she'd consider giving a lecture on the Uffizi, and she was excited about it. She typed the entire lecture out in braille. She gave her first talk at the end of January, and it was a big success.

Candy left for Paris in the third week of January, to do the couture shows. She was going to be Karl Lagerfeld's bride for Chanel. They paid her an enormous fee to be exclusive only to them, and she had a ball staying at the Ritz. And on the plane coming back from Paris, she met a man. He was working as a photographer's assistant, as part of a graduate program he was in at Brown. He was twenty-four years old, and they laughed all the way from Paris to New York. His name was Paul Smith. He was getting his master's in photography in June. He was planning to open his own photography studio after that. He said he had worked on a shoot with her in Rome two years before, but he had been a lowly intern then, and they had never met.

She told him about Annie, and losing her mother in July, and then she told him that her father was getting married in two weeks, to a girl who was thirty-three years old.

"Wow, that's heavy," he said, looking sympathetic. His parents had gotten divorced when he was ten, and both of them were remarried. But he said his stepparents were cool. "How do you feel about that?" he asked about her father's remarriage.

"Actually, like shit," she said honestly.

"Have you met her?" he asked with interest.

"Not really, not since I was a kid. My sisters always called her 'the slut.' She tried to steal my sister's boyfriend when she was fifteen."

"Maybe you should give her a chance," he said cautiously.

"Maybe. It just seems way too soon for him to get married."

"People do stupid things when they're in love," he said sensibly, and then they got off the subject onto other things. He was from Maine and loved to sail, and told her about his racing adventures.

They shared a cab into the city, and when he dropped her off at her house, he told her he'd give her a call the next time he was in town. He was going back to Brown the next day, which was in Rhode Island. He was going to be there until graduation in June. It was nice for Candy to be with someone her own age for a change, engaged in wholesome pursuits, going to college, and doing things appropriate for their age.

When Candy walked back into the house, everyone was out.

Sabrina was working even longer hours now that she was no longer seeing Chris. Tammy was going crazy with her show, as always. And Annie seemed to be taking more classes than ever at school, and seeing a lot of Brad on weekends. It was a relief when Paul invited Candy to visit him at Brown two weeks later. He was having a show of his photographic work. It was a great weekend for both of them, and she loved meeting his friends. They were startled when they realized who she was, but for once everyone treated her like just another kid. It was more fun than she had had in years, better than the party scene in New York.

Tammy was having meetings with the network again when she ran into the man she'd met right before the holidays, the one who was going to St. Bart's with his family, and never called her when he got back. She hadn't thought he would, so she hadn't been disappointed. He introduced himself to her again after the network meetings. He said his name was John Sperry, and said he was sorry he hadn't called her.

"I've been out with the flu for two weeks," he said when he saw her. It was a lame excuse, but as good as any other. Tammy looked at him and smiled. If he'd been a freak, he would have called. "You think I'm lying, don't you? I swear, I've been sick as a dog. I nearly had pneumonia."

She almost laughed at him. She'd heard it all before. "I lost your number. That always works for me too." Although he could have called her at the show.

"I didn't have your number," he reminded her, looking embarrassed. "But come to think of it, why don't you give it to me now?" She felt silly giving it to him. She didn't have time to go out with him anyway. They were having a million problems on the show. Their host's contract was up and he wanted double the money. He'd been shot once and assaulted twice. He felt he deserved combat pay for being on the show, and he wasn't wrong. The trouble was the audience loved him, which gave him a choke hold on them now. She had been discussing the problem with Irving Solomon and the network people all morning. Tammy was tempted to let him go, but she was afraid their ratings would show it, and the sponsors wouldn't like it.

She went back to her office and forgot about John Sperry again. Something crossed her desk about a special Valentine's show, and when she saw it, she thought of her father. He was getting married on Valentine's Day, and none of them had spoken to him since the day after Christmas when he told them. She wasn't sure what to do. They couldn't ignore him forever, but she wasn't ready to deal with Leslie and his marriage yet either. None of them were.

She brought it up that night at dinner at the house. She threw the question out to her sisters. "What are we going to do about Dad?" He hadn't called them either. He was obviously hurt by their reaction, and they were horrified by what he was doing. They all felt he was betraying their mother. It had been five weeks since any of them had spoken to him, which had never happened before.

"Maybe one of us should call him," Sabrina suggested, but no one volunteered.

"I don't want to go to the wedding," Candy said quickly.

"None of us do," Tammy said with a sigh. "How could we? It would be such a disrespect to Mom."

"But he is our dad," Candy said hesitantly.

"Why don't we take him to lunch and talk, or invite him here?" Annie said softly. She had been thinking about it for weeks too. And the fact was they all missed him. They just didn't want Leslie in their lives, at least not yet, and maybe never, depending on how she behaved. None of them were ready to include her in their family. It was a terrible dilemma, but they didn't want to lose their father either.

"Do you realize they might have a baby?" Sabrina mentioned, and Tammy groaned audibly.

"Please. You're making me sick," Tammy said miserably.

In the end, after hours of discussion, they decided to invite him to the house for a drink. It was less stressful than sitting through a meal in a restaurant, with strangers all around them. As the oldest, they appointed Sabrina to call him. She was hesitant and nervous when she called the house in Connecticut. What if Leslie answered?

He answered on the second ring, and he sounded so thrilled to hear her, that she felt sorry for him. He obviously didn't want to lose them either. And he agreed to come to the city the next day. He never mentioned Leslie once. For a brief moment, Sabrina hoped he had changed his mind. But she knew that if he had, he would have called.

They all came home early from work to meet with him. And they noticed that he looked nervous when he arrived. They walked into the living room as a group and sat down.

"We assume you're still getting married on Valentine's Day," Tammy began, with hope in her eyes that was quickly dashed.

"Yes, I am. We're actually flying to Las Vegas to do it, which sounds a little silly. But I knew none of you would want to be there, and it's too soon to make a big fuss."

"It's too soon to be getting married," Tammy said, and her father looked her in the eye.

"You're not going to talk me out of it, if that's what you asked me here for. I know it seems early to you, but at my age, you don't have a lot of time. There's no reason for us to wait."

"You could have waited for us," Sabrina pointed out to him, "and for Mom."

"Would six months make that much difference to you?" he asked them. "Would you really be happier about Leslie then? I don't think you would. And this is our life, not yours. I don't interfere with what you do. I don't tell Sabrina that she should be married, that Chris is a great guy, and she should be doing something about it, if she wants kids. I don't tell Tammy that she should stop working on all these crazy shows and find a decent guy. Or Candy that she needs to go back to school. Or Annie that she needs to find a job even if she's blind. Your mother and I always respected you. We didn't always agree with what you did, but we gave you room to make your own mistakes and decisions. Now you need to give me the space to make mine. Maybe what I'm doing really is insane. Maybe Leslie will walk out on me in six months and find a younger guy, or maybe we'll be happy for the rest of our lives, and she'll treat me well in my old age. But I need to find out. This is what I want. It's not what you want, for yourselves or for me, but it's what I want to do, and what I think I need. She's a good woman and we love each other. And whatever I do, or don't do, no matter what, your mother isn't coming back. And she was the love of my life. But she's gone, and the truth is, I don't want to be alone. I can't. I'm too unhappy by myself. And Leslie is good company. We love each other, although differently than I loved your mother. But why shouldn't I have a second chance?" They listened to him without interrupting him, and some of what he said made sense. Collectively they took a breath, and without saying anything, Candy put her arms around him and hugged him. She was thinking about what Paul had said on the plane, about giving Leslie another chance. Time would tell. For her father's sake, she hoped Leslie was a decent woman, whether they liked her or not. It was just too soon for them.

"We love you, Dad," Tammy said. "We just don't want you to make a mistake, or get hurt."

"Why not? You do. We all do. Mistakes are part of life. If it's a big mistake, I'll call Sabrina and do something about it." He and his oldest daughter exchanged a smile.

"I hope it works out for you, Dad," she said softly. It was so nice to see him again. They had all missed him so much.

"So do I. All I can do is try. And I'm sorry you're all upset. I know this is hard for you. It's a big change for me too." And it was so much too soon for them.

"Do we have to see her, Dad?" Annie was the one who asked. None of them wanted to see her, but they assumed that he'd expect them to. He was more reasonable than they thought. He was still the father that they all loved so much.

"Let's go easy for a while," he said sensibly. "Let's get us back on track first. I thought I was never going to hear from any of you again." He had been sick over it for a month.

"We missed you a lot," Candy said.

"I missed you too," he admitted, as Sabrina opened a bottle of wine. They each had a drink with him, they all hugged each other and promised to get together again soon. And a short while later, he left. The meeting had gone better than any of them had hoped. He was marrying her, but at least he and his children were talking again, and he wasn't expecting them to embrace her with open arms, or even see her for a while. He was hoping they'd get used to the idea in time. And he had told them that there would be no Fourth of July party this year. It would be too hard for all of them, and now it was the anniversary of their mother's death, not just a party. He said that he and Leslie were going to Europe in July, and they were free to make other plans. It was a relief for all of them. None of them could have faced that party ever again, and even less with Leslie around.

"What are we going to do for the Fourth of July?" Candy asked.

"Let's not worry about that now," Sabrina said wisely. At least they were speaking to their father again. And they collectively agreed to send them flowers and champagne in Las Vegas on Valentine's Day. It was a gesture of truce that they knew would please him. There was no question though, it was more than odd to realize that they would now have a stepmother younger than their oldest sister. This was not what any of them expected when their mother died. But then again, neither had their father. Leslie had just dropped by, and love had happened.

They were still talking about it when Tammy's cell phone rang. She couldn't imagine who it was at that hour. It was John Sperry asking her to lunch the next day. She was stunned to hear him.

"I can't believe you called me," she said, sounding amazed.

"I told you I would. Why do you seem so surprised?" She wanted to answer, "Because normal guys never call me. I'm a magnet for freaks and weirdos." Maybe he was, and only appeared to be normal. Who could tell anymore? She wasn't sure she'd know a regular guy if he bit her on the nose.

"I don't know why I'm surprised. I guess because most people don't do what they say. How was St. Bart's, by the way?"

"Fun. I go there with my family every Christmas. I have three brothers, and they all bring their wives and kids."

"I have three sisters," she said, smiling. The picture he painted of his family was appealing, and similar to hers, except that none of her sisters were married and had kids.

"I know. You said you quit your job to come here and take care of your sister. I was impressed by that." Very impressed, in fact. "What happened to her?" Tammy had walked out of the living room with her cell phone to talk to him.

"It's a long story, but she's doing really well." As she said it, she suddenly realized they were halfway through their lease, and she felt sad. She loved living with them. Maybe when their current lease expired, they'd find another house. None of them seemed to be going anywhere. Maybe they would live together forever. Four spinsters in a house. The only one finding true love these days was their father. And Annie seemed to be doing well with Brad. And she liked the boy Candy had met on the plane. Her love life and Sabrina's were in the tank. Her own had been for years. She had a reality show instead.

"You said your sister had an accident. What happened?" He seemed to be interested. Maybe he was only curious, but talking to him was pleasant. He seemed like a nice guy. He was intelligent, good-looking, and had a relatively important job.

"She lost her sight. It was very dramatic for her. She's an artist, or was. She's doing special training at the Parker School for the Blind."

"How strange," John said, sounding pensive. "One of my brothers is deaf, and we all sign. He was born that way. It must be a huge adjustment for her to lose her sight."

"It is. She's been amazing. And very brave."

"Does she use a guide dog?" he asked with interest.

"No." Tammy smiled. "She hates dogs. We have three here, the rest of us all have one each, but they're little, or two of them are. My older sister has a basset named Beulah. She suffers from chronic depression." He laughed at the vision.

"Maybe she needs a shrink," he said, joking with her.

"We have several of those too."

"That reminds me. Now tell me the truth about Désirée Lafayette. Did she used to be a guy?" Tammy laughed out loud.

"I've always wondered that myself."

"She sounds like a stripper."

"She'd probably love that. She wants me to get her a wardrobe, designed specially for her by Oscar de la Renta. I haven't had the guts to ask him yet. Or the budget."

"I'm sure it could be arranged."

"I hope not."

They laughed about the show for a few minutes, and he repeated his invitation for lunch. He suggested a restaurant that she liked. It sounded appealing, and it was nice to get out of the office for a change. She didn't do it often, she was usually too busy putting out fires to stop and eat. They made a date for one o'clock the next day.

The others asked her who it was when she hung up and came back into the room.

"Someone from the network I keep running into at meetings. He invited me to lunch," she said noncommittally.

"That sounds like fun," Sabrina said with a sad smile. She hadn't gone out since she and Chris broke up a month before. All she did was work and come straight home. She didn't have the heart to do anything else. All she'd done was think about him since he left. She missed him horribly. And she hadn't heard a word from him. She kept thinking about the beautiful ring. And the proposal that had terrified her. She wasn't as brave as her dad. Or as foolish. She didn't see how his marriage to Leslie could ever work. But she wished him well. Even though she thought the way he had gone about it was a huge disrespect to their mom. But she loved him nonetheless, and she was relieved that they had talked. At least the lines of communication were open again. That was something at least. But like the others, she was worried about how his marriage to Leslie would impact them, and their relationship with their dad.

Tammy met John Sperry for lunch the next day. He was intelligent, interesting, and she liked him. He had a million projects in the works, lots of interests, played a lot of sports, loved the theater, was ambitious about his job. He was extremely close to his family, and thirty-four years old. It appeared to both of them by the end of lunch that they had a lot in common.

"So what do we do next?" he asked her as they left the restaurant. "Dinner or another lunch?" Then he had a different idea. "How about tennis at my club on Saturday morning?"

"I'm a lousy player," she warned. But it sounded like fun.

"So am I," he admitted. "But I enjoy it anyway. We can have lunch at the club afterward, or somewhere else, if you have time." He was starting slow, and she liked that too. She didn't like men who took her out to dinner once and tried to rush her into bed. And she would be perfectly content if they just wound up friends. She didn't have many friends in New York. All of her friends were in L.A., and she never had time to see them anyway.

She was in good spirits when she went back to the office and he called her the next day just to say hello. He sent her an interoffice memo with a joke in it, and she laughed out loud at her desk. He was a nice addition to her life. Not a bolt of lightning, which she didn't want. It was more like a quiet entrance of someone solid into the room. She felt his presence, but it didn't shake her up or unnerve her, which felt much more comfortable to her. And he wasn't on any unusual diets, and didn't belong to any cults. That in itself was a marvel.

She said very little about him to her sisters. Their contact didn't warrant it yet. She came home happy and relaxed on Saturday, tired after a game of tennis, which he had won easily. He played much better than he said, but she had held her own. And afterward they'd had lunch and gone for a walk in the park. It was still cold, but not too much to enjoy a walk. She ran into Brad and Annie on their way out as she got home. Brad was taking her to some sort of tactile conceptual art exhibit he had read about that he thought she'd enjoy, and they were chatting animatedly. He wanted her to do another lecture at the school. He thought she should do a museum series, or one about the art in each city in Italy she had visited. Her memory was excellent, and there was much she could share with her fellow students.

"Where've you been?" Annie asked her. She looked happy with Brad, and Tammy was pleased to see it. Candy was at Brown for the weekend again, visiting Paul. It was the second weekend in a row.

"I played tennis with a friend," Tammy said easily. "Is Sabrina home?"

"She's upstairs. I think she's getting sick. She sounds awful."

Tammy nodded. Sabrina had looked sick since New Year's Eve.

"Have a good time, you two. See you later."

"We won't be back till late. We're having dinner after the exhibit."

"Good. Have fun." Tammy was smiling to herself as she walked into the house. Annie looked so radiant with Brad, and they looked so comfortable together. Everything about it seemed right. She was happy Sabrina had won the bet.

She walked upstairs to check on Sabrina, and found her lying on her bed in the dark. She suspected she wasn't sick, but depressed.

Tammy hated to see things end with Chris. He was such a good man, and had been so good to Sabrina for so long. It was a shame she had such an aversion to marriage. If ever she had been inclined to get married, Chris would have been the right man. But apparently she just couldn't. Sabrina seemed to prefer losing him to marrying him.

"How're you doing?" she asked Sabrina gently, and her older sister shrugged. She looked pale and tired and worn out, with dark circles under her eyes. The breakup hadn't been a liberation, as some were. It had been a major loss, and still was. She had been mourning him for a month.

"Not so great," Sabrina said, and rolled over to look up at the ceiling. "Maybe Dad is right. Maybe you have to take chances in life, and risks. But I just can't see myself married to anyone, ever. Or having kids. It's so much goddamn responsibility, and way too scary."

"You take care of all of us," Tammy reminded her. "You mother all three of us, especially Annie and Candy. What's the difference if it's your sisters or your kids?"

"I can tell you guys to take a hike." She smiled ruefully. "You can't do that to your kids. And if you screw it up, you fuck them up for life. I see it all the time at work."

"You should have been a wedding planner instead of a divorce lawyer. It would have been better for your future." Sabrina smiled in answer.

"Yeah. Maybe so. Chris must absolutely hate me. He was so sweet with the ring that night, but I just couldn't do it. Not even for him. And God knows I love the man. I wouldn't mind living with him at some point. I just don't want the paperwork. It's too big a mess to undo it if you have to. This way, if you want out, you say goodbye and that's it. You don't need a buzz saw to pull your lives apart."

"And you're the buzz saw?" Tammy asked her.

"That's my job," she confirmed. It was how she saw it. "I chew right through everything you've got, your heart, your head, your wallet, your kids. Saw the little suckers in half and give half to each parent, fair and square. Christ, who'd ever want to go through that?"

"Lots of people do." Tammy wasn't as worried about it as Sabrina, but it concerned her too. "That reminds me. I didn't want to say anything to him, but I hope to hell Dad gets a pre-nup."

"He can't be that stupid," Sabrina said, sitting up finally. She had been lying there for hours, thinking about Chris. "I'll send him an e-mail and remind him. It's none of my business, but someone has to tell him, or should."

"See what I mean? You take care of all of us, Sabrina. Why not do it for your own kids, instead of a bunch of adults? It might be more fun with kids."

"Maybe so." She smiled, but didn't look convinced.

She went downstairs to get something to eat, and offered to get Tammy something too. Candy called in a little while later, to let them know she was okay. After the terrifying incident with Marcello, she checked in constantly now, and always told them where she was. She never went to anyone's apartment, and even in Rhode Island, visiting Paul, she was staying at a hotel, and Sabrina didn't think they had slept with each other yet. She was being extremely cautious, and Paul didn't seem to mind, which said good things about him. And he was young and wholesome. He wasn't some sleazy player looking to hit on young girls. The one who was considerably older, for Annie, was Brad. But somehow the age difference between them didn't seem to matter. Annie was mature for her age, especially now. And Brad was so protective of her, which was a comfort to both of her older sisters, and even to Candy. They all approved of Brad and Annie's romance.

Sabrina and Tammy spent a quiet night together, watching movies, doing the *Times* crossword puzzle together, and relaxing after their hectic weeks. John called Tammy on Sunday, and just chatted with her for a while. And Tammy bathed all the dogs on Sunday night. Annie was out with Brad again. They were having dinner with friends.

"We lead an exotic life, don't we?" Tammy commented, as she dried one of the dogs, and Sabrina came by with a load of clean towels. They smiled at each other, and were happy to see Candy when she got home.

"How was it?" Tammy asked her, as she set down her bag.

"Great. We spent time with all his friends." She was full of the excitement of the weekend, and seemed to be enjoying being with people her own age.

All four girls were home that night eventually. Their bedroom doors were open, and they called out their goodnights to each other. And each one lay in bed, smiling, thinking how lucky they were to have each other, no matter what happened with the men in their lives.

Chapter 25

Valentine's Day was a mixed blessing at their house. They all woke up knowing that their father was getting married in Las Vegas that day, and it weighed heavy on their hearts. It made them miss their mother even more. They were solemn and uncommunicative at breakfast. They had sent their father and Leslie flowers to their hotel room, and champagne. And Sabrina had sent him the e-mail about the pre-nup two weeks before. He had answered, saying that he had thought of it himself and taken care of it, which reassured her. At least, if it didn't work out, Leslie wouldn't walk off with everything he owned.

As for Valentine celebrations, Brad was taking Annie to dinner that night. Tammy was amazed that John had asked her out for the evening. He had suggested they go to dinner and a movie, which sounded perfect to her, without seeming awkward or overly romantic to either of them, since they had just started dating. And Paul was planning to come down from Brown for the night to see Candy. Everyone had something to do except Sabrina, who was planning to stay home, and do some work. The others felt terrible when they left her. She was making herself a bowl of soup when Tammy went out, and felt guilty leaving her there alone.

"Don't be silly," Sabrina reassured her. "I'll be fine." She smiled encouragingly, and told Tammy how pretty she looked. And she had already told her how much she liked John. He was nice-looking, but more than that, he seemed like an intelligent, kind man, with a lively mind. And he was as full of energy and bright ideas as Tammy, and worked in the same field. And she liked Paul Smith too. He was a breath of fresh air compared to the men she usually saw circling Candy, waiting to take advantage of her in some way. And she loved Brad. She told Annie how lovely she looked when she went out. Tammy had helped her dress, and Candy did her hair, and trimmed it a little again. She seemed absolutely elfin when Brad appeared. And he was bowled over by how beautiful she looked. He was obviously crazy about her, and Annie was visibly in love with him. Things seemed to be taking a serious turn.

By nine o'clock, Sabrina was alone, and she sat at the kitchen table, staring at her soup, thinking of Chris, and wondering how it had come to this. She had lost the man she had loved for nearly four years. She finally gave up and poured the soup down the sink. She couldn't eat, or work. All she could do was think of him, and all she missed about him. She hadn't heard a word from him since New Year's Eve. He had never called her again from the moment he left the house, with the engagement ring in his pocket that she had refused to accept.

She wandered around the living room for a while, tried sitting in the den and watching TV. She couldn't concentrate, and finally walked back up to her room and stared out the window as it began to snow, and then finally she couldn't stand it anymore. She needed to see him, if only just once more. She went back downstairs, put on her boots, grabbed a coat out of the closet, and walked toward his apartment in the snow. She buzzed the intercom downstairs and heard his voice for the first time in almost two months. Just hearing him was like the oxygen she had lacked for six weeks.

"Who is it?"

"It's me. Can I come up?"

There was a long pause, and then the buzzer sounded, which released the door. She pushed it and walked up the stairs to his apartment. He was standing in the doorway, frowning, in a sweater, jeans, and bare feet. Their eyes met for a long time as she looked at him and walked slowly toward him, and he stepped aside as she came through the door. As she walked in and looked around, nothing had changed, and neither had he. He was still the man she loved, but couldn't bring herself to marry.

"Is something wrong?" he asked her with a look of concern. She looked a mess, and didn't look well. "Are you okay?"

She turned to look at him sadly. "No, I'm not. Are you?" He shrugged in answer. It had been a miserable six weeks.

"Do you want something to drink?" he offered, and she shook her head. She was still cold, and sat down on the couch, wearing her coat. "Why are you here?" She didn't remind him that it was Valentine's Day. It was beside the point, for them at least, though not for her sisters, who were out with the men in their lives, even if newly arrived.

"I don't know why I'm here," she said honestly. "I had to come. Everything's been so awful without you. I don't know what's wrong with me, Chris. I'm scared to death of marriage. It's not you, it's me. And here's my father marrying some bimbo, five minutes after my mother died. Why isn't he scared? He should be. Instead I am. I hate what marriage does to people after it goes wrong."

"It doesn't always go wrong," he said gently, as he sat down across from her, in a big leather chair he loved. He used to sit there for hours with the dog. "Sometimes it works."

"Not often. And I guess those are the ones I never see. Do we have to get married? Isn't there something else we can do?"

"We've already done that. I don't want to run in place forever, Sabrina. I want more out of life than that. So should you. I've been meaning to call you." He hesitated. "I've been thinking about all this too. I hate to give up what I really want, and you shouldn't either. What if we live together for a while? Not forever, but maybe six months, till you get used to the idea. Maybe when you and your sisters give up the house. We could try it out for a while. If you want, you could live here. Or we could get a place of our own. I don't know. Maybe the paperwork isn't as important as I think it is. Maybe we should just live together, and see what happens. And maybe then you wouldn't be so scared of the next step." His voice trailed off as she shook her head no.

"Don't do that, if it isn't what you want. Don't settle, Chris," she said miserably, trying to defend his interests, because she loved him, but they were in conflict with her own.

"I want you," he said clearly. "That's all I want, Sabrina. It's all I ever wanted since the day I met you. You and your crazy life, your sisters, your father, our silly dog... and one day, kids of our own. You take care of your sisters as though they were your kids. Let them grow up. They will anyway. We could have our kids."

"What if they hate us? Or they're drug addicts or juvenile delinquents? Doesn't that scare you?" Her eyes were two dark pools of fear. He felt sorry for her, and wanted to put his arms around her. But he didn't. He kept looking at her, wishing it was easier for her.

"It doesn't scare me with you," he said clearly. "Nothing does. And if they're juvenile delinquents, we'll get rid of them and get new ones." He smiled at her. "I just want you, sweetheart. However it works for you. If you'd rather live togther, we'll do it. Just promise me, if we have kids, we'll get married. I'd like them to be legitimate. It might make a difference to them one day." She nodded, and smiled slowly at him.

"Maybe after six months of living together, I'd be okay."

"I hope so," he said, as he stood up and came to sit down next to her. He put his arms around her and held her, as she leaned her head against him. This was the part of her that had been missing since New Year's Eve. Losing Chris had been worse than losing a limb.

"I'm sorry I was such a jerk on New Year's Eve," she said softly. "I was scared."

"I know. It's okay, Sabrina. It's going to be okay...you'll see...."

"Why are you so sure, and I'm such a freak?" But a lot had happened in the past year that had scared her more than ever. With her mother gone, she was even more frightened than before. It had knocked the pins out from under her somehow. And he was right. She took care of everyone else in the world, why not him? And maybe even their kids. "I love you, Chris," she said, looking up at him.

"I love you too. I was miserable without you. I was thinking about coming over tonight. I was afraid you'd slam the door in my face." She shook her head, and he kissed her. They hadn't solved all their problems, but it was a beginning.

"I'll move in when we give up the house," she promised. "I'm going to miss it though. It's been so wonderful."

"How's Annie doing?" he asked her. He had missed all of them so much. They were like his family now, and had been for so long. They were a lot to lose, and Sabrina even more. She felt the same way about Chris, which was why she had walked over to see him.

"She's doing fine. She's falling in love with Brad. I think it's serious.

He's got her taking all kinds of classes, doing sculpture, giving lectures on art in Florence. He wants her to teach there next year. And he's trying to talk her into getting a dog."

"He's a good man. I like him." He didn't ask Sabrina if she thought they'd get married. It was still too soon. They had only been dating for two months. And the only person who seemed to be getting married in their family was the one who shouldn't, their father. The whole world was upside down.

He took her to bed then, and she spent the night with him. She remembered to call her sisters, and said she was okay, but didn't say where she was. Tammy was convinced she was with Chris, and they didn't want to call.

She and Chris both went back to the house in the morning, looking a little sheepish, but happy to be together again. Her sisters threw their arms around him and hugged him, like their long-lost brother. It was a happy reunion for them all.

"Welcome home," Sabrina said softly as she kissed him, and Beulah barked frantically and wagged her tail like a metronome.

Chapter 26

March was an exciting month for them all. Tammy was having a great time with John Sperry, and on St. Patrick's Day, she got a call she would never have expected in a thousand years. The network had an idea for a new show, and they wanted her to develop it, for prime-time TV, out of New York. It was about three young women living together—they were a doctor, a lawyer, and an actress—and the crises that arise in their lives. They were going to shoot it and base it in New York. They wanted big-name actresses in it, and important visiting actors on the show. They already had sponsors for it, and they wanted Tammy to produce it. It was just like what she had done in Los Angeles, only bigger and better. It was exactly what she would have wanted, if she had dreamed it up herself. She couldn't believe her good luck. It was a fabulous opportunity. She accepted it immediately. They wanted it on the air by the following spring, which meant she would be staying in the city, even after they gave up the house. And she realized it probably meant she would sell her house in L.A. now, and buy something here. A brownstone of her own.

Maybe her sisters could even live with her, since their current arrangement had worked so well.

The network already had an office for her, an assistant, and a secretary. She could pick her own associate producers. They were giving her carte blanche and a budget that blew her mind. All they wanted was an Emmy down the road, and they felt certain she could win one for them.

She couldn't wait to tell John as soon as she left the office. They wanted her to start by June, and her schedule was her own. It allowed her to give the show she was working on a decent three months' notice to find someone else to produce *Can This Relationship Be Saved? It's Up to You!* It was probably the worst show she had ever worked on, but she had actually enjoyed it a lot more than she expected to. And in a way, she'd miss some of the people she'd worked with. The show had served her well, kept her busy, made her some decent money, and it had only taken six months for something better to come along. The new show was the biggest opportunity of her career. And when she told John, he was ecstatic for her. He said he had known nothing about it, and Tammy believed him.

"It's going to be the hottest show on the air," he confirmed to her. They talked about it animatedly over lunch, and she told her sisters as soon as she got home that night.

"Cool!" Candy said excitedly. She was leaving the next day for a two-week shoot in Japan. It was big money for her, and she had already made plans to visit Paul at Brown when she got back. Annie was happy with Brad. Chris was back. All was well in their world.

Her sisters congratulated Tammy on the new job. And she gave notice on *Relationship* the next day. Irving Solomon was sorry to lose her, but he told her that she had done a great job with his show, and pulled the ratings way up. It was what Tammy did best.

Annie was supposed to graduate that month, but Brad had convinced her to extend it and train with a seeing-eye dog. She wasn't enthusiastic about it, but she said she'd try it. She had picked out her own chocolate lab, and would graduate in May with the dog. Baxter left school at the end of March, but they promised to stay in touch. He had become a very special friend, and had made school better for her right from the first. Now he was passing the baton to Brad, who wanted her to teach several art classes in the spring. Both history and painting. She didn't see how she could paint without seeing, but Brad suggested she do abstract work, and see how it went. She had discovered that sculpture wasn't her thing, but she liked working with pottery and a kiln, and had made some beautiful pieces she gave to Brad.

The best thing they did when Candy got back from Japan in early April was plan a trip together. Tammy and John organized a ski trip in Vermont for all of them. They spent a weekend at a house he rented. Everyone skied except Annie, but she had a good time going for long walks. She had brought her new dog up just for company. They hadn't done their training yet. She had named her Jessica, and she was very sweet. She got along with all the other dogs in the house.

The ski weekend was utter perfection. Annie rode the ski lift up and down. And Brad took Annie skating at night, which she had always loved, and found she could still do, as long as she held his arm. They had a fantastic time, and Paul had even driven over from Brown to be with Candy. Sabrina and Chris had never been happier. They were comfortable with their new agreement. Nothing would change until the sisters gave up the house in four months. And then she and Chris would move in together. And all of them had spoken to their father when he got back from his honeymoon in Las Vegas. He said everything was fine. They were planning to see him soon, but were giving it some time before they did, for everything to settle down.

And on the last day of the ski trip, they agreed to take a trip together the next summer. They wracked their minds about where, until Annie suggested a boat. She had always loved boats and was an avid sailor. They agreed to a price they could all put in it, and planned it for July. Brad, Paul, and Annie would be out of school, and Chris and Sabrina could take time off. John said he could steal some time. Candy would be back from the couture shows and Tammy could make her own schedule while developing the new show. The only big decision they faced was what kind of boat, motor or sail. They could hardly wait.

Two weeks after their ski trip, the girls called their father and invited him to lunch. They met him at the '21' Club, and he looked uncomfortable the entire time, even more than he had before. The last time, when he told them about Leslie after Christmas, he had looked panicked. This time, as Sabrina agreed later, he looked embarrassed.

He waited until the end of lunch again to tell them. It was a shock for all of them, but nothing really surprised them anymore. He finally got the words out, and told them Leslie was having a baby in November. She had just found out, and they thought it had been conceived on their wedding night, a detail they didn't want or need.

"You leave me speechless, Dad," Tammy said. "Good luck, I guess, but can you see yourself bringing up another child? I can't even face doing it at my age. You'll be seventy-eight years old when it goes to college."

"I can't deprive Leslie of having children," he said calmly. "It's very important to her."

"I'll bet," Candy said. Once Leslie had a baby, she had far more rights if they got divorced, but no one said it to their father. He had to have a few illusions left. He was convinced that they had married for love. And who was she to say they were wrong? Sabrina hadn't even reacted when he said they were having a baby. Compared to everything else that had happened to them in the past year, the baby their father was having wasn't the end of the world. Sabrina was just grateful it wasn't twins.

Annie's graduation from school was very moving, and was attended by everyone's family and friends. Annie had done a huge amount of work toward her diploma, and was doing well with the dog, although they still needed to do some more work.

She had asked her father to attend the graduation, preferably without his wife. At first he was very hurt by the request. He still wanted them to warm to Leslie, but then he realized that Annie's request only meant that what they really wanted was to be with him, not share his love with his new wife. None of them mentioned Leslie's pregnancy, or her at all in fact. They wanted to continue to pretend that the situation didn't exist for as long as they could. After November, that wasn't going to be possible at all. It wouldn't just be about Leslie then, but about their father's baby with her. Sabrina said it was a terrifying thought, and the others agreed. Their father with a new baby was a daunting prospect. He seemed so old to have more children. It was lucky that Leslie was young.

They had had no contact with her since she came to drop off her pie. She certainly got a lot of mileage out of a single apple pie and a porcelain plate that had to be returned. The girls were unsure if they were right about her or not. They hoped that they were wrong, and their father right. In the meantime, they wished him well. But things were not quite back to normal. They all realized, as did their father, that it would take time. They loved their father just as they always had. But opening their hearts to his new wife so soon was still too hard. Maybe one day. But not yet.

In May they chartered a sailboat out of Newport, Rhode Island, to use in July on a communal trip. The boat was well staffed with an efficient crew, and from the brochure it looked like a beautiful boat. There was a captain, two crew members, and four cabins for them. It was going to be a memorable trip.

And two days before they picked the boat up in Newport, Tammy was shaken to the core by an offer she got. A rival show to the one she was going to develop wanted her to produce their show in the coming season. It would mean moving back to Los Angeles, her friends, her house, all the things she had been so anxious not to leave in September, but had anyway. And now she had an abundance of offers, both the show she was working on in New York, and the new one they had just offered her in L.A. She could be back there shortly after they gave up the house in New York. It was a tough decision, but after a night of careful thought, she decided that she liked the show she was working on in New York, and she wanted to be closer to her sisters. She turned down the L.A. offer, the day before they left for their boat trip. She told John about it after she made the decision, and he was enormously relieved. Their relationship had flourished for the past six months. Tammy was happier than she had been in years. The freaks and weirdos in her life were history. She couldn't believe she'd actually found the right man at last. He was well adjusted, sensible, intelligent, and they were crazy about each other. And they loved each other's families.

The call that shook them all was the one they got the night before they took the boat. All four sisters were frantically packing. Candy was bringing five suitcases, and each of the others were packing one. The dogs had been boarded. Annie's dog was still in training, they hadn't completely bonded yet, but they were getting there. And the realtor called them about the house. Their landlord had fallen in love with Vienna, his research project was taking longer than planned, and he wondered if they wanted to keep the house until the end of the year, and extend their lease by another five months.

They had a serious family discussion about it, and regretfully Sabrina bowed out. She couldn't do that to Chris—she had promised to move in with him on the first of August. He had been patient for so long that she didn't dare ask him to extend it. Candy's tenant was moving out of the penthouse, and she was thinking of going back there, but it was tempting to stay on at the house. Tammy was delighted. She was so busy working on the new show that she didn't have time to look for anyplace else or move, and Annie smiled mischievously and said it worked perfectly with her plans. She had just turned twenty-seven. So at least two of the sisters wanted to stay on, and maybe three. They said that they'd miss Sabrina, but they all agreed that it was time for her to move in with Chris. He had waited long enough.

All eight of them flew to Providence the next morning, the four sisters and their men. A van took them from the airport to the dock in Newport, where the sailboat they had chartered was waiting for them. It was the first of July, and they had it for two weeks. They were planning to sail around Martha's Vineyard and Nantucket, and visit friends along the way. And during the second week, they were going to visit Paul's family in Maine.

It was hardest of all for the girls to believe their mother had been gone a year. They were grateful that their father had canceled the party. This was a much better way to spend their mother's anniversary. Together, among people they loved, in a different setting than the place they'd been the year before when the accident happened.

On the morning of the Fourth, the girls held a quiet ceremony on deck, and each of them threw a single flower into the water. Tammy noticed that Annie threw in two.

"What was the second one for?" she asked her quietly afterward. Annie hesitated and then answered, "My eyes."

They set sail shortly after and spent the day around Martha's Vineyard, and at dinnertime they motored into port for the night. It had been a magical cruise so far, and at dinner Brad squeezed her hand to give her the sign. Annie took a breath, and waited for a lull in the conversation. Moments of silent and rapt attention were hard to come by, so Brad clinked a glass with his knife. Annie was smiling and holding his hand.

"We have something to tell you," she said, sounding excited and breathless. Sabrina and Chris exchanged a look and smiled. If it was what he thought, Chris was hoping it would be contagious. But he couldn't complain. Sabrina was seeming a lot braver about their future these days. She had even mentioned having children once or twice. "We're getting married in December," Annie said, looking in Brad's direction. "I'm going to work at the school with Brad . . . and be his wife . . ." she added, as the group erupted in hearty congratulations.

"Damn," Sabrina said a minute later. "I should have made it a two- or three-part bet. What was that you said a year ago? You'd never have another date, and you'd be an old maid . . . and you'd never have kids. I could have made a fortune." They all laughed, as Brad put an arm around Annie and kissed her. They looked blissfully happy as Annie nestled next to him. Chris kissed Sabrina and put an arm around her. And Tammy mentioned a little later that she was going on vacation with John and his brothers in August. Candy and Paul just laughed. At their age, marriage was the farthest thing from their minds. They just wanted to hang out with each other and have a good time, as they had been for the past five months.

As they sat on the boat, the four women looked at each other. They didn't have to say anything. They were thinking of their mother. The gift she had given them, of each other, was in fact the best gift of all.

"To sisters!" Sabrina raised her glass to all of them. "And their men!" All eight glasses were raised, and they silently toasted their mother as well for the love she had shared, the lessons she had taught them, and the bond she had woven between them that could never be broken. As hard as it had been, in some ways, this had been the best year of their lives.

Danielle
by
Danielle Steel

The new fragrance.

Believe
in happy endings.

www.daniellesteelbeauty.com

Available at selected stores.